ADVANCE PRAISE FOR *HAVEN*

"Dangerous, dark, and a definite page-turner.
And the romance... Swoon!"
—**C.C. Hunter,** *New York Times* **bestselling author
of the Shadow Falls series**

"A smoking-hot hero and spine-chilling mystery = total win."
—**Jennifer L. Armentrout, #1** *New York Times* **bestselling author**

"This electrifying tale will take you on an unexpected journey into
a secret world of witchcraft and shape-shifters. Romance, adventure,
and magic! Lindsey leaves you breathless and wanting more."
—**Adriana Mather, #1** *New York Times* **bestselling author
of** *How to Hang a Witch*

"This is not your mama's paranormal!
Sexy, dark, and intense. Unputdownable!"
—**Sophie Jordan,** *New York Times* **bestselling author of** *Firelight*

"Gripping and gritty, *Haven* had me glued to the pages from
beginning to end! Rain is the best kind of hero—tough, sexy, sweet,
loyal. He charges through this action-packed tale that had me tearing
up more than once, and I was perfectly happy to follow!"
—**Pintip Dunn,** *New York Times* **bestselling author
of** *Forget Tomorrow*

"An utterly gritty and satisfying resurrection of the monster genre.
Rain is an intense narrator and you won't know whether to
scream or swoon. *Haven* is an instant classic!"
—**Courtney Allison Moulton, author of** *Angelfire*

"Darkly compelling and deliciously chilling, *Haven* hooks you from
the first line and never lets up. Gritty, spine-tingling,
and full of nail-biting tension."
—**Amalie Howard, bestselling author of** *Bloodspell*

"Lindsey writes a hero with fire and gasoline. Then she lights a match
with breakneck pacing and scorches a path to readers' hearts.
Don't blink for a moment."
—**Victoria Scott, bestselling author of** *Fire & Flood*

"Dark, different, sexy, and edge-of-your-seat intense."
—**Shawna Stringer, bookseller**

MARY LINDSEY

HAVEN

Entangled Publishing, LLC
2614 South Timberline Road
Suite 109
Fort Collins, CO 80525

Entangled Teen is an imprint of Entangled Publishing, LLC.

Visit our website at www.entangledpublishing.com.

Edited by Liz Pelletier
Cover design by Liz Pelletier
Interior design by Toni Kerr

ISBN: 978-1-63375-883-4
Ebook ISBN 978-1-63375-884-1

Manufactured in the United States of America

First Edition November 2017

10 9 8 7 6 5 4 3 2 1

an imprint of Entangled Publishing LLC

"We all hold a beast inside. The only difference is what form it takes when freed."

For Hannah

I tried to find a cool quote to sum up
my feelings, Bee, but words aren't sufficient.
So, instead, do this: Close your eyes and reach
for me with your heart. My love will always
be there, ready to pull you close.
Always.

ONE

A strangled scream accompanied the gratifying crunch of breaking bones.

"We gotta go," Moth said, turning the pockets of the guy at his feet.

Rain relaxed his fists and stared down at the thug he'd been pounding. Blood pulsed under the swastika inked on the guy's temple, making the tattoo move like a living thing. He wanted to kill it.

From beyond the park, a siren wailed.

"Seriously, dude. Drop it." Moth's voice was as shrill as the siren.

A quick glance over his shoulder confirmed the girl, huddled against the wire mesh trash can overflowing with beer bottles and garbage, was okay—well, alive at least, which might not have been true if things had gone down differently.

Even in the dark, he could tell she wasn't from this part of Houston. Girls from this inner-city neighborhood had a harder edge. She was a few years younger than him, closer to Moth's age—maybe fifteen or sixteen—dark, terrified eyes pleading above the duct tape strapped across her mouth and chin and all the way around her head. Her wrists were bound with zip ties behind her back.

God only knew what the assholes' plan for her had

been, if they'd had a plan at all. These guys often acted spontaneously and indiscriminately—ironic for a group powered by discrimination. He gave the one at his feet a hard kick in the ribs for good measure but only received a weak moan in response. Good. The bastard wasn't going anywhere anytime soon.

"Rain!" Moth's tone bordered on panic.

"Yeah." He examined his bloody knuckles in the moonlight and his stomach turned over. The guy had better not die. Rain's DNA was all over him. With one last glance at the girl, he followed Moth into the dark moon shadows of the heavy oaks lining the back edge of the park, where he paused to watch the police cruiser skid to a halt. Only when he was sure the girl was in the care of the cops did his sense of self-preservation kick in, and he leaped the back fence of the park into the adjoining churchyard.

"What the hell is wrong with you?" Moth hissed through his teeth. "We almost got caught."

Gravel on the walkway behind the church crackled like Rice Krispies under his boots. He liked Rice Krispies. They served them every morning at the shelter.

He fell into step beside his friend, who was at least a head shorter. Rain had always been grateful for his size. He was taller and bulkier than most, so people left him alone as a general rule. That wasn't true of Moth. "You should get off the streets," Rain said.

Moth replied with a go-to-hell glare.

Slinking into the shadows that clung to the side of the building, they had a clear shot to the other end of the churchyard. They emerged on a side street, slowed, and assumed their typical defiant, don't-give-a-shit teen thug personas, which fit Moth like a glove.

"But I like the streets," he said as they neared the corner.

"I've got freedom here."

Yeah, freedom until one of the gangs or the cops or worse found the chance to grab him up.

When they passed the bus stop, Old Jim wasn't stretched out on the bench like he'd been every night since Rain and his mom had moved in down the street three months ago. Jim's bag was there, though, tucked under the bench next to his blanket. He never went anywhere without his stuff.

"Oh, cool. Let's see what the old guy guards like a pit bull." But before Moth could get his hands on the backpack, Rain shoved him against the wall of the bus stop rain shelter, causing the graffiti-covered Plexiglas panels to rattle in their metal frames like thunder.

"No. Don't touch his shit."

Moth nonchalantly brushed his T-shirt as if he'd gotten crumbs on it, but Rain knew he'd surprised him and it was a nervous gesture. He fluttered when rattled, hence his nickname. "Since when have you been so righteous, Rain?"

"Since when have you been—" A siren drowned out his voice.

"Jeezus, I thought that was the cops for a second." Moth's fingers twitched at his chest as an ambulance sped past and then slowed to turn at the light a block up.

Red and blue lights pulsed across the surface of the boarded-up Family Dollar store on the far side of the intersection as the vehicle made the turn.

"I hope it's not Old Jim," Rain said.

For a long time, his friend studied him, then wiped the bottom of his shirt over his face, smearing dirt, rather than wiping it away. "You're acting weird tonight." He struck out up the street, not looking back as he spoke. "Really weird. You almost killed a guy back there, but you're worried about an old dude who sleeps at the stop?"

It must be nice to be so callous—to be Moth. To see things

only in terms of what could serve a purpose. Somehow, even after all this time, Rain couldn't do it—couldn't give in to the every-man-for-himself hopelessness surrounding him like a cage. There was a way out of here. There had to be. And that's why he got on that school bus every morning and didn't drop out, like Moth, Dig, Twitchy, and the others in his loosely formed gang of non-gangsters.

"The only reason I beat the skinhead is because he was gonna hurt that girl." Regret spiraled through him as the adrenaline burned off, leaving him weak and nauseated. He usually had better control, but seeing those guys dragging that girl...

Moth stopped and smirked. "Riiiiiiight. Because it wasn't fun at all."

Remorse churned to life again in Rain's gut, and his hands shook. He hated feeling this out of control. Maybe he was screwed up because he hadn't eaten all day. Hopefully his mom had saved him some food at the shelter. "Beating those guys was fun to you?"

Moth shrugged. "Yeah. Of course it was."

Turning the corner, Rain glanced back at the stop and sighed with relief. Old Jim was back on his bench. He must've been off taking a piss or something. The man gave him a thumbs-up, then flipped the bird at Moth. Clearly, he hadn't wandered off too far to keep an eye on his stuff.

After turning the corner, both of them stopped short in the middle of the sidewalk.

"Oh shit," Moth said.

Not only was an ambulance in front of the shelter where Rain and his mother lived, several police cruisers were parked at odd angles to the curb, like they'd come down the one-way street the wrong way. Kind of like Rain had lived every day of his life.

"We need to split," Moth said, turning to run the way they'd come.

"No."

Moth grabbed the back of Rain's shirt and pulled. "No? Are you out of your mind? They're here to pin us for beating those guys in the park."

A paramedic rolled a gurney out the front door, and even from a block away, Rain knew exactly who was on it from her almost skeletal build and bright-red hair.

"They're here to bust us." The younger boy's voice bordered on a whine.

"That's my mom."

Fluttering fingers tightened in the fabric of his shirt. "She probably got loaded and passed out in the hall. C'mon, Rain, let's go."

She probably *had* overdone it again, but he couldn't just run away. Pulling his friend with him, he flattened against the side of the building.

Moth had a family on the other side of town he could go to. Even if he didn't want them, they were there. Mom was all Rain had. Ideal or not, she was it. This time when his stomach rolled over, it wasn't from hunger or anger; it was from dread.

A paramedic spoke with two of the officers. Miss Gill, the lady who answered the phone at the shelter, joined them, wringing a tissue in her hands. She scanned the street in both directions, and he motioned to his friend to stop fidgeting as they blended further into the shadows. Shoving the tissue in her pocket, she said something to the men. In unison, they turned and looked in Moth and Rain's direction.

"Fuck you, man. I'm out," Moth called as he ran back down the street the other way.

Rain's heart hammered in his chest until he thought he might vomit, and then, right as he made up his mind to run, too, the paramedic pulled the sheet over his mother's face.

TWO

With a gasp of diesel fumes, the Greyhound bus pulled away from the stop at the Stripes gas station, leaving Rain completely alone for the first time he could remember. There had always been someone around—his mom, the person in the next bunk at the shelter, a kid in the next desk at school or the neighboring cell in juvie.

Stuffed in a cramped seat between the window and a guy who talked on his phone the entire five-hour trip had left him stiff. He shifted his duffel bag to his other shoulder and stretched, spine popping twice like brittle twigs.

The sun had set hours ago, and the moon hung low and fat in the night sky, illuminating the trailer park across the side street to the west and an empty pasture just beyond.

Checking out the gas station, he shook his head at his usual shitty luck. The word "closed" blinked rapidly in time to his hammering heartbeat from a lit sign in the station window. Ordinarily, it took a pretty big badass to rattle Rain, but for some reason, the prospect of meeting his mom's sister for the first time gave him the jitters.

He leaned against the rustic wooden post at the front of the building and let his bag slide from his shoulder to the pavement with a *thud*. At his court hearing, the judge ordered him into the custody of his next of kin, since he wasn't of legal age. Hell, he hadn't even known he had a next of kin other than his mom. Then a social worker handed him an envelope containing a letter on frilly pink paper from someone calling herself "Aunt Ruby," who said she couldn't wait to meet him and would pick him up here, tonight. The envelope even included the bus ticket to a tiny town in the middle of the Texas Hill Country and some cash.

He scanned the empty parking lot in front and the crop field to his right. Bugs made a racket all around, rivaling the sound of the traffic on the Pierce Elevated overpass back home where his group of guys usually hung out. They were probably there now, planning how to get enough cash to score a six-pack or something harder.

He didn't miss them. He didn't miss any of his life, really, especially the last year. Time had simply been a bookmark. Something that held his place while he waited to finish the story.

Sucking in a breath of warm air, he rolled his shoulders to release tension. At least he didn't have to worry about retaliation from the skinheads anymore. Nothing in this small town could hold a candle to that kind of threat. Hell, kids around here most likely didn't even know what real danger was. Their biggest concerns were probably falling off a tractor or getting rained out of the high school football game.

A semi hummed and rattled on the main highway in the distance, then faded, leaving him alone with the bug chatter.

What if this Aunt Ruby person had forgotten this was the day he'd arrive? Maybe his social worker had filled her in and she'd changed her mind. He knew no one here. This town was so small it probably didn't even have a shelter. A siren wailed in the distance, maybe on the highway. They had cops, though, and probably a jail.

"Whatever," he muttered, feeling anything but noncommittal. "Squid ink," his mom had called it when he said something that covered up how he really felt.

"Yeah, whatever," he said again, kicking a pebble toward the gas pumps standing guard in the flickering fluorescent lights under the overhang.

The bugs in the crop field to his right fell silent, and a bird spooked to flight from somewhere in the middle, catching air with a wild flapping of wings. He held his breath, but only silence followed. Probably a feral cat had scared it. Happened with the pigeons in the city all the time.

"Whatever."

The hair on the back of his neck prickled as he waited for the bugs to kick back up with their radio static. Nothing but insects far off in the distance, a car passing up on the main highway, and the relentless hum of the fluorescent tubes over the gas pumps.

He grabbed his bag and slung it over his shoulder, searching the area for what had stood his hair on end. He had a great sixth sense about danger—he always had—and something was off.

The silence out here in the middle of nowhere was unnerving. At least in the city he knew what to listen for.

With light steps, he crossed to the far end of the building toward the field where the bird had spooked. It might've been a trick of the eerie light from the moon, but it appeared something was moving through the rows of what looked like waist-high corn. Not tall enough to clear the tops but big enough to cause ripples as it parted the stalks in its path.

"Probably sheep or goats," he told himself, heart pounding.

Then, with a screech and flapping of wings as loud as hand claps, a whole flock of birds burst from the field, dashing over his head, causing him to instinctively duck and cover but only for a moment. Whatever had startled them needed to be faced straight on, not in a cowering ball.

Leaving the bag on the ground, he unfurled from his crouch, fists at the ready, feet apart, knees slightly bent as he'd done hundreds of times. Adrenaline pumped through his body in a familiar, heated wave, readying him for the fight.

But no fight came. The stalks remained still, except for a slight swaying from a gentle breeze. After a few minutes, the bugs cranked up again with their grating song, and he took a deep breath.

"What-fucking-ever."

He picked up his bag and wandered again to the front of the building. Headlights approached from the side street. The familiar shape of a Crown Vic with overheads sent him slinking back to the far end of the station, where he ducked behind the dumpster. He heard the police cruiser slow, followed by the grind of wheels turning on loose gravel as it pulled into the parking lot. *What now?*

Motor still running, a woman's voice called: "Aaron? Aaron Ryland?"

How did the cops in New Wurzburg get his name? His aunt was the only one who knew he was coming. His eyes flitted to the cornfield. For a brief moment, he considered taking off and leaving this whole court-ordered mess behind. But experience had taught him that facing shit head on was usually best, so he took a deep breath and stayed put.

The engine cut off, and the car door opened with a metallic groan. "Aaron, it's me, Aunt Ruby."

Sonofabitch. She'd brought the cops with her to pick him up. What had the social worker told her about him?

"Aaron? Was that you I saw a minute ago?"

Well, he couldn't lurk in the shadows all night. She'd obviously seen him before he bolted. "Yeah. I'm…" What the hell could he say to explain why he was hiding behind the dumpster? "Uh, yeah. Be right there."

Behind him, the corn-looking stuff rustled, and he experienced the spider-crawling-up-the-back-of-his-neck feeling he got when he was being watched.

"Fuck off," he growled at the corn, feeling like the dumbass he would have appeared if anyone were close enough to actually hear. "Seriously, fuck off and go scare some more little birdies. You don't want to mess with me."

The field answered with silence and stillness. Probably because there was nothing there. He shook his head. He hadn't slept more than a few short spurts in days, which would explain why he was issuing threats to cornfields. Hopefully, a bed was in his near future, even if it was at the police station.

Time to get on it. "Hey, sorry I held you up, I…" He stopped dead in his tracks as he rounded the corner.

Leaning against the police cruiser was a dead ringer for his deceased mom. Freaky doppelganger stuff, only where his mom had been sickly with sunken shadows under her glassy eyes, this woman was healthy and alert. Her red hair was pulled back in a severe bun on the back of her head, and she wore blue or black cop garb—it was hard to tell in the flickering fluorescent–enhanced moonlight.

"Holy shit." The words came out before he could stop himself.

The woman looked as stunned as he felt. "Yeah, holy shit is right." She pushed away from where she'd been leaning against the car and hooked her thumbs in her gun belt, never taking her eyes off him. "You look exactly like your father. Scary, even. God, for a minute, I…" She looked away for a moment, blinking rapidly. After a deep breath, she met his gaze again and extended her hand. "I'm your aunt Ruby. I'm sorry, I thought you knew. Your mom and I are…" A line creased her brow making her seem older, somehow. "We *were* twins."

His mom had a twin. His chest tightened. Why hadn't she told him? He took Ruby's offered hand and shook, surprised by her firm grip. "Nice to meet you. Thanks for the bus ticket."

She stepped back and looked him up and down. "It's uncanny, the resemblance."

"You knew my dad?" His mother had never spoken of him other than to say he knocked her up and then died.

Her eyes narrowed as she studied the field behind him. "Let's talk about this somewhere else." She gestured to the car with a tilt of her head. "You hungry?"

"Yeah." He followed her to the cruiser with its driver door still open.

"Good. My neighbor Sharon dropped off some pot roast and lemon pie at the house. Let's hit it." She slid into the driver's seat as he strode to the other side, stopping next to the door.

"Well, what are you waiting for?" she asked through the open window.

It was impossible to hold back his goofy grin as he climbed into the passenger seat. Aunt Ruby chuckled and delivered a friendly punch to his shoulder. "First time in a police car?"

He barked a laugh. "No. First time in the front." He regretted saying it the second it came out of his mouth, but the tension in his shoulders lessened when her smile broadened.

She stared at him a moment before putting the car in gear. "More like your old man than simply looks, then."

Rain's jaw clenched at the mention of the father he'd never known. He fought back the urge to grill this stranger with the dozens of questions he'd wanted to ask since he could talk. Taking a deep breath through his nose, he consciously relaxed. His questions had gone unanswered for his entire life. They could wait one more day.

As they pulled out of the parking lot, he glanced back at the cornfield. It was probably the reflection of the lights from the trailer park on the rear window glass, but a chill skittered down Rain's spine at the possibility the shiny gold dots among the stalks were actually multiple pairs of eyes watching them drive away.

THREE

No matter the size of the city or school, all-in-one desk/ chair combos were a universal, and way too small for a guy Rain's height. He shifted but only managed to knock his knee on the chair of the girl in front of him, who demonstrated another high school universal: the screw-you look.

Math after lunch sucked. At least a quarter of the class was asleep or had their heads down. The others, judging by their glazed expressions, wished they were asleep. The teacher, a middle-aged guy named Mr. Pratt, with a bad comb-over and wearing a short-sleeve plaid dress shirt, launched into a senior slump pep talk. "I know most of you have already received your college acceptance letters, but I need you to hang in here just a few months more."

College acceptance letter. Rain almost laughed out loud. What college would accept him? No money, no parents, and mediocre grades because he was never at any school more than a few months.

The teacher tapped the shoulder of a boy in the front row. He startled awake with a jerk, and a girl with long, wild, tangled light-brown hair sitting in the next desk laughed. Sleepy Guy twisted toward her, delivering a vicious glare. The huge red spot on his forehead from where he'd rested it against his desk made him look ridiculous. The girl pointed to the corner of her mouth and then to his, indicating he had drool or something going on. He wiped his mouth with his sleeve. She tucked her head down and went back to messing with her phone under her desk.

"As we discussed at the beginning of last semester," Mr. Pratt continued, "calculus is the mathematical study of change…"

Change. A topic Rain knew all about. Always the new guy. His mom had bounced around from place to place so many times, he'd lost count. It'd bothered him when he was little because it was impossible to make close friends—something he'd wanted more than anything. As he'd gotten older, he realized not forming bonds was a good thing. It meant no regrets for leaving someone behind.

A girl one row over gave Rain a shy smile, then returned her attention to Mr. Pratt. She had light hair and fair skin, like most of the kids in the class. Aunt Ruby had explained that New Wurzburg, like the other small towns around it, was comprised primarily of descendants of German immigrants who settled the area a couple hundred years ago, which he supposed accounted for the sameness so unlike any of his schools before.

His gaze was drawn again to the girl with her waist-length, tangled hair and rumpled T-shirt in the front row. She didn't have the groomed civility of her classmates, which intrigued him. When Mr. Pratt stopped right in front of her and laid his fingers on the top of her desk, still yacking about the wonders of mathematics, she tucked her phone between her thighs.

A big guy two seats in front of Rain elbowed the tall, skinny guy next to him and nodded toward her as his fingers flew over his phone screen. He chuckled and placed his phone in his back pocket right about the time the girl in the front seat flinched and her phone went off, playing "Highway to

Hell" as its ringtone.

The teacher stopped his lecture, and the girl sunk low in her chair. Wordlessly, he held out his hand.

"Mr. Pratt. I can explain," she said.

His only response was unmoving silence and a wiggle of his fingers. Clearly, this had happened before. With a sigh, she placed her phone in his palm, and the girl with short hair and another wearing a bow in her ponytail snickered, but they fell silent when she twisted in her chair and whispered something under her breath.

The guy who'd phoned her coughed to cover his laugh. *Asshole.*

"You may collect your phone in the principal's office after school," the teacher said, depositing it in his desk drawer with a slam.

The girl slumped back down in her chair, and the guy two rows up fist-bumped across the aisle with the skinny guy next to him. Rain's fingers curled.

For the rest of the period, he found it hard to keep his eyes off the girl in the front row. Her hair had streaks running through it that reminded him of the little square golden caramels that his social worker kept on her desk to use as bribes. At one point, she looked over her shoulder and glared at the boys two rows back, and Rain almost gasped aloud. She had the weirdest eyes he'd ever seen. They were pale, pale blue, making the pupils stand out like they were hole-punches through paper.

The guy blew her a kiss, and she flipped him the bird.

"Later," he whispered.

"Miss Burkhart," Mr. Pratt said. "Is there something you'd like to share with the class?"

"No. They already know that I want Thomas to eff off, but thanks." Nervous laughs erupted from some of the students.

There was an odd tension in the class, like people were scared to react or something.

"You know, there are better ways to communicate than crude gestures and swear words."

The guy she'd called Thomas wore a smirk Rain wanted to pound off.

"Yes, Mr. Pratt. I'm well aware. But I'm afraid better communication would be lost on him. I'm speaking the only language he understands."

The teacher opened his mouth, but the bell rang before he could get any words out. Students shot to their feet with loud voices and scraping of chairs over terrazzo. Mr. Pratt scurried to his desk, snatched the phone, and rushed from the room, probably to take it to the office.

Leaving her backpack on the floor, the girl rose and strode to stand right next to the guy she'd called Thomas, the one who had set off her phone. Her unnerving eyes locked on his face as the rest of the class emptied with the exception of the guy from the front row and the skinny guy in the next desk. None of them seemed to notice or care that Rain remained seated in his desk in the back corner.

"Like what you see, Friederike?" Thomas leaned back in the chair and straightened his legs out in front of him, thrusting up in an un-subtle display.

She leisurely scanned his body from head to toe and back up again. The heat in her gaze raking over the guy caused Rain to shift in his chair. Leaning so close their noses almost touched, she said, "Do I like what I see?"

The skinny guy chuckled and exchanged a look with the dark-haired boy who'd been asleep in the front row. Clearly, they all knew one another well, based on the nonverbal exchanges that took time to develop.

In one swift movement, the girl he'd called Friederike

grabbed the desk attached to Thomas's chair and yanked up, flipping him backward, desk and all. If his hands hadn't been behind his head, his skull might have cracked. "*Now* I like what I see," she said. "You laying at my feet."

"Holy shit, Freddie. You could have hurt him," the skinny guy said.

Thomas untangled from the metal and fake wood and kicked the desk to the side. An eerie, threatening growl came from the guy's throat that made the hair on the nape of Rain's neck lift as Thomas crouched as if preparing to lunge.

Neither of the other boys seemed ready to come to Freddie's defense. In fact, they appeared nervous and ready to bolt as they eyed the door.

Rain's fists tightened into balls. His muscles tensed, readying to jump out of his desk if the guy made a move.

"What's going on in here?" A teacher wearing a striped dress and wire-rimmed glasses stuck her head in from the hallway. "Is everything okay?"

All four of them answered "Yes" at the same time. Definitely running buddies, to cover and answer in unison.

"I leaned back too far," Thomas said, placing the desk on its feet. "It's cool."

The teacher gave them a skeptical look, then her eyes found Rain in the back of the room. "Oh. You're the new student. Ruby's nephew, Aaron."

And then, it was as if he'd materialized from invisibility. All four of the kids in the room turned to him, and their eyes narrowed. Yeah. He was used to this. Having to prove up to the existing gang—only this wasn't a gang. It was a group of kids in a tiny rural town. Harmless.

"What happened here?" the teacher asked him.

Rain didn't need to look to know four sets of eyes were trained on him. He could feel it. "Like he said, he just tipped back in his chair and lost his balance. No big deal." He slung his backpack over his shoulder and strode toward the door. "Nobody got hurt."

As he passed, he slid a warning look at Thomas, whose eyes narrowed. When he looked at the girl, she gave him a grateful, almost imperceptible nod, then glanced away.

"So, Ruby tells me you're now a full-time resident of New Wurzburg," the teacher said, moving aside so Rain could join her in the hallway right outside the door. She came up to his shoulder and was much younger than his aunt.

News traveled fast around here. He'd only been in town for three days. He answered with a noncommittal shrug.

"Well, I'm sure I'll see you around," she continued. "Our book club meets at Ruby's every Wednesday. I'm Ms. James, the world history teacher. Welcome to Wurzburg High."

"Yeah, thanks."

Together, the three guys and the girl left the classroom, all shooting him wary glances. He forced himself to focus on Ms. James as they strode down the hall.

"Um, a word of advice," she whispered. "Avoid those four. Especially the girl. They're nothing but trouble."

Trouble. Rain almost laughed. He and trouble were on a first-name basis, and these country-grown kids weren't even acquainted with it.

Shaking his head, still amused by the girl flipping the desk, he headed out to find his next class, track. The school was larger than he expected because it served several Hill Country towns. As he rounded the corner to the gym, something felt off. Stopping, he scanned the hallway, lined on both sides with banks of lockers, only to find students rushing to class. Still, he remained frozen in place as the hallway cleared, the fine hairs on his neck crawling, warning of danger.

A locker slammed behind him, and he turned to meet

the odd pale eyes of the girl from his last class. He must have walked right past her before the bell rang and emptied the place. She wasn't traditionally pretty, like prom-queen pretty. She was tall and strong with high cheekbones and those crazy-cool eyes. She arched an eyebrow as if daring him to say something about what had happened earlier, but no words came. All he could manage was a dumbfounded stare as she turned away dismissively and wandered down the hall with a purposeful, sensual gait that took his breath away.

No wonder his body sensed danger. The girl was killer.

Before she turned the corner, she glanced over her shoulder with an expression warning him to be on guard. Yeah. He planned on it. Not only with those guys in Calculus class, but with her as well. Maybe this little town wouldn't be so boring after all.

He shifted his backpack to his other shoulder and struck out with a huge grin as he thought about seeing her again tomorrow. For the first time in his life, he was looking forward to his next math class.

FOUR

Rain had lost count of how many first days as the new kid he'd endured. He'd always assumed that it'd get easier, but it never did. His innate loner instinct constantly warred with his desire to fit in—something he'd never achieved. At least *this* first day was over, and he had a nice, comfortable bed and roof over his head. Not to mention a TV with loads of channels. He switched to an episode of *Law & Order* and propped his feet up on Aunt Ruby's coffee table, which was worn and scratched like it had doubled as a footstool for decades.

A cop on the show was interviewing a teenage boy who appeared terrified, and his mind wandered to Moth. The kid had never made sense to him. Why would someone with parents and a home choose to live out on the streets? Rain never had a choice. Maybe he never would, but for now, he planned to enjoy the gift fate had given him and ride it out until he was forced to move on. He had no doubt that would happen as soon as his aunt discovered what kind of shit he'd rolled in for the past few years.

The door creaked open, and he slid his feet from the table.

"Hey," Aunt Ruby said, closing the door but not locking it behind her. He'd noticed she'd left it unlocked last night, too. "How was your first day of school?"

"Good. Over."

She smiled and unclasped her weapon belt. "Same here. Day over. Sorry I'm so late. Chief had me run an errand at the last minute."

"Ah. Is that code for busting someone?"

After locking her gun belt in the file drawer near the coat closet, she joined him on the sofa. "No. It's non-code for running an errand. We needed coffee and stir sticks at the station. The chief likes a special brand of coffee that's only carried in the next town."

"Can't the chief go get his own coffee?"

"*Her* own." She sat back and rolled her shoulders. "And no. She was out investigating a couple of reports that came in, and honestly, I was bored stiff and glad to get out of my desk chair."

That didn't meet his expectations of what he knew about cops at all. He figured she was out in the cruiser gleefully issuing tickets and responding to 911 calls, knocking heads and taking people down.

She stared at the TV screen. The detective was cuffing the teen. "You like cop shows?"

"Sure."

"You ever thought about becoming a police officer?"

"Me?"

"No, I was talking to the wasp on the wall behind you. Figured it had high aspirations in law enforcement."

Sure enough, a large red wasp was crawling up the wall. Rain crossed the room, hand raised.

"You might want to use your shoe or something," Aunt Ruby warned. "The red ones sting like crazy."

Not if he hit it right. And that was the one thing Rain knew how to do: hit. In one sweeping move, he lunged and slapped the wasp with an open palm, then stepped on it when it hit the floor.

Staring down at the broken pieces, he felt a pang of regret for killing it. It had been out of its element and looking for a way to escape—a victim of bad timing and worse reputation. Like him. He took the paper towel offered by his aunt and scooped up the body parts.

"Careful, they can still sting after they're dead," she warned.

He folded the paper towel with the insect parts inside.

"You're fast," she said. "And really accurate. Have you ever studied martial arts or taken boxing classes or anything? You'd be good at it."

He shook his head. He'd had real-life instruction on the streets.

"You hungry?" Before he could respond, she struck out for the kitchen. "Go throw that thing away and wash up. I'll scramble some eggs. Does that work?"

He nodded.

"Breakfast for dinner," she said. "Your dad's favorite." An odd, stricken look crossed her face, and her lips drew into a thin line. Without another word, she disappeared into the kitchen.

By the time he'd ditched the bug, washed his hands, and made it to the kitchen, Aunt Ruby was beating the shit out of some eggs in a bowl. "Grab that skillet in the bottom drawer." She nodded at the wide drawer under the stove. "And put it on that right front burner."

She lit the flame and drizzled some oil into the skillet out of a wine bottle with a silver spout. "Do you cook?" she asked as she poured the eggs into the pan.

"No."

"Me neither, but eggs are easy."

He leaned against the counter and watched her jerky

movements as she scraped the eggs from the bottom of the pan once they'd cooked and solidified. It took all his willpower to not push her for information about his dad and how she knew him, but she seemed shaken.

"So, how much do you know about Roger?" she asked finally without eye contact.

Roger. The guy had never had a name until now. His heart pounded painfully.

Aunt Ruby dumped the eggs on two plates, with one having at least twice as much as the other, before returning the skillet to the cooktop with a *bang*. She handed him the fuller plate.

"Nothing. Mom never talked about him."

She stilled for a moment, and it appeared her eyes got wetter, but she turned away before Rain could be certain.

"He was a good man. Did dumb things but good deep down." She sat at the table, and Rain slid into the chair opposite, studying her face, which she'd schooled into a noncommittal *whatever* expression. He knew that look. He'd mastered it for when the cops or authorities questioned him.

He took a bite of eggs and waited. He was good at waiting. He'd done it his whole life.

Aunt Ruby set down her fork. "I'm sad you didn't get to meet him."

His mom had led him to believe her dealings with his father were nothing more than a hook-up with a stranger resulting in a bad outcome: him. Yet, here was her twin sister talking about the guy like they were close and calling him a good man. He dug into the eggs, hoping she'd continue.

"We grew up in this house, your mom and I." She looked around the small kitchen. "I always thought she'd come back home. I'd hoped…" She shook her head and took a bite of her eggs.

His mind flew back to Moth. Like him, Rain's mom had a place to go, but even with the burden of a tiny child, she'd preferred the streets. His insides twisted as anger and sadness warred painfully.

Aunt Ruby's phone rang, and they both flinched. "Sorry," she said, reading the screen. "Chief is calling."

"Yes?" she answered. Her eyes flicked to Rain's face then back to her eggs. "Um, sure. I'll go right now."

She hung up and grabbed her weapon belt from the file cabinet. "Wanna go on a ride-along?"

He shoved the last bite of eggs in his mouth. "Sure."

"Don't get your hopes up. It'll be boring." She fastened the belt around her waist as he cleared both plates from the table. "The most exciting calls I've been on recently were a treed raccoon and the sparrow that flew through Mrs. Whittaker's window and got stuck in her sunroom." She grinned. "And I didn't even get to cuff anybody."

He dried his hands and followed her out the door, sliding into the front passenger seat of the cruiser. "What's the call about this time?"

She shook her head and put the car in gear. "Oh, it's Helga Goff again. She lives all by herself out past the east end of the rock. Honestly, if I lived out there, I'd get spooked, too. She's spotted everything from space aliens to Sasquatch to Wolf Man over the years. I suspect she's just lonely and likes the attention. Always has fresh baked cookies."

She turned onto the highway and headed toward a large stone hill, rising in the moonlight like the shell of a huge, smooth turtle. "Beware of the cookies. She always leaves out one thing or another. They're terrible."

"Thanks for the warning."

"This time she swears there's a mermaid behind her back hedge."

He chuckled.

"Yeah, I always get the winners."

"How many people are on the police force here?"

"Just the chief, me, and Gerald, the guy who does dispatch, filing, answers phones, works on the cruiser, and is the station handyman."

"Does he want to be a cop?"

"I've no idea. I doubt it. He'd be a menace to society with a weapon. Can't even use the stapler safely."

A huge hill loomed to the left of the car now, and it seemed to glow in the moonlight. "What's that?"

"Oh. Enchanted Rock. It's a giant dome of pink granite pushed up by volcanic activity. People come from all over to climb it. The Parks and Wildlife Department oversees a couple thousand acres of recreational land, including Enchanted Rock."

"Enchanted."

"Yeah. The Native Americans indigenous to this area believed it held magic. Later, the German settlers had a legend about it. Some of their descendants still believe it." She shook her head and laughed. "It's said that on a full moon, the power of the earth reaches for the heavens at that one spot, infusing the surrounding area with magic strong enough to change man to beast."

He stared at the menacing rock, crouching as if ready to rise from the ground in the eerie glow of the full moon. "What kind of beast?"

"Dunno. Maybe a mermaid." She winked. "Let's ask Mrs. Goff. Her people go way back around here."

Gravel crunched under the tires as she turned onto a dirt road running toward the hill, ending at a small cottage with ornate wooden cutouts around the porch.

An elderly white-haired woman wearing a bathrobe

waited on the porch.

"Remember, the cookies are at your own risk," Aunt Ruby warned with a grin as she pushed open her car door.

"Took you long enough to get here," the woman said.

Rain joined his aunt on the sidewalk. "This is my sister's boy, Aaron," Aunt Ruby said.

The woman eyed him, eyebrows raised. "Yes, I know."

Ruby shifted uncomfortably. "You called about seeing something suspicious?"

The old woman's eyes were still fixed on him as if she were trying to look inside him, and his throat tightened under her unnerving stare. "Yes." Finally, she looked away, and he could breathe. "There's a mermaid behind my back hedge." She held out a plate of cookies. "I baked some cookies for you. Would you like one?"

Aunt Ruby shot Rain an amused glance. "Thank you. We'd love one."

She took a small, oddly shaped cookie with blackened edges, and so did he, and Mrs. Goff smiled.

"I'll, um, go check the back hedge. You get the barn, okay, Aaron? If you see a mermaid, the code word is 'Ariel.' Yell it and I'll come take it into custody. Periodically, let's give an all clear as we go."

He bit back a smile. "Will do."

Mrs. Goff's brow furrowed with disappointment. "Aren't you going to eat your cookies?"

"Work before reward. Let's go, Aaron."

His aunt pulled him around the side of the house. "Throw it away in the bushes and tell her it was delicious. You'll thank me for this." When he looked over his shoulder, the woman was peering around the side of the porch.

"Make this look good," she said, pulling out her flashlight. "Give her a fun night. Barn is that way." She pointed to the left at a structure the size of a two-car garage before stalking toward a row of shoulder-high bushes lining the back of the property, swinging the flashlight dramatically left and right. "All clear!" she shouted.

With a chuckle, he followed a foot trail over the rocky terrain to the wooden barn. After touching his tongue to the edge of the cookie, he grimaced, spit, and then dropped the nasty-tasting thing between a cactus and a jagged rock the height of a bench. It tasted like the woman had used salt instead of sugar.

He opened the double doors and looked inside, finding nothing but some old buckets and empty, open-topped wooden crates. Obviously, this building hadn't been used in a while. "All clear!" he shouted, playing along with Ruby's game.

He closed the doors and circled toward the back of the building, picking his way over rocks and patches of cacti, grateful for his steel-toed boots. When he made the turn behind the barn, tension clawed his spine, and his adrenaline spiked. Frozen in place, he held his breath. Something was here, and it sure as hell wasn't a mermaid. This was the same feeling he'd had at the cornfield last night—the unmistakable sensation of being watched.

Scanning from one side to the other, he searched the rugged area behind the barn that stretched for miles all the way to the base of Enchanted Rock. If someone were out there, it would be impossible to spot him.

"All clear!" his aunt shouted in the distance.

He took a shallow breath, still not moving, as something slunk through the shadows past a copse of trees fifty or so yards out. Another something followed it. They moved quickly, at least three of them, like dogs or coyotes or maybe mountain lions, low to the ground, before disappearing behind a cluster of boulders.

Just animals doing what animals do. Nothing sinister. He took a deep breath and relaxed, almost giddy with relief. There were no skinheads or gangs hunting him around here. He was safe for the first time in years, he reminded himself.

"All clear!" he yelled to his aunt as he headed along the side of the barn, cursing internally for losing his shit over nothing.

Right before he made it to the path, something crashed inside the barn, like a bucket falling over.

Heart hammering, he snuck back to the building, grabbing a two-by-four board leaning against the outside that would make a good weapon, before swinging the doors open.

He stood in the doorway, blinking as his eyes adjusted to the darkness of the barn. Nothing was there. Maybe it had been a raccoon, like his aunt had mentioned at the house. Or a feral cat. He squinted into darkness broken only by moonlight spilling through the open doors across the dirt floor.

"Aaron?" Ruby's voice called.

Board in hand, he prowled along the left side, across the back to the right corner, the most shadowed spot in the space. By now, his eyes had adjusted to the dark.

And there, crouched in a ball, tucked up tight behind a crate, was the mermaid.

Wild, tangled hair partially screened pale shoulders, arms, and breasts. And then, her eerie, familiar eyes met his, her expression as naked and exposed as her body.

"Aaron," his aunt called again. "All clear?"

Holy shit. No. Nothing was clear. Why was the girl from his calculus class naked in Mrs. Goff's barn? Here, in the middle of nowhere.

"You okay?" he whispered.

She nodded once.

"Need help?"

She shook her head, hard.

"Need a ride home?"

Again, she shook her head.

He stared, spellbound by her primal, terrifying beauty. Like she'd sprung from the earth itself.

"Aaron?" His aunt's voice sounded closer.

The girl shrank further into the shadows. His eyes locked on hers, unsure what to do. He wasn't comfortable leaving her alone, naked, in the middle of this harsh place. He should reveal her. Tell his aunt what he'd found and make sure she got home safely. That guy named Thomas had called her Friederike. The other one, Kurt, had called her Freddie.

Wordlessly, she pleaded. He knew this look. It was the same one he'd seen only weeks before on the girl in the park. *Help me. Don't let them hurt me.*

"All clear," he shouted. Her eyes never left his, as if she was as confused by his actions as he was by hers. "Nothing here. All clear."

FIVE

Rain relaxed in his desk when Freddie and her three buddies skidded into the calculus classroom right as the bell rang. He'd been uneasy all night about leaving her in Mrs. Goff's barn. Not having wheels or any way to go check on her was messed up. At least in the city, he could catch a bus. And then to make things worse, Ruby clammed up tight on the way home and said she was too tired to talk about his mom or dad.

Taking a deep breath, he willed his heart to slow as he watched Freddie slip into her seat, giving the dark-haired guy scrambling to his desk next to hers one of the finest go-to-hell looks he'd ever seen. Then, his heart turned back into a jackhammer when she twisted and stared directly at him. He stared right back, and to his surprise, she looked away first.

All night, he'd tossed and turned, wondering how she'd ended up naked in that barn—trying really hard not to focus too much on the naked part. Maybe her clothes had been stashed somewhere in the building—or maybe she'd had a ride nearby. Either way, she must've had shoes with her. No way could she have gotten far barefoot with all those prickly plants and rocks.

All logical conclusions pointed to her being there to hook up with someone. Why else would she have been naked? But he'd seen no evidence of anyone else, and her clothes would have been there. She'd also seemed scared—beyond being caught fooling around.

A middle-aged woman with short brown hair entered the classroom and shut the door behind her, then wrote her name on the board. "I'm Miss Kendleton. Mr. Pratt had a family emergency and won't be here today."

Again, Freddie gave the guy next to her a vicious glare, and he recoiled, tucking his chin like a scolded toddler.

"Please pull out your homework, and I'll come by to check it," Miss Kendleton said.

Rain tore the page of work out of his binder that he'd half-assed his way through between classes and placed it on his desk. Neither Freddie nor her three friends made any move to get their homework.

The substitute worked her way around the room and eventually reached Rain's desk. She took his paper and, without even looking at the work, put a checkmark on the top next to his name, then ran her fingers down the grade-book page. "You wrote Rain, but the only Ryland here is Aaron. Is that you?"

He could feel his classmates' eyes on him as he nodded.

"Any relation to Ruby and Lynn?"

"My aunt and mom." His voice was barely above a whisper.

"I went to school with them. I'm in Ruby's book club."

Ms. James had mentioned the book club yesterday. Did everyone in this hick town know everyone else? And was every person who lived here in Aunt Ruby's book club? Evidently, and it made him uncomfortable. It was easy to get lost in a big city. Here, everyone was up in your business.

As she moved on to the guy in front of him, Rain glanced up to find several students staring at him with interest, including Freddie. Her hair was tamed into a ponytail today, but she wore the same clothes as yesterday. Her wrinkled jeans were smeared with dirt and green stains like she'd rolled down a hill or something. And she had some wicked scratches on her arms.

Those hadn't been there in the barn. He'd seen every inch of her arms—as well as other parts that had kept him up all night—and there had been no scratches.

Her eyes narrowed as she noticed he was staring at the marks, and she whipped back around in her chair.

As the teacher explained a formula and worked several problems on the board, he studied Freddie's three friends. They appeared to be in the same clothes as yesterday, too, though he hadn't paid as much attention to them as he had her. The dark-haired guy in the front row cast occasional nervous glances at Freddie, who ignored him. The skinny guy she'd called Kurt, sitting next to the big one named Thomas, had a cut lip and a grass stain on his shirt, and neither of the boys wore the cocky attitude he'd seen the day before.

The teacher erased the board and wrote a new problem, then announced, "Okay. I want you to pair up in groups of two or three to solve this. It's due by the end of the period."

Perfect. Maybe he could get some answers—and not to the math problem. He shot to his feet and walked along the outside wall to stand right in front of the desk of the dark-haired guy in the first row. After the boys had teamed up yesterday, he had no desire to make nice. "Move," was all he said. The guy's eyes were as dark as the Freddie's were pale. He made no move, but the girl stood, as if to leave. Rain took her hand. "Please sit. We need to talk."

She jerked her hand away and glared at the two girls a row back who quit staring and lowered their heads, suddenly entranced with their work. "I'd rather not."

"I can't imagine why." He narrowed his eyes at the guy.

"Move. Now."

As if she were in charge of him in some way, she nodded, and he scooted out of his seat and joined his two friends several rows back.

So stiff she looked brittle, she lowered herself into her chair, studying him.

"Gimme a piece of paper," he said. "We need to look like we're working."

She passed a piece of notebook paper and crossed her arms over her ribs. "What do you want?"

"Answers."

"Well, you're shit out of luck, because I suck at math."

"Not math, and you know it."

She slumped low in her desk and frowned. "Look. I appreciate you not ratting me out last night, but that's all you're going to get: appreciation." She snatched the paper back and copied the problem from the board, pencil rasping over the surface. He was surprised the lead didn't break, or maybe even the entire pencil, as hard as she gripped it.

The hairs prickled on his neck, and he glanced over his shoulder at her three friends, who had perfected the you're-a-dead-man glare.

"Your boyfriends don't like me."

She stared at him, face unreadable. He'd hoped she'd clarify her relationship with them, but instead, she shrugged and resumed scribbling. "Neither do I."

"You don't even know me."

"Don't want to."

He knew he should throw his hands up and go back to his own desk, but his curiosity was bigger than his pride.

One of the scratches on her arm widened as it disappeared up into her T-shirt sleeve. He reached to pull up the sleeve to see how bad it was, and without even turning her head, she clamped her hand around his wrist with a surprisingly strong grip. Pale, narrowed eyes met his. "Touch me and you'll regret it."

He glanced over his shoulder to find her friends leaning forward, gripping the edges of their desks. He suspected she wasn't referring to them making him regret it, though.

"That's a really bad scratch. You should get it looked at. Might need stitches."

She slammed down her pencil. "Look, Emily, or Erin, or whatever your name is."

"Aaron. But I go by Rain."

"Right. Sprinkles." She picked up the pencil again. "I really do appreciate your not exposing me last night, but get out of my business."

He leaned close. It was risky, but if she could tease about his name, he could tease right back. "Not sure you could have been any more exposed. Though maybe if your hair had been pulled back like it is now…" He arched an eyebrow and stared pointedly at the skulls on the Thirty Seconds to Mars T-shirt stretched across her chest.

Her face flushed red, and she resumed scratching numbers across the page. Then the corner of her mouth quirked up in a half smile.

He let out his breath and smiled, too.

"You flirting with me, Sprinkles?"

"Maybe." He was dying to find out more about her. He'd never been this intrigued by a person. He shifted in the undersize desk to face her more. "Wanna tell me why you were in that barn last night?"

"Nope." She set down the pencil, and it rolled off the sloped surface. She caught it before it hit the floor. Her reflexes were lightning fast.

"Wanna tell me about the scratches on your arms?"

"If I tell you, will you drop it?"

"Probably not. Depends on the explanation."

She tapped the pencil on her desk and rolled her eyes. "I walked through some thorn bushes on my way back home. Looks much worse than it is."

"You walked home? That means you live near Enchanted Rock and had clothes nearby, then."

"Wrong on all counts. Don't quit your day job, Sherlock."

Man, she wasn't making this easy. He'd almost gone mad last night, seeing her in his mind and not knowing if she'd made it home safely. He'd walked to school early and staked out the senior lot, hoping to speak with her before school, but she'd never arrived. Maybe, like him, she didn't drive. Then, he'd spent the entire lunch period looking for her with no results.

She placed the paper on his desk. "Truly, I suck at math. If you value your grade, you'll do this."

He looked around, and everyone except her three buddies were hard at work, many of them using calculators. "Do you have a calculator?"

"Yeah." She pulled one out of her backpack and handed it to him. "Never turned it on. Not sure if it even works."

It was one of the super-expensive kinds the rich kids at his last school had. When he slid the case back, there were words written in silver Sharpie inside. YOU MAKE ME PROUD. LOVE, DAD.

His chest tightened at the words he'd never hear from his own father—a man he'd never known. "You and your dad must be close, huh?"

She cleared her throat and tugged the zipper shut on her backpack. "Just do the work, okay?"

"Yes, ma'am." He'd inadvertently hit a hot button with the dad. As he filled in a couple of empty spaces in the problem, his mind worked to fill in some blank spaces about this girl. "So, I noticed you seemed a little scared yesterday."

"Maybe *you* should be scared."

"Of you?" He met her eyes.

The side of her mouth quirked up again. "Nah. I'm no threat to you at all."

He nodded and filled in another blank. "That's good to know, because your friends want to rip out my throat."

She glanced over her shoulder at them. "That's a weird phrase, but yeah, you're not high on their list of favorite people."

"Why?"

"Just do the work, okay?"

He put the paper back on her desk. "You do it." It was a dick move, but he was testing something. He'd stayed alive this long by being a good judge of people, and he had a hunch this girl's tough act was just that—an act born of necessity, not choice. She had to appear tough to these boys for some reason.

She stared at the paper and sighed rather than snap orders at him again, confirming his hunch. He retrieved the paper and completed the problem, then leaned close as he placed it on her desk.

"Why were you in that barn last night?"

She leaned in as well, shoulder touching his, causing warmth to radiate from where they met. "None of your damn business."

"It's totally my business. That makes twice I've lied to cover up for you, and I'd like to know why."

Cold air replaced her warm shoulder when she pulled away. "Lying was your choice."

"Everything cool, Freddie?" Thomas called from behind them.

She stilled, then turned. "Yeah. Butt out."

"Hey, she's got a thing for your butt, Tommy," Kurt teased.

"It's not my butt she wants," Thomas said, leaning back. "Is it, Freddie?"

Surely she wasn't dating this guy. He tensed at the thought.

"Quiet," the teacher called from the desk at the front.

Freddie crossed her arms over her chest, mouth clamped tight in a thin line.

"Okay, if I guess right, will you tell me?" Rain asked.

"It's out of your league, Sprinkles. *I'm* out of your league."

He leaned in again and spoke so quietly, she would have to listen very closely to hear him at all. "Yes, you're way, way out of my league, but I pride myself on aiming high. Simple yes or no answers to two questions. Just two and I'll drop it, okay?"

She stared at him for a long moment, then looked away and nodded.

"Were you in the barn to hide from those guys?"

Her eyes shot to his briefly, then back to the board at the front of the room.

"Yes or no?"

"No."

She'd said it without expression, staring straight ahead. She was lying.

His desk made a metallic shriek as he scooted it closer to hers. "I know what it's like to have problems. To hide and hope to hell I don't get caught."

She snorted. "That's not your second question."

"If you need help with those guys…or with anything at all—"

Her eyes narrowed. "Oh, so you see yourself as some big-city superhero who can swoop in and rescue little ol' helpless me?" Her voice dropped back to a low whisper. "From what, Sprinkles? You don't even have a clue what's going on."

"You're right, but I want to." His instincts told him this girl was in some real trouble, which was something he *did* understand.

The bell rang, and she stood and scooped up her backpack.

"Turn in your papers in the basket on the teacher's desk," the substitute called. "Be sure your names are on them."

He wrapped his fingers around her wrist. "I'm serious about being here if you need anything. I've been in deep myself." He shot a glance at her friends, who were heading their way. "I'm also good at beating the shit out of people."

She tugged her arm free. "Pretty sure I've got this."

"I'm sure you do. In fact, I'm certain of it. But I know from experience, sometimes it's nice to know someone's got your back, even if you don't need it."

She stared as if seeing him for the first time.

"I still have my second question," he said, determined not to waste this connection.

"Everything okay, Freddie baby?" Thomas asked, snaking his arm around her waist. The other two guys flanked on either side defensively.

She slammed her elbow into Thomas's ribs, and he withdrew his arm and grabbed his side. "Shit, Freddie," he gasped. The other two boys took a step away from her.

"What's the question?" she said to Rain, as if she hadn't just rib-checked the crap out of someone.

"Wanna go out sometime? You know. Just hang out or something?"

The guys gaped as if he'd just stepped out of a flying saucer.

Her eyes widened, and she appeared to hold her breath. He'd surprised her.

"Yes or no?" he pushed.

She glanced at Thomas then ratcheted her chin up a notch,

meeting Rain's gaze directly. "Yeah. That'd be cool."

Now her friends exchanged looks like she was from outer space, too.

Freddie's sudden smile made his heart hammer.

"And thanks for…" She evidently decided against whatever she was going to say. "For helping with the assignment today. You're right. It's good to have backup sometimes."

After she left the room, her friends shot him angry glares promising retaliation as they slunk out the door after her. Rain found it hard to contain his smile. He'd never met anyone quite like this girl—fierce and smart and painfully sexy. He dropped the paper in the box on the desk.

"If you're at your aunt's tomorrow night during our book club, I'll see you then," Miss Kendleton said.

"Yeah, great." Hopefully, he'd be as far away from that shit as possible, and out with hot, mysterious Freddie Burkhart.

SIX

Rain heard Freddie's angry voice and paused before he rounded the corner to the bank of lockers where he'd seen her yesterday. The tardy bell was about to ring, so the hallway was clear of students for the most part.

"I'll do whatever I want with whomever I want, Thomas. You have zero say. None of you do."

"What do you think Uncle Ulrich will say?"

"Uncle Ulrich isn't going to know. If he finds out," she said, voice deep and raspy, "then he's going to find out a lot of things the three of you've been doing."

"Fine," he said. "Just remember our dads' agreement and keep your jeans zipped."

"Screw you, Thomas. This isn't the Middle Ages."

"Screw me's right."

"Not in your wildest dreams is that gonna happen," she answered.

"Happens in my dreams all the time. And yeah, it's pretty wild."

"You sonofa—" Her words ended in a growl.

"Hey, hey, hey!" one of the other guys said over sneaker squeaks and grunts. "Break it up."

"Yeah, we need to get to class."

Rain recognized the last voice as that of the dark-haired

kid from the front row.

Freddie gave a frustrated huff. "Forget class, Merrick. You need to find Mr. Pratt's cat," she snapped. "Find it or you'll be singing soprano tomorrow, we clear?"

"Yeah." Merrick rounded the corner and almost bumped into Rain. He was followed by Kurt, and then Thomas, who had a nasty scratch across his cheek.

Rain flashed a fuck-you smile, which didn't go over well. The three guys squared off shoulder to shoulder, and he resigned himself to the inevitable. The odds weren't great, but he'd been in a lot worse situations. He'd really hoped to not get suspended, though. The gig with Aunt Ruby was new and the best he'd ever had. Now this.

"Come on," he said. The tardy bell drowned out the thud of his backpack hitting the floor. "Which one of you pricks wants to start some shit, because it sure as hell isn't gonna be me. I've no beef with you."

Kurt snickered. "Beef," he repeated.

"Moo," the dark-haired one named Merrick said.

Thomas cupped his hands around his mouth and did a cow imitation. "Mooooo!"

"Stop it." Freddie rounded the corner, hands balled into fists on her hips.

"Mooooo!" Thomas bellowed, and the other boys laughed. "He brought up livestock, we didn't."

What the hell? It was like they'd snapped and reverted back to grade school. The three guys high-fived one another and sauntered off down the hall, lowing like cattle the whole way.

Freddie dropped her arms to her sides. "Sorry. They're total assholes."

And completely out of their minds. At least he wasn't nursing injuries and an expulsion slip. He grabbed his backpack from the floor and slung it over his shoulder.

"I, uh… Well, gotta get to study hall," she said. "The teacher never takes attendance, so I won't be counted tardy."

"Yeah. I've got track. Same story."

"Oh, you run?"

"Only if I'm losing a fight."

She smiled and leaned against the bank of lockers. "Do you run a lot?"

"Never had to yet."

She smirked. "Because you're just that good."

"Because I know when to fight and when to walk away."

"Didn't look like you were walking away from the boys." She arched an eyebrow. "Do you really think you could beat all three of them?"

"I'd have kicked their asses."

"You're pretty cocky there, Sprinkles."

And he knew she liked it. Understood it. "Maybe, but it really boils down to motivation. What I want is a lot more important to me than what they want is to them."

"And what is it you want?"

You. The thought came out of nowhere, and the truth of it startled him. He shifted his backpack to his other shoulder and leaned back against the lockers next to her. "I wanna just lay low for a while without having to always watch my back or wonder what's coming at me, you know?"

She turned sideways to face him. "Yeah, I do."

Silence stretched between them like a tense bowstring, and all he could do was stare. Something was happening. Something fragile and rare and terrifying. And he loved it. Reveled in the conflicted, complicated silence as their bodies and minds acknowledged the unusual nature of their attraction—a raw, animal need on a level so basic, it was all he could do to keep his hands off her right there in the middle of the school hallway.

"You kids don't want a detention the week before spring break, now do you?" a short, bald guy in tight coach shorts called from down the hall.

Freddie cursed under her breath.

"Sorry," Rain said. "I'm new. I stopped her to ask for directions to the gym. Totally my fault."

The guy looked him up and down. "I'm Jack Jones. Head football coach. What's your name?"

"Aaron Ryland."

"Ruby's nephew, then."

He nodded.

The only thing that would make this worse was if the guy told him he was a member of Ruby's book club.

"You a senior?"

"I am."

"You look like you could take some hits. Too bad we didn't get you on our football team a couple of years ago."

Yeah. Hits.

"Follow me, I'll show you where the gym is." He delivered a pointed stare to Freddie. "Get to class, missy."

She gave the coach a middle-finger salute behind his back, then she winked at Rain, causing that jackhammer in his chest to crank back into action. Good thing he was about to run laps; it would help him work off some of this tension that pushed the needle into the red zone every time she was near.

"Good job, gentlemen!" the gym teacher shouted as Rain's group crossed the finish line after a 440. He bent at the waist, hands on knees, catching his breath while fighting the urge to throw up. It felt good to push that hard and take his body to the limit. He'd much rather be taking his body to the limit another way, but that wasn't likely to happen anytime soon—if he was lucky enough for it to happen at all. Freddie wasn't like anyone he'd ever known. She was guarded and clearly carrying a lot of baggage she wasn't ready to unpack.

"You sure you don't want to run varsity?" a guy with curly blond hair and a dark tan asked. "Coach was serious, you know. We still have a few meets this year."

Rain straightened, catching his breath. The guy was so tall, they stood eye to eye, only he didn't bear that hardened look of the streets. He was more the college-prep jock type. "Yeah. Totally sure. Heading straight from here to look for a job. Hopefully I'll find one and won't have time for after-school training."

"Have you tried Ericksen Hardware?"

"No. They looking?"

"They are if you tell them I sent you." The guy grinned, showing perfect, straight teeth. "I'm Grant Ericksen." He extended his hand. "My family owns it."

"Rain Ryland."

"I know." The guy had a strong grip and a genuine smile. It usually took Rain a while to trust people, but a strange warmth traveled from their clasped hands up his arm, disarming his usual suspicion. He liked Grant immediately, which struck him as odd.

"Well, go check out the store, and if it's not a good fit, come join the track team. I'm the captain. We need another sprinter, and the coach is interested in you." His eyes traveled past Rain's shoulder to the bleachers. "I think someone else is interested in you, too."

Freddie was seated on the top row, long legs crossed and arms draped casually over the back of the railing like she owned the place.

"Proceed with caution," Grant said. "She and her kind are a whole mess of trouble."

So much for liking the guy. "What do you mean, 'her kind'?"

Grant's smile slipped for a moment then flashed again. "Oh, I mean her family. They're a rare breed." He studied Rain for a moment, then arched an eyebrow. "But, hey, you look like you're up for a challenge. If she's your kind of thing…" He delivered a friendly punch on the shoulder. "See you tomorrow."

Kind of thing? "Yeah. Tomorrow." Grant was the third person to warn him off Freddie. Either he was getting his signals all wrong, or everyone else was. Ridiculous small-town bullshit.

When he looked back up at the bleachers, Freddie was gone.

SEVEN

Aunt Ruby's house was only a few blocks from the high school, so ordinarily, Rain would walk to and from. Not today. On the way back from Mrs. Goff's place last night, he'd told his aunt that he wanted to look for a job, and she'd offered to pick him up from school and introduce him to people in town. Having a cop introduce you surely couldn't hurt a job search.

"Hey," she called from the open cruiser window as she pulled to the curb. He'd never warmed up to someone as fast as he had his aunt Ruby. Maybe it was the fact she was his mother's twin and looked so familiar. Maybe it was her genuine friendliness. But as much as she put him at ease, he was certain he'd never be comfortable getting into a police car. "Thanks for picking me up."

"No biggie. My shift ended at three." She signaled and pulled out onto the street. "How'd your day go?"

An image of Freddie leaning against the lockers wearing that sexy, confident smile flickered in his mind, and he fought back a grin, shrugging noncommittally instead. "Nobody got hurt." Which was true, but just barely.

She turned the corner at the stop sign, heading toward the main strip, if you could call it that. Downtown New Wurzburg was nothing more than a few knickknack stores, a gas station, and a beer garden. Nearby Fredericksburg was bigger—and that didn't say much.

"Well, nobody getting hurt is a ringing endorsement," she said.

"It is where I come from."

She glanced over momentarily, and her face clouded. Pity? Regret? Hard to tell. Whatever it was, he didn't like it.

"Any idea what kind of job you want?" she asked.

"Got a line on an opening at Ericksen Hardware. You know it?"

"Sure do." She smiled and hooked a U-turn.

"That was an illegal turn!"

"Livin' on the edge. Hopefully I won't catch myself and give me a ticket."

She winked, and he thought of how his mom's life could have been so different—how *their* lives could have been different. He placed his palm over the dull pain in the center of his chest. Her warm, funny twin was everything his mother hadn't been.

"Why did my mom leave here?"

Her expression went completely flat, like Old Jim's did when he talked about serving in Vietnam. "Some people just don't like small-town life, I guess."

But his mom hadn't had any kind of life. They'd bounced from one shelter to the next, even sleeping on the streets and eating out of dumpsters when things were really bad. They could have been here, living in a Christmas card town with its old-fashioned storefronts and single stoplight. He could have grown up in a warm house instead of a living hell. Why had she done it?

"You okay, Aaron?"

He hadn't realized they'd stopped until the car motor fell silent. Relaxing his clenched fists, he took a deep breath. "Yeah."

"I read your files."

Ah, here it comes. "Juvie or CPS?"

"Both."

Great. No doubt she'd find a way to send him away now that she knew what kind of shitstorm she'd taken on. He stared at his hands and waited for the hammer to drop.

"I had them sent right after I got the call from your social worker—the night Lynn died."

That was weeks ago. "What took you so long to read them?"

She lifted her hand from the steering wheel, and for a moment, he thought she was going to touch him, but instead, her arm dropped limply in her lap. "I read them all the next morning when they were faxed to the station. Then several more times the following day. That's when I decided to agree to the judge's request to bring you here."

His throat tightened to the point it was hard to swallow. She'd brought him here knowing who and what he was. Studying her face, he realized there were some tiny lines on the outside of her eyes he hadn't noticed before, the kind that come from laughing a lot. But there was also a little wrinkle down the middle of her forehead, like a permanent reminder of a dark expression.

"I'm here if you ever need someone to talk to," she said.

Those were the same words he'd said to Freddie. He shook his head to clear it. Ruby knew all the shit he'd done. All the trouble he'd been in, and still, she offered kindness. "Thanks."

"Now, go get that job so you can afford some wheels. Chauffeuring you around is going to grow old real quick."

"Yes, ma'am." Warm wind swirled around him, ruffling his hair as he stepped out of the car that had suddenly seemed way too cramped.

"I've got an errand to run. I'll be back in thirty, okay?"

"Sure." He paused halfway through closing the door. "Hey, Aunt Ruby…" Leaning down to see inside the cruiser, he marveled again at how similar she looked to his mother. "Thanks…you know, for taking me on and all. I'm not gonna let you down."

With a tightening of her lips, she nodded and started the car. And as he watched her back out of the parking space, that line on her forehead that had only been a shadow before became a deep crease.

The woman behind the counter at Ericksen Hardware and Feed leaned closer to get a better look at Rain through her thick glasses. "You say Grant sent you here about a job?"

"Yes, ma'am."

One painted-on eyebrow arched, and she gave him another once-over. The kind of skeptical look you give a coat at the resale store before you pass on it—or maybe more like the look you give a piece of garbage as you pitch it in the dumpster.

"Stay," she ordered, then disappeared through a set of swinging double doors behind her.

Stay? Weird, but whatever. The place seemed okay enough. Old-fashioned, but that was probably the norm around here. Shovels, rakes, and yard tools hung in racks on the wall to his right, and on shelves beyond, fertilizers and bug poisons. Down the left wall, power tools, screws, nails, and hardware were displayed in bins, buckets, and on hooks. There was only enough room to house a couple of racks in the middle, containing everything from windbreakers to rain boots to camping equipment. Ropes, garden hoses, and other stuff hung from hooks on the ceiling, giving the small store a cramped, cave-like feel.

After several minutes, a girl who looked to be in middle school came out from the same doorway. Like Grant, she was attractive with blond curls. She stared at him for a long time, and he resisted the urge to look down to make sure he still had clothes on. He'd never been scrutinized like this before. First the woman, now this kid. What was with these people?

"You're the new guy in town everyone's talking about." Her voice was calm and low, mature, like she was a much older person stuck in a kid's body. "The police officer's nephew."

"Yeah."

She raised her chin. "You should be more respectful."

"So should you."

"Saying 'yeah' is rude."

"So is staring."

Her eyebrow arched, just like the woman's had a few moments ago. "You're dark."

What did that mean?

"You should have red hair. You come from redheaded stock. Your sire was dark-haired, though, I'm told."

What a weird kid. If the words weren't off-putting enough, her haughty tone certainly was.

"But you have height and strength, which is what we need."

So, they must be looking for a stocker, or maybe someone to deal with the small lumberyard he saw out back when Ruby dropped him off.

The woman stuck her head through the doorway. "How old are you?"

"Seventeen."

"When will you be eighteen?"

"Next month."

"I need a few minutes to discuss this with my husband."

She nodded and disappeared again.

The kid gave him the creeps the way she never took her eyes off him. She didn't even blink. "There a bathroom I can use?" he asked.

"Through there." She pointed to a door just past the fertilizer on the right side of the store. He didn't really need to take a leak, but getting away from the freaky kid for a few minutes worked. He closed and locked the door to the small bathroom and leaned against the paneling next to the sink with a sigh, then tensed all over again when the woman's voice drifted through the wall behind him.

"Grant texted. He believes this one's a good fit."

Rain held his breath, listening to the muffled voice. The bathroom must've backed up to whatever room the woman was in.

"Well, he said that last time, too, and we know how that one turned out," a male voice replied.

"That was unfortunate, but Grant believes—"

"Grant is not in charge yet."

"But this is his responsibility. You turned her over to him."

Huh. They referred to the store as a "her" like you would a ship or a car. The dude was only a senior in high school, and he already owned a business. Lucky bastard.

"Compatibility?" the male asked.

"He just texted that there was a display of receptiveness, which is more than we've had with the others."

What the hell? They must have a hard time hanging on to employees. No wonder, with the freaky behavior.

"Well, give him a job and keep him close. Maybe this one will last long enough to settle things down. If not, I'm revoking Grant's sponsorship."

"Charles, no."

"We can't afford another loss. No matter what or who. Go

hire the kid and warn your son what's at stake."

What kind of place was this if they couldn't keep employees? No way was he working here. No way in hell.

"Oh, and call Ulrich Burkhart. Tell him to keep his niece in line this time, or I'll deal with her myself."

Ulrich... Freddie and her three friends mentioned Uncle Ulrich. These people were talking about Freddie.

The male cleared his throat. "And one more thing. Tell Ulrich if she isn't willing to step up once she graduates, she's finished. We'd be better off with Kurt anyway."

"You wouldn't. Charles, no. It would break Grant's heart."

"Try me."

What the actual hell was going on here? Whatever it was, it didn't sound good for Freddie. A door opened and closed on the other side of the wall.

Gooseflesh crept up Rain's arms and back. Something here was off. Way off. He should head straight from this bathroom out the front door and not look back. And he would have, were it not for Freddie. He'd told her she could trust him. What kind of chickenshit move would it be to bail after hearing that kind of craziness? He had no clue what they were talking about, but he was damn sure going to find out.

He flushed the toilet just in case someone was nearby, then ran the sink for good measure. Yeah. He'd take this job and get to the bottom of whatever creepy shit was happening. As for "this one" lasting long enough, they could damn well bet on it. He'd dealt with a lot more crap than any stupid job could dish out. *Bring it, assholes.*

EIGHT

"So, how'd it go?" Ruby asked as Rain got in the car in the Ericksen Hardware and Feed parking lot.

"Well, I got the job." He hoped he came across as normal and not nervous.

"That's great news, Aaron! Did you get to meet Ellen and Charles Ericksen? Ellen's in my book club and is super nice."

Well, wasn't that interesting? Maybe he needed to hang around the house during that meeting after all. "Didn't meet him, but she seemed okay. I start on Monday."

"Oh, that's fabulous. What will you be doing?"

When he glanced through the windshield at the building, the weird girl was watching him through the window. *Figuring out what the hell is going on around here.* No wonder Freddie had that scared look in her eyes when she thought no one was watching. "Stocking shelves, mostly."

For a moment, he thought she was going to hug him, which honestly would've been okay considering how uptight he was, but she started the car instead. "We should celebrate."

Yeah. Celebrate a job where they can't keep employees and the owner had some kind of problem with Freddie.

"First, this." She pulled a brand-new cell phone from a bag stowed between her and the door.

"Aunt Ruby. I can't—"

She thrust it into his palm. "You can, and you will. It's as much for me as you. It'll be much easier for both of us if I can reach you. Besides, I'm hoping you'll make some friends and this will be useful when that happens, too. Right?"

"Yeah, I guess." He turned it over in his hand. He'd never had a cell phone before. Most of the guys back home did, usually jacked from somebody or cheap burner phones, but since he didn't deal or use, he hadn't needed one. His lungs felt tight, like he couldn't take a deep breath. "I don't know what to say."

"Thank you?" she teased.

"Thanks." He smiled, which was no easy feat, and she smiled back, making it worth the effort.

"It's hard for you to accept gifts, isn't it?" she asked.

He shrugged. "Not really. I've taken handouts my whole life."

"This isn't a handout." She squeezed his shoulder. "We're family, Aaron. You're my only family left."

Something in him clicked into place. She was in the same boat as he was—they were in this *together*. The thought alone made his lungs feel less constricted.

She sniffed, started the car, and backed out of the parking space. "I've already programmed some numbers in your phone. My cell, the police station, and the pizza delivery place. You should probably add the hardware store now, too."

The girl was still watching through the storefront window. Yeah. Enter it as *Hell's Hardware and Freak Show Feed*.

Instead of heading east toward home, she turned west and soon pulled into a fenced lot with several corrugated-metal storage sheds. "But the phone's not the best part." She looked younger when she grinned, and he found her obvious joy contagious. She turned over a cinderblock next to the door of the end unit and snatched a small silver key from the block's rectangular footprint in the dirt. "The best part," she said, inserting and turning the key in the lock. "Is…" The lock clicked open, and she yanked on the door with a grunt, swinging it wide to reveal what appeared to be old car-engine parts, several large toolboxes on wheels, a painted wooden rowboat, and two bright-red motorcycles. No, not motorcycles—they were more like the motocross bikes Rain had seen on those insane X-game shows in the shelter lobby. "This!" She propped the door open with the cinderblock and strolled inside to stand between the bikes.

Her grin seemed forced as she patted the seat of the larger one. "This one's yours."

He'd heard of people being speechless, but this was the first time it had ever happened to him. She couldn't possibly be serious.

She rolled it out into the sunlight, and he noticed her smile had faded. "Well, it used to be your dad's, but it's yours now." She blinked several times rapidly and took a deep breath. Something was off. "Ever ridden one?"

"No."

She rolled it close and leaned the bike toward him. "Hold this."

"Aunt Ruby—"

"Just hold it while I get the other one, okay?"

Yeah, something was definitely off. She wiped away a tear with the back of her hand as he took the bike by the handlebars and balanced it upright.

She rolled the other one from the shed. "Riding these bikes is easy. Do you have a driver's license?"

"No."

"Have you taken driver's ed?" Her voice was strained, like she was struggling hard to not lose it.

"Took the book part. It was offered at school. I couldn't

afford the practical driving part of the course, and I didn't figure I'd ever drive… Aunt Ruby, we need to talk."

"Well, at least you have a general understanding of the rules of the road." She was talking faster now. Like it was a rehearsed speech.

"Aunt Ruby, stop." He put down the kickstand and rolled the bike back until it was locked in place while she rattled on like her life depended on it.

"I know you don't have a license yet, but nobody around here cares if you stay on the small back roads and you don't ride like a jackass." By this point, tears were rolling unchecked down her face as she gripped the bike.

Taking her by the shoulders, he gave a slight shake "Ruby!"

"Oh God." She shook her head. "I'm so sorry, Aaron. I thought I could…"

He put down the kickstand on her bike, then rounded it to pull her into a hug. Something he'd never done in his lifetime. His mother recoiled from his touch, and he'd never been close enough to anyone else to offer comfort.

As he held the sobbing woman, he realized it was as beneficial for him as it was for her. He needed this. Human contact. Messy. Complicated. Essential. Something he hadn't known he was missing.

She sniffed loudly and stepped away. "Thanks. It always seems to catch me by surprise." With an awkward half laugh, she shook her head. "Just when I think I've got myself together, *bam*!" She sniffed again and pushed some hair back behind her ear that had come loose from her bun. "Lynn was such a part of me, you know? The same soul in different skins. We lived in that house together our entire lives until…"

Until I came along. Yeah. His mom told him over and over how he'd screwed up her life. She'd omitted to mention her twin, though. And the fact his dad was not a one-and-done, like she'd called him so many times. This was his bike. He'd been involved with his mom before she left New Wurzburg. She'd said they'd met and hooked up at a bar in Houston, and she never saw him again. She'd lied. *Why?* "Tell me about my dad."

Ruby looked startled.

"Please," he continued. "I guess I'm just looking to make sense of things. She never mentioned family. Said she didn't know my dad."

Ruby walked to the shed and pushed the door closed. "She knew him all right. Everyone did. Roger Blain moved here our senior year in high school, and as you've discovered, new people are novelties in a town this small."

She had that right. He felt like something squished flat enough to see clear through on a microscope slide every time he set foot in the school. And it had been worse at the hardware store.

Ruby pulled the cinderblock out of the way and swung the door shut. She put the lock in place and snapped it closed, then returned the key to its place under the concrete block. When she turned back to him, she seemed more composed. "I don't know why Lynn lied about Roger—or me. The three of us were best friends for almost a decade."

"What happened?"

"Life happened, Aaron. Sometimes stuff just…happens." She grabbed the handlebars of her dirt bike and flipped the kickstand up with a boot. "But you know all about that, don't you?"

"Yeah."

Her blue eyes met his. "Let's let the past be past. You're here now, and we're family. That's what matters."

A small lump formed in his throat.

"Welcome home, Aaron."

The lump grew to golf-ball size, and his eyes stung.

She cleared her throat as she fiddled with the brake lever. "Well, we're gonna lose daylight if we don't get started now, and these really need to be run. It's been a while, but Gerald took care of them for me last week before you arrived."

"The guy who can't operate a stapler?"

Her smile made his chest feel warm inside. "The only things Gerald can do right are motorbikes and tractors. He came out here, cleaned and tuned them up, and put in all new fluids. They should run great. You ready?"

"I don't know how—"

She straddled her bike and turned the key. The thing roared to life. "S'easy. Just do what I do."

After copying her every move and following instructions, he found himself speeding down a long dirt road next to her, and for a moment his heart pinched. He was riding his dad's bike next to his aunt, who was laughing like she was flying. If only his mom had chosen this way to fly instead of the drugs and booze. If only…

No. Ruby was right. Let the past be the past. New town. New start. He had a great place to live, the hottest girl he'd ever met had agreed to go out with him, and now he even had a job—probably a shitty one but still a job. When Mrs. Ericksen had come out and offered him a position at the store, she'd seemed almost normal. Maybe he'd misunderstood the conversation through the wall. Maybe it wasn't Freddie they were talking about at all.

Yeah, and maybe he was the Easter Bunny. Something weird was going on at that place. Weird shit was going on everywhere, including whatever Freddie had been up to in Mrs. Goff's barn. Shit that clearly had Freddie rattled, too. And one way or another, he'd find out what all of it was about. But for now, he'd just enjoy the feel of the wind and setting sun on his skin and the hum of the bike under him.

Enchanted Rock loomed ahead several miles in the distance, powerful and primal. Like Freddie. Like him.

Moth had said he liked the streets because they offered freedom. But he was wrong. The streets were an intricate prison. *This* was freedom—simple, pure, and absolute. For the first time in his life, Rain had hope—not the pie-in-the-sky far-fetched kind of nonsense he'd dreamed of as a kid but something real and tangible and possible. Maybe, just maybe, he'd finally found a place where he belonged.

NINE

At first, Rain thought the tapping was Aunt Ruby at his bedroom door, but when it happened the second time, he realized it was coming from his window.

Rubbing the sleep from his eyes, he checked the time on his phone. Two fifteen in the morning.

Tap-tap-tap.

He slid out of bed, wrapped the sheet around himself, and grabbed the baseball bat that he'd found in the back of his closet the day he moved in.

Tap-tap-tap.

With a jerk, he pulled aside the heavy curtains to find nothing other than the narrow street glowing blue in the bright moonlight and the houses across it.

Then he saw the pale eyes just below the windowsill.

From where she crouched in the bushes, Freddie gestured for him to open the window, then shot a glance behind her as if looking for someone.

He flipped the lock and pushed up, but the window didn't budge.

Again, she scanned over her shoulder. Between the tall hedge outside his window and her curtain of hair, he didn't have a clear view, but it was obvious she was naked again. *What the hell?*

He tried the window once more but realized it was sealed shut with multiple coats of paint. It probably hadn't been opened in his lifetime.

Go to the front door, he mouthed, pointing in that direction. She shook her head.

Shit. Sheet still clutched around his waist, he grabbed his jeans from the floor and dug out his pocketknife. She glanced behind her several times as he sliced through the paint all the way around the wooden window frame. She was definitely evading someone. Finally, the window budged, opening an inch or so but no more.

"Hurry," she whispered.

"Go to the front door," he said.

"Can't." She appeared shaken, just like she had in the barn. She stood, slid her fingers under the opening, and pulled up, giving him a full view.

Holy shit. This was the kind of thing that happened only in dreams. Really good ones.

"Don't just stand there," she whispered, tugging hard on the window with dirt-covered hands. In fact, she had dirt smeared in several places on her body and leaves in her hair. "Help me." He pushed from the inside and the window broke loose all at once, slamming against the top of the frame with a *bang*.

She instantly dropped into a crouch in the bushes and placed her forefinger to her lips to silence him. "Keep your room light off," she whispered. "Walk out the front door. Act like you're looking for what made that noise. Be obvious."

When he stepped onto the porch, he flipped on the light. "Anybody here?" he said, still clutching the sheet to his waist. "Hello?" His voice sounded super loud in the stillness.

"Hey," Ruby answered from a bench hanging from chains at the far end of the porch, nearly making him drop his sheet.

She popped a chocolate in her mouth from a box on the seat next to her. "Having a toga party?"

A dog whined, then howled nearby. Another answered in the distance.

"What are you doing up?" he asked.

"I could ask you the same thing."

"Oh, um." He scanned the street but saw nothing out of the ordinary. "I thought I heard something. Guess it was you."

"Sounded to me like your bedroom window opening."

Damn. "Yeah, I opened it to check things out."

"Probably just the dogs," Ruby said, popping another candy. She lifted the box. "Want a chocolate?"

"No, thanks. Dogs?"

She swallowed and nodded. "Yep. It's not uncommon in the country for a wild pack of dogs to form up. I've never seen any, but I've heard them, and sometimes livestock gets killed or goes missing. We get calls at the station about them occasionally." She popped another chocolate in her mouth. "Sometimes it sounds like there are dozens of them over near Enchanted Rock. I used to think it was coyotes, but people swear they've seen big dogs. Some even say they're wolves, but those don't live around here." She shrugged.

Why, he wondered, was he on the porch talking about dogs when Freddie was in the bushes outside his room? "Well, since it's nothing to worry about, I'll just go back to bed."

She nodded, mouth drawn in a line.

"You okay, Aunt Ruby?"

"I will be. I always am. Good night, Aaron. Kill the light on your way in, okay?"

He felt terrible leaving her out there, clearly unhappy, wallowing in a chocolate binge, but Freddie had something going on, and that was more pressing. On more levels than he cared to think about.

When he got to his room, the window was shut and the drapes pulled together. Through the closed bathroom door, he could hear the shower running.

Yeah. Again, like a really great dream.

The water cut off. He pitched the sheet on the bed and pulled on his jeans, heart pounding.

The front door closed. Ruby coming back inside, no doubt. Maybe she'd open up to him one day. Tell him what caused that worry line down her forehead that was in complete opposition to her older, deeper smile lines.

A drawer opened and closed in the bathroom as he pulled his shirt over his head.

But first, he needed Freddie to tell him why she had been in that barn last night and outside his window tonight. He wasn't one to gamble, but he'd bet most anything it had to do with those three guys in calculus class.

With the drapes closed, it was dark. So dark that he could barely make out the bookshelf and desk on the far wall.

He shuffled over to the desk and sat in the chair, thinking it a wiser choice than the bed considering…well, considering.

His body tightened and his heart pounded in his ears when a shaft of light from the bathroom sliced through the darkness, then widened as Freddie pulled the door open all the way. She'd raided his closet while he was on the porch and now wore his red Nike shirt and a pair of his track shorts, which made her legs look even longer. She'd wrapped her hair in a towel wound up like a turban. In her fist, she clutched his comb.

She sat on the foot of his bed, and for the longest time, they simply stared at each other in silence as steam wafted from the bathroom, dancing in wispy tendrils through the shaft of light between them.

He wanted to ask her a million questions but knew it was

better to wait her out. To let her tell him what was going on when she was ready.

Finally, she spoke. "So, you're not going to quiz me?"

"No." It was all he could do to sit still. Like when he used to feed the squirrels in the park, he remained quiet and unmoving, hoping to gain her trust. And since she'd sought him out tonight, he believed he'd made a good start.

"Thanks for...well, you know." She looked toward the window and shrugged. "Letting me in."

He sat in silence while she unwound the towel from her head. Her hair tumbled down her back in a wet tangle.

She scooted back a few inches on the bed. "Made myself at home in your bathroom. Didn't think you'd care."

Oh, he cared. He cared a lot, but he certainly didn't object. She was in his room, which was awesome and scary as hell at the same time. Fascinated, he watched her methodically untangle the bottom few inches of her hair with his comb.

"You're weird," she said.

"In what way?"

"In that you're not interrogating me. The boys would be firing questions left and right."

He assumed she meant the three guys from calculus. "I'm not one of the boys."

Comb mid-pull, she paused. Then met his gaze directly. "No. You're not."

His vision had adjusted to the darkness, and he could see her face more clearly now. The smears of dirt were gone, and her pale eyes looked like colorless, clear glass in the dim light. Long lashes cast slanted shadows across her skin. Beautiful.

"I know you came from Houston. Did you live there all your life?"

"We moved around a lot. Mostly in Houston, yes."

"Why are you in New Wurzburg?" She resumed her

detangling. She'd made it about six inches up now.

Ah, so she was going to interrogate *him* instead. "Court order."

Her eyebrows rose in surprise. "What did you do?"

I existed. "My mom died. Ruby's my only relative. The judge ordered that I live with her until I'm eighteen."

The surprise clouded with something else. Sadness? "Sorry about your mom."

He gave a one-shouldered shrug.

She tugged on a particularly stubborn tangle. "Your name is Aaron. Where did Rain come from?"

"It's sort of an inside joke." *Not a funny one.* "Mom always said that from the moment she got knocked up, a rain cloud followed her around—a storm of trouble and ruin. She called me her little rain cloud, and Rain just stuck."

The tangle broke free, and she moved to one higher up. "And your dad?"

"Never met him. Died working on an offshore oil rig in the Gulf before I was born. Mom said she didn't know the guy—it was a one-night thing—but she said she saw his picture in the paper and recognized him." Which he now knew was a total lie.

"That sucks."

"Yeah."

For a long time, she worked her way up her hair, clearing tangles without talking. He noticed the scratches on her arm weren't as deep as he'd originally thought.

He leaned back in the chair. She seemed more at ease with him now. "Tell me about those guys you hang with. Who are they to you?"

"Jealous?"

"Maybe."

She pulled the comb through her hair from the part to the ends on the left side. "It's complicated."

"Everything is. Welcome to life."

Her eyes shot to his, and she opened her mouth as if to speak but closed it, sliding the comb through her hair farther back.

He rolled the chair closer to where she sat on the foot of the bed. "Look. Clearly, the four of you grew up together based on the way you interact."

"Yeah. We're cousins." Evidently surprise showed on his face because she spoke more quickly. "I have a really large family. Almost everybody at Haven Winery is related in one way or another."

"That's your home?" There were tons of vineyards and wineries around this part of the Hill Country.

"Yes."

"Thomas doesn't act like your cousin."

"We're third cousins a billion times removed or some such thing."

As long as she was being honest, he might as well go there himself. "I don't like him. And I don't like the way he talks to you—like he owns you. Are you dating?"

"No."

"Let's be honest with each other."

"I'm not lying."

Maybe not, but she wasn't being totally honest, either. "The one named Merrick seems frightened of you, but you appear afraid of the other two."

She snorted. "The day I'm afraid of Thomas and Kurt will be the day hell freezes over."

"Then why are you hiding from them in my room right now?"

"Not because I'm afraid of them."

But she was. He knew fear, and that was what he'd seen both in the barn and outside his window. Pure, undiluted fear.

Rain scooted the rolling desk chair even closer, to where their knees almost touched. He could feel the heat from her through his jeans.

She went back to slipping the comb through her hair. "In class, you said I could trust you. I needed a place to hang out for a while."

"Why?"

"It's a game. A twisted game." Her voice was strained and fractionally higher. She was lying.

The chair creaked when he leaned back and crossed his arms over his chest. His knees touched hers, but she didn't pull away.

"Sort of like hide-and-go-seek," she added.

"Naked?"

"Like I said, twisted."

God, she was pretty. Even lying through her teeth she was pretty. "How often do you play this game?"

She set the comb on the bed next to her and pulled her sleek, damp hair over the front of her shoulder. It was so long, the ends folded in her lap. "Not often. I…" She wrapped the hair around her hand and closed her fist. "I don't like to lose. I can't lose."

Running around naked with her cousins in the middle of the night made no sense to Rain, but *that* he understood. "I don't like to lose, either."

When she drew a deep breath in through her nose, he realized he'd leaned in and so had she. She inhaled again, as if smelling him. Then she made a rumbly sound that shot adrenaline from his chest to his fingers and toes and everything in between in a hot, buzzy wave.

Instinct deep inside him warned him to back away. Something else, something stronger and more primal urged him forward. He placed his hands on her thighs, just above her knees. Her breaths quickened and her pupils expanded to push the pale irises to the edge. Neither moved. Neither spoke.

Beneath his palms, her smooth skin heated, and his entire body hardened. Hesitant to move and break the moment, he could only stare as his heart tried to chisel its way out of his rib cage.

Her gaze dropped to his lips, and she covered his hands with hers, giving approval to his touch.

He slid his hands higher over her smooth skin and leaned in, bringing their lips within an inch of each other. Heads tilted. Breaths mingling. He'd never felt like this—like he was on fire from inside out.

Then she closed the distance, and when their lips met, it was like a match hitting kerosene. No gentle, polite, getting-to-know-you first kiss from Freddie. She all but consumed him, wrapping her arms around his neck and digging her nails into his skin. Hot. Demanding. *Perfect.*

Before she broke the kiss, she'd managed to crawl into his lap on the desk chair that he was certain he'd never be able to do homework in again without needing a cold shower.

She pulled away and stared at him like she'd discovered something new and amazing. Heaven knew *he* certainly had. Never had he been kissed like that—like the world revolved around that moment. And he wanted more. He wanted everything.

TEN

With one hand braced behind Freddie's back, Rain threaded the fingers of his other in her thick, shower-wet hair at the back of her head and pulled her in for another kiss. The desk chair creaked as she shifted on his lap and fisted the back of his T-shirt, her tongue tangling with his.

The embrace could have lasted ten seconds, or ten minutes, or ten hours. It was as if Rain's mind and sense of reality flipped off like a wall switch when he kissed this girl. Nothing but pounding blood and heat and *her*.

She pulled away, both of them breathing hard, faces only inches apart. Then her expression changed completely—like she'd remembered something horrible all of a sudden. Her eyebrows drew together, and she shook her head. "No." She scrambled out of his lap and backed toward the bathroom door. "No. We can't."

What the hell? She'd been on fire a moment ago. Now this? "Why not?"

"I didn't come here for this."

"I never thought you did. Doesn't mean we should stop. Sometimes things just happen."

"This can never happen. I made a huge mistake. This is all my fault. I'm sorry."

He took several cautious steps toward her. "What was a

mistake? Coming here or kissing me?"

"Both. Bad ideas. Terrible, terrible ideas." She backed into the bathroom.

"Tell me why this"—he gestured to himself, then her—"is a bad idea."

"Nothing in this town is what it seems."

"Things rarely are."

"And to make it worse, you live with a cop."

"Kissing isn't illegal, Freddie. She's not going to come in here and bust us."

She rolled her eyes. "That's not what I meant."

He took several steps closer. "Yes, I live with a cop. Ironic, since I've spent my whole life running from them."

"Why?"

"Because things aren't always what they seem." He repeated it in the same cadence and inflection she'd used. He braced a hand on the doorframe. "This isn't about me. It's about why you're pushing me away. You trusted me enough to come here. Now trust me enough to tell me why you've changed your mind."

Freddie paced Rain's bathroom like a caged animal. She pulled her hair in front of her shoulder again and twisted it around her hand. "I'm in danger, and I'll put you in danger."

"What kind of danger?"

"I don't know."

With most people, he would chalk this whole scene up to drama, but with Freddie, he expected that danger meant the real deal.

"You're talking to someone who lived on the streets and was hunted by gangs."

She stopped pacing and faced him. Good. She was listening.

"You asked where I'd lived before this? It was a homeless shelter. Before that, it was a tent city under an overpass, then juvie. Before that, an abandoned warehouse where a guy killed another guy just to see what it felt like. I can handle danger. Let me help you." He risked it and stroked her cheek with his fingertips. For a moment, she leaned into his touch, then she pulled away. "Let me in," he said. "You can't do this alone. Everyone needs someone." Even him. "Please, Freddie."

Her expression changed several times as she warred in her head. "Bad things are going on. I think lots of people are involved, but I don't know who, and I don't know why, and…" A tear breached her lid and stalled halfway down her cheek. She scrubbed it away with the back of her hand. "You wanna know why I hadn't used the calculator? It's because my dad gave it to me the day he was murdered. I'd made an A on a test, and he gave it to me as a reward before school the next day. It was the last time I saw him alive."

Murdered. "When did he die?"

"October."

Only six months ago. No wonder she was screwed up. He wanted to bombard her with questions but held his tongue.

Her brow furrowed. "I don't know who did it, and I'm scared I'll be next."

"Are the police investigating it?"

"I think the police are *in* on it…"

Please no. "Ruby, too?"

She shook her head. "No. Not your aunt. She's li— An outsider."

Outsider? Interesting and specific, considering there were only two other people on the police force. Ruby had lived in New Wurzburg her entire life. She and his mom had grown up in this very house.

He leaned his shoulder against the bathroom doorframe. "Do your cousins know you're looking for the killer? That you think you're next?"

"No. Nobody does. Well, except you now. Everyone says it was an accident, but it wasn't."

"Let me help you." If he could help her search for answers, he could stay close and keep her safe.

She was silent, as if considering his words, and his heart ached for her. He knew what it was like to be completely alone and afraid with no one to trust.

He shoved his hands in his pockets to keep from touching her again. "Coming from outside, I have a fresh perspective."

"I can't get you involved."

"But I *am* involved. And maybe my aunt knows something you don't."

She gave a choked laugh. "Your aunt is in danger, too. You can't tell her I'm looking for his killer."

He held up his hands. "Okay. We'll keep it between the two of us. Our secret."

After splashing water on her face, Freddie sniffled as she dried off with a hand towel.

"I've gotta go."

She hadn't agreed to let him help, but she hadn't said no, either. Rain nodded and stepped back from the bathroom doorway.

"Do me a favor," she said. "Go do the routine on the porch again to draw attention away from your window, just in case."

"So you don't lose."

She smiled. "Well, I did say I like to win."

His throat constricted at the possibility that someone out there was waiting for a chance to hurt her. No way in hell would he stand back and let that happen. "So do I."

After flipping on the porch light and calling, "Who's there?" a couple of times, he returned to his room, finding it empty, as expected. When he went to pull the window closed, he found his red Nike T-shirt and gym shorts folded neatly on the sill.

ELEVEN

Freddie wasn't at school the next day, but her cousins were. From the moment they hit the calculus classroom, they fired gonna-fuck-you-up looks at Rain. He answered in kind.

Mr. Pratt was back and acted no different than before, even giving the same senioritis speech before taking attendance. When he called Freddie's name, Thomas told him she was home sick. Then he shot a threatening look at Rain who stared right back, relieved to know she'd at least made it home.

The boys' body language was hostile, not only toward Rain but toward their other classmates, too. The students sitting near them leaned away, most likely subconsciously. Others darted worried looks in their direction. He wasn't sure whether it was Freddie's absence that fueled their aggression or something else.

After a lesson he paid no attention to, Rain held in his desk as the ending bell finally rang, not wanting a conflict with the guys. He'd wait until they cleared out, but they didn't. Like him, they made no move to leave. Once the room emptied, they stood and so did he. No way was he getting trapped in that idiotic desk to have his skull cracked.

The tall, skinny guy, Kurt, was the first to speak. "Stay away from Freddie."

He wondered if she was really ill. "Is she okay?"

Thomas spoke this time. "She must have gotten into something rotten last night that made her sick."

"Yeah. Some disease," Kurt added.

"Mad cow disease, maybe?" Thomas snorted, and he and Kurt fist-bumped.

The third guy, Merrick, held back from the other two and didn't seem as into the game. He was the weak link. If shit started, it was only a two-on-one situation. Piece of cake. If something was going to go down, though, Rain wouldn't be the one to start it. He kept his expression mild and said nothing.

"First and last warning," Kurt said. "Stay the hell away."

"Or what?" *Dammit.* He couldn't just keep his mouth shut. Inwardly, he kicked himself for being stupid and poking the wasp's nest.

Thomas moved within punching distance. "Or I'll slowly peel your skin from your body with my teeth while you scream and then eat you for dinner."

Whoa. That was unexpectedly fucked up. Not the run-of-the-mill threat.

"Careful. That might give you mad cow disease or something," Rain said, still reeling that the sick asshole had gone all Hannibal Lecter.

"Let's go," Merrick said. "He got the message."

The boys grabbed their backpacks, and all three left the room without a backward glance.

Rain had exchanged a lot of trash talk in his life, but that was some of the freakiest shit he'd ever encountered. Peel his skin from his body? He shuddered, adrenaline still pulsing through his veins.

In the hallway, he caught sight of the guys following a group of girls. He sped up to get closer. They were making the same mooing sounds they'd made at him the day before. Every now and then, Kurt bleated like a sheep. The girls didn't look angry, as Rain would have expected; they looked terrified. In fact, students parted when they passed, like in the video he'd seen one time when a shark passed through a school of fish.

The boys split up right before the tardy bell rang, and Rain leaned against the wall of lockers, puzzling out what he'd witnessed. The first time he'd seen Freddie and her cousins, he'd equated them with a gang. Maybe they were, and it was Freddie who kept these guys in check. Maybe she was the gang leader, and in her absence, they went rogue. He needed to keep an eye on them until she returned, which he hoped was soon.

Evidently, she'd told her cousins where she'd been last night. That, or they'd put two and two together and figured it out on their own.

He wondered if she was really sick or simply avoiding him. Maybe he shouldn't have kissed her. Perhaps he'd moved too fast. *No.* She'd kissed *him.* Practically climbed him like a jungle gym. His body heated at the memory, and he shook his head to clear it. A long, hard run was just the thing he needed right now.

The school workout gym smelled like plastic mats, metal, and sweat. It was raining, so the coach told the guys they could lift weights instead of run today.

"I'll spot," Grant offered when Rain stopped at the bench press.

"Cool." Rain slid another set of forty-five-pound plates onto the bar and lay back on the bench, testing the bar before lifting it.

Grant took his place behind him to catch the bar if it

didn't make the hooks. "So, Friederike Burkhart, huh?"

Rain relaxed his grip before he even attempted the lift. *What the hell?* Had Freddie taken out an ad announcing she'd dropped by his place?

He positioned his hands and pushed up, lifting the bar from the hooks. Just right. Enough weight to be a challenge but totally manageable. He lowered the bar to his chest and pushed up with a grunt. Three reps should do it.

"I was surprised, honestly. She's usually not receptive," Grant said, voice conversational.

Rain took another breath before lowering the bar again. *Receptive.* What kind of term was that? With a grunt, he raised the bar back and kept it suspended, muscles vibrating under the stress. One more rep at this weight.

"You good?"

"Yeah" With a deep breath, he lowered the bar to his chest and shoved it back up with a fierce growl.

Grant assisted as he let the bar fall back into place. "Hmm. I guess I can see your appeal."

What was with this guy?

"Mom and Dad said you came by the store for a job."

Rain sat up. "Yeah. I start Monday. Thanks for that."

"No big deal. Glad I could steer you in the right direction." He took a seat on the bench, evidently planning to press the same amount of weight. He pushed the bar out of the brackets and centered it. "You made an impression on my little sister. She wouldn't shut up about you all through dinner."

She'd made an impression on Rain, too. Not a good one.

Grant lowered the bar and pushed it back up with what appeared to be little effort.

"Where is Friederike today?" Grant asked after another rep.

"How am I supposed to know?"

"Because she was at your place last night."

Was everyone in this town a member of some online gossip chat room or something?

Grant did another rep, and his muscles vibrated on the press. Rain spotted the bar back to its bracket. "You and Freddie must be close for her to share her private life with you."

He barked a laugh as he sat up. "Her cousin told me."

It seemed odd she would have told her cousins, since she had been hiding from them in the first place.

"Merrick saw her climb out of your window." Grant punched his shoulder in that conspiratorial, macho guy kind of way.

Rain wanted to punch him back in a knock-his-teeth-out kind of way. "Another round?"

"Nah. I'm done." Grant extended his hand. "Thanks for the spot."

Warily, Rain took his hand. Like yesterday on the track, a warm buzz traveled up his arm and a strange appreciation for the guy washed through him. *Not right.* Nothing about this was right. This whole town was off somehow, and he planned to get to the bottom of it, starting with the mystery of Freddie's dad's murder and who might be out to harm Freddie.

"Take care, Aaron Ryland," Grant said before Rain reached the door. Somehow, it sounded more like a warning than a friendly parting comment.

TWELVE

Rain pulled the hood of his jacket lower over his face and crossed the street. The one-story, tan brick building looked more like a post office than a police station. A dented blue Toyota Corolla with a red right front quarter panel from another car, a sleek pearl-finish Mercedes, and Ruby's cruiser were the only vehicles parked out front.

He took a deep breath. Moth would get a huge kick out of this: Rain Ryland entering a police station by choice. Man, oh man, how his life had changed.

Under the overhang, he shook off the water and pulled back the hood. The door stuck when he pulled the handle but eventually broke free with a loud squeak of the hinges. Ruby'd said Gerald was the catchall guy, from dispatch to handyman. Hopefully he was better with the phone than he was with a screwdriver and a can of WD-40, which was all it would take to repair the door. The interior of the station was in no better shape. The first thing that caught his eye was the dinginess of the place, punctuated by the hum and flicker of fluorescent tube lights in the yellowed tile grid ceiling, half of which were burned out. Gerald should be fired as handyman for sure. At least he was good with dirt bikes.

"What do you want?" a balding middle-aged man said from a scratched metal desk in the back left corner of the room.

What kind of greeting was that?

"Hey, Aaron!" Ruby rose from behind a desk in the opposite corner outside a door labeled CHIEF WANDA RICHTER. "He's here to see me, Gerald. Thanks."

"Oh, this is your nephew." The man scanned him up and down with a grimace that looked like he'd just chewed up a bug. *Screw you, too, buddy.*

"What are you doing here?" his aunt asked, helping him out of the rain coat and hanging it on a hook inside the door. She gestured to the metal folding chair in front of her desk.

"Just dropping in to say hi." That sounded lame. Better than the truth: *I came to see if I can find out what's going on in this crazy town, specifically with regard to Freddie's dad's death.*

"Have a seat. How was school?"

Weird as hell. "Good." He slipped out of his backpack—still dry because he'd worn it under his coat—and shoved it under the chair with his foot. "So…" He gestured to a novel opened facedown on her desk as he sat. "Is this your typical day?"

"Yep. It's a safe, quiet little town."

Safe, my ass.

A glance at Gerald confirmed he was listening in.

Ruby picked up the novel. "My book club meets tonight. I haven't finished this week's chapters." It had an orange and black cover with a guy dressed in black on the front. "It's about space aliens in high school. You might like it. You could catch up easily by next week. Wanna sit in tonight?"

The chief's door opened, and a woman dressed in a black pantsuit like on the TV detective shows stepped out. It was hard to tell how old she was. Maybe sixtyish. She had shiny blond hair with silver streaks in it, coiled in a braid around the top of her head like a crown—the kind of hairstyle that looked like it was a pain to do and uncomfortable to wear, which suited. The Mercedes out front made sense now.

"I need the Schmidt Ranch file," she ordered Gerald. "Fetch. Now."

Holy shit. She commanded him like he was a pet dog or something. Rain hated her immediately.

"Anything new, Ruby?" Her tone for his aunt was civil in comparison.

"No, Chief. Not a single call."

"I'm going to check out that report from the ranch. They lost another calf last night." Her gaze froze on Rain, and he felt pinned in place. Unable to move or even breathe for a moment.

With a low growl in his throat, he broke free of whatever had frozen him up and stood. What was wrong with him? Maybe it was the lack of sleep last night.

"Uh, Chief. This is my nephew, Aaron. Lynn's boy."

The woman didn't move a muscle. "That's obvious."

Again, he felt that odd paralysis, and once more he shook it off, staggering back a few steps.

The chief's eyebrow arched.

"He came by to say hi." Ruby sounded tense.

"I'm told you've befriended the Burkhart girl," the chief said.

"We've only just met." As weird as he felt, it was a wonder his voice worked. His mom used to complain of migraines. From her description, he might be about to have one based on the painful swirling in his skull.

"You discussed her father, I assume."

What the actual fuck was going on here? "Only that he died."

"And that came up because?"

What a bitch. "Because I told her both my parents were dead and hey, I guess we had that little special something in common."

"Hans Burkhart died in an accident involving a grape harvester. Terrible tragedy. He was too mangled for the girl to see. I'm sure she's suffering from a lack of closure." She walked closer, and the weird sensation in his head grew stronger, along with his dislike of the woman. She smiled. "Yes. You'll do nicely, Aaron Ryland."

"What the hell does that mean?" *Oh shit.* He'd blurted that out before he thought. The headache was messing with his usual control.

From across the room, Gerald's mouth gaped open. Aunt Ruby shifted uncomfortably on the other side of the desk. Maybe he should dial it back. This woman might be a royal bitch, but she was also Aunt Ruby's boss. "Sorry, I — "

"Welcome to New Wurzburg, Aaron Ryland." She turned her back to him and ordered, "Gerald. File. Now."

And as if he were the dog she treated him like, Gerald came running, file in hand, passing it to her as she strode out the door. But the look he gave as he watched her leave through the window was anything but that of an obedient puppy. His expression was one of pure hatred. Rain had seen it hundreds of times. Hate had a look and feel unlike anything else in the world — toxic, overwhelming, all-consuming — and it was the same wherever he went, this tiny town included.

The weird swirling sensation in his brain had stopped, at least. He sat and covered his face with his hands.

"You okay?" Ruby asked.

"Have the start of a wicked headache."

She pulled a bottle of aspirin out of her desk and slid it to him. "Happens to me all the time. Probably the flickering lights."

Gerald made a choking sound but looked away when Ruby glanced in his direction.

She grabbed a bottle of water from a flat of them on the

shelf behind her and passed it to Rain. "What was with the chief's questions?"

"I have no idea what that was about." He popped the aspirin and took a swig of water.

Gerald made another choking sound and covered it with a hacking cough.

Ruby smiled, and the little lines around her eyes deepened. "She mentioned a girl."

"Just someone I met." Maybe with the chief gone, it was a good time to see what Ruby knew. "You happen to know anything about the death of a guy named Hans Burkhart? He died last October."

"The girl's father."

"Yeah."

She sighed. "I'm on coffee and varmint duty. The chief takes all the bigger stuff. She'd be the one to ask."

Like hell he was going to ask her anything.

Aunt Ruby's phone rang, and she picked it up before the second ring. "Ryland... Yes, Chief." Her eyes darted to Gerald, shuffling files on his desk. He had a stack of them at least a foot tall. "I'm sure it was an honest mistake. I'll do that right now. I'll scan and send it to you in five." She hung up without saying good-bye.

"You gave her the wrong file, Gerald." Ruby crossed to the file cabinet. "You gave her Schneider Grain Company, not Schmidt Ranch."

He shrugged.

"Gotta scan it. I'll be right back, Aaron." File in hand, she disappeared into the chief's office.

"Weren't no headache." Gerald had a thick accent.

Rain remained silent, meeting the guy's glare.

"Weren't no harvester accident, neither." He moved a file from under the stack on his desk. His hands trembled like Old Jim's did when he needed a fix, causing the folder to vibrate. "The shed. The boat. Follow the body." He placed the folder hanging over the edge and slammed his palm down on the metal desk, never taking his eyes off Rain. "Tell them people no."

"What people?"

He stood, his breathing labored. "Say no. Normal people can't handle it. The pull of it. The *power*. It's like crack. You'll break. It'll kill ya."

The guy was acting like *he* was on crack. He wasn't making any sense.

"If I was you, I'd get the hell outta here, as far away as possible. Get on that motorbike of your old man's and leave before it's too late." And with that, he stormed out the door into the pouring rain.

Through the window, Rain watched Gerald speed off in the Corolla like he was running from the cops. He leaned his forehead against the glass, trying to make sense of the guy's rant. Over the ticking clock above Ruby's desk and the hum of fluorescent tubes, the muted click and groan of a scanner came from the chief's office as Aunt Ruby prepared the correct file.

File. He crossed to Gerald's desk and picked up the folder he'd left hanging over the edge. It was labeled HANS BURKHART. Gerald had clearly left it there for him, but Rain didn't have time to check it out right now. Ruby was going to finish her task any second, and who knew when the chief would return. He'd have to borrow the file. Surely he could sneak it back in easily. Nothing unusual about visiting his aunt, right? He'd just put it right back on Gerald's desk tomorrow. He stuffed the file in his backpack under the folding chair and zipped it.

"Hey!" Ruby said.

He straightened with a jerk like a kid caught stealing from the cookie jar. Fortunately, she didn't seem to notice he was acting weird. Proof that people only see what they want to see.

"All done. Want a ride home?"

"Sure."

"Gerald gone?"

"Yeah. He took off a few minutes ago."

She shook her head as she replaced the file she'd just scanned. "Sometimes I think he screws up on purpose. I just can't for the life of me figure out why."

Rain couldn't figure out a lot of things, but he was sure as hell going to try. Starting with the crazy things Gerald had said. Maybe Freddie could make sense of it. He slung his backpack over one shoulder.

"Have much homework?"

He grabbed his rain coat and followed Ruby through the door, waiting while she locked up. "Just some reading." One file to be precise.

"Oh, I hope it's not much. I'd love you to join our group tonight."

"I'll be there." Never had he imagined going to a book club meeting. But this was one get-together he wouldn't miss if his life depended on it. From the way Gerald was acting, maybe it did.

THIRTEEN

Smells of freshly brewed coffee and baked cookies filled the house. The first guest, Ms. Kendleton, Mr. Pratt's substitute, arrived right as Aunt Ruby placed a plate of cheese and crackers on the coffee table.

Rain endured the mandatory pleasantries but struggled to stay focused. He'd read the file several times when they'd gotten home but hadn't seen any evidence Freddie's father's death had been a murder. Actually, he hadn't seen anything indicating it was a harvesting accident, either. No description of the body and no autopsy report, which he thought was required with something like this. At the top of the single page were the deceased's name, the date, estimated time of death, and the Haven Winery address. "Northwest corner third row" was scrawled above the words "accidental death." Nothing more, really, other than signatures from Ulrich Burkhart, a rep from a funeral home, and Chief Richter.

Rain still didn't know what to make of Gerald's bizarre ramble about a shed, following a body, and telling people no. As soon as this thing was over, he'd check out the file again and write down everything Gerald had said and try to make sense of it, if there was anything useful. The guy seemed out of his head.

More book club members arrived, bringing food and wine.

It didn't take long to draw the conclusion that this weekly get-together wasn't solely focused on books.

In addition to Miss Kendleton were Ruby's neighbors Eliza and Sharon—the one who'd made that delicious pot roast and lemon pie he'd eaten his first night. Also present was Susie James, the teacher who'd shown up when Friederike dumped Thomas in his desk. Ruby laughed with a woman named Mrs. Whittaker about getting a bird out of her sunroom. And last, but not least, was Ellen Ericksen, Grant's mother, who arrived with a huge wicker basket. At first, Rain thought it contained food, but it didn't. It was some kind of sewing basket.

The snacks were all spread out on the coffee table, and a couple of dining chairs had been added to the room so that everyone fit. Rain held back, not willing to join the circle. He sat instead in a worn armchair in the corner behind Mrs. Ericksen. As soon as he settled, she moved to the opposite side of the circle, facing him. *Hell.* He couldn't move without it being an obvious attempt to get out of her line of vision.

For a moment, he considered ditching altogether, but since the file held nothing, he decided to stay. Aunt Ruby had said she'd try to bring up the topic of Freddie's father to see if anyone knew anything, which was really cool of her.

"Where's Sophia?" Mrs. Whittaker asked, pouring wine into a plastic cup before sitting on the sofa along with Sharon and Eliza.

"She had to go to Corsicana to take care of her sister," Miss Kendleton said from a dining chair to her right.

From a wing chair across from the sofa, Susie James squealed. "Oh yay! The baby came?"

"Not yet," Eliza said with a huge grin. "Any time now."

Miss Kendleton grabbed a cookie from the table. "How's your husband's vertigo, Eliza?"

"Much better, which suits me fine. I was sick of fetching him things like one of his bird dogs." She panted like an eager puppy, and the other women laughed.

They went on like this for a while. Everyone seemed to have news about everyone and everything with the exception of Mrs. Ericksen. She pushed her needle in and out of some fabric pulled tight in a round wooden frame, listening but not contributing. Instead, she did her needlework and periodically studied Rain, which made him want to squirm. Her fingers moved quickly as she pierced the material, rarely glancing at her work. She even rethreaded her needle with a different color without looking down.

"I hear there was another calf killed at Schmidt Ranch," Mrs. Whittaker said.

Ms. James reached for a cracker. "Dogs again?"

Ellen Ericksen's fingers stilled.

"Probably. My husband says if it doesn't stop, he's going to get a group of guys together and take matters into his own hands."

"That's a terrible idea, Sharon," Ruby said. "You know what the mayor and chief said about that."

"Yeah, well, I don't see them doing anything about it." Sharon eyed Mrs. Ericksen. "Sorry, Ellen. I know Chief Richter is your sister, but we've gotta do something. The traps aren't working, and we can't afford to lose any more calves this year."

Mrs. Ericksen plunged her needle into the fabric inside the round frame and resumed her sewing.

Whoa. Mrs. Ericksen was Chief Richter's sister. On closer look, Rain could see the resemblance. Their mom must have given them look-regal-while-being-creepy-as-shit lessons.

"Poor Lud Pratt. He was so distraught when his cat went missing, he called in a sick day and I had to sub. He was certain that whatever had been killing the chickens in his neighborhood had gotten his cat." Miss Kendleton spooned some sugar into her coffee. "I'm so relieved it showed up the next day."

"I hear he found it safe and sound inside his house when he woke up the next morning," Sharon said.

"It probably was inside the whole time," Ruby added.

Rain knew better. He'd seen Merrick's face after Freddie threatened to make him sing soprano and told him to find that cat. Merrick was probably as relieved by the outcome as Mr. Pratt. It would have been entertaining to watch the kid break in to return it, though.

Ms. James pushed from her chair and grabbed her coffee cup, then walked to the kitchen to refill it. "Do any of you know who's clearing that land near the highway?"

There was a unanimous shaking of heads.

"It is going to be a new vineyard," Mrs. Ericksen said. "Haven Winery is expanding."

Rain's stomach lurched when she met his eyes directly, like it was some kind of challenge.

"Speaking of Haven, did any of you hear what happened to the owner, Hans Burkhart?" Ruby asked.

Well, that caused Mrs. Ericksen to break eye contact. Her lids narrowed as she studied Aunt Ruby.

Again, unanimous shaking of heads. How was it they knew everything about everyone but didn't have a clue about Haven or Freddie's dad?

Eliza set down her wineglass. "I wasn't aware anything had happened, but then, that bunch out at Haven Winery keeps to themselves. It's like they're a cult or something."

Mrs. Whittaker raised her Solo cup. "They sure do make good wine, though."

"The kids don't mingle at school," Ms. James added. "They

stick together like glue. I worry about the girl. She was in my class last year, and I never saw her speak to another student outside of her cousins."

"Her father died last October," Ruby said.

Mrs. Ericksen's fingers stilled again, gaze steady on Ruby. "He died in a harvesting accident. It was a terrible tragedy."

Those were almost the exact words the police chief had used. Goose bumps rose on Rain's arms.

Ms. James set down her coffee cup. "That poor girl."

"Harvesting accident?" Sharon's brow furrowed. "I had no idea."

"It wasn't in the paper," Mrs. Whittaker added.

Mrs. Ericksen stabbed the needle in and out with incredible speed. "You know how those people are. Like Eliza said, they keep to themselves."

The hairs on the back of Rain's neck prickled at her words. They reminded him of the "her kind" remark her son had made. Like Freddie's family were less, somehow.

"Well, let's get on to this week's chapters, shall we?" Ruby suggested. The women chattered and laughed as they pulled out their books and notes. Rain didn't have the stomach to sit through a book discussion with Mrs. Ericksen studying him like a science experiment, but it would be rude to leave at this point. At least this hadn't been a total waste. He hadn't learned much about Freddie's dad, but he now knew three things he hadn't before: Freddie's family's business was expanding; her father's death had been swept under the rug for some reason, since the town gossip group knew nothing of it; and Mrs. Ericksen was not only spectacularly weird, she was the police chief's sister.

He needed to talk to Freddie. Maybe he could go after this. She said she lived at Haven Winery. Google showed it was only a few miles down the highway. He had wheels now. Ruby had let him bring the motorcycle home instead of leaving it with hers in the shed…

He shot to his feet. *Shit.*

The shed. There had been a wooden boat in the shed. *The boat*, Gerald had said. *Follow the body*, he'd said.

Dread bordering on panic caused a wave of nausea to tumble through him. There could be a body in the shed. *Shit, shit, shit.* "I gotta go."

"Oh. We're just about to start the book discussion," Ruby said.

He took a few steps toward his room. "Yeah, uh. Well, I totally forgot I have a history quiz tomorrow. I'm really sorry."

The women said good-bye interspersed with things like "school first" and "what a nice boy." Mrs. Ericksen said nothing, she simply watched him over her reading glasses, needle stabbing in and out.

FOURTEEN

Rain climbed out his bedroom window and moved through the shadows to the garage, opening it as quietly as possible. With luck, he'd be back well before the book club ended, and nobody would even know he'd been gone.

As he rolled the dirt bike down the street so he could start it without being heard, his chest ached. He hated sneaking out behind Aunt Ruby's back—and he wouldn't have if there hadn't been a full house. He needed to get to that shed right now, and walking through the living room wasn't an option with creepy Mrs. Ericksen watching his every move. Something about her wasn't right. Hell, something about this whole town wasn't right.

Once out of earshot, he started the bike and took off for the shed, feeling dread rather than freedom as the wind whipped his face.

By the time he'd made the short distance to the storage lot, his imagination had run wild with what he'd find under that boat, and he seriously considered turning back around and returning with Ruby once her meeting was over. He'd promised Freddie he'd keep Ruby out of it, though, so he sucked it up and stuck to his original plan.

The gate to the storage lot was unlocked and open, just like before. There were no lights, but the low moon, just a day or so past full, lit up the place enough to make out the gravel and crushed-shell road ringing the lot, surrounded by long grass bending in the wind from the east. Parking the bike just outside the unit that belonged to Ruby, he pulled the key from under the cinderblock where she'd stashed it when they'd been here before.

The lock clicked with some effort. He pulled it out and hooked it through the eye after flipping the hasp open. Swinging the door wide, he stared into the yawning blackness. Surely there was a light or something.

He swiped across his phone and accessed the flashlight mode, then searched for a switch or pull cord. Nothing.

The flashlight on the phone was probably not enough for this, and he was running low on battery, so he rolled his bike closer, turned the key, and angled the headlight to shine at the back wall.

The contents of the shed took on a strange life of their own in the horizontal light. The boat motor cast a long, irregular shadow that crawled across the room like a monster. The shadows from the handles of the toolboxes gaped like toothless mouths on the drawers. Everything assumed a sinister look and feel; even the paint on Ruby's dirt bike brought to mind images of wet blood.

Rain shook his head and swallowed the lump in his throat. It felt like he'd stepped into a horror movie as he moved farther in, the wind and his rasping breaths the only sounds.

Maybe he should wait until morning when the light was better. The dirt bike headlight wasn't right for what he was doing.

Which was what, exactly? Turning the boat over. That's all he needed to do. Gerald had said, *Under the boat.* And, *Follow the body.*

Body.

Surely there wasn't a body under the boat. He took another step and shoved his phone in his pocket. Hans Burkhart's body had been taken to a funeral home, according to the file Gerald had made available.

He took a deep breath through his nose. There'd probably still be an odor…unless the body had been buried in the dirt floor.

Wind lashed the shed, causing the corrugated panels to rattle and groan, and his heart rate skyrocketed.

Back in the city, he'd done a lot scarier shit than this, but he understood the city. This was different. Something about this town—these people—wasn't right. The unknown was far more terrifying than the familiar. He wiped his hands on his jeans. He was tougher than this. *Nut up, Ryland.*

He shoved one of the rolling tool chests to the side, then cleared some boxes stacked around the boat to the edge of the space, making room to tip over the boat.

Whatever was under that boat wasn't nearly as horrible as what Freddie was going through not knowing what happened to her dad, what might happen to her. And he liked her. Really liked her in a way that surprised him and caused him to do creepy shit like look for bodies in sheds at night.

With a deep breath, he leaned down and slipped his fingers under the edge of the boat, wind still moaning through the shed walls. With a grunt, he lifted, and…

Bam!

He fell to all fours reflexively in the pitch darkness, as he would if gunfire had broken out in his old neighborhood. His mind registered that the wind had simply slammed the door shut, but his body reacted as if he were under attack. More than once, his instincts had saved his life when his mind had found ways to explain away the situation, so he remained low to the ground for a moment.

Wind rattled the metal sheeting, and the door groaned, then slammed back open. He squinted in the headlight glow.

"Only the wind," he said. This time, thank God, his body had been wrong.

Last time he was here, Ruby had propped the door with the cinderblock that hid the key, so he did the same, sliding it into place, then checking out the storage yard for good measure. It was a fenced lot in the middle of fields off a dirt road. As safe as safe could be. No gangs. No thugs casing it out. Nobody coming to jack him up. Just grass and wind and moonlight—and that unmistakable sensation of being watched.

"Hello?"

Only the wind answered. This place was screwing with his head.

"Whatever."

He needed to just get on with it and get out. Now. Right now. Like ten minutes ago, now.

Just for good measure, he pulled out his phone and turned on the flashlight.

The boat was wooden with chipped blue paint. RUBY was hand-painted in sloppy red letters.

"Ruby," he read out loud. Maybe it was his aunt's boat. No. People labeled gym clothes, not boats. This was the boat's name. His aunt had said this was his dad's stuff. Why would he name his boat "Ruby"?

He set the phone on a rolling tool chest, the light shining on the cobwebs clinging to the wood frame supporting the metal sheets that made up the roof overhead. "The shed. The boat. Follow the body," he said in an almost chant, like it had run though his head since Gerald had first said it.

Again, he reached under the edge of the boat, breaths shallow, and lifted, rolling the boat over and upright with a crash. It rocked side to side twice, then stilled. For a moment, he stared at the bald dirt where it had rested, then he picked up the flashlight to see if there was evidence of digging. Nothing. Flat, smooth dirt. Nothing else.

He turned off his phone light. "Dammit!" he yelled. "Nothing."

Nothing at all—which was better than a rotting body, he supposed. Still, he'd lied to Ruby about the test for nothing and was no closer to helping Freddie. Gerald had sent him on a goose chase. *The asshole.*

His phone rang, causing him to jump back and bang his elbow on a tool chest. It was his aunt.

He rubbed his elbow. *Dammit.* This was the last thing he needed. "Hey." Gritting his teeth, he waited for the onslaught.

"You okay?"

No anger. No grilling. No "Where are you?" Nothing but concern in her voice.

And for some reason, that made his eyes burn and his throat itch. His whole life he'd bluffed and covered, and with two words, this woman cut to his heart. "Yeah. I, uh…" His mind raced through credible excuses for why he'd snuck out, ranging from: he needed to get the study guide from a kid in class to he was studying with a friend. Instead, he told the truth, which surprised him. "I'm at the shed. I needed to check something out." He scrambled to figure out what he'd tell her he was checking out because looking for a body was not an over-the-phone topic.

"Okay. Just making sure you're all right. See you when you get home."

The call disconnected. No questions. He shook his head in disbelief. She trusted him. An adult. A cop. Trusted *him.*

A scratching sound, like a mouse or rat would make, came from the corner of the shed, and he turned on his flashlight again. As he swung the light toward the corner, something in the upturned boat caught his eye. Duct-taped to the bench seat in the boat was an envelope—the big brown kind like his school had put his records in every time he transferred. He hadn't noticed it before because he had looked under the boat, not in it. The tape made an unnerving rip, pulling chunks of blue paint with it as he yanked it loose from the wood.

He shined the light on the front of the envelope. It was preprinted with the New Wurzburg Police Department logo. This must be what Gerald wanted him to find.

More scratching from the corner. He'd had enough of the creepy shed. His phone battery was running low anyway.

After rolling the boat over, he tucked the envelope under his arm and put the shed contents back like he'd found them, then locked up. Again, that feeling like he wasn't alone oozed through him in a prickly wave. A scan of the lot and fields revealed nothing out of the ordinary.

He pulled the envelope from under his arm and held it in front of his headlight. He knew he should probably wait until he got home in good lighting and out of this creepy lot in the middle of nowhere, but his curiosity was out of control.

It was sealed with only a simple metal brad, which was good, because his heart raced and fingers shook. Again, he glanced around to check he was alone.

Large glossy photos were inside but nothing else. He held the small stack of photos up to the headlight. On top was a picture of a field of plants...vines strung on wires and what looked like someone leaning against them a few yards in the distance.

The second photograph revealed it wasn't someone leaning against the vines in the first photo, it was someone tied to them. The shot was from the back, and the man's head slumped down and over his right shoulder. His wrists were bound with zip ties to the thick wire supporting the vines, reminding Rain of the crucifix Ms. Gill had behind her desk at the shelter. Facing the guy tied to the wires were Chief Richter, a huge guy with gray hair, and Mrs. Ericksen.

"What the hell?" His breaths came in quick puffs as he realized these were probably pictures of Freddie's dad. If so, she was right; he'd been murdered. The guy couldn't have tied himself up like that.

Fingers trembling, he shifted the third and fourth photo to the top of the pile and tilted it to the light.

"Holy shit." *Holy, holy shit.* Dropping the photos in the dirt, he backed away a few steps, mouth covered. Rain had seen some freaky shit in his day—bodies in dumpsters, the results of local gang blood-ins—but never, ever had he seen anything like this. Shuffling a few steps farther from the picture, which thank God had landed facedown, he lowered his hand and took several huge gulps of air, but it wasn't enough. Grabbing his knees, he leaned over and vomited on the dirt drive, wishing to hell he hadn't opened that envelope. Hoping to heaven Freddie never saw it.

What if the killer does that to Freddie next?

He retched again, trying to push the image from his mind.

He couldn't let her see those photos. Too much. Maybe that's why they had kept it from her. Nobody deserved to see their dad like that. To see anyone like that. *God.*

Soon, his breathing and heart rate slowed.

What was he supposed to do with this information? *Follow the body*, Gerald had said. The body had been taken to a funeral home. Perhaps that's where he'd start.

That niggling, eyes-on-him feeling was back, and he spun around to find no one. Time to listen to his instincts and get the hell out of here.

Without looking at them, he shoved the photos back in the

envelope, stuffed it in his waistband, and pulled his shirt down over it, then got on his bike. The rev of the motor drowned out his hammering pulse. As he took the turn out of the lot, he shot a look back at the shed. Then stopped, feet hitting the gravel road with a crunch on either side of the bike.

From the far end of the building, a large brown dog with patches of missing fur stared back for a moment then disappeared into the brush.

He placed his hand over the envelope he'd shoved in the front of his shirt. "Whatever."

FIFTEEN

Bleary-eyed, Rain shuffled down the stairs at the end of the school hallway. He hadn't slept a minute last night, and the combination of exhaustion and horror had taken its toll. He'd gone back and forth between showing Freddie the photos and not telling her about them at least a hundred times. Hell, she might be a no-show again, and all the worry would be for nothing.

He rounded the corner to the math wing and stopped short. There she was, tilting her head as Grant whispered in her ear. Her cousins appeared furious, their faces grim and fists clenched. She pulled back and pointed a finger at the classroom. The boys reluctantly followed her direction, slinking away to class. Then she turned back to Grant, who was leaning against the wall like he didn't have a care in the world. He crooked his finger, and she moved closer. Rain's heart hammered when Grant reached for her, circling her neck beneath her hair. Rain's body tensed, and it took all his restraint not to interrupt the embrace.

Grant pulled his hands away and put something in his shirt pocket, then removed a small box from his front pants pocket. He opened it, and she looked inside with no change of expression. Rain bit back a curse when Grant placed a gold chain from the box around her neck. Her reaction wasn't typical for a girl receiving a gift. She simply walked away from him without a word, face expressionless, and went to class.

As if Grant could feel Rain's stare, he turned to him, smiled, and gave him a thumbs-up.

That motherfu—

"Mr. Ryland. You're going to be tardy," Mr. Pratt said, tapping him on the shoulder as he passed.

Rain entered the classroom expecting Freddie to acknowledge him in some way or at least act guilty, but she didn't even look up from her phone, so he walked the longer route to his chair, across the front of the room, stopping at her desk.

She remained focused on her screen. He cleared his throat.

"Keep walking," was all she said, her voice flat and toneless.

He fought back a wince and took a deep breath, eyes locked on the gold chain of the necklace where it disappeared into her cleavage under her V-neck Death Eater T-shirt.

From several rows back, Thomas snickered.

Bad move, asshole. He met the guy's gaze directly, and the snicker died out. At this point, Rain was itching for a fight. Exhausted and pissy, he'd been played, and he didn't like it. She should have told him she was with Grant before she kissed him like that. Not that he'd take it back. No way. He just wouldn't have gotten his hopes up for more. And then there was the issue of her dad. He shuddered at the memory of the photos.

"We need to talk," he said.

She didn't react, just moved colorful squares around on her screen. Merrick shifted uncomfortably in the desk next to hers while she acted like Rain didn't exist.

He slid into his desk and spent the rest of the class period in turmoil. Maybe he should just turn the envelope over to her and let her find her father's killer with Grant. No. Grant's mom had been in that photo. She knew the man had been murdered, yet at the book club, she'd said it was a harvester accident. Rain fought back the urge to throw up again. Gerald had been right. That was no accident.

And Freddie had accepted a necklace from Grant, which got under Rain's skin a lot more than it should have. But honestly, he had no right to be pissed. He'd asked about Thomas, not Grant. He'd never once asked if she was dating anyone else. Nor had she asked him.

She said going to his room had been a mistake—that it couldn't happen again. Maybe because there was something brewing with Grant. *Fine. Shit happens.* He'd just do what he always did—wait and see. He needed to focus on what was important: Freddie's safety and her father's murder. He'd promised to help her, and he would. He could handle just being friends and not kissing again.

Yeah.

Right.

No way in hell…

The bell rang, and Freddie and her cousins headed straight for the door. No hassling or mooing at girls this time. Rain gave them a brief head start, hoping he could catch her at the lockers, and he did. Only Grant arrived first. Before he got close enough to hear what was said, Thomas charged Grant, who was not as big, but strong, as Rain knew from the bench workout. With a quick sidestep and little other effort, Grant pinned Thomas to the locker by the throat.

Rain expected Freddie to jump into the fray in her usual style, but she didn't. She stood aside, expressionless, as Thomas's face turned red, then purple.

"Stop," Merrick said. "Please, Grant."

He pulled his hand away, and Thomas slid down the lockers to a heap on the floor, clutching his throat and gasping.

"The agreement. The promise," Thomas wheezed.

"Was among yourselves. We weren't a part of it. The book overrides. You know that." Grant took a deep breath, and his shoulders relaxed. "I'm sorry, Thomas. It would be a lot easier your way. There's just no chance it'll happen, even if Friederike wanted it."

"She does."

Freddie didn't react, arms crossed over her chest. She didn't seem herself. It was like she was zoned out or something.

"You're delusional, dude." Grant picked up his backpack. "So's your old man. Don't let him screw you over, Thomas. Things are changing fast. Keep up or you're out."

He turned his attention to Freddie. "It'll be okay. The test won't be for a while. I have a really good feeling about this one." He touched her cheek with his fingertips, and she shook her head, as if to clear it.

"It's cool, Freddie. We're here," Merrick said, placing a hand on her shoulder. "Stay cool."

Grant patted her head and strolled off toward the gym. Thomas struggled to his feet, studying her face, like Kurt and Merrick.

She shook her head again, then covered her face. "Go," she ordered, lowering her hands. "Leave me alone. Go, all of you."

And they did. The bell rang, and she didn't move other than to pull the necklace out of her shirt and rub it.

"Hey." Rain kept his voice soft, barely loud enough for her to hear.

She snapped her head in his direction, eyes brimming with tears. He recognized the hopeless, haunted look on her face because he'd worn it so many times himself. This girl was trapped by something or someone and needed help.

She held up a palm like a traffic cop. "Stay away from me."

Of course, he did just the opposite, moving within inches so that she had no option other than to deal with him.

"So...Grant?"

She looked to the side, then after a few deep breaths said, "Stay away from him, too."

"I work for Ericksen Hardware. That's going to be hard."

"You do?"

He nodded.

"You need to quit."

"Why?"

"You wouldn't believe me if I told you. Just...." Her breath was ragged. "Please go."

"Let me help you."

She laughed then. Threw her head back and laughed, almost maniacally. "I'm not the one who needs help, Aaron Ryland. You are."

"Okay, then you help *me*."

"That's what I'm trying to do. Why can't you let it go? Stay away from the Ericksens and stay away from me. Just do the safe thing and walk away."

"Freddie, I've never been safe a single day in my life until I came here, and now you're telling me I'm not, which just makes things status quo. Big fucking deal." He hadn't meant to raise his voice. He took a deep breath, then dropped his backpack and unzipped it. He ripped out a piece of paper, and, using a pencil he dug out of the bottom of the pack, scribbled his phone number. "I have information about your dad's death. I'm not going to talk about it here and now." He handed her the paper. "If you want to hear about it, call or shoot me a text, and we can meet up."

He zipped his backpack and stood. "I'm not quitting my job, and I'm not going away." He slung the pack over his shoulder. "I'm here to stay." He gestured to the paper she clutched. "Use that number."

He headed toward the gym but hit the back door instead. No way in hell was he going to track. He was likely to do something stupid to Grant, and the last thing he wanted right now was to draw attention to himself. Something was up with Freddie, and until he figured out what it was, he was going to lay low.

He was almost home when the text came: *NW corner Haven. 9:00*. It was the first time he'd smiled all day.

SIXTEEN

F reddie was already there when Rain arrived at the northwest corner of the Haven Winery property. He parked the bike in the grass next to the whitewashed wooden fence and climbed over to join her on a boulder at the end of one of the rows of grapevines.

She didn't speak. Didn't even look at him. He knew why: Based on the photos and the description in the file, her father's body was recovered a couple of yards from where they sat.

Even though she'd repeatedly warned him off, he leaned close until their shoulders touched.

She closed her eyes. "I still hear his voice sometimes."

A breeze rustled the leathery grapevine leaves, and she sighed. "I wake up every day thinking it was all a bad dream, and he'll be at the table when I go in for breakfast." She opened her eyes. "But he's not. I'm totally alone."

The pain in her voice cut through his chest like a blade. He wanted to take her in his arms and hold her until her pain went away—until *his* pain went away—which was impossible of course. But this girl made him believe in impossibilities. For the first time, he felt like a true connection with someone else was possible. Not just possible. *Necessary.*

She stood and walked between the rows, stopping at a stretch of exposed wire. "He died here, I'm told." Tracing her fingers over the wire, a tear ran down her cheek. Again, Rain was overcome by an uncustomary urge to hold her. "The grapevines won't grow here. It's like the earth is mourning right along with me." She made a choked sound and turned her back to him.

He pushed his hands in his pockets and stood still, giving her time to recover. What would it be like to have a connection like that? A bond so profound, it impacted everything.

"Where's your mom?"

She didn't turn around. "Left to go live with…family in Germany soon after I was born. I never met her. I've never missed her."

Her dad had been everything to this girl. And now she was adrift. Like him.

Her long hair blew toward the south, in the direction of a cluster of buildings he assumed made up the winery compound. "What did you find out about my dad's death?"

"Gerald gave me a file."

She spun to face him. "Gerald?"

"Yeah, middle-aged balding dude at the police station."

"I know who he is. How did you meet him?"

"My aunt…"

"Oh, right." Her expression relaxed. "He gave you a file?"

He didn't want to get the guy busted, so he backpedaled. "Well, it was on his desk, so I borrowed it."

She took a few steps toward him. "And?"

"The file says it was an accident, but too many things are missing—like an actual report. I think you're right."

"I know I am."

So did he, but he couldn't bring himself to tell her why. Not yet.

She turned her head sharply, like she'd heard something. "Shit."

"What is it?"

"The boys. Let's get out of here."

He looked in the direction she'd turned her head and heard a faint call of her name. Damn, she had good hearing.

They climbed the fence, and she got on the dirt bike behind him without hesitation.

"Ready?" he asked. She answered by tightening her grip around his waist, and they took off. Sticking to back roads, he made his way toward Enchanted Rock.

Her thighs tight against his and her arms wound around his waist made him forget everything but the moment. She leaned her head against his shoulder, pressing her breasts into his back, and his whole body heated. When she slid one of her hands inside his shirt and ran her warm fingers over his abdomen, he slowed and fought for focus.

"Turn left here," she said, pointing with her free hand to a trail off the side road. It was barely wide enough for the bike, but in a short distance, it opened onto a wider path that ended at a locked gate. She trailed her hand across the top of his waistband, making him one step short of crazy and hard as a rock as she slid off the bike. "What else did you find out?" She climbed the gate and struck out on the footpath, not even checking to see if he followed.

God. She wanted to talk again. He wasn't sure he could form words, much less walk after she touched him like that. He climbed the fence, trying to get it together before he answered. "Well, Gerald acted weird."

"He always does." She moved up the trail as if she knew it by heart, easily stepping over clumps of cacti and ducking under low, scruffy tree limbs with unusual agility.

"You know him?"

"Yeah."

He stopped, hoping she'd elaborate.

"We hung out a couple of times," she said over her shoulder.

Well, that seemed strange. "He told me to say no."

It was her turn to stop now. "To what?"

"I was hoping you'd know."

She shrugged, but the motion was jerky and awkward. She was hiding something.

"He said I should get out of here."

"Wise words. I wonder where you've heard that before?" She ducked under a tree limb covered in thorns. As he followed her up the trail, he remembered she'd said she walked home that night from Mrs. Goff's. No way in hell she could have walked through this stuff without shoes.

"He said things about normal people not being able to handle the power of it."

She didn't respond.

"Any idea what 'it' is?"

"Nope." She picked up her pace.

"He said it was like crack and would kill me."

"He's kinda nuts," she shot over her shoulder, ducking under another low, thorny limb.

"He also said your dad's death wasn't an accident."

That got her attention, and she stopped. "What else did he say?"

This would've been the perfect time to tell her about the photos, but he couldn't. For a moment, that haunted, vulnerable look he'd seen before flickered across her face. She did a good job keeping up a tough facade, but like him, it was only a mask. "He said to follow the body, which, according to the file, went to Reinhardt Funeral Home."

She shrugged. "That's a logical suggestion."

"Listen, Freddie. Nothing about the guy was logical. He seemed totally strung out. He said it would *kill* me—whatever *it* is."

She shoved her hair out of her face, gaze flitting back the way they came. "We shouldn't have come here. I've made another mistake. I've put you in danger."

"Now you're acting like Gerald."

"Gerald was right."

He rolled his eyes in frustration. The way everyone in this town talked in circles was on his last nerve.

She put her hands on her hips, eyes narrowed. "Tell me the truth. Has there ever been a moment when you felt fear around me? Fear *of* me?"

He thought back to when he'd sat next to her in class. "Yeah. But it was silly. Made no sense, especially now that I know you."

"You don't know me." She advanced on him, and he took a step back, surprised by her intensity. "And it's not silly. There are things that defy logic—things that speak to the instinctual fear we cloak with reason to explain them away. Listen to that fear, Rain. Follow it." She made an exasperated huff. "Get on your bike and go home."

No way. This girl was in trouble, and he was determined to keep her safe and get to the bottom of it. No way was he running away scared. He moved closer. Very close. So close he could feel the heat rolling off her body. "Is that what you really want?"

"Yes." Her voice trembled, making it come out almost like a question.

He leaned down so that his lips were a breath away from hers. "Liar."

She pulled back. "What's right and what I want aren't the same. I'm trying to do what's right."

Moonlight glinted off the gold chain peeking out from the neckline of her T-shirt, and his stomach knotted with something dark and unfamiliar. "Does this have to do with Grant?"

Her brow furrowed. "Grant?"

"I saw him give you that necklace." As he said the words, he realized the uncomfortable sensation in his gut was jealousy.

"It's a replacement. They make them at Ericksen Hardware. He just delivered it." Then she barked a harsh laugh. "Oh, you thought Grant and I…" She shook her head again. "No. Absolutely not."

He took a breath and let it out slowly. Well, that was a relief at least. "So, you want me to listen to my instincts."

"Yes."

He reached out and pulled her to him by a belt loop on her jeans. Her eyes widened as she crashed into him. The contact with her long, muscular body made the blood roar in his ears and other places. "My instincts aren't telling me to go home. They're telling me to do this." He took her face in his hands and covered her mouth with his.

SEVENTEEN

F reddie's lips were soft and warm—reserved at first, but soon she met Rain's tongue stroke for stroke, setting his entire body on fire. She grabbed the back of his shirt as his hands roamed up and down her spine. He'd never get enough of this girl. Her wild, sensual heat and her feral noises deep in her throat drove him wild. Too soon, she pulled away from the kiss, leaving him achy and breathless.

"Not here," she said, moving soundlessly up the trail ahead of him.

"Not here" implied "somewhere else," which sounded promising. Hopefully somewhere close. He felt awkward and overly noisy following her, branches crunching and bushes rustling as he passed.

Soon, they broke into a clearing that gave them a view of the granite dome in the bright moonlight. Nighttime campers and hikers milled across it, their flashlights sweeping back and forth like drunk fireflies.

"Enchanted Rock," she said, brushing the hair out of her face. "The Apache and Tonkawa tribes believed it held magic."

"Ruby told me the German settlers here did, too."

She resumed her climb. "Really? I didn't know that."

"Yeah," he said, finding it odd she hadn't heard the legend.

"Something about the power of the earth turning men into beasts or some such nonsense."

"Huh…" was all she said as she took a trail to the right. They climbed silently for what felt like forever, until they came into a clearing on top of a smaller dome, similar in form to the large one in the distance. The surface was the same pink granite. Facets in the stone twinkled like glitter in the moonlight. Every here and there, a hole in the otherwise flat surface held water and plants—like one of those biome projects from biology his sophomore year. He turned a full three-sixty, marveling at the beauty of the terrain. Strips of wild brush and trees cut groomed, mowed pastures and fields of crops into straight-edge wedges. A lake reflected the low-lying clouds and moon. Were it not for the people on the dome in the distance, so small they looked like ants from here, he could easily imagine what it was like before this area was settled. Harsh, terrible, and beautiful at the same time.

When he turned back to Freddie, he bit down a gasp of surprise. She'd stripped off her shirt and tipped her face to the moon, eyes closed, like one would do to the sun at the beach. And here he'd thought the landscape was the most beautiful thing he'd ever seen.

The air was still. Eerily still, and her smooth skin appeared to glow from inside in the moonlight—her black lace bra sheer enough to make him a little dizzy.

Without opening her eyes, she said, "Take off your shirt."

No way in hell was he going to argue with that. He yanked off his shirt, clutching it in his fist, waiting for his next instruction.

He forgot how to breathe when she opened her pale eyes and moved toward him. Her gaze wasn't focused on his face, though. It was on his chest. Stopping in front of him, she traced her fingers over the ink.

"Raindrops?" she asked, finger outlining one of the shapes.

"Tears," he replied, again light-headed as she ran her fingertips over his pec.

"For your mom?"

"No. For all of us."

She stepped back and, for a long time, stared at the tattoo comprised of dozens of drops in a random pattern over his chest, spilling down his ribs.

She traced a scar on his side with the tip of her finger. One of many marring his body from fights. "Your life has been sad."

And so had hers recently. Maybe that was why he felt so connected to her. Their shared grief, their shared stand against a harsh, unfeeling, screwed-up world. Their shared solitude.

She turned back to the moon and raised her arms. "Do you feel it?"

Well, that was a wide-open question. He was feeling lots of things.

"The moon," she said. "It's like aloe when you're sunburned. Try it."

He imitated her posture, head back, arms out, but felt nothing other than the throbbing hardness he always felt around her.

"So, what do you think about that legend your aunt told you?" she asked.

He opened his eyes to find her studying him. "That the rock can turn men into beasts?" His mind raced, wondering what would prompt that question and what answer she was looking for. Men *were* beasts. Horrible monsters at times. He'd seen it firsthand. "I believe we all hide a beast inside. The only difference is what form it takes when freed."

There it was again. That strange warm pull in his chest while she studied him. Like she totally got him—something no one else had ever bothered to do. He'd never been understood or accepted. People saw his size and found out his background and immediately wrote him off as dangerous or not worth the trouble. Not Freddie.

She obviously found his answer acceptable, because she wound her fingers in his hair and hauled him against her for another kiss. Raw, open-mouthed, and hungry. He'd never met anyone like this, who made him burn so hot he thought he might die from need. Recovering from surprise, he placed his hands on either side of her bare rib cage, feeling her body expand and contract with each quick breath. Bones and hard muscle working beneath smooth, soft skin. Skin he wanted to touch all over.

"I like you, Rain Ryland," she said, dragging her nails down his back.

"Like" didn't even come close. He was on fire for her. Had thought of her night and day since he first saw those eerily pale eyes and badass attitude. She was smart, strong, and terribly, terribly dangerous, which turned him on like crazy. "I like you, too."

"How much?"

Something was going on here. Something other than foreplay. "More than I've ever liked anyone." Which was true and unexpected. This was more than physical, which was a terrifying thought for him. Maybe this time he could stay. Maybe this time he'd actually found a home and wouldn't have to leave everything behind.

He kissed her again, not wanting to think about legends, or leaving, or anything else for that matter. He wanted to just live in this moment as long as it lasted. Running his hands lower, his thumb brushed the unmistakable shape of a condom in her back pocket. He froze, and she smiled against his lips.

"You scared, Sprinkles?"

"Yes."

"Of me?" It was like she *wanted* him to fear her.

"No." He pulled back, amazed at how her eyes reflected the moon like clear glass. "Of this." He gestured to the space he'd put between them. "Of whatever this is." The intensity of it. The urgency. And worse, much worse—the potential loss of it. He'd never feared losing something before because he'd never had anything worth keeping. This girl, though. She was different. And he wanted her.

Snatching up her discarded shirt and tucking it into her waistband, she took his hand and led him down the side of the hill to a small trickle of a stream gurgling over rocks as it made its way to the foot of the huge dome of Enchanted Rock itself. But instead of climbing the rock, she led him around the base as he followed, mesmerized by her skin glowing in the moonlight, and then ducked inside a small cave.

"You seem to know the area well," he said, squinting in the darkness of the cave, still clutching his shirt in his fist.

"I've lived here my whole life. Grew up exploring this area. Close your eyes."

"No need. I can't see a thing."

"That's why I want you to close your eyes."

He did, focusing on his other senses. The sound of the stream nearby, the chorus of insects in the still night outside the cave entrance, her raspy breaths and salty smell—natural and perfect.

"Now open them."

He did, and could see her, mere inches away. Closing his eyes had allowed them to adjust to seeing in the dark. Smart girl. Unable to resist it any longer, he ran his fingers over the lace of her bra, fascinated by her sharp intake of breath and her reaction to his touch. This was, without a doubt, the high point of his entire life. And from the way it was going, it might even get better.

With a flip, she popped his blue jeans button and lowered the zipper.

Hell yeah. Definitely getting better.

She pushed on his shoulders and he sat. Crouching over him, she placed her palm on his chest and urged him to his back on the dirt floor. Knees on either side of him, she crawled up his body like an animal. The necklace dangled between them, and he captured it. It was a little glass bubble with leaves inside. Like a cooking spice or weed or something. "What is it?"

"A good-luck charm."

"It works. I'm feeling really lucky right about now."

"You're about to get luckier."

He released the necklace and placed his palms on her thighs on either side of him, happy to let her take the lead completely, and she did, kissing her way down his body as he groaned with pleasure. "Freddie," he said as her cool fingers met his heated flesh.

He looked up at her pale eyes, staring at him intensely over her straight, slim nose and full lips. Lips he wanted to kiss.

"I shouldn't like you," was all she said. She leaned down, running her lips from his sternum to his chin, her hot breath fanning across his skin causing his hips to buck instinctually. *Instinct.* The thing she kept telling him to listen to. Well, he was listening. Hard.

And right as she lifted up and grabbed the waistline of his jeans, she froze, head twisting to the side as if listening to something outside the cave. Her hand flew to the necklace charm, and her wide eyes met his before she squeezed them shut. A strange growl churned from her throat. She swallowed hard, as if trying to force the sound back down. "No," she whispered. "Oh no." Then her hands flew to her face, feeling the flesh, practically clawing her own skin. "Not now."

Picking up on her alarm, Rain sat, and she swung around to a crouch beside him. "What is it?" he asked.

"Listen to me, Rain." Her tone was desperate. "Whatever happens. Don't speak. Don't say a single word."

"Wha—"

"Promise me."

He nodded, and then a couple of things happened at once: Voices came from nearby, and her expression changed into one of fury. Her lip pulled up from her teeth in a snarl, right about the time three forms filled the entrance to the cave.

"Away," she ordered, her voice a growl. "Get out."

"We're here to bring you back," Kurt said. "Ulrich sent us."

Rain folded his legs under him so he could get to his feet if the guys made a move, but he was far more worried about Freddie at that moment. Her posture changed, her back bowed, arms rotating to where the elbows pointed toward her body. Neck stiffening. She seemed to have gone into a trance or something. Her eyes grew unfocused, and her face contorted. "Get out now," she warned. Voice gravelly and unnatural.

"No, Freddie," Merrick yelled from outside the cave opening. "Don't."

"She's losing it," Kurt said, backing up a step.

Merrick pushed past the other boys and dropped to his knees in front of her. "Keep it together, Freddie. Please. Stay cool." He looked over his shoulder at the other two. "Something's wrong. The new charm isn't working." Then he turned his brown eyes back to Freddie. Speaking as he would to a drunk person—slowly and clearly. "You need to get away from him so you don't hurt him. Do you understand?"

She nodded, and he took her elbow and pulled. To Rain's surprise, she went willingly.

Thomas and Kurt stood aside as Merrick led her out of

the cave. Clouds covered the moon, making the scene even freakier than it already was. Crouching to not bump his head, Rain moved to the entrance, zipping his fly, not sure what to do other than keep his mouth shut like he'd promised.

Freddie didn't look right—didn't sound right—as her breaths came in loud, erratic pants. Hands on knees, she leaned over, back bowed, like she'd just run sprints. Merrick took her necklace and rubbed the glass bubble on her lip. "Bite," he said. "C'mon, Freddie. You like this guy. Keep it together. For him. For *us*."

She bit the bubble. Rain heard the glass crush between her teeth.

"Where's her shirt?" Kurt asked. "Quick before the moon comes out from the cloud cover."

Giving Rain a go-to-hell look as he shoved by him, Thomas ran inside and grabbed her shirt from the floor, pitching it to Merrick on his way out.

But before her cousin could pull the shirt over Freddie's head, something happened. Face covered with the black T-shirt, her body convulsed, her abdomen and ribs heaving then contracting. She cried out "No!" as her spine protruded in raised knobs beneath the skin of her back, and she fell to her knees. Hair, silver and thick, appeared in patches on her shoulders, expanding to cover her arms and back, like it was sprouting in time lapse. She ripped the shirt off her head, tearing it to shreds in the process, and twisted to stare at Rain. Directly at him.

Like hate, regret had a look unlike anything else. And in her now foreign eyes he saw an unmistakable apology. He placed his hand over his heart—over the inked cascade of tears—to let her know he understood.

And what he saw then was more terrifying than anything he'd ever imagined. Perhaps more frightening than the photos of her murdered father. Fangs and fur and a shocking change in ear shape were what he noticed first. Not human. Not animal. But somewhere between, as the bones of her face elongated to a disfigured mask, and she screamed. His heart hammered painfully in his chest as he fought the urge to scream himself.

Then, before Rain's horrified eyes, Merrick ripped a chain holding a glass bubble exactly like Freddie's out from under his own shirt and looped it over her head. With one last look at Rain, he sprinted down the trail away from them. But before he disappeared from sight, Rain swore he saw him drop to all fours, body contracting in places and expanding in others, but his mind didn't register it fast enough to be certain before Merrick disappeared into the brush.

Freddie pressed Merrick's necklace to her chest, sucking in deep breaths. She looked like herself now. Breathing heavily with tangled hair, smooth skin, and closed eyes.

Thomas patted her shoulder, but she didn't react. "We've got it from here," he said. "We'll take care of him."

"Looks to me like she was taking care of him just fine," Kurt said. "Weren't you, Freddie?"

"Don't." Her voice was ragged. "Saw nothing. Knows nothing."

"Come on, Freds. You knew it would come to this if you kept messing with him. You can't play with your food, honey." Thomas's smile at Rain made his hair stand on end.

I'll slowly peel your skin from your body with my teeth while you scream and then eat you for dinner, he'd said. After what Rain had just seen, reality had taken a hard left, and that now seemed entirely possible.

"Two-legged livestock is off-limits," Kurt added.

What the hell was going on? Rain's eyes darted from the two boys to Freddie, who still didn't look well. Sweat beaded on her face, and her hands shook. "He knows nothing."

"He's been talking to Gerald. He knows a lot more than he should. It's over, baby. There's no choice. You know this."

Thomas tugged a chain from under his shirt, but before he could pull it off, she grabbed his wrist. "No. I say no. If you kill him—" Her frantic expression morphed to anger, and she straightened. Thomas twisted his wrist, but she held firm, knuckles white from pressure. "If you so much as bruise him, I swear to you both, I won't wait until I graduate to make my decision. I'll step up tomorrow as leader and have the two of you put down. You've committed enough infractions for three death sentences, and you know it."

"He saw!"

She gestured in Rain's direction. "Look at him. He's totally wasted. Dropped acid two hours ago," she lied. "He doesn't even know who he is. He won't have a clue about this tomorrow, and if he does, he'll think it was one hell of a weird trip, that's all."

Rain looked up at the moon, letting his jaw go slack to play along with her story. He wasn't sure exactly what was going on, but he knew she was trying to keep him alive.

"Why him?" Thomas's voice cracked with the words. He cleared his throat.

She turned and studied him. "I was only playing with him. You know that."

Rain's stomach dropped at her words, which wasn't rational considering what he'd just seen. He should be relieved she'd planned to discard him. Oddly, he wasn't.

"Okay," Kurt said. "We'll let him go tonight, but you're coming back with us. And if he shows any signs of knowledge, he's done."

She shrugged. "Fine."

"Call Grant. The formula of your charm was way off,"

Thomas said. "He clearly didn't up it enough."

"Underestimated that he was dealing with a bitch in heat." Kurt snickered and high-fived Thomas.

Her voice was almost normal now. Clear and strong. "I hear the SPCA is doing a two-for-one neuter deal right now. If you don't get your asses down that trail to wait for me by the gate, I'm making an appointment for you."

Laughing and shaking their heads, they headed out. "Stop taking advantage of stoned livestock, Friederike," Thomas shouted as they disappeared from view. A couple of moos and baas were thrown in as they went.

And then, they were alone.

So many thoughts swirled in Rain's head that it felt like a tornado twisting through his skull. Nothing was clear or coherent except that this girl, who he'd grown to like more than anyone he'd ever met, was not who or what he thought she was. Hell, she might not even be human.

She held up her hands. "You didn't see anything."

"The fuck I didn't."

"Freddie!" one of the boys called from a distance.

"Listen to me, Rain. You have to act like what you saw…" She closed her eyes and took a couple of deep breaths. "It didn't happen. It should never have happened."

"Gee, ya think?" Here he'd been thinking he was helping her. That she'd liked him. *I was only playing with him.*

"Something went wrong. I never intended for you—"

He took a step toward her. "To what? To find out you turn into some…*thing*? Some scary hairy thing and your crazy-ass relatives want to skin me and eat me for dinner? When did you plan to tell me this? Right after we…" His voice trailed off as he gestured to the cave. His chest ached so bad, it felt like it was going to split open. He ran his hands through his hair, hating himself for the hurt look on her face. "My God."

"I had planned to never tell you."

At least she was being honest.

"Freddie!" The tone from down the trail was uglier now.

"I've gotta go. Listen." She placed her hand on his shoulder, and he pulled away, out of reach. "I know this is asking a lot, but it's the only way I know to keep you alive. You've gotta act like you didn't see a thing tonight. Like you're still into me." Her eyes filled, the unshed tears reflecting the moonlight. "I'm really, really sorry. I never intended to hurt you."

He gave a single nod, his emotions tangled and confused. He wanted so badly to believe her. To believe the connection he'd felt had been real and not some game she'd been playing.

"We eat lunch under the big oak tree at the front drop-off at the school. Meet me there tomorrow and act like you're still hot on me. I know that's a stretch after what just happened." She looked down and took a breath before continuing. "I'll be rude and end it with you in a day or so, and this will all be over."

But the thing was, he didn't want this to be over. He was deep down more troubled by the prospect of losing her than anything else at that moment. Which was wrong in a million ways. "What are you?"

"I can't. I…I wish I could." She took several steps back, the regret and hurt on her face so genuine it made his chest ache. "I'll see you tomorrow?"

He stared out over the trees below, still trying to untangle his conflicted thoughts and emotions. "Yeah."

She turned to go, her shirtless, slim back looking so vulnerable—so un-monsterlike.

"Freddie."

With a deep breath, she turned around.

He strode into the cave and scooped up his shirt from the floor where she'd kissed him senseless, and a wave of sadness

poured through him at their missed opportunity. He shook his head to clear the ridiculous thoughts away. Yeah. The missed opportunity to make out with a...whatever she was.

"Arms up," he said. He slipped his shirt over her head. Something in him rebelled at her spending time with Thomas shirtless. He shouldn't care, right?

But he did. He cared a lot.

And as she walked down the trail away from him, never looking back, he shuffled puzzle pieces: the eyes glowing from the field his first night here. The feral dogs Aunt Ruby mentioned. The dog at the shed last night.

All easily explained away.

Listen to your instincts. There are things that defy logic.

She disappeared from view, and his chest tightened, everything in him wanting to call her back.

Still, his mind clicked more pieces into place one by one: Gerald's weird warnings. The chief going to the ranch because an animal had been taken down. Ruby's story of the legend of the rock changing man to beast. Freddie twice turning up naked and covered in dirt and leaves in the middle of the night.

But most of all, what he'd just seen. Skin stretching. Bones morphing. Hair and claws and fangs. His heart beat even faster, possibilities blurring rational explanations.

You wouldn't believe me if I told you, she'd said.

Maybe not, but he'd sure believe her now.

His mind returned to the old adage. *People see only what they want to see.* Something in him had always recognized she was different. From the moment he saw those strange pale eyes, he'd known she wasn't like other people. And the things that should have warned him off—her aggressive behavior, her harsh demeanor, her evasiveness, not to mention her verbal warnings—had been the things that had attracted him the most.

While having witnessed whatever he'd witnessed—her changing into something else—had shaken him, deep down he couldn't say he was surprised. Something in him knew. Something in him *liked* it.

Something in him was sick.

He held out his arms and tipped his face to the moon as she had done, hoping to feel it. To feel *something*, but all he found was sad, hollow loneliness. He opened his eyes and stared out over the brutal, beautiful surrounding countryside and considered his own words.

We all hide a beast inside us. The only difference is what form it takes when freed.

Yep. Fucking nailed it.

EIGHTEEN

The next day at lunch, Rain found Freddie and her cousins exactly where she'd said they'd be—under the oak tree in front of the school. No wonder he'd never seen her in the cafeteria or courtyard. He shifted his backpack higher on his shoulder and tried to look casual. Not easy when approaching what might be a pack of wild animals. No. What was *certainly* a pack of wild animals.

He needed to keep this craziness in perspective, though. This couldn't be much different than the gangs back in Houston.

They lounged in a loose circle at the base of the trunk—Thomas leaning against the tree flanked by Kurt and Merrick, facing Freddie, whose back was to Rain. Thomas was the first one to notice him heading their way. An elbow nudge alerted Kurt, and their change of focus drew Merrick's attention. Freddie didn't turn around, but her shoulders rose a little, and she stiffened, indicating her awareness of him.

If there was anything Rain had learned about gang mentality, it was to never show weakness. Go all in. Well, he'd thought long and hard about this last night on that hill, and there was no debate; he was all in. He wanted Freddie, monster or no monster. He'd liked her before last night. He liked her now. End of story.

Keeping his breath even and his gait loose, he ploughed

ahead. Best tactic, he found, in dealing with a hostile group was to communicate directly with the leader, generally cutting straight to the point with no bullshit. There was no doubt in his mind who led this gang.

When he stopped directly behind Freddie, the boys looked ready to launch up and tear him apart, no doubt thinking he was going to cause a scene about last night. He wanted a scene, but not the kind they expected.

"Hey," he said, ignoring the others as he crouched behind Freddie, pulling her hair over her shoulder, exposing the long column of her neck. She made no response, other than a small shudder probably only he could see. He knew this was a risk, not only with regard to her but with the boys, too. In order to be accepted by a gang, you had to take a stand they would understand and respect.

Wrapping his arms around her, knees on either side of where she sat in the grass, he leaned down and nuzzled her neck. God, she smelled good. Like soap and fresh-cut grass. He kissed the area just behind her ear.

"Uh…" Her voice was breathy with surprise.

One of the boys growled.

No halfway with a gang. No show of weakness. He ran his lips down her neck. He didn't like public displays of affection, hated seeing them, but this was absolutely necessary. He was making a statement. A big one. He wasn't scared of Freddie's cousins. And most of all, he wasn't scared of Freddie. He wanted her to know that. Understand it on that same primal level they shared last night.

He wasn't livestock, and he wasn't going away, and he planned to get that across in a way that every single one of them would understand. So once he felt her relax a little under his lips, he made his statement. He bit her on that sensitive area between her neck and shoulder. Not hard enough to break the skin but definitely hard enough to leave a mark.

He'd expected her to flinch or protest, but instead, a rumbling met his lips as she made that deep growl he'd liked so much in his room and the cave. She wasn't the only one growling, though. He lifted his head to find Thomas's eyes narrowed, teeth bared.

He wanted to growl and snarl back but decided to keep it low-key, since he wasn't supposed to remember anything unusual from his fake drug trip. "Sorry about last night. I must have zoned out or something," he whispered, knowing the boys could hear.

He sat next to her on the grass, stretching his legs in front of him, staking out a large area of space in the middle of the circle, getting his point across: *I belong here.*

A rare roast beef sandwich sat half eaten on a piece of foil in front of her. Certainly not school food. She picked it up and took a bite, clearly aware he was studying her. "Want some?"

"I ate a piece of pizza on my way out here." He'd left class right as the bell rang and made it through the line first so he could make it there in time to see her.

"Ugh. Not the school pizza, I hope," Kurt said, nose wrinkled. "That shit's awful."

"Not if you grew up eating out of trash cans and dumpsters so you wouldn't starve." He wanted them to know he wasn't soft. He was establishing his place in the pecking order: *I'm big, I'm bad, and I do what it takes to survive. Moo, my ass, motherfuckers.*

Kurt's eyebrow arched. He'd impressed one of them, anyway. Merrick seemed cool with him, too. He was back to stuffing chips in his mouth with both hands. Moth used to do that. Rain wondered if the kid was okay without him there to keep him out of trouble. Hopefully he'd gone back to his family.

"So, what did you think of Enchanted Rock last night?" Thomas asked in an obvious attempt to test him.

Freddie stiffened, and Merrick stopped chewing.

"It was cool…" He furrowed his brow. "The sunrise this morning was…" He turned to Freddie. "I'm sorry. How bad did I blow it?"

"Pretty bad," she said.

"Dude, you were wasted," Merrick said with a laugh.

Kurt and Thomas glared at their cousin as if he'd spoken out of turn. Clearly Merrick occupied the lowest rung of the ladder.

"You were there?" Rain shot a surprised look at Merrick, then at Freddie, who rolled her eyes. He could win an Oscar for this performance.

"Sorry. Let me make it up to you." He kissed the red mark rising on her neck. Behind her, he caught a glimpse of Grant watching from several yards away. Well, wasn't that interesting?

She closed her eyes, and he knew she was psyching up for something. "Look, Rain. You're a cool guy, but this isn't working for me."

His gut did a somersault. *Wait.* She said she'd end it in a few days. He needed those days to convince her he was cool with whatever the hell she was. That they could find a work-around.

She scooped up her sandwich and backpack and struck out for the school.

Oh, hell no. No way was he letting her do this.

"Easy come, easy go," Thomas said.

One hard punch, and his teeth would go easy. But he didn't have time to demonstrate.

"Freddie!" He grabbed his backpack and caught up with her in just a few strides. "Stop." He blocked her way and was surprised to find tears in her eyes.

"Don't make this more difficult than it has to be," she said under her breath, eyes focused on the ground. Students had taken notice of them. Probably not a good thing, considering…

"It's already difficult but not impossible. Hear me out."

She hugged her backpack to her chest. "I'm trying to save your life."

"I'm trying to make my life *mean* something."

Her gaze snapped to his face. "What are you saying?"

"Don't end this."

She kept her voice barely a whisper, far too low for anyone else to hear. "But you saw me last night. What I *am*…" She shook her head as if to clear it. "You should hate me. Be terrified. Hide from me." She pointed to the boys under the tree. "Instead, you bit me in front of my pack. That's like a throw-down."

Exactly. He smiled.

"You're taking the act too far. I had to stop you."

"It's not an act." He lifted her backpack from her arms and slung it over his shoulder next to his. "We need to talk." He raised the sandwich in her hand to his mouth and took a bite. "Delicious." He arched an eyebrow. "Almost as delicious as your neck."

"You must have a death wish. You're not normal."

"Says the girl who morphs into Moon Creature."

Finally, she smiled, and he could take a full breath for the first time since last night. Over her shoulder, Rain checked on the boys. Grant had joined them and he, Kurt, and Thomas appeared to be in a serious discussion while Merrick calmly watched Freddie. When he noticed Rain staring, Merrick smiled and gave a nod. One simple action that said something incredibly profound: *I accept you.* Now if only he could get Freddie to do the same.

NINETEEN

Rain needed to talk to Freddie in private—without interruption. After rejecting several empty classrooms, he stopped outside a door labeled AUTHORIZED PERSONNEL ONLY. Of course it was locked. "Watch for teachers," he said, pulling out his lock pick. He'd considered not carrying it anymore, thinking it useless here. Fortunately, old habits die hard, and he'd grabbed it up this morning, along with his pocketknife. With a few practiced moves, the lock popped easily.

Her surprised eyes widened when he grabbed her hand. He pulled her inside, closing and locking the door behind, plunging them into jet-black darkness.

"Well," she said, voice breathy. "That's a useful skill."

The warmth of her body, so near to his, made it hard to focus. "I have lots of useful skills."

"I bet you do."

For a moment, he did nothing except listen to her deep breaths, finding his own chest expanding and contracting in sync with hers, then he lit his phone screen and located the light switch. Both blinked in the harsh light of the bald bulb housed behind a safety cage on the wall. The room held maintenance supplies—tools, ceiling tiles, long fluorescent light tubes.

"This is a bad idea." She brushed her hair over her shoulder.

"You say that a lot."

"Well, you have a lot of bad ideas."

He slid both backpacks down his arms and leaned them against a metal shelf. "I have some really good ones, too."

They stared at each other for a moment, and he imagined how she'd looked last night when the hair had sprouted and her face had elongated. He'd expected seeing her today would bring back that horror, but none came. Just an additional burst of intrigue added to his already raging curiosity.

No time for bullshit. They only had a short while before the bell rang. He leaned back against the locked door. "What are you?"

Suddenly, her tattered black Converse high-tops were the most interesting things in the room.

"Around your cousins and everyone else, I'll act like I didn't see anything last night," he said, "but I *did* see something. I want to know what the hell it was."

She gave a one-shouldered shrug. "I'm not allowed to talk about it."

"Or what?"

Her cool eyes met his. "Or we die. Revealing the magic results in a death sentence for both of us."

Magic. "So, what if I guess it?"

Again, she studied her shoes.

"Because I think I've got this figured out."

"I need to go. The guys'll come looking."

She was so closed off. Arms crossed, head turned away.

"I'm calling bullshit. You're scared to hear what I have to say. Scared I'm right. Scared I want to be with you anyway. Most of all, you're scared of how I make you feel."

The bell to end lunch rang, and she flinched. "I asked you to not make this harder than it has to be."

He took her hand and placed it over the front of his jeans, and her breath hitched. "It can't be harder." It was a shitty move, but he wanted her to know he was for real about this.

She didn't pull away when he removed his hand. Instead, she traced his zipper on the way up to hook her finger through his belt loop and met his eyes. He had her attention now. "Listen to me. I don't care what you are. I care *who* you are."

"Only because you don't know me. You don't get it." She dropped her arms to her sides. Her breaths quickened, he suspected from some kind of fear of her own.

"I get this." He took her face in his hands and lowered his face to hers, meeting her lips with a gentle, soft kiss. She didn't kiss him back. *Hear me*, he willed her. She pulled away, shaking her head. Closing him out. *No. Not going to happen.* Time to lay his cards on the table.

"I'm not exactly sure how the necklace or Grant or your cousins play into things," he said, figuring he needed to let her know he understood more than she gave him credit for. "But I know your anger brought on the change last night. It's also tied to the moon and maybe Enchanted Rock."

She held her breath, unmoving, like someone about to jump off a cliff into the ocean for the first time.

"I know the necklace works like an antidote or suppressant, but yours malfunctioned. All three of your cousins wear them, so I assume they transform as well."

Her only response was to look away.

He tipped her chin up to force her to look at him. "Grant doesn't wear a charm, but he provides them. I don't get that connection, but I'm working on it." Her breaths came in quick, shallow pants.

"You referred to your cousins as a pack," he continued.

She paled.

"Your cousins call people livestock."

Undoubtedly uncomfortable that he was nearing the heart of it, she took a step back.

"You didn't change enough last night for me to see exactly

what you turn into, but I saw one of your pack at the shed the night before last."

"What shed? What did you see?"

"A large brown dog with missing patches of hair."

She shook her head. "Not one of us."

"Wolves." He took her by the shoulder. "You and your cousins change into wolves."

She stilled completely, eyes wide.

"You're a werewolf."

Then she squeezed her eyes shut as if willing his words away. *Boom. Direct hit.* He waited, hands on her shoulders, steadying her.

"Go away, Rain. Go now and go fast. Back to Houston. Anywhere but here."

"No."

When she opened her eyes, they were full of tears. "People are going to die."

"People already have."

Her brow furrowed as she undoubtedly thought about her dad.

"I'm not scared. I can handle it," he said.

She rolled her eyes.

"I'm not some sheltered starry-eyed kid just looking to get laid."

One dark eyebrow arched.

He threw his hands up. "Okay. Getting laid would be great, but you know what I mean. I can handle rough times. I can handle danger. I can handle you—what you are."

After a moment, she took a deep, shuddering breath. "Watchers." She blinked rapidly a few times, and he released her shoulders, giving her space. "We're Watchers. We protect the Weavers."

"Watchers are werewolves," he prompted. She didn't

respond, as if it were difficult to admit. He pulled her hair over her shoulder and wrapped it around his hand as he'd seen her do in his room. She watched as he wound it around again.

"We shift into wolf form."

There it was. Straight up. He should have been freaked or at least troubled, but instead, he was intrigued and surprisingly turned on. "And what do Weavers do?" He wound the hair around one more time, pulling them together, bodies touching from chest to knee.

"They weave the spells that hold the magic in place."

Werewolves and witches. *Holy fuck.*

"You realize what will happen if you tell anyone, right? Like your aunt. It would be a bloodbath."

The thought of something happening to Aunt Ruby made his body feel colder—like ice filled his veins. "I would never reveal you. You need to trust me."

She barked a laugh. "I'm in a closet that you broke into, telling you secrets that could get us both killed. We're past trust, Sprinkles."

He leaned down and tugged on her hair just enough to pull her face up to his. "Yeah, we are." This time when he kissed her, she kissed him back, and his body roared to life. Her hands roamed his body. Urgent. Bold. When the tardy bell rang, neither of them even acknowledged it.

"I think you must be insane," she whispered against his lips as he ran his hands under her shirt, unclasping her bra. "Or have a death wish."

"I have one wish right now, Freddie Burkhart. Only one."

Her smile broadened into a grin he could only describe as wolfish.

TWENTY

F reddie suggested they should show up to calculus at different times, but Rain insisted they arrive together. He wanted the boys to know they were good. Tardy slips in hand, they entered the room and took the quiz that was already in progress.

Every now and then, one of the boys would glance back, and Rain would smile, knowing they could see the bite mark Freddie had left on his neck. He figured there'd be hell to pay for it, but he didn't care. She was worth it.

Before they'd left the closet, he'd asked her to meet him for a ride tonight, but she said she couldn't, that she had to work late every Friday night. She'd also asked him to lay low until she ironed things out with the boys, so he held back when the end-of-class bell rang, letting her leave flanked by her cousins.

Right as he finished packing up, his phone vibrated in his pocket. It was a message from Aunt Ruby asking him to call, which was unusual.

Hitting the hallway, he dialed her.

"Hi, Aaron," she said. "Sorry to bug you at school."

He shifted the phone to his other ear, pressing it close to muffle the noise of students filling the hall. "No problem. What's up?"

"Um, well, did Gerald say anything to you when you were

in the office Wednesday?"

Like heat lightning, his adrenaline flashed, and he froze. "Like what?" He covered his other ear with his palm to block out the noise.

"I dunno, like anything unusual? He left before I finished scanning that file and he usually says good-bye."

Every red flag in his system went up. "Has something happened?"

"Yes. No. Well, I don't know."

He stepped out of the way of students rushing to class and flattened against the wall, stomach roiling.

Ruby continued. "He didn't show up for work yesterday, and he never called in. He didn't come in again today. I went by his house, and it was unlocked, but he wasn't there. His car was in the driveway. He's done this before, so it's probably not a big deal."

"No, he didn't say anything unusual." He felt like shit lying, but at this point, he wasn't sure how dangerous the situation with Freddie really was, and mentioning what Gerald had said could put Ruby in danger—something he'd never do.

"I didn't figure. Worth a try. Hey, I won't be home until really late tonight. My shift ends at two a.m."

"That's late."

"Yeah. All the wineries have bands and stuff going on Friday nights. It's my big night. Somebody might lose a phone or lock keys in their car or something."

He smiled at the sarcasm in her voice. "There's always the possibility of a rogue raccoon."

"Or a mermaid."

His heart stuttered. "Yeah. That, too."

"Well, get to class. See you tomorrow. Let me know if you head out somewhere or need anything."

"Will do."

Shit, shit, shit. Keeping Aunt Ruby in the dark about the wolf business was going to be a constant challenge. He'd sensed something was up from the moment he set foot in New Wurzburg. It was a wonder she hadn't picked up on it, as long as she'd lived here.

In track, they ran sprints, taking the top two from each of four rounds to progress to the final race that day. He was the only one in the final round not on the varsity track team, all of whom were in this class and stayed over to practice after school. Of course, there would be no practice after school today because it was the last day of classes before spring break.

"Sure you don't want to join varsity?" Grant asked, taking his spot in the lane next to him.

"Positive. Got a job, remember?"

The guy grinned, like he knew the punch line to a joke.

The coach called, "On your marks," and then the whistle blew. Rain and Grant were in the front of the field from the start, neck and neck, arms pumping and legs screaming from maxing out. Wouldn't let him win. Couldn't let him win. Within ten strides of the finish, Grant migrated over into his lane, foot somehow getting in front and tangling up with Rain's, sending them both down on the track.

For a moment, Rain was too stunned to speak. The guy had done it on purpose. Both of them could've been hurt. He glared over at Grant, who had gotten to his knees, eyes trained on Rain.

"You did that on purpose," Rain accused through gritted teeth.

There was that shit-eating grin again.

He had the urge to punch the guy, but he kept it together, instead asking in a controlled, low voice, "What the hell is wrong with you?"

One of the coaches arrived. "You boys okay?"

Grant didn't respond, just continued to study Rain in that same creepy way his kid sister had the day he came in to the hardware store for the job.

"Yeah," Rain said, pulling a rock out of the skinned area on his knee. "Just an accident."

"Well then, get off your butts and go change. Bell rings in ten. Have a good spring break, guys."

"Wanna tell me what the hell you're doing?" Rain asked after the coach wandered off.

"Testing something."

"What? How much bullshit I can take before I kick your ass?"

He laughed. "Yes, actually."

Rain straightened his shirt and struck out toward the locker room, determined to not let this guy get to him.

"Hey, Ryland. There's a decent blues band at Haven tonight. You should check it out."

Rain consciously relaxed his hands that had curled into fists.

"A bunch of us will be there."

So the asshole trips him, then invites him to hang out? The whole town was nuts. "No, thanks."

"Friederike will be there."

Just hearing her name made his heart kick up. Freddie had said she was working tonight; maybe he'd see her if he went. He turned and Grant arched an eyebrow, and for the hundredth time that day, Rain wondered how this guy figured into what he'd seen last night. Maybe if he went to Haven, he'd find some clues.

"We're meeting around seven. You should join us. I think you'd fit right in."

With what he knew about this town, he was pretty sure that wasn't a compliment.

TWENTY-ONE

The party scene at Haven Winery was already in full swing when Rain arrived. Mercedes, BMWs, and high-end pickup trucks packed the gravel parking lot in front. Party buses labeled TEXAS HILL COUNTRY WINE TOURS and A TASTE OF THE HILLS lined the far end. He parked his dirt bike near the fence surrounding the main building and took a deep breath of fresh night air, scented with wine and perfume.

Maybe this wasn't a good idea. Grant's behavior on the track had been strange. He shook his head and bit back a laugh. He was hot for a girl who morphed into a wolf. Strange was relative.

"Shit." He patted his pockets, already knowing his phone wasn't there. He'd accidentally left it on the kitchen counter back at the house. No big deal. He'd be home way before Ruby. The only person he wanted to call or text was here, anyway. Hopefully he'd get a chance to see her face-to-face.

Rain swallowed hard. He didn't like crowds, and as he looked over the waist-high fence, there was no denying this was a full-on party. Loud blues music wailed, while people danced on a concrete floor under a rough-hewn wood pavilion. Picnic tables decorated with candles in hurricane globes surrounded the edges of the crowded dance floor and spilled out into the garden. Wineglasses sparkled under the strings of multicolored decorative lighting zigzagging overhead. Freddie's people knew how to throw a party.

"Rain!" Grant called from a table at the back corner of the garden. Thomas, Kurt, and Merrick were with him. At a table nearby, he recognized Grant's mother and sister and a man with curly blond hair he assumed was Grant's dad. Of course, they were all watching him—because that's what creepy assholes do. He met Mr. Ericksen's stare directly, and the man's eyes narrowed. *Yeah. Screw you, too.*

Grant stood and gestured him over. As he made his way, he scanned for Freddie but didn't see her in the crowd.

"She's inside," Grant said, gesturing to the opposite end of the bench on his side, facing the three boys.

Am I that obvious? Clearly, he was.

"She has some formal dinner party with out-of-town guests her uncle's making her go to in the wine-tasting room."

Well, that sucked. She was the only reason he was here.

Freddie's cousins looked uncomfortable. Stiff. Rain's adrenaline spiked in response. The guys flitted looks at one another, making a bizarre situation even weirder. After a few awkward minutes in which Rain refused to be the first to talk, Thomas broke the silence.

"So, how do you like New Wurzburg High?"

He schooled his expression to keep it neutral and not draw attention, but he was certain his outrage was obvious from his tone of voice. "Are you kidding me?"

Thomas's brow furrowed. "Look. Uh, we got off to a bad start."

"No shit. You threatened to skin me alive and eat me for dinner."

Grant tensed beside him, eyes narrowed on Thomas, who cleared his throat. Thomas turned his phone a quarter turn on the tabletop, then another. "Yeah. That was uncool. I…" After a quick glance at Grant, he dropped his hand to his lap.

"I wanna forget all about that and start over."

Rain had no clue what was going on, but a threat like that wasn't something he was ready to forget, especially in light of the fact the guy had the ability to change into a monster that could make good on the threat.

Thomas stared at the bruise on Rain's neck, and a muscle in his jaw twitched. This was hard for him. Forced. "I mean, it looks like you're not going away any time soon. You and Freddie… Well. Anyway, I'd rather not be enemies."

Grant gave an almost imperceptible nod, like an approving parent.

No wonder it felt forced. It *was*. For some reason, Thomas was doing this for Grant, or maybe because of him. Rain folded his arms on the table, waiting to see who would chime in next.

"Well, great. Let's celebrate a truce, then," Grant said. "I'll be right back." His curly gold hair reflected the multicolored strings of lights overhead as he strode through the crowd.

Another awkward silence fell over the four of them. A forced peace was better than none, Rain supposed. He met each of their eyes briefly, then spoke. "I know you guys and Freddie are close, and you're hostile because you want to protect her and your family. I like her and won't be a dick to her. I like her no matter what." He stressed the last words, knowing he was on thin ice here, hinting that he knew their secret, but it was vague enough for denial.

The only one to react physically was Merrick, whose eyebrows rose in surprise.

"What do you mean by that?" Kurt asked.

Rain shrugged. "You know exactly what I mean."

"Here we go!" Grant set a stack of Solo cups on the table along with a bottle of wine and slid onto the bench.

Rain glanced around, but nobody nearby seemed to be watching them. Maybe they could score a bottle of wine without ID because the boys lived here. A scan to the right confirmed Grant's family was interested, however, making no attempt to hide their stares.

Grant poured and handed a cup to Rain, then poured three more, passing them to the boys. "To Haven," Grant said, lifting an empty cup.

"To Haven," the three boys repeated.

"You're not drinking?" Rain asked.

Grant shook his head. "Nah. Wine allergy."

"You'll like this, Rain," Thomas said. "It's Haven's private label made in small batches. We don't sell it to the public."

Rain turned the bottle to check out the label—like he knew the first thing about wine. FULL MOON was scrawled in a dramatic font over a photo of a full moon peeking through gnarled tree branches. The significance wasn't lost on him. *Private family label. Right.*

They all watched him like they were waiting for his reaction. Maybe it was pride in their product.

He raised the glass to his lips and took a sip. It was as if they were holding their breaths. The flavor was strange. Uncomfortably bitter, but he wasn't a wine connoisseur by any means. Maybe all good wine was bitter. He took another sip and set the cup down. "Why don't you guys sell it to the public?"

Thomas and Kurt exchanged glances.

"It's not something that would generate much demand," Merrick said, taking a sip.

The band started a new song, and Rain tapped his finger in time.

"Most of the visitors to Haven are business people with money to burn from Austin and even cities farther out. Houston. Dallas. They hit the shops in Fredericksburg and wineries all along the highway, Haven included," Grant explained.

"Drink up," Kurt said.

Rain swallowed the remainder in one swig, hoping it tasted better if shot fast. It didn't. His body shuddered involuntarily at the bitterness, then he winced at the heat when it hit his stomach. It was different than any wine he'd tasted. Merrick was right; it wouldn't have broad appeal.

Grant refilled his cup before Rain could object. He'd rather drink cough syrup, but the guys sipped theirs like it was delicious.

"To Freddie!" Thomas said, raising his cup.

Well, shit. It would be rude to not join the toast. "To Freddie," Rain, Kurt, and Merrick repeated. The three cousins downed it like it was a chugging contest and then looked to Rain expectantly, as if challenging him to follow.

Whatever. He choked it down, determined that he would refuse more.

From a table in the opposite corner, a shrill peal of laughter broke out that made him want to cover his ears. The band had upped the volume as well to a nearly deafening level.

"You okay?" Grant asked.

"Yeah. It's just kinda loud."

The boys didn't react. Simply stared, like they expected him to elaborate or something. Merrick rubbed his palm over the lump under his shirt that Rain knew was his glass charm like Freddie's. He must have gotten a replacement for the one he'd given her at the cave.

They'd dimmed the lights or something—more like they'd dimmed the colors. The vibrant colors of the light strings overhead, and even the clothes worn by the people dancing in front of the band, now seemed faded. Wait. You couldn't dim colors.

And the odors… Instead of sweet wine and women's perfume, it now smelled like dirt and sweat. Heavy, oppressive, and stifling. His stomach rolled over. God. Maybe he had a wine allergy, too.

"You cool?" Kurt asked.

Why did they keep asking him that? "Yeah."

"Want a tour?" Thomas stacked the boys' cups.

Not really. In fact, his brain felt too large for his skull, and he was overwhelmed by the assault of sounds and smells. Crap. He was wasted, but he'd only had the equivalent of a glass of wine. "Yeah. A tour. Sure." Maybe he'd see Freddie. At least he'd be away from the band that was about to rupture his eardrums.

None of them made a move. They just watched him— including Grant's family several tables away.

Well, shit. Maybe they were waiting on him to get up first. He slid to the end of the bench and stood, which seemed to surprise them.

"So, Rain, I'll see you Monday at work, right?" Grant said.

"You leaving?" For some reason this panicked him.

"Yep. Gotta work early. Glad you showed up." He opened his mouth like he was going to say something but didn't. Instead, he turned to Thomas. "You've got it from here. Get him to the back just in case."

"In case of what?" The band and partiers were so deafening, Rain wasn't sure he'd even said it out loud.

"In case the wine goes to your head." Grant ran a hand through his hair. "It's very strong. Most people would pass out after what you drank."

Perfect.

"But you're doing great, like I knew you would." Eyes on Merrick, Grant gestured with a tilt of his head to a big building to the east.

"Follow me," Merrick said.

As Rain trailed Merrick with Thomas and Kurt close behind, the skin on the back of his neck prickled. He felt trapped somehow, like he was being herded. Like *livestock*.

TWENTY-TWO

Rain followed Merrick through the back door of Haven Winery's main building. He shook his head to clear it before staggering down a dark, paneled corridor with offices opening up on either side. The building smelled like chemicals and grapes.

The grape odor was a no-brainer, but the other smells were weird. He took a deep sniff, and the air stung his nose.

"How ya doing, man?" Thomas asked from behind him.

"Fine." But he wasn't. Something was seriously screwed up. Not only the smells and sounds, his balance and everything was way off—like he couldn't control his own body.

They took a turn and entered a large triple-height room with five huge stainless-steel tanks at least twenty feet tall on one side. Workbenches, blue storage drums, and hoses on hooks lined the walls. Several machines on wheels stood shoulder to shoulder in the middle of the space.

"Those take the stems off the grapes," Kurt said.

They'd take off fingers and possibly hands, too, Rain noticed as he peered inside the machine at the workings that looked like a huge drill bit on its side.

He turned full circle in the middle of the room—or maybe the room spun a circle around him, it was hard to tell, as messed up as he was. His eyes traveled up one of the tanks to what looked like a submarine hatch door.

"From the tanks, the wine goes into the barrels, which are stored in here," Merrick explained.

With Thomas and Kurt close behind like herding dogs with a stray sheep, he followed Merrick into a dark room with brick walls and a vaulted ceiling. Tall racks supported wooden barrels on their sides.

The brick walls put off a strong earthy stone odor that mixed with the wood of the barrels, overwhelming him for a moment. He took a deep breath and shook his head again. Hopefully the wine had reached max effect. If not, he was going to pass out, which, considering he was surrounded by apex predators, could be lethal.

Kurt's face wavered in and out of focus. "You okay?"

"I don't know." He placed a palm on a barrel for a moment as the room closed in, heart banging around in his chest like he'd just run a 440.

"Maybe we should go get Ulrich or Grant's dad." Merrick's voice echoed off the hard surfaces of the room.

Rain placed a fist against his chest and pressed hard, willing his heart to calm. His chest ached like it was going to explode.

"No. Grant said to wait it out unless he got critical."

What the fuck? Rain leaned against the rack of barrels and closed his eyes. It wasn't like when he'd gotten loaded before. This was unlike anything he'd ever experienced. Like the ligaments between his bones had melted and his insides were rioting to rip through his skin.

Like he was dying.

He cracked his eyelids open and studied Merrick's scuffed boots as the boy shuffled back and forth nervously, like Moth used to do. Sweat broke out on Rain's forehead, and he closed his eyes again. "I think I'm gonna puke."

"We need to get him out of here—to somewhere not warded. Ulrich will skin us alive if he gets sick," Merrick said.

"Or dies in here," Thomas added.

"Freddie's going to kill us if he dies at all," Kurt said.

"I'm going to kill you anyway." Freddie's voice was like a bucket of cold water dumped over Rain's head, bringing clarity for a moment.

He tried to stand up straight, but his body had disconnected from his mind. He couldn't even open his eyes or turn his head to look at her.

"But I'm going to kill Grant first."

Cool fingers pierced the hair at his temples, leaving soothing trails on his scalp. "You okay, Rain?"

His voice didn't work, but he nodded, eyes closed. Her touch seemed to negate some of the nausea.

Still, she ran her hands through his hair. "Grant swore he'd wait until we were sure."

"He must have been sure." Thomas's voice answered.

"No. He was in a hurry. Just like last time." She trailed her fingers down the sides of Rain's neck. "Which elder approved this?"

"Mr. Ericksen."

"I'm gonna kill him, too. The asshole."

Rain would have agreed if he'd been able to talk.

"Why didn't you stop Grant?"

"We, uh…"

There was a long pause, or maybe his brain just hit the mute button for a moment.

A low growl came from Freddie's throat. "Holy shit. You three were in on it."

None of the boys said anything.

"Oh my God. You helped him. You're all murderers." Her voice was shrill. Panicked, which did nothing to calm Rain's erratic heartbeat. "My dad would never have let this happen. If he were here, he'd—"

"See, that's the problem, Freddie," Thomas said. "He's not here. You've gotta let go of the way he did things. Move on."

"Move on?" Her voice had gone from shrill to deep and gravelly. Deadly. "Unless you want to lose your balls right here and now, I'd suggest you three move on. Straight through that door and out of my sight as fast as you can."

"Listen, Freddie…"

Rain couldn't tell who'd spoken. A wave of nausea rolled through his gut, and he groaned, sliding down the rack, crumpling in a heap on the cool concrete floor. She joined him, pulling him close, cradling his head on her chest, her almost bare chest. He cracked his eyes to see she was wearing some kind of sleeveless shiny dress of indeterminate color. Or maybe his eyes still weren't working right. And she smelled good. So good.

"S'gonna be okay, Rain. You just hang in there, okay? Focus on staying awake."

Hell, at this point, he was pretty sure he needed to focus on staying *alive*.

As his heart thumped in his chest like a kick drum, the rest of his body's senses blurred until there was nothing but the steady *whack-whack, whack-whack* of his blood pushing through his brain and Freddie's soft breasts under his cheek.

Heat. All over, emanating from the inside out. Rain shook his head and opened his eyes to near darkness. Smells assaulted him—unfamiliar, like paint and plastic. And then there was a smell he'd recognize anywhere. The scent of grass and salt. Freddie.

"There you are. Welcome back." Her voice was close. "The worst is over. You're going to be okay. Just relax."

A cool hand cupped his cheek, turning his head. In the darkness, he could barely make out the features of her face, only inches from his.

"You're in my cabin," she said. "You're safe."

Safe. "I was poisoned."

"You survived."

So he had. And he was in a bed. With Freddie—which beat the shit out of dying. Cautiously, he wiggled his fingers and toes, then stretched, relieved to have control of his body again. "How long was I out?"

"A while. It's about two in the morning."

Shit. He sat up, and the room spun.

"Shhh," she soothed. "You need to take it easy for a while. It hasn't worn off yet."

A wave of nausea surged, and he lay back with a groan. "What?"

She placed her palm on his chest. "Sleep. We can talk later."

Sleep? Hell no. He wanted answers. He *deserved* answers. It was time for Freddie to come clean. He'd nearly died—he still felt like he was going to die—and he wanted to know why. "What hasn't worn off?"

"The wine."

"That wasn't wine, and we both know it. Stop screwing with me." He pushed to his elbows, and when the room remained steady, he sat upright, staring down at her in the near darkness. Reaching up, he slid the curtains above her headboard open, and moonlight streamed in. Her hair was slicked back into some kind of fancy knot on the back of her head, and she had on makeup. She looked like a goddess. Sensual, powerful, mysterious. And so hot, he couldn't think straight—or maybe that was the residual effect of the wine or whatever that was. *Focus*. He needed some answers. "Why did Grant poison me?"

She sat up, putting them almost nose to nose. She was wearing a formal-looking dress with no sleeves that seemed like it would fall right down if she lifted her arms. "It's not poison—at least not to Watchers."

That explained why Thomas, Kurt, and Merrick hadn't gotten sick.

Never taking her eyes off his face, she added, "It's one hundred percent fatal to average humans. Kills 'em every time."

And he'd lived… "So you're saying I'm a Watcher."

"Not exactly."

He ran his hands through his hair and fought down another wave of nausea, followed by a chill. "What does that mean, 'not exactly'?"

"It means you might have the capacity to become one of us." She placed her palm against his forehead. "Your body is cooling, finally." She slipped out of bed and into the shadows on the far side of the room. Her dress was long, like the kind movie stars wore, and though it was amazing, it didn't suit her like torn jeans. Rain squinted at the bright beam of light slicing through the room as she opened a refrigerator door

Become one of us… That should scare the hell out of him. He wasn't even sure what becoming one of them entailed. He'd avoided gangs his whole life, skirting the edge just enough to know where and when things were going down so he could stay out of trouble. This had trouble written all over it.

Her scent filled his head, and the bed dipped. The dress rustled when she slipped in next to him with a plastic sandwich bag full of ice. She piled the pillows behind him, and once he rested back against them, she placed the bag of ice on his forehead. "You'll be back to normal soon."

Normal. He didn't even know what that meant anymore. "Why me?"

Her nails grazed his scalp as she brushed his hair back and moved the bag of ice higher on his head. "Feeling better?"

He stilled her wrist. "Why me?"

She looked away, avoiding his question. Rage like fire billowed up in his chest. He took a deep breath and consciously loosened his grip on her wrist to be sure he wouldn't break her bones. Something was wrong with him. Really wrong. Everything was heightened. His sense of hearing, his ability to smell, and now, even his emotions—especially his emotions. An unexpected growl rose from his throat as he grabbed the bag of ice with his free hand and flung it across the room.

His outburst apparently startled him more than Freddie, who arched an eyebrow as if waiting for him to do or say something else.

His nausea had completely disappeared, which would have been a relief, were it not for the aggression that had taken its place. Heart pounding, he released her wrist and scooted away. Her scent wrapped around him, making it impossible to focus on anything else but her—her pale eyes; her thick hair; her smooth, silky skin he wanted to touch all over. Skin he wanted to kiss…and bite.

Shit.

He scrambled out of the bed and retreated to the far corner of the room, spearing his fingers into his hair as he paced like a caged animal.

"What you're feeling is normal, Rain."

No. Wanting to bite a girl—really bite her—was *not* normal. Through the window over her bed, moonlight streamed in, bathing her in a cool glow, causing her satin gown to shimmer. Never had he wanted anything as badly as he wanted Friederike Burkhart at that moment, and if he didn't get out of her bedroom, he was going to do something monumentally stupid. "I've gotta go."

Stepping in his way, she held her arms out to block him from reaching her door. "Sorry. I can't let you go out like this."

He shoved by her, but before he reached the doorknob, she spun him around and slammed him up against the wall, knocking the wind out of his lungs. *Damn*, she was strong.

"Can't let you leave, Rain."

He sucked in a wheezing breath and met her eyes directly. "What's happening to me?"

"Remember in the cave at Enchanted Rock when you told me everyone has a beast inside?" Hands still on his shoulders, she took a step nearer. "You were right, and yours is close to the surface. It's what the wine does—it heightens the beast. Watchers drink it two days before the full moon to wake our wolves so we can shift quickly. In your case, you won't turn because there's another step, but the beast is roused."

He closed his eyes and let his head fall back against the wall with a *thump*. *Beast*. He sure felt like one. "How long will it last?"

Her body met his as she relaxed into him. "Hard to say. You're feeling better now, right? The queasiness is gone, isn't it?"

"Yes."

"Good. You're out of the woods, then."

"Why did Grant do this to me?"

She took a deep breath, and her brow furrowed. "Because I showed interest in you. This should never have happened. It's all my fault. I'll make sure it never happens again."

He stopped her from pulling away, and it was all he could do to not crush her against him and kiss her. She was right. The wine had certainly brought out something animal in him. "And what is Grant's role? He's not a wolf."

Her body remained tense. "He's a Weaver. And his job, like his father before him, is to maintain pack balance. We're low on new members. Through history, people with a strong beast inside have been singled out by the Weavers and put through this test to keep the pack strong by adding new stock to the bloodline."

He ran his fingers up and down her spine, loving the silkiness of her dress and the feel of her body against his, surprised this news didn't scare the shit out of him. "So they're looking to add me to your pack."

Palms on his chest, she pushed back, but he held her firm at the waist. "It's not gonna happen. Ever. I won't allow them to do this to you."

"And they always do what you say?"

Her eyes narrowed. "I'm the Alpha."

"I thought your uncle was in charge."

"Only until I'm eighteen. Youth is an asset in the pack. When the heir is of age, power transfers and the exiting Alpha stays on as adviser."

"And I have no say in this?" Not that he had enough information to decide either way, but he wanted to know where he stood.

"None whatsoever. You don't have a clue how horrible it would be. The danger you'd be in." Her eyes filled with tears. "Presuming you lived through the transformation at all." She turned her face to the side. She looked different with makeup and earrings and her hair pulled back—elegant. And completely wrong. He preferred her earthy and primal. "I refuse to let this happen again," she continued. "The test is risky enough; you're lucky to have lived through it. The next step is much, much worse."

Again… This had happened before. "Is this how you became a Watcher?"

"No. I'm a natural-born shifter. My ancestors were turned centuries ago."

Millions of questions swirled in his brain, but he found it hard to focus with her this near. It was as if his body had a will of its own. All he wanted was to rip off his shirt so he could feel her against his skin. He shook his head to clear it. "So what exactly are Weavers?"

"Not now." She placed her finger over his lips. "I don't want to waste time talking." She traced his lips with her fingertip. "We won't get this chance ever again."

He opened his mouth to object, but she cut him off with a kiss. "This will be your only time to feel your wolf rise, and it's the best part." She ran her hands down the planes of his chest, stopping at the waist of his jeans, and his heart rate kicked up even further.

"What part is that?"

"The part where the wolf is near the surface but can be controlled." She popped the button on his jeans, and he sucked in a raspy breath.

"Controlled by whom?" His voice came out deep and strained.

She grinned as she slid down his zipper. "By me. Because you, Rain Ryland, are about to completely *lose* control."

TWENTY-THREE

Rain sifted his fingers through Freddie's hair as the light from the window above them bathed the room in the warm amber light of sunrise.

His nausea had returned right before the sun had come up, but it was more manageable now. Hell, everything was more manageable now. Never, ever in his wildest dreams had he imagined someone like this girl. Smart, powerful, and holy shit, the things she did to his body and mind. She'd said they'd never be together like this again because it put him in danger. Well, that was a load of shit. He didn't scare that easily.

Bang, bang, bang, bang.

Freddie shot upright in bed and shouted at the door, "This had better be good or you're dead!" She snatched her dress from the footboard and stepped into it.

More banging.

Grumbling about her cousins, she staggered to the door, holding the back of the dress together with one hand and rubbing her eyes with the other.

Rain didn't even have his jeans all the way up when she yanked open the door, but it wasn't one of her cousins, it was Chief Richter standing there.

Shit, shit, shit. He fought back another wave of nausea and zipped his fly. Leaning over to grab his T-shirt caused his head to almost explode.

"What do you want?" Freddie's tone struck him as abnormally hostile.

The chief's response was controlled and frigid. "Him."

Freddie defensively blocked the doorway. "Why?"

"It's none of your business."

"Oh, it's my business all right. Just like it should've been my business with Gerald." Her fancy hairstyle had fallen apart last night. She reached under the tangles to fasten the buttons on the back of the dress. "The answer is no. It will always be no."

A horrible gloat stretched Chief Richter's face. "It appears to me…" She paused to look both Freddie and Rain up and down, then pointedly studied the rumpled bed before returning her gaze to Freddie. "That 'no' is not in your vocabulary."

Rain caught Freddie around the waist before she lunged at the chief, pulling her against him. "Don't," he whispered in her ear as much for himself as for her. With his splitting headache and acute nausea, he'd love nothing more than to let Freddie go nuts on the woman, or shove the chief back on her ass himself, but it would only be one moment of gratification, paid for with days/weeks/months, maybe even years of regret.

Freddie stilled in his arms, a low growl rumbling deep in her throat. Chief Richter's only response was a dramatic arch of one eyebrow.

"Am I under arrest?" Rain asked.

"Should you be?"

"No."

"Well, that's reassuring at least. I'm taking you home. Your aunt is worried sick about you."

Shit. Poor Ruby. "I'll drive home now. I should've called her. Sorry you had to come out."

"You'll do no such thing. You don't have a license." She gave Freddie a glare. "Besides, you and I need to have a chat, Aaron Ryland."

"I said no," Freddie snapped. "He's not going to be a part of this."

"That's his choice now, isn't it?"

"No. It's mine. I don't want him. I won't accept him. Ever."

Again, the chief's eyes roved over her bed and the tangled sheets. "Really?" She snapped her fingers. "Come, Ryland."

What the hell? "Um…" His pounding head and roiling gut made it impossible to form thoughts. It was like his brain had short-circuited.

Chief Richter smiled and crooked a finger. As if on their own, his feet shuffled forward.

"Stop it," Freddie shouted. "Leave him alone." She grabbed Rain's arm and pulled hard, but he shook her off easily despite the fact he hadn't intended to. It was like he was a puppet controlled by invisible strings propelling him toward the waiting squad car.

"He doesn't know anything. He can be set free and moved away from New Wurzburg." Freddie's voice sounded desperate now.

The chief paused only long enough to open the back door for Rain. "He can end up in a terrible accident and be found dead in a ditch at the side of a country road, too." She opened the driver's door and slid in. "Or maybe discovered in a field, the victim of a tragic wild animal attack. There have been a lot of those recently, haven't there?" She made a *tsk*ing sound as she closed the door.

"You bitch!" Freddie screamed before the chief sped from the lot.

Heart hammering, Rain noticed there was no handle in the back of the squad car. He was trapped. Obviously, the chief had manipulated him mentally, somehow, which was probably why he'd felt weird during their first meeting at the station. Maybe the wine last night weakened him to where he couldn't defend himself like he had then. Only, until now, he hadn't been certain that was what had happened.

Over his shoulder, Haven Winery disappeared behind a hill. The chief's voice ran through his head. *Found dead in a ditch at the side of a country road.* This car ride could be the last moments of his life. The final chapter of a story that went nowhere.

"So, you drank the wine and lived."

So far.

She glanced at him in the oversize rearview mirror. "I'm impressed. Not convinced, though. What has the girl told you?"

Back to familiar routine: cop asks questions. He remains silent.

The dewy grass on the rolling hills sparkled in the sunlight as they whizzed past acre after acre.

"You see me as the enemy, but I'm not. She has it all wrong. The Weavers make it possible for her pack to live among humans. To thrive. We're the reason they exist in the first place."

The tension in his chest unlocked a bit when she turned in the correct direction to take him home. Maybe she didn't intend to leave him dead somewhere.

Then, she turned down a single-lane dirt road.

Maybe she did…

She stopped the car and twisted in the front seat to face him.

"You are the last hope that girl has. Either she settles down and straightens up, or she'll be kenneled or destroyed."

He shifted his gaze from the field of tall grass to her face. "What does that have to do with me?"

"You know what she is, right?"

"She's my friend."

One side of her mouth quirked up. "Okay, you can play ignorant." She narrowed her eyes. "If you want her to live… If *you* want to live… If you want your aunt Ruby to live, you will exhibit common sense and go along with this. You will attempt the change. Are we clear?"

He clenched his jaw so tight, he was sure his teeth would crack as he maintained eye contact. All his life he'd dealt with gangs and bullies. Chief Richter was just one more bully— there was a difference, though. In the past, the threats had been against only him. This was aimed at people he cared for.

She ripped the car into gear and backed onto the highway, then wordlessly drove him to Ruby's house.

He could hardly believe it when he stepped out onto the driveway. Blinking in the bright sun, he took a deep breath, nausea welling and head pounding, glad to still be alive.

Ruby ran out and threw her arms around him. "Oh, thank God you're okay. Thank you, Chief, for finding him and bringing him home. I was so worried."

The chief remained in her car. "He's very capable, Ruby, and has a strong survival instinct. Hopefully he has common sense as well."

Without another word, she took off, leaving him with Ruby, a sick stomach, a pounding head, and a billion unanswered questions.

TWENTY-FOUR

The word "hangover" didn't even begin to cover Rain's condition when he woke up. He'd never felt this bad in his life. Chief Richter's threats and the fact he'd upset Aunt Ruby made him feel even worse. Then, add to that the girl who drove him wild had actually said they'd never be together again and she didn't want him, and he was in a royal shit mood.

"Hey." At least his aunt had whispered and left the lights off.

He could manage only a grunt in response.

"I'm off to work." She stepped into the room and put his phone on the nightstand next to him. "It's been dinging since yesterday morning." She patted his shoulder. "Someone's worried about you."

Yesterday morning? He pushed up to sitting, and his head spun. "Wha—?"

"You've been out for a whole day." In the light shining around the curtains, he could just make out her face. She smiled. "Must've been one hell of a party."

"Uh…yeah."

"See ya tonight. Sandwich makings in the fridge. Fresh bread on the counter."

The mention of food made him want to puke, but he groaned instead.

"There's aspirin in the top drawer of my bedroom dresser. Drink lots of water."

"Thanks." At least he could finally form words. "Sorry."

She paused in the doorway. "No need for that. We all do stuff we regret. No one got hurt, and that's all that matters." She took a deep breath, and the furrow in her brow smoothed. "Better let the girl who's been texting you nonstop know you're okay." She winked. "Looks like you've got a friend."

He closed his eyes for a moment after she left. A friend. She was so much more, and yet he wasn't sure where they stood. *I won't accept him…ever*, she'd said. And she'd mentioned Gerald as if his situation were parallel. As he went to the bathroom to splash water on his face, his stomach rolled over. Bloodshot eyes stared back at him in the mirror. He looked like hell… He felt like hell. He barely made it to the toilet before he was sick.

Ding.

He wasn't up to dealing with her right now. Not while his head felt like it was inside a goldfish bowl. He might text something he'd regret, and there was way too much at stake. He put down his toothbrush and turned on the shower.

Ding.

Hopefully a shower would clear his head. Cool water ran down his feverish body, helping with the headache but not the anxiety that had escalated since leaving Haven Winery. Chief Richter had threatened him if he didn't go through with the next step, whatever that was, which Freddie clearly opposed. Was he ready to become something other than what he already was? Hell, he didn't even know what all was involved.

"Shit, shit, shit!"

Shouting was a mistake that sent him to his knees in the shower.

The first thing he needed to do was clear his head enough to talk to Freddie and get some straight answers. Telling him that being with her was dangerous wasn't good enough. He wanted specifics. He wanted the truth. First, though, he needed aspirin.

Ding.

He scooped up his phone and saw the last three messages from Freddie. All said, *You okay? Worried.*

I'm ok. Will call later, he shot back.

After pulling on clean clothes, he staggered into the hallway, right about the time someone banged on the door. Loud. Well, maybe it wasn't that loud, but with his headache, it was painful.

"Who is it?" he called though the door, adrenaline swirling. *What the hell is wrong with me?* He'd never done something cautious and fearful like that before. This place—these people—was getting to him.

"Open the door, Rain," Freddie said from the other side.

When he peeked through the window near the door, he saw his motorbike on the driveway. He opened the door, and she pushed by without hesitation, then she slammed the door shut and locked it.

"Way to scare the shit out of me," she said. "Why didn't you text back?"

"I did."

"Yeah. Five seconds ago! I thought you were dead."

She pitched her backpack on a chair and paced the living room like a caged animal, shoulders slumped and fists clenched, reminding him of the strange posture right before she went all Moon Creature at Enchanted Rock. Her hair was a tangled mess, and her clothes were ripped in a couple of places. "I thought Wanda Richter had made good on her threat." She took a deep breath and released it as if fighting for control.

He couldn't help but be flattered by her intense reaction—and relieved. He leaned back against the closed door, smiling. "Admit it."

She stopped pacing. "Admit what?"

"You like me."

Her mouth opened and closed, then she crossed her arms over her ribs. "Of course I like you or I wouldn't have… We wouldn't have…" Her neck and face flushed red, and she made a wild, exasperated gesture to the ceiling. "You know."

He found it interesting that as bold as she was about everything else, she seemed shy about what had happened in her cabin.

"Hold that thought," he said. "I really need some aspirin." She grabbed her backpack and followed as he pushed open Ruby's bedroom door. "And some answers."

"No. What you really need is this." She pulled a half-empty wine bottle out of her backpack.

"Hell no. That shit almost killed me." He strode to the tall dresser against the wall of his aunt's bedroom and pulled the top left drawer open. There was nothing inside but loose change. The right drawer had what he was looking for. He pulled out the aspirin and unscrewed the top.

"You need this, not aspirin," she said, pushing the bottle toward him. "It's not the same formula you drank before. It's like an antidote." She set the bottle on top of the dresser when he didn't take it. It was a tall green bottle with a gold label bearing the name HAIR OF THE DOG.

"Clever name." He shook three aspirin into his hand.

"Clever product. Why don't *you* be clever and drink some. Aspirin won't help moon sickness. In fact, it'll make you barf."

Moon sickness. He dropped the pills back into the bottle, screwed on the cap, and placed it on top of the dresser. He took the wine bottle and removed the cork. "How much do I drink?"

"Depends on how bad you feel."

Pretty damn bad. He took a sip and shuddered at the bitter medicinal taste before reaching to put it back on top of the dresser. A framed photograph caught his eye, and he almost dropped the wine bottle as he stared at what could have been his twin, only a couple of years older, and his mother, who looked gorgeous in a flowing white wedding dress.

He took another swig of the wine, hoping to hell it worked and his head would clear enough to form a coherent thought. His mom had lied about this, too. He grabbed the framed photo and carried it to the window to check it out in better light.

"You okay?" Freddie asked.

"Yeah." But he wasn't—not even close. Staring at the photo, he took a deep breath and released it slowly, already feeling the clearing effects of the wine. He ran his thumb over the glass covering the picture of a familiar stranger. Aunt Ruby had been right. Rain's resemblance to his father was uncanny. His mom grinned out of the photo at him. It was the first genuine smile he'd ever seen on her face. Equally natural was his father's smile. The man and woman in the photo were so happy. They'd had a wedding. What the hell happened that turned her into a lonely, bitter addict? It was almost worse knowing where she came from and what she could have had. What *he* could have had.

Instead of a life here, growing up with both parents and his aunt in a comfortable house, he had been raised as an unwanted mistake on the streets. Her rain cloud. And it was all lies.

"So, wanna tell me what's going on?" Freddie asked, picking up the wine bottle from the dresser and offering it to him.

"My parents were *married.*" He showed her the photo.

She swapped the bottle for the photo and studied it. "I knew Ruby Ryland had a twin, but I never met her. It's cool they were married, though, right?" She handed the frame back.

He put it in place again and took another swallow of wine.

"Here's another picture of them." Freddie pointed to a photo thumbtacked to the wall near the closet. His mom and dad, wearing goofy hats, were in the boat from the shed—the one named *Ruby.* Again, their happiness as they grinned at the camera seemed to make his childhood even bleaker.

As he stared at the couple in the faded photo, Freddie wandered into the open walk-in closet. Metal hangers clicked together as she passed toward the back. "There are a bunch of men's clothes in here," she said.

"Probably Ruby's dad's."

"Hey. Look at this!" She held up a white wedding dress covered in a clear plastic cleaners bag. Rain had no doubt it was the same dress in the framed photo.

She hung the dress back on the rod. "Maybe this was your mom's room."

"There are only two bedrooms. This was Mom and Ruby's parents' room, and they shared the one I'm staying in. Aunt Ruby moved over to this room when her folks died. My mom had already left New Wurzburg."

She'd been right. He didn't need aspirin. The wine had worked a miracle, and he felt almost human. He grabbed the aspirin bottle and opened the drawer to put it away, stopping short. In the back of the drawer was a diamond ring. A wedding ring. He pulled it out and stared at the photo—at the same ring on his mother's finger.

Swallowing hard, he put the ring back where he'd found it and joined Freddie at his aunt's desk, which was piled with junk—old birthday cards, clipped coupons, and a ton of bills.

Freddie shuffled through some cards and letters in the back corner of the desk and handed him a stack of papers.

"What are these?" he asked.

"I have no idea. There may be something in them about your mom and dad." She picked up a bunch of envelopes and rolled off the rubber band binding them.

Rain glanced over his shoulder at the door. "Maybe we shouldn't—"

"Hey, check this out. These are letters and notes between Ruby and a guy named Roger. That was your dad's name, right?"

"Yeah. Roger Blain. What kind of letters?"

"Love letters." She put one down and picked up another. "And whoa. They're hot."

His mouth went dry, and he almost wished his head were still fuzzy so the truth wouldn't sting so much. His dad had cheated on his mom with her own twin. No wonder his mom hated him and never mentioned she had a sister.

No wonder Ruby felt compelled to bring him to New Wurzburg. She was making amends to her dead twin. *Damn.* He pressed his palm over his chest to stop the sharp ache under his ribs.

His mom must have been pregnant when she found out her husband had cheated with Ruby, and she just took off rather than stay and deal with it. She'd only been twenty when he was born.

"Huh…" She turned over the piece of notebook paper and read the back. "Um…"

"What?"

She glanced at the photo on the dresser, then handed him the paper. "I think we got it wrong."

He squinted to read it in the dim bedroom light. *"I know you don't believe me, but I didn't seduce Roger. You accused me of planning it all out, but I didn't. Neither did he. It just happened, you know? I hope some day you'll forgive me for ruining your marriage."* It was signed, *Lynn.*

"That makes no sense."

"Yes it does if you look at it the right way."

He stared down at his mother's familiar scrawl, totally confused.

Freddie picked up the photo. "What if that's not your mom in the wedding dress? What if it's Ruby?"

His knees and legs grew soft, like Jell-O, and he slumped onto the end of the bed.

She handed him the photo, then opened and scanned a letter from her stack, put it back in its envelope, and picked up another. "I mean, look at the name of the boat." She pointed at the photo thumbtacked by the closet. "And why would your aunt have kept her sister's wedding dress?"

Somewhere deep down, those had all been disconnects because he wanted so badly to believe his mom had experienced at least a brief time of love and happiness with his dad. That he wasn't the product of an unhappy drunk one-and-done. He saw what he wanted to see.

"Oh, yeah. Here we go." She turned an envelope toward him addressed to Mr. and Mrs. Blain. "It's a Christmas card." She pulled it out and flipped it open, then read, *"Dear Ruby and Roger, Wishing you a happy first Christmas as husband and wife. Love, Mom and Dad."*

Shit. From the end of Ruby's bed, he stared at the wedding picture in his lap. Poor Ruby. Every day since Rain had moved in, she not only saw a face that looked remarkably like her cheating, dead husband, she saw the result of the worst kind of betrayal.

Freddie straightened the stack of envelopes and came to stand immediately in front of him, and laid her cool palm against his jaw. "You okay?" Her voice was soft and soothing, bringing him back from the edge like he imagined a lullaby would a small child.

No. He wasn't okay, but the fact Freddie was with him made it bearable. "Why did she bring me here? It has to be tearing her apart." So many things clicked into place: the matching bikes, Ruby's reaction to cooking eggs that night, her shock when she saw him the first time. "Poor Ruby." Gently, he placed the framed photo back on the dresser.

Freddie took both of his hands in hers. Her eyes brimmed with unshed tears. "Maybe having you here makes her feel better. Maybe she's looking for something good in all of it. That's what we do when we're grieving. Look for a reason to justify senseless loss."

He fought back a pathetic laugh. If an English teacher had asked a class to write a paper on the central theme of his life story, it would have been about senseless loss.

She raised the scarred knuckles he'd used to pound so many people over the years to her soft lips and brushed light kisses across them, sharpening the hollow ache in his chest with hope. He closed his eyes against the emotion welling up inside brought on by her one tender gesture.

"Do you want me to go?" she asked. "Give you some time alone?"

"God, no." The words came out faster and louder than he'd intended. He opened his eyes and met her gaze. "I want you to stay." He *needed* her to stay. "I want…" He didn't know exactly what he wanted, but holding her seemed like a good start. He pulled her close and she wrapped her arms around him, leaning her head against his shoulder like she craved the comfort as much as he did.

He wanted to tell her that everything was okay. That all of this was just a road bump and everything would be back to normal soon, but he knew the words would be hollow. Neither of them would reach normal. His life had been screwed up from the time he was born, and her situation was worse. The loss of her father had been devastating and the threat to her safety was real. Too real. Purpose pushed the ache of loss aside, and he took a deep breath.

He ran a hand from her neck down her spine to her waist and back up again to reassure himself as much as her. He'd find the killer. He'd keep her safe.

Trailing his hands down her arms, he froze when she flinched in pain. He stepped back and studied her carefully. The last time he'd seen her, she was wearing an evening gown that revealed a lot of skin and not a single visible injury except for the one cut on her arm that was partially healed. As she put down the bottle, he noticed there were several new gashes on her upper arms, peeking out from under her shirt. He reached out and lifted up on the bottom of her shirt, pulling it over her head, revealing multiple injuries.

"I guess you're feeling better, huh?" She grinned, adjusting her sports bra.

Rain focused on the multiple distinct canine bite marks on her shoulders and upper arms. "Who did this?" Adrenaline raged through him, making it hard to stay calm, especially when her only response was a smile. He wanted to know. Wanted to kill him…or her. Shit. Obviously there were girl wolves, too. He was looking at one. "Who did it?" His voice was gravelly.

She remained relaxed and still. "You know who did it."

"Thomas."

She shrugged. "I think Kurt got a nip in, too."

"A nip." He was so pissed, he wanted to go hunt them down.

"Down, boy. I don't need a defender." She took a step back.

"See, here's the thing. Bites on the front of the body—the head, shoulders, nape—those mean you stood your ground. Bites on the legs, back, and lower half of the body mean you were running away." She slipped her jeans off and did a full circle, exhibiting a maddening amount of unmarked skin. "As you see, I was not running away, but Thomas and Kurt are gonna have trouble sitting for at least a week."

He smiled at that image.

She scooped up her shirt and pants and pulled them back on.

Closing his eyes, he forced himself to focus on something other than her skin. "I need you to answer some questions for me."

"Sorry. Gotta get back to the winery." She stepped into her shoes and headed to the door of Aunt Ruby's room.

He followed. "You drove my bike here. How are you getting back?"

"I was hoping you'd take me."

Maybe that raise-the-beast wine he drank last night hadn't worn off, because his body was tuned to her like a radio station, and her smart-ass smirk made him want to kiss her senseless, which would be really uncool in his aunt's room.

Taking her hand, he led her down the hallway to his own room. Her eyes flitted to the bed, and she gave him that grin he was beginning to recognize as a signal that things were going to get interesting. This wasn't the time, though. If he was going to keep her safe—keep himself safe—he needed answers. *Focus Ryland.*

Stopping in the center of the room, he crossed his arms over his chest to keep from touching her and getting distracted. "The way I see it, you owe me some answers."

"The way I see it, I don't owe you anything." Her gaze dropped to his mouth, and she leaned closer. "But I'd like to give you something."

He took her by the shoulders and gave her a gentle shake, wishing he could shake himself hard enough to make his teeth rattle and his body stop responding to her long enough to get some answers. "Stop this. I almost died because of that wine your cousins and Grant gave me."

Her expression hardened, brow furrowing. "God, I hate that I pulled you in to all this. I know you want answers, but the more you know, the more danger you're in. You're better off not knowing any specifics."

"Way too late for that." He ran both hands through his hair. "The chief threatened to kill me if I didn't turn into a Watcher. She thinks I know everything, so I intend to. I want to know what I might die for." He sat on the foot of his bed and buried his face in his hands, frustrated by the helplessness caused by his unfamiliarity with this world he'd fallen into.

"The chief thinks you know everything, huh?"

"Absolutely. And she brought me home anyway."

With a huff, she sat next to him on the bed. It seemed like forever before she finally spoke. "The Weavers came first. They brag about how they were here from the beginning of man. Watchers weren't around until the mid-1500s, when the European covens created them for protection."

So they were like magical guard dogs. "Protection from what?"

"Humans." She drew her knees up to her chest. "Magic started freaking out normal people. Weavers will tell you the fear resulted from humans' jealousy, because all Weavers are self-absorbed assholes. History books will tell you it was simply the ignorance and superstition of the Middle Ages in Europe as well as changes in the Church."

"So how did Weavers and Watchers end up in Texas Hill Country?"

She played with the white threads on the frayed edge of the hole in her jeans. "My pack settled this area in the late 1800s but came to the United States as early as the 1600s after fleeing from the Bamberg and Wurzburg witch trials in Germany." She shuddered. "Village leaders over there kind of went nuts and were burning people left and right. Watchers guided as many Weavers as possible to safety in the forests, protecting them from witch-hunting parties, but not everyone got out. Hundreds of innocent humans were murdered alongside the remaining Weavers in the frenzy." Her gaze was on the calendar above his desk, but her focus was far away. "They tortured them first. Some were just little kids. Four years old. Burned alive."

She shook her head and sighed. "Can you imagine burning a four-year-old? Fear makes people crazy. Get enough crazy people together and the insanity makes sense in some bizarre way, and the weaker ones will follow authority, even if it's out of control."

Yeah, he'd seen that enough times with gangs. "Pack mentality."

Eyes narrowed, she snapped her head toward him. "Crowd mentality. Packs have order and discipline if the Alpha is strong."

He nodded. "Fair enough."

That seemed to satisfy her, and she relaxed, running her fingers over his thigh, once again making it impossible to concentrate.

"You're intentionally distracting me so that I'll stop asking questions," he said closing his eyes as she ran her forefinger up the inseam of his jeans. His breath hitched as she moved higher.

"It appears to be working," she whispered in his ear.

"I wish you'd stop." He stilled her hand, which caused his body to riot and hers to tense.

"Well, you're shit out of luck," she said tugging her hand away and standing. "Because I'm not a genie granting wishes."

He stood, too. "No, you're a wolf girl answering my questions because the chief of police threatened to kill me if I didn't become a wolf boy or die trying. I'd rather not die for either reason. Knowledge is power. I'm into power. Talk."

"You don't know anything about power." She stomped to the door. "Or danger. Or the kind of evil you're bringing down on your head." She gestured in the direction of Ruby's bedroom. "And your aunt's head."

"The chief threatened to kill her, too."

She slumped against the doorframe. "Oh shit…"

"Yeah. I'm deep in this. Way, way deep."

TWENTY-FIVE

Seated next to Rain on the foot of his bed, Freddie fiddled with the ends of her hair, twining strands between her fingers. He recalled how he'd been immediately drawn to her the moment he'd first seen her. How she'd seemed extraordinary and he'd recognized her feral nature from the start, even if he'd not known the extent of it. Somewhere, deep down, he believed her classmates recognized the difference too, based on the way they parted the hallway when she and her cousins walked through.

"How come regular people don't call out this magic and monster shit going on?"

She shrugged and released her hair. "People only see what they want to see. A girl who's aggressive and in charge isn't an alpha wolf; she's a rebellious troublemaker. A Weaver with the power of influence simply comes across as a good-looking, friendly, popular track star, because that's what people are looking for."

The power of influence. That explained the warm fuzzies when Rain shook Grant's hand.

"A police chief is supposed to be authoritarian and into everyone's business," Freddie continued. "Nobody would ever suspect she's the head of a Weaver coven and has the power of compulsion. Same with the mayor, city council members, school superintendent… Hell, even the head cafeteria lady at school. Humans see only what they expect."

Rain had known that all his life. People expected a big, rough-looking guy from the streets to be aggressive and violent, so that's what they saw. His mom saw only disappointment when she looked at him. And after a while, he'd lived up to everyone's expectations—or lived down to them. Hell, he'd started to believe it himself until he moved here.

Freddie shifted to face him. "After what happened in Germany in the 1600s, the Weavers made sure the magic was safe. Rather than keep to themselves, like in the old days, they infiltrated and took over most local government positions where they lived, so that if the witch-hunt hysteria ever caught on again, they'd be in a position to put an end to it before it started."

He ran his finger under the chain on her neck and pulled it out of the collar of her shirt, rolling the small, glass bubble between his thumb and forefinger. "I'm still not clear on how you're tied to Grant and his family."

As if following a protective impulse, she pulled the charm from his fingers and tucked it back inside her shirt. "It's complicated. Weavers maintain the magic and are only really vulnerable as a coven four times a year, on the equinoxes and solstices, when they have to recast the spells that keep their territory safe from revenants and local humans who see past the facade."

He must have looked confused because she patted his knee.

"Revenants are sort of like vampires, but not sexy in any way." She shuddered. "They're nasty, more like the zombie myth than Dracula legend."

Great. There were vampires, too.

"Anyway," she continued, "our pack circles the coven to

keep them safe when they zone out during the spell-casting and are defenseless. We're also on call if an emergency comes up and they need to get out, like they did back during the Wurzburg and Bamberg witch trials in the 1600s." She turned to him and placed her hands on his shoulders. "And that, class, is the end of today's history lesson." She swung her leg over him to straddle his lap and nipped his earlobe.

With a groan, he wrapped his arms around her and she scraped her nails down his back, making him lose track of reality. Witches and magic and werewolves took a back seat to the desire that burned him up like flames whenever she touched him, and he wondered if she'd have that effect on everyone or if it was something unique to him. His stomach lurched. Had Gerald felt it too? Gently, he pulled back and met her eyes. "I need to know about Gerald."

"Gerald is a sad, sad story," she said, shaking her head. "He moved here after he dropped out of college his sophomore year."

He was relieved she answered so easily. He tucked her hair behind her ear. "So he's been here a long time."

She rolled her eyes as she untangled herself from his legs and moved to sit beside him. "No. He's been here a little more than a year. He's only twenty."

Holy shit. He looked at least forty, maybe older.

"He moved into the apartments on First Street and took a job with Ericksen Hardware. As always, the Ericksens stuck their noses into my business and arranged a meeting."

His heart rate kicked up a notch. "Why would they pair you up like that?"

"It's not important." She made to stand, but he placed a hand on her shoulder to keep her near.

"It is to me," he whispered, fighting back a wave of dread.

For a moment, she studied him as if debating, brow

furrowed. Then she closed her eyes and took a deep breath. "I have to be secured to a mate by the time I'm twenty-one or power goes to the next in line."

"That's seriously screwed up."

She barked a half-choked laugh. "Hey, I'm lucky. Until the 1800s, the Alpha had to be paired with a mate by the age of fourteen." She shook her head. "Low life expectancy."

The whole thing was like something out of a fairy tale. One of those messed-up, scary ones. He couldn't help but glance down at her full lips, wishing things were different— that they had nothing to fear but normal, everyday things, like bad grades and not making curfew. "So, was Gerald down with becoming a Watcher?"

"I don't think Gerald knew anything about what was going on when they gave him the wine the first time," she said. "He was just a small-town hick with no immediate family. Perfect for this purpose."

Chills danced down his spine. "Perfect in what way?'

"Being converted to a Watcher usually doesn't end well for humans. Someone with no immediate family is perfect, because nobody asks questions when the person disappears or mysteriously dies in an 'accident.' The Weavers call them *disposables.*"

Another reason he'd been selected. Only Ruby would know if he went missing, and obviously the chief considered her disposable as well.

"He almost died when he drank the wine," she said.

"So did I."

"Nah. You fared much better." She ran her finger from his sternum to his waistband.

Her intimate touch caused irritation to flare, rather than lust.

Her grin widened. "Now you want to know if I slept with him."

He didn't answer. It couldn't go in his favor no matter which way he responded.

"Does it matter if I slept with him, Rain?"

"Yes." He regretted his answer immediately, but anything else would have been a lie. He wanted honesty from her. She deserved it from him.

Her eyebrows rose. "Why?"

This was a land mine. He closed his eyes and took a deep breath. He had one shot to get this right. The truth was the best path, so he stuck with it. "Because I want to know if what happened between us was a choice you made or just a part of some sick plan. I don't give a shit who you've been with. I'm only interested in what's going on between you and me."

"Would you be jealous if I told you I did?"

"I'd be disappointed. You've never expressed an attachment to the guy, and it would reduce what happened between us in your cabin to a meaningless part of changing me into one of you." He wasn't being entirely honest. He wouldn't be disappointed. He'd be devastated.

Her brow furrowed as she studied his face. "I didn't sleep with Gerald. I didn't even kiss the guy."

The tightness in Rain's chest relaxed and was replaced by a warm bloom of hope.

"They converted him without my approval or knowledge. By the time I found out, Gerald had already spun off." She folded her legs under her. "What happened between you and me wasn't meaningless, Rain." She turned his face to hers. "That's why I don't want you to do this. It's too risky. I mean, look at Gerald. He's twenty years old but will die in a year if he doesn't stop shifting."

"I thought the charm you wear stops that."

"It does. He refuses to wear one." She rose and crossed to his desk, picking up an arrowhead his aunt had given him

last week. Ruby had told Rain it had belonged to his father…
The cheating bastard. *Focus.*

"We try to only shift when it's free. Gerald is so addicted
to the high of turning, he can't stop."

"Free?" Rain had learned at a very early age that
everything had a price. It made sense that magic did, too.

"Yeah. The price we pay is lost time. If we shift within two
days of the full moon—two before, the night of the full, and
two after—we don't age in our wolf skin. We call it *The Five.*
If we are outside that window of The Five, we age in…" She
rolled her eyes and put the arrowhead back down on his desk.
"It sounds stupid, but we age in wolf years—which is worse
than dog years. The average wolf in the wild lives only six to
eight years. Thirteen if she's really lucky. Shifting outside The
Five is a huge price to pay. Every hour takes ten hours off
your life span. Every day ages you ten days—sometimes more.
The time loss is even more dramatic in converted humans.
Sometimes three or four times faster. Gerald has aged thirty
years in a little over one."

"He seems unhinged."

She trailed her fingers over his dresser. "That's part of it.
Staying in our wolf form too long can make us nuts. We're
humans made wolf, not the other way around." She joined
him again on the bed. "Gerald won't wear the charm, and he
won't accept help. In fact, he's disappeared again on one of his
runabouts. If he doesn't turn up for work on Monday, the pack
is supposed to go and track him and bring him back to the
Weavers. It's too risky to have him out there where humans
could discover him. He knows it but can't help himself. Gerald
is addicted to the feeling of being in his wolf skin."

"It feels good to be a wolf?" he asked.

With an arch of an eyebrow, she smiled. "Yeah. It feels
good. Really good."

"As good as our time together in your cabin?"

"Not quite." She grinned and flopped to her back, the mattress bouncing as she landed. He lay back next to her and neither of them spoke for a while. They just stared at the fan moving in slow circles on the ceiling, and Rain wondered what she was thinking about.

"Poor Gerald," he said. It was hard to believe a guy in his twenties looked so old.

She sighed. "Yeah. He was just in the wrong place at the wrong time. Because the pack needs new blood and bringing in a loaner mate from Europe is super expensive, the Weavers will snatch up the first available *disposable* who comes along, hoping he'll live through the process." She stiffened, probably because she'd realized she'd made a clear reference to him being disposable. "I was never interested in Gerald. He wasn't my type."

Rain would've killed to know what kind of guy was her type.

"Since I'm the next Alpha, they have to bring in a strong match for me. Thomas has always thought he was my designated mate, but they want to find someone who's not blood-related. He's a third cousin. Kurt and Merrick are my first cousins, so they're totally out. Everyone else in the pack is related, married, ancient, or a combination of the three."

He propped up on an elbow. "And you guys call *humans* livestock."

"Don't be an asshole."

"I'm being honest. It's a breeding program."

"It's supposed to be a *voluntary, informed* breeding program. The Ericksens didn't receive that memo, evidently. They never asked me if I wanted Gerald. I didn't. Now, he's going to die an old man at twenty-two because they forced him into something he didn't understand and can't control."

Well, that added a few dozen questions to Rain's list. But right now, he wanted to get answers that would would help him figure out who wanted Freddie dead. He rose from the bed and reached under the mattress, pulling out the file Gerald had slipped him at the station and the envelope of photos from the boat shed. As long as they were being honest, he needed to go all in. "Who do you think killed your dad?"

She clearly hadn't expected that question, because her eyes widened and her mouth pulled tight into a thin line as she sat up. After a moment, she whispered, "I don't know."

Rain couldn't imagine how much it must hurt to lose someone like that. Someone you trusted and depended on. Someone who loved you back. Her pain was written all over her body as she seemed to draw in on herself like she had in the vineyard that first time he picked her up on the motorbike.

"I promised I'd help you find his killer. I never break a promise," he said.

"That's the file you told me about. The one Gerald gave you."

"Yes. And also absolute proof your dad was murdered, despite what the police told you."

Her eyes dashed to the file and envelope. "What is it?"

"First, I want to know why you don't think it's an accident."

She closed her eyes and took a deep breath through her nose. "Dad couldn't have been in a harvester accident. We weren't harvesting at the time. Also, we don't own the machinery. We pay for the service. And I would know; I'm the one who arranges for harvester rentals. It was an out-and-out lie, and it was like they *wanted* me to know as a warning or something but needed a story for the humans in the area. They wanted me scared."

"Who do you think killed him?"

"At first, I thought it was my uncle Ulrich because he

had the most to gain from Dad's death. Then, he pushed the Weavers to keep me on as Alpha presumptive. Now, I don't know what to think." Again, her eyes flitted to the file and envelope.

"Could your uncle have done that to throw you off?"

"Anything is possible. I want to know what Gerald gave you."

He handed her the file. "This is the police report. It says cause of death is an accident, but there's nothing there, really." He couldn't bring himself to show her the photos, and he tightened his grip on the envelope as she scanned the file.

"This is worthless. What's that?"

He sat next to her and placed the envelope in his lap. "Photographs. I don't know who took them or how Gerald got them."

She inhaled a shuddering breath, never taking her eyes off the envelope. "It's Daddy."

"Yes."

"Is it bad?"

"Yes."

"Not an accident?"

"Not even close."

She bowed her head as if praying. "I don't want to see them. Tell me."

God, in a way, he wished she'd look at them for herself to spare him this. But at least this way, she could create an image her mind could handle, rather than see the unimaginable. Bile rose in Rain's throat at the memory of the images in his lap. "In the pictures, a man is bound to grapevines by his wrists with zip ties. Arms horizontal. His head is tilted to the side. His eyes are open." He shuddered.

A tear trailed down her cheek but she made no sound.

"He… His mouth is sewn shut."

Her entire body stilled, then stiffened. "I'll kill them." She shot to her feet. "I'll kill every last one of them."

He grabbed her wrist. "Who?"

"The Weavers!" she shouted. "His mouth was sewn shut." Her eyes narrowed. "I'm going to single-handedly slaughter every one of them and liberate my pack once and for all."

She fought to free herself from his grip, but he refused to let her go. He'd been like this. Enraged to the point of murder. Acting on this would do her no good.

"Stop."

She growled, and when she tried to knee him in the crotch, he spun her, catching her arm behind her back.

"Lemme go!"

"No. Listen to me." She continued to struggle, so he pulled up on her wrist, twisting her arm even more. He'd never dealt with anyone this physically strong. "Listen. I'm trying to help you. Are you hearing me?"

He'd been too mad to hear many times. Enraged to the point of mindlessness. He knew how it felt. How *she* felt.

After another minute or so of thrashing, she stopped and slumped against him, tears soaking her face. "I want them dead."

"I know," he whispered. "But this isn't the time or the way."

"All of them need to die." Her voice broke on the last word.

He turned her to face him, then pulled her into his arms. "Even the ones who are innocent?"

Sniffing, she nodded.

"Even the four-year-olds?"

She stiffened. He was fairly sure she wasn't breathing, but he knew for a fact she was finally listening.

"We don't need pitchforks and torches, Freddie. We need to use our brains and get the evidence to do this the right way, not the way that feels right at the moment." He ran his hand up and down her spine, and after a while, she melted into him.

"I just want it to stop. The wondering what happened. The pain. The fear." She wrapped her arms around his shoulders and scraped her nails along his scalp like he loved. He pulled her even closer.

"Make it go away," she whispered against his chest. "For just a little while, let's be normal people, with normal lives, doing normal things."

And as he held her close, Rain knew that nothing about this entire situation, especially his attachment to Freddie, was normal. From the first moment he'd seen her, he'd known an attraction this intense was unnatural.

He smiled and kissed her forehead. Yeah. Unnatural, which suited somehow. He'd always felt outside of society and different. Maybe it wasn't because he was off or wrong. Maybe it was because everyone else was. Until now. He lowered his mouth to hers, knowing that the kiss would be anything but normal.

TWENTY-SIX

"I still think we should go straight to the top and confront Wanda Richter," Freddie said as they passed Bean's Coffee Shop and turned right onto Magnolia Street.

Rain squinted in the afternoon sun, loving the feel of Freddie on the bike behind him. "This is a better place to start." Gerald had said to follow the body. "Do you know anything about Reinhardt Funeral Home?"

Freddie put her chin on his shoulder. "Yeah. The Reinhardts are one of the original Weaver families in New Wurzburg. Petra, the youngest one, is a freak. She had to be homeschooled starting in sixth grade because she drew too much attention. She still does, but they keep her pretty well contained."

Being a freak in this freaky world was an accomplishment. Rain pulled into the packed funeral home parking lot where a black hearse waited under a green awning. "Must be a funeral going on."

Freddie got off and did a three-sixty, checking out the cars. "I don't recognize any of these, so it's a human funeral."

"Maybe we should come back later."

She struck out toward the front door. "Nah. This is a great time to catch Petra. They keep her hidden when there are regular people around. She creeps everyone out."

He fell into step beside her on the pebble walk leading to the oak front doors. "You think Petra's the one we need to see here?"

"Yep. She's the only one who would have touched my dad once he was brought here."

He arched an eyebrow in question, stopping on the bottom step.

"She's a Sealer," she said from a step above, which put her a bit taller than him. "She's the only one who can secure the magic into the body so it doesn't escape all at once, and she makes sure the body's prepped right to not return as a revenant."

He followed her through the doors into a lobby with dark, formal-looking furniture and stark white marble floors. A box of tissues was perched on top of most every flat surface. Organ music droned from a room off to their right, and through the glass doors, he could see people in pews facing a coffin draped in white roses.

He'd never been inside a funeral home before. Because they'd been penniless, his mother's body was taken care of by the county. He'd brought her ashes to the wooded area near the church, and he and Moth had returned her to nature. It seemed the right thing to do. She would've hated something public like this.

His breath caught as he stared through the glass at the mourners, imagining Freddie sitting in that front row at her father's funeral, holding in her grief and rage. Clearly, she'd had the same thought because she stopped for a moment, staring in with wide, glazed eyes, then squared her shoulders.

"Let's go before one of the Reinhardts spots us. Weavers are thick as thieves. Chief Richter will know we've been here within minutes," she said.

The hairs on the back of Rain's neck prickled as they

walked down a dark paneled hallway toward a door labeled EMPLOYEES ONLY. The organ continued to moan from behind. "So, is this Petra a friend of yours or an enemy?" he whispered.

"Neither. We went to school together until she quit. I always kind of felt sorry for her. She's a Weaver, though, so we were never really close."

"Watchers and Weavers can't be friends?"

She stopped outside the door, hand on the knob. "No."

"You're friends with Grant."

"We have a business relationship. He's my sponsor. We're not friends."

He'd seen Grant with her. The way he watched her. He'd love to be friends with Freddie. Which begged the question, what the hell was a sponsor? Before he could ask, she shoved open the door and took off down an even darker hallway toward a metal door at the end.

"Have you been here before?" he asked, shooting a look over his shoulder.

"Only for Dad's funeral, but never back here." She nodded at the metal door at the end of the hall. "That has to be where we'll find her, though. Magic is sealed inside steel walls. Doctor Perkins died three days ago. It's a five-day process, so chances are, she's here."

The Watchers could shift during The Five, and it took five days to prep a body. "Five seems to be a theme," he said.

"The number five holds power," she said as they reached the door. "The culture of the Watchers and Weavers is wound up in the number. The five senses. Five elements—"

"I thought there were four elements."

"Aristotle said five: Earth, water, fire, air and aether."

"Aether?"

"That which is beyond the material world." She shrugged. "At least that's what I've been told. Weavers are weird."

To his surprise, she didn't open the door and walk in like she had the others. Instead, she gently knocked. When there was no response, she knocked again.

The organ music had faded to nothing, and the dim, flickering light of the hallway, along with the thoughts of aether and things beyond the material world, had him completely spooked.

"Ready?" she said.

No. Hell no. God only knew what was behind a metal door at the end of a creepy dark hallway at the very back of a funeral home. "Sure."

Slowly, she reached for the door, and he held his breath, heart pounding. It felt like forever as she rotated the handle to the right, then soundlessly cracked open the door. A faint red light spilled from inside the room across the tile floor like blood.

A noise behind them nearly sent him launching out of his skin.

"Jeezus, Petra. You scared the shit out of us," Freddie said, hand to her chest. "Don't sneak up on people."

The girl with shoulder-length inky hair, dressed all in black, stood no taller than Rain's chest, but her presence was enormous. "It seems to me that you're the one doing the sneaking, Friederike Burkhart." Lowering her chin, she studied Rain with her huge black eyes that were way too large for her face. Sort of like a nocturnal creature that had adapted to see better in the dark.

A shiver passed through him as she scanned him up and down. Her gaze paused briefly on the envelope of photos in his hand before returning to his face. It was as if she looked through him rather than at him, and he fought the urge to squirm. A jet-black eyebrow arched and a side of her mouth quirked in a bizarre half smile, then her expression moved to one of horror, with wide eyes and dropped jaw. Rain looked behind him to be sure the bogeyman wasn't there. When he looked back, Petra's pale face reflected his least favorite emotion: pity.

"What?" Not the best greeting when meeting someone new, but this was beyond weird.

She shook her head as if clearing it, then pushed by them. Swinging the metal door wide, she gestured for them to follow, her long black skirt flowing around her like a cloud of heavy smoke.

"Told you she was a freak," Freddie whispered before following her into the room.

Rain swallowed a lump in his throat as he entered the space that looked like something out of a spook house. Every surface was covered in brushed stainless steel. Walls, floor, even the ceiling were clad in metal that reflected the light from the raw red bulb in the center of the ceiling, heightening the eerie feel of the place.

In the middle was a metal table with a draped body on it. A wave of relief flooded over him when he realized the entire corpse was covered, even the face.

"Doctor Perkins?" Freddie asked.

"Yeah. Two more days left," Petra responded, placing her hand on his chest. Her pale skin was almost the same shade of the white drape—at least Rain assumed it was white. Hard to tell with everything soaked in red light.

"You're here about your dad." Petra picked up a large, curved needle from a metal tray near the body. "Your friend here talked you out of a mass slaughter. Now you're seeking to justify what you perceive as a moment of weakness when you followed his advice." Freddie and Petra stared at each other over the draped body.

"Freak here can read minds," Freddie explained.

Needle still in hand, Petra picked up the end of a long string of some kind. It looked black in the eerie red light. "Freak here sees events. She can't read minds. I see things that have occurred or will occur." She threaded an end of the string through the needle. "You believe a Weaver murdered your father because his mouth was sewn shut." With steady hands, she pulled the string to where it was doubled evenly through the needle. "You're not aware that I've been accused of his murder and an inquiry has begun based on your uncle's accusation."

Freddie's hands balled into fists at her sides as the girl slid the string over a block of something that looked like a blob of wax in a dish on the tray. Petra smoothed the thread from needle to end between her thumb and forefinger. "I didn't do it."

"Who did?" Freddie asked. "You can see stuff. Tell me who did it."

The girl gently folded down the sheet, exposing the head of the body on the table. It was an elderly man with a beard. His eyes and mouth gaped open as if he'd seen something remarkable. Freddie immediately turned her back, but Rain couldn't bring himself to look away. He'd seen quite a few dead bodies when living on the streets, and it always struck him how compelling they were. How intense the fascination was with the worthless shell the spirit leaves behind. For some reason, though, he was still unable to look at the pictures of Freddie's dad.

"I don't know who murdered your father, Friederike," Petra said. "I can't see the events experienced by other Weavers. I also can't read humans and Watchers unless I see their eyes. As you know, I don't see many people other than my own family. The murderer could be anyone outside of you and your uncle." Her eyes slid to Rain. "Or him... But I seriously doubt it was a Weaver."

"Why?" Freddie asked, back still turned.

"Because it was done all wrong. Totally out of order. A Weaver would probably have been closer to accurate, especially if attempting to frame me."

Freddie's voice shook. "What was out of order?"

"The sealing of the body." The girl took a sprig of something that looked like a dried plant from a bowl on her tray and placed it in the dead man's mouth. Then, she forced the jaw closed with the palm of her hand. She picked up the needle and string and held it under his bottom lip. "If it's done out of order, the magic doesn't release properly and it can take over the body. You know what happens then."

"No!" Freddie spun to face her. "Tell me you fixed it. Tell me he won't rise."

"He won't, because I sealed him properly when they brought him here." She pricked the needle through the man's bottom lip, and Freddie covered her mouth.

Rain put his arm around Freddie's trembling shoulders. "Can we talk somewhere else, Petra?" *Preferably someplace without a dead man in the center of the room.*

"There's a rigid timeline. I can't leave for a while. Not until the mouth is sewn shut, and it needs to be done right now." She pierced the upper lip and drew the thread through. Freddie buried her head in his shoulder. No doubt, she imagined her father on that table.

"Hey," he said, turning Freddie away. "Why don't you wait at the coffee shop at the corner for me. I'll meet you there in a bit."

"I'm not some fragile, weak chick you need to protect," she said through gritted teeth.

"No, you're a tough, kick-ass girl whose father was murdered and shouldn't have to watch something like this.

It's too much. I'm amazed you could even set foot in this place. It's not weakness. It's self-preservation."

"You're going to leave this room, Watcher, and go to the coffee shop and have a beverage, and you're going to feel so much better. Also, he's going to get some key information, and you're going to have crazy sex later," Petra said, needle still in hand.

"You're a freak, Weaver," Freddie shot over her shoulder as she headed for the door.

"Yeah, but I'm right." She met Rain's eyes. "Most of the time, anyway."

The door slammed behind Freddie, and Petra's shoulders dropped a little like she was relieved to see her go.

"So, did you really see all that?" Rain asked.

"I totally made all of that up. It doesn't take special powers to predict the obvious."

TWENTY-SEVEN

"How did you become a mortician?" Rain asked Petra.

"I'm not a mortician. I'm a Sealer. I was born into it and then forced into work way too early. I'm not supposed to begin sealing until I'm twenty-one."

That clearly wasn't the case. "What are you, fourteen?"

"Eighteen. I've been sealing since I was nine."

Holy shit. At nine years old, a little girl should be playing with dolls, not corpses. "Why?"

"Lust and bad luck." She snipped her thread and made a tight knot. "Mrs. Goff was the Sealer before me. She fell in love with the wrong guy and ruined my life." She made a new stitch in the lips of the man on the table. "Weavers and Watchers can't have relationships. They get physical with each other every now and then, of course, because Watchers are beasts and that's the nature of a beast." She gave Rain a pointed look before pulling her string tight and snipping it. "Everyone likes a walk on the wild side, including Helga Goff, but then she got all stupid and fell in love with the guy."

Ruby had told him Helga Goff lived alone. "Where's the Watcher now?"

Again, she made a tight, tidy knot. "He died while hiking in Utah. Buried in an avalanche." She snipped the edges of the knot and picked up the needle. "By the time the snow melted enough to find the body, it had already reanimated."

"As a revenant."

Her gaze moved from where her needle sunk into the doctor's skin to Rain's face. "Yes. They always return to the source of their magic. They consume magical flesh as fuel in order to stay animated."

Zombies. "They eat Watchers and Weavers."

"They eat Weavers. We contain the most magic." She returned her attention to Doctor Perkins and completed another stitch while Rain's mind churned with questions.

"That doesn't explain why you had to start doing this at nine years old."

"Magic is tied to confidence and truth of purpose. Helga Goff lost her power to seal." Her pale, strong fingers completed another stitch. Rain found himself less and less creeped out as she worked, and he began seeing the craftsmanship in her stitches. "Her dead lover sought her out when he rose, of course." She shook her head and sighed. "After she killed him, she sealed him herself in her barn, then tended the body for the required amount of time. She was never the same again."

The more he knew about Watchers and Weavers, the more screwed-up the whole thing was.

"She still sees things." She threaded another piece of string through the curved needle. "Three years ago, she told me you would come to New Wurzburg."

Yeah. Totally screwed up. "I need you to tell me everything about the day they brought Hans Burkhart here, Petra. Who came with the body, what everyone said, and what you believe really happened."

"Chief Richter, Ulrich Burkhart, and Ellen Ericksen brought in Hans Burkhart's body. They didn't talk at all during my examination of the outside of the body. Ulrich Burkhart paced and growled a lot. When I was done, the chief asked me what I thought happened. I told her I thought it was someone trying to incite a pack riot by making it look like a Weaver did it. That set Mrs. Ericksen off on a tangent about how I was unstable and saw conspiracies everywhere."

"Why would she say that?"

"Because there *are* conspiracies everywhere. I see things, remember?"

"Why did you believe it was someone framing a Weaver?"

"They were framing *me*, actually." She made the final push through the upper lip. "From the outside, it looked like a proper job of sealing the magic. It wasn't until later that I discovered what really killed him."

"Did you tell them?"

"No." Again her eyes sought out the envelope in his hand. "Like you, I have photographs. I saved the evidence for the trial."

"What trial?"

"A tribunal of Elders from other covens will assemble next month. If the real murderer isn't found by then, I'll be tried. If I'm found guilty, I'll be burned at the stake and my magic destroyed forever."

What the actual fuck is going on here?

She smiled at him as she tied the last stitch. "But now that I've met you, I am pretty sure that won't happen."

"Pretty sure."

"Yeah. I saw…" She shook her head. "Hard to explain. I saw something in your forward memory."

"What did you see?"

"I can't tell you or it'll come out at trial that I led you. There are others who see future and past actions, and they'll examine this conversation thoroughly."

"Okay, so tell me about your private examination of Hans Burkhart."

She wiped an ointment of some kind on the stitches as she spoke. "When the magic is sealed into a body, it is sort of like a time-release capsule that allows the magic to seep out at a safe rate. The steps are precise. First, the body is allowed to rest for twenty-four hours. That's probably just a remaining precaution from olden days to be sure the person is really dead and not passed out drunk or in a stupor or something. Day two: Family is allowed in to say good-bye one last time. Services can be held this day, open casket and all, if the family wishes. In Hans Burkhart's case, the service was closed casket, obviously." She gestured to the body on the table. "Doctor Perkins had a huge service yesterday. It's not only good for the family, it keeps human suspicions down that it fits tradition."

She smoothed the doctor's hair. "This is day three. On the third day, the tongue is cut out—"

"Why?" Rain ran his hand through his own hair, stomach flipping at the thought of a nine-year-old cutting out a corpse's tongue. No wonder she was different.

She laid a hand on Doctor Perkins's chest. "You don't want to know."

"I do." He needed to know everything about the process in order to figure out who killed Freddie's father and might be out to hurt her as well. Any random thing might be the key.

"It keeps revenants from talking. They're very persuasive. It also makes it to where they can't swallow. Hard to eat a Weaver if you don't have a tongue."

For a moment, he thought she might be kidding, but her expression was completely sincere. "Then what do you do next?"

"Then, wolfsbane is placed in the mouth. In Weavers, it slows the magic's release, but it's necessary with Watchers to keep them from turning to wolf form during the full moon in death and giving us away if the grave is exhumed for some reason. Opening a casket of a man to find a wolf carcass makes for really bad press."

He remembered the photos Gerald had led him to and shuddered. "Then you sew the mouth shut."

She gestured to the body in front of her. "In case my spell isn't strong enough and they try to rise or spit out the wolfsbane." She rolled her eyes. "Like that would ever happen with a body I've sealed. It's mandated, though. One more safety layer. Then, the fourth day, I weave the spell and on the fifth, the body is buried."

"Why is the room metal?"

"It dampens the magic trail. Weavers can't pirate any of it because it's contained so completely."

"Magic can be pirated?"

She rolled the table with the tray close to the outer wall. "Oh yeah. All the time."

It got weirder and weirder. "Why do you work under red light?"

"I like it. It's soothing."

Whatever. "So, you said something was wrong with Hans Burkhart's body?"

"Other than it was dead?" She pulled the sheet over the doctor's face. "That was a joke, by the way."

"Hilarious."

She scrubbed her hands at a sink and dried them. "Pull out your photos, and I'll show you."

Shit, shit, shit. He didn't want to see them again. He handed the envelope to her, and she opened it, laying the glossy shots on top of the doctor's body. "I knew the envelope contained photos because I saw them in your past." She put the one shot from the back on top of the stack. "Okay. First off, stringing someone up is a ballsy move, but this was more than display." She pointed at the zip ties. "Look how the skin is torn. He struggled. They did this not only to leave a statement but to contain the guy."

She placed the picture of the front of him on top. Again, Rain felt the urge to vomit as he stared at the open eyes. It was nothing like the doctor's eyes that stared at the ceiling as if in wonder. These eyes were open in terror.

"Look at the stitches. I sew from bottom to top. These were sewn top to bottom—you can tell by the indentations—and the knot is different. I'm left-handed, so they look different than knots tied right-handed."

Rain couldn't tell the difference based on the photo and had no desire to look more closely at it or at the doctor's body. "I'll take your word for it."

"Everything from the outside and oral examination seemed perfect. The tongue had been removed and wolfsbane was introduced into the oral cavity as required, but there was a big difference. After everyone left, I did a full examination because I noticed something way off." She pointed at the photo balanced on the doctor's chest. "Look at the stretching of the skin around the stitches on Hans Burkhart's mouth."

He didn't look.

"I found blood and wolfsbane in his stomach, which means it had been swallowed." She stacked and straightened the photos, then slid them in the envelope and handed them to Rain. "Whoever did this sealing procedure didn't do it to secure Hans Burkhart's magic after his death. They did it as a form of torture. The entire process was done while he was still alive."

TWENTY-EIGHT

When Petra led Rain to the lobby of Reinhardt Funeral Home, the place was empty. "Where did everyone go?" he asked.

"To the cemetery," she said, picking up a memorial service program from the floor and pitching it into a trash can. "My family, too. They went to finish the service and inter the body. I'm not allowed to go."

In regular light, she didn't look quite as unusual, just pale like she never went outside and, of course, there were those weird, oversized eyes and flowing black clothes.

"Why aren't you allowed to go?" he asked. Freddie had given her take on it, but he wanted to know why Petra thought she was kept away from "normal" people.

"Because I'm a freak."

Having skirted the edges of society himself for so long, he got where she was coming from. "Aren't we all?"

She tipped her chin down and stared at him like she had that first time she saw him. "I suppose we are."

He ran his finger over the edge of a rose in a huge arrangement on a table. It was soft and pliable like Freddie's skin. His chest ached for her and her father. "Who do you think killed Hans Burkhart? Is Freddie in danger?"

"I'm not certain."

He picked up a pen with the funeral home information on it from a display next to the flowers. He forced the last question around the lump forming in his throat. "Who would want them dead?"

She stood unnaturally still, like a statue. "Everyone." A grandfather clock behind her chimed, and she flinched. "You should go before my family gets back."

Freddie had told him it would be bad if Petra's family saw them there, but he really needed answers, and he suspected this girl had some. "Want to go get coffee?"

She looked around, like she wasn't sure what to do or say. Like she was lost. "I…"

"Come on. Freddie's probably got caffeine jitters by now. I need to catch up if I'm going to keep up with her, right?"

Statue-still, she studied him with her chin down and her eyebrow quirked up in surprise.

"You're looking into my memories and future memories. You know you're going to come with me, so what's the holdup?"

"I've never…" A single tear rolled down her unnaturally pale face. "Nobody has ever invited me to do anything before."

Rage burrowed into his bones as he followed the tear's progression down her cheek. This girl had been locked in this place full of death with no friends except corpses. Maybe that's why fate had dumped him in the middle of all this. Maybe if he became one of them, he could make life better for this girl who had been hacking off dead people's tongues since she was in second grade.

His fists curled at his sides. What the hell was wrong with these people? Well, other than they were witches and werewolves. Surely, even with that kind of freaky crap going on, there should still be a code of basic human—or nonhuman—decency.

"Come with me, Petra." He gestured to the door.

"You're not embarrassed to be seen with me?"

At that moment, he wanted to kick some Weavers' asses. "No. Not at all."

For a long time, she stared at her black lace-up boots, then lifted her chin. "I can't go in the shop, but I'll walk there with you. I know a back way where we won't be seen from the street."

Once out the back door of the funeral home, she turned right, then opened a gate into a lot filled with junk. Abandoned, rusting car parts and ancient kitchen appliances along with unidentifiable hunks of metal were strewn about in the knee-high grass. "Watch your step. And look for snakes, too."

Rain knew he needed to make the most of this short walk. "You said everyone wanted Hans Burkhart dead. Why?"

She lifted her skirt to navigate the tall grass, making her look like something out of an old-timey movie. "He wanted a revolution of sorts. The original system is obsolete. Hans Burkhart knew this and wanted to change the way things are done. It angered a lot of people, including my parents and most other Weavers."

"Who was the most pissed off?" That would most likely be the person who wanted to hurt Freddie.

"Like I said, *everybody*." She leaned down to check out something in the grass before striking out again. "Some had more to gain by his death than others, though. Obviously, Ulrich Burkhart and his sons, Kurt and Merrick, would benefit because after Ulrich, Kurt would become Alpha if Freddie was skipped over...or *unavailable*. Kurt is favored in some circles because Freddie is...difficult."

He'd never made that connection that the boys were Ulrich's sons. "What about Freddie's cousin Thomas?"

"Him, too. His father, Klaus Weigl, had planned for Thomas to be paired with Friederike, which would put him in a pack leader position, behind her, of course, but if something happened to her before they had kids, he would be Alpha. Friederike's father wouldn't consider it because he didn't trust Klaus. Everyone was surprised when Ulrich followed Hans's wishes that a new Watcher be found. So far, Ulrich Burkhart has kept to his brother's plan to put his daughter in as Alpha, but he's also expanded the Winery, which Hans was completely against."

Every bit of information only raised more questions for Rain. He waited, though, letting her spin the story her way.

Her skin almost looked normal in the pink hue of sunset. She picked up a metal bar from the grass and twirled it in her strong, pale fingers, like a band drum major—only this girl had never even gotten to go to high school, much less watch halftime at a football game. Rain's heart twisted painfully in his chest as he watched her. Her life must have been horrible. No school. No life outside the funeral home.

She stopped and stared back at him, then dropped the rod into the grass. "If she takes her uncle's place when she's old enough, Friederike will be the second female Alpha in the history of this pack. It's been more than one hundred years since the last one." She tilted her head and watched a plane cross the sky before striking out through the long grass again.

"Who else had a lot a stake?"

"Some Weavers' existences are wrapped up in managing the pack. The entire Ericksen family will be out of a job if the pack becomes autonomous as Hans Burkhart wished."

"The hardware store will shut down?"

She stepped over a rusted car bumper. "No. Their role within the coven will become obsolete. They fear that irrelevance will lessen their status and power in the coven."

"They're in charge of the breeding program."

Her eyebrow arched. "Interesting way to put it. They call

it *lupine primogeniture."*

"Well isn't that fancy. Sounds like a PBS TV documentary."

"Kind of softens the blow, doesn't it? Give something a pretty name, and it can't be ugly."

They walked along in silence for a few minutes, interrupted occasionally by a startled cricket chirping as it sprung from the tall grass as they passed.

He paused by an old rusted-out Chevy truck hull. "It sounds like you might be in favor of Hans Burkhart's revolution."

"Most of the younger generation in both the pack and coven favor change."

"You say most. Who isn't in favor?"

She leaned against the hood of the truck. "Like I said, there are members of the Watcher pack who would benefit from sticking to the old ways." She crossed her arms over her ribs and stared at the sky, like it was a novel thing—which it might have been. He didn't know the extent of her isolation.

After a few more minutes, they reached a gate with a lock on it. The fence was too tall for Petra to climb in her skirt, so Rain reached into his pocket for his lock pick.

She placed her hand on the lock, and it popped open.

"Nice." He slid the tool back in his pocket.

"I can seal and unseal more than magic in dead bodies."

"Very cool."

She beamed up at him as if he'd just given her the best compliment ever. On the other side of the gate was an alley behind a row of businesses.

"I walk this way at night to go to the park near the library," she explained. "I like to look in the windows at all the books. One of these days, I'm going to get up the nerve to go inside." She said it in the same tone Moth used when he talked about winning the lotto someday.

Rain shoved his hands farther in his pockets and vowed to make sure that happened for her.

They were only a few stores away from where the back of the coffee shop should be. "Tell me about Grant Ericksen." The guy made him uneasy.

She stepped over an old Crisco can that had fallen out of a dumpster to their left. "Grant hates me. He's hated me since we were seven years old and I knocked him on his butt with magic. His father gave him a hard time for being bested by a girl. I wouldn't put it past him to frame me while getting rid of Hans Burkhart and gaining unfettered use of Friederike in the bargain: win, win, win."

He stopped short. "What do you mean, unfettered use of Friederike?"

She covered her mouth, and her eyes grew even larger. "I've said too much."

Oh shit. He couldn't afford for her to clam up now. Maybe if he appealed to her dislike for Grant. "Look, I don't want to talk about this in front of Freddie. Please tell me what the deal is with her and Grant. I don't like the guy."

"That's odd. Everyone likes Grant. He makes sure they do."

"And you don't have that power to make people like you, do you?"

She struck out down the alley. "No. People see me as I really am, not as I want them to see me."

"And how do you want to be seen?"

"As…" She skimmed her fingers over the bricks in the building as she continued down the alley ahead of him. "As something other than a freak."

Poor Petra. She was smart and sensitive under all that Goth clothing and pale skin. "You might be surprised how people really see you if you give them a chance."

She made a defeated noise in the back of her throat.

In only three strides, he caught up with her. "Grant's power of influence doesn't work on me."

Her eyebrow arched. "Grant's dad is old school and believes that Watchers serve Weavers. He controls Grant completely. If Friederike is anything but docile, Charles Ericksen will see to it that she's put down or kenneled. If it's the latter, she'll be administered an obedience spell, and Grant Ericksen will own her...like a pet." She shrugged. "Unfettered use."

Anger roiled in his gut. *Oh, hell no.* "What you're describing is slavery."

"Weavers call it *ordained service.* Again, if it has a pretty name, it can't be ugly, right?"

Rain felt like his insides were boiling. How could something like this be going on in the twenty-first century? "You know that I was given the Full Moon wine, right?"

"Yes, I saw that in your memories."

"Grant was the one who did it."

"I know."

"What else do you know?"

"That you start work at Ericksen Hardware and Feed tomorrow."

"When you first met me, you saw something else."

Her boots became very interesting all of a sudden. "Friederike is waiting for you. She's anxious and wants to go home."

He bent down to put his face in her line of vision, and she looked away. "When you first met me, you saw something that scared you and then made you feel sorry for me. What was it?"

She shook her head. "My abilities are limited. I'm not always accurate. You need to go see Mrs. Goff. Her visions are very clear."

He barked a laugh. "Mrs. Goff sees imaginary creatures in her yard and calls in the police. She's not reliable."

"Mrs. Goff doesn't call the police. She calls Ruby Ryland." She looked at the sky as if she'd lost her train of thought.

"Why Ruby?"

"To get to you. You asked what I saw." She shuddered. "I'm not the person to share that. If you want to know, you need to go see Helga Goff."

He stared at her a long time, pulled between frustration and fear. For him, for her, for Freddie. If this girl, who saw the unimaginable every day at work, was freaked out by something enough to shudder at the thought, it had to be bad.

"I really need to get back home now," she said, shifting her weight from foot to foot. "But you must go see Helga Goff. Promise me you'll go see her soon."

"I promise. I'll go by her place tomorrow after work."

She gave a quick nod and pivoted to head back to the funeral home.

Rain caught her hand and stopped her. "Now, I want you to make *me* a promise." He pulled the pen he'd snagged at the funeral home out of his pocket and wrote his number on the back of her hand. "Call me if you need anything. Even if it's just to talk to a friend."

"Friend?" Her eyes widened as she stared up at him.

"I'm your friend, Petra. Call me anytime."

She stared at the numbers on her hand.

"Well, see ya." He headed toward the corner of the building.

"Be careful at work tomorrow, Rain Ryland," she warned from the shadows of the alley.

"Is that what you saw? Something that happens to me at Ericksen Hardware?"

"No. But the Ericksens are very powerful." She stared at the concrete as she pushed a rock around with the toe of her boot. "I've never had a friend before. I'd like that friend to stay alive."

TWENTY-NINE

Rain pulled into the Ericksen Hardware and Feed store parking lot at seven forty-five the next morning. Even with the brilliant morning sun bathing everything in a cheerful golden glow, his stomach churned with dread.

Petra's voice chanted through his head in an ominous loop. *Be careful at work tomorrow, Rain Ryland.*

Grant's little sister was seated behind the counter studying a large book when Rain stepped inside. She didn't look up as the bells above the door made way too much racket for his frayed nerves. He'd hung out with Freddie in her cabin after the coffee shop. Around midnight, he made it home and went straight into bed but couldn't fall asleep. Maybe it was because Freddie tied his insides up in knots, or maybe he'd slept so long after drinking the wine the boys had given him, but his mind couldn't stop trying to put puzzle pieces in place. The problem was that there were too many missing pieces to get a feel for the full picture. Hopefully, Grant and his creepy family would fill in some of the blanks for him.

"Is Grant here?" he asked.

"Not yet." The girl flipped a yellowed page in what looked like an ancient book. "Are you going to run away now?"

What the everlovin' hell? "From you?"

"No. From yourself."

He didn't answer. He simply watched as she turned another page.

"Blood will tell, I suppose." She raised her eyes to his. "Cowardice is genetic."

Well, creepiness was certainly genetic. Rain leaned against a lawn sprinkler display and stared. "Are you talking about my mom or my dad when you mention cowardice?"

"When your father found out he'd been chosen, he did several foolish things. First, he got married, thinking that would make him less desirable to us. Then, he tried to convince his wife to leave New Wurzburg." She wrote something in the book. "Like we wouldn't have found them."

She was skirting around and not coming straight out and giving anything away. It could all be interpreted without any wolf or witch twist. His palms had become sweaty, and he fought to control his breathing. He'd never let this girl see his discomfort. Ever.

"Then a miracle happened." She returned her attention to her book.

"What?"

Her smile belonged in a horror movie. Nothing creepier than a knowing, smug smile on a child. "You."

They'd planned to convert his father into a Watcher. A chill crept up his spine. "You planned to hook my dad up with Freddie? That's sick."

A blond eyebrow quirked up. "So you know about Freddie—about New Wurzburg." She gestured to the yellowing tome in front of her. "Exactly how much do you know?"

Oh shit. So much for playing dumb. She'd clearly baited him to see how much he knew. He gritted his teeth, refusing to look away. "I know enough."

"We never intended a pairing between your father and

Freddie. She wasn't born yet. We planned a pairing between him and any suitable female to produce new stock to dilute the bloodline. But like I said, we got something much better because you are appropriately aged for the next Alpha." She shrugged. "That is, unless you're a chicken like your father."

He moved closer to the counter to get a better look at her book, which appeared to be handwritten names in lines with lines drawn between them. "I'm not scared of anything or anyone."

"You should be."

The bells on the door clanged, and Rain spun to find Grant striding in with a grin on his face. "Hey, Rain."

"He knows," the girl behind the counter announced. "He knows everything, which means this won't be anything like Gerald Loche."

Grant's happy expression fell into one of confusion and possibly anger. "How did you find out?"

Rain answered with a noncommittal shrug.

"If Freddie told you, she…" He didn't finish the sentence.

"The penalty is death for revealing our true natures to a human," the girl said as if she were remarking on a flavor of ice cream. "And that would make my big brother sad."

The death penalty. "Freddie didn't tell me."

Grant paced back and forth in front of the counter. "She must have."

"He specifically knew of the lupine primogeniture program," the creepy little sister announced.

"How?" Grant's question was leveled at Rain.

"I figured it out," Rain said, shoving his hands in his pockets to hide the trembling. "Not hard. It's pretty obvious."

Grant looked from Rain to his sister and back again.

He had to turn this away from Freddie. "Well, I suspected when I overheard you talking to the boys in the hallway. You even got physical with Thomas. Then, there was the night at the winery. Like I wouldn't know something was up from that shit you pulled." The guy's face paled. "And then, back in Freddie's cabin, I totally figured it out without her saying a word. I mean, it's not in my nature to want to bite a girl unless my nature's been altered, right? The wine you gave me did a serious number on my brain and body. A wolf's a wolf, right? Nothing subtle there."

Grant went from sickly pale to red. He looked to his sister as if for advice.

She flipped another worn page of her book. "Well, if his beast rose far enough, he could have figured it out on his own, especially if you were that obvious, Grant."

It was the first time Rain had liked the little freak.

"The chief knew you'd given me the wine," Rain added to twist the knife. "She didn't seem to mind that I was in on New Wurzburg's dirty little secret."

Grant's face got even redder. His sister cleared her throat and turned a page in her book. "My suggestion is to either submit a termination request and have him put down, which will bring a lot of questions your way, or make the best of it and go forward." She studied Rain a moment, and he schooled his expression to his go-to who-gives-a-shit look. "It could work in our favor that he knows and is still here, as opposed to running away like his sire did."

The door bells jangled, and all three tensed.

"Good morning, everyone," Grant's dad said, pushing his glasses up on his nose. His gaze stopped on Rain and stayed there. "Ready for a hard day's work?"

"You bet." Rain was relieved his voice came out steady.

After a long once-over that somehow felt like a threat, Charles Ericksen jerked his head toward the back of the store. "Need deliveries made to Carter Ranch and Haven Winery.

Clipboard is on the truck seat."

"Got it," Grant said. "Follow me, Rain." With a tug on Rain's sleeve, they headed to the back of the store at almost a run. It struck Rain that Grant was as anxious to get away from his dad as he was.

"You can drive if you want, but it might be easier if I do, since I know the area," Grant said, yanking open the driver's door of a white panel truck.

"I don't have a license."

He grabbed a clipboard off the seat of the truck and shot Rain a surprised look. "You drive a motorcycle."

"Different kind of license." He didn't have one of those, either, but Grant didn't need to know that. Information needed to flow one direction today.

After a quick inventory of rolls of barbed wire, wire staples, and rope for Carter Ranch and two oak barrels and half a dozen blue drums of chemicals for Haven, they struck out.

Grant changed the tuner from a talk-radio station to classic country music. Didn't make much difference what he played, really; the truck didn't have AC, and the wind through the open windows made it hard to hear. "So, you still getting along with Freddie?"

Info one way, he reminded himself. "Going good, I guess."

The guy looked over but didn't reply. After they pulled onto the highway, he cleared his throat. "So, you know your purpose in all this."

"To make the world a better place," he said in a singsong voice with a smirk.

Again, Grant glanced over. "You will make the world a better place if you can convince Freddie to step up as Alpha."

"Why wouldn't she?"

"She's still messed up from her father's death."

"She doesn't talk much about that. What happened?"

He shifted in the seat and checked his mirrors. "Accident. She didn't tell you about it?"

Info flows one way. "Not really. Where's her mom? She never mentions her."

He switched off the radio, lips in a grim line. "Her mother was on loan from Germany. She was returned three days after Freddie's birth."

"On loan, like breeding stock in a zoo? Do you know how messed up that is, man?"

"Yeah. Pretty messed up." He flipped on a blinker and turned onto a dirt road. "The alternatives are worse."

Rain really wanted to confront the guy but was afraid of giving away too much or being overly specific and putting Freddie, Gerald, or Petra in jeopardy. He hadn't heard mention of using female *disposables*. Only males. Maybe women were more likely to have loved ones who gave a shit about them and would notice if they went missing than guys like him did. Maybe it was harder to successfully convert them. Who knew.

They backed the truck up to a huge metal barn and unloaded the items. It felt good to lift heavy stuff. It knocked off some of the edge and nervous energy. Neither spoke again until they pulled into the Haven Winery parking lot.

"Freddie's pretty special," Grant said, taking a small road off the back of the lot that ran behind the main building.

Rain opted to stay silent and see where the guy was going with this. He was still steamed over the loaner-mom thing.

"You were carefully picked," he added.

"Yeah, because I can be gotten rid of easily."

"Because Freddie likes you, and I thought you two would suit."

Rain gritted his teeth.

"She requested we cancel your conversion." Grant waited as if Rain would respond. Fat chance. "Any idea why?"

Rain didn't even move a muscle in response, but his chest ached at the thought she'd cut him out of her life like that.

"She's afraid the process will kill or mess you up, like Gerald." Grant looked over at him. "Are you afraid?"

He met his eyes directly. "No."

The road led to a metal roll-up loading door in the side of the main building. Grant backed the truck up and Merrick, Kurt, and Thomas came out to meet them. Freddie joined last and waited by the side of the building.

Grant put the truck in park and killed the motor. "Don't hurt her, Ryland."

Rain kept his voice low enough to not be heard through the open windows. "Says the fucking *zookeeper.*"

"Hey! It's about time," Kurt shouted from the loading dock. "You barely beat the storm."

As if on cue, a clap of thunder vibrated the air.

"I'm not the bad guy, Ryland." Grant pulled the keys out of the ignition. "I'm on her side."

Grant opened the door and stepped down on the pavement. "I'll help you guys get the full drums loaded in, and Rain and Freddie can go get the empties for us to take back."

"I'll show you where they are, Rain," Freddie said.

When they entered the dark hallway that he recalled from Friday night, he took her hand and pulled her to a stop. "Hey." He kissed the spot on her neck he'd bitten in front of the guys at school. There was barely even a bruise now.

"Hey, yourself. I'm surprised you actually went to work today." She leaned into him, and all that anger and tension he'd felt in the truck cab with Grant melted into the wall behind him.

Leaning his head back against the paneling, Rain closed his eyes and marveled at how simply being near Freddie made him feel better, like cool fingers on a sunburn. "Why would

I not go? The antidote wine worked fine."

"I was hoping you'd get smart and quit the job at Ericksen Hardware like I suggested."

He ran his hands down her back and up to her shoulders again. "Some of your suggestions are really good. Some suck."

"It was a good suggestion."

"Like asking Grant to cut me loose?"

She pulled away, but not before he saw the stricken expression on her face. "We need to get the empty chemical drums out of the way before my cousins come down this hallway with full ones and there's no place to put them."

He followed her into the big room with the stainless steel tanks he remembered from his "tour" with Thomas, Kurt, and Merrick.

"Here you go." Not making eye contact, she rolled a handcart to him and pointed to a line of blue plastic storage drums. "Those go back to the truck, and the new ones go in their place. They're light, but they don't stack."

He tipped one easily and slid the handcart under the edge.

From the hallway, laughter drifted into the large room. The guys needed a place to put the full drums, so instead of taking them all the way to the truck one at a time, he decided to first move them out of the way so the new ones could slip in their places. Without using the handcart, he shoved one across the concrete floor to a spot near the closest tall metal tank. A second one followed.

"How's Ruby?" she asked, sweeping the empty spots he'd cleared.

"She's fine." He grabbed the third drum but couldn't slide it easily like the others. "This one's not empty. Want me to leave it?"

"It's empty. They all are." She set the broom against the wall. "I cleaned and tagged them myself on Friday."

A yellow label that said RETURN was stuck to the top of the barrel.

He shoved it again. "Nope. Definitely not empty."

There was a metal band around the top that had a lever handle attached. He pulled out on the handle, but it wouldn't budge. Freddie joined him with a short pry bar. She inserted it under the handle, using the lip of the barrel as a fulcrum, and ripped up. The band came loose with a metallic *pop* and Freddie instantly stepped back, nose wrinkled.

"Man, you guys are slow," Kurt said from the doorway, pushing a cart with a barrel from the truck on it. "What have you been doing? No, wait. I don't want to know. Keep that stuff private."

"There's…" Freddie covered her mouth. "Something rotten in there."

It must have been her super wolf nose making her that sensitive, because Rain only smelled something rank, like slightly spoiled milk, but nothing to make him back up to the opposite side of the room. Maybe the chemicals that they'd stored in the drums smelled like that. He pitched the ring to the side and pried the top off the drum.

With an instinctual step back, his stomach flipped over, and like Freddie, he covered his mouth.

"What is it?" Kurt peered into the drum. "Oh shit."

Rain replaced the top but didn't put the tension band back in place. "We need to call the cops. Nobody touch it."

"We should open the garbage bag and see what's inside," Kurt said, pulling a pocketknife out of his jeans.

Before he reached the drum, Rain grabbed his wrist. "I said, nobody touches it."

"What's going on?" Grant asked from the doorway. Merrick held the other end of a rolling dolly with two barrels on it.

Kurt yanked his arm out of Rain's grip. "There's something dead in a garbage bag in that barrel, and Livestock here won't let me take a look."

Thomas pushed his way around Merrick into the room. "We need to see what it is."

"We shouldn't touch anything until the cops are here." Rain stood defensively between the barrel and the boys.

"Things don't work like that around here," Thomas said, moving closer. "The family protects its own."

"What if it's one of your own in this barrel?" Rain asked.

"Like I said. We'll deal with it." Thomas moved closer and squared off.

Rain couldn't let him touch it. If it was a human in there, they could blow all the evidence. "What if it's *not* one of your own?"

Kurt, knife still in hand, moved shoulder to shoulder with Thomas. "We'll deal with that, too."

"Back off, you two," Freddie said.

"Come on, Freds. It's probably just garbage someone was too lazy to take out." Kurt looked to Thomas as if seeking affirmation. The pecking order was clear. If Petra was right, and they passed Freddie over and Kurt was made Alpha, it would be an uphill climb for the guy and the whole pack. He was a born follower.

"Cut it open, Merrick," Thomas ordered from the doorway.

Thomas, on the other hand, was not a follower, but he was unpredictable, and Rain didn't trust him.

Merrick's eyes flew straight to Freddie, who pulled out her phone. "Don't move, Merrick. Let me think."

Rain hated to make his next move, because it would hurt Freddie, but after what Petra had told him, he knew this was the perfect time to watch everyone's reactions to see if any of these guys knew about the cover-up of Freddie's dad's death.

"The family protects its own? Kinda like you did when Hans Burkhart was murdered?"

All three boys appeared stunned, but it might have been because Rain knew about it rather than they were unaware it was murder. Grant, however, gave no reaction at all, confirming this wasn't new news to him.

Thomas's fists balled. "He got crushed by a harvester."

"It was an accident," Kurt said.

Jaw dropped, Merrick simply stared at Freddie.

"No, it wasn't. There was no harvester." Freddie's voice was muffled by her hand. "He was murdered." Her eyes flitted to the barrel. "And I'm not going to let another one get swept under the rug."

Merrick abandoned the dolly and moved close to Freddie.

"I don't know what you're up to, Ryland, but no way are you going to tell us what to do," Thomas growled.

"Call the cops, Freddie," Rain said.

"And don't tell *her* what to do, either," Thomas added.

"I think we should leave the chief out of it for now." Grant was still in the doorway. "Someone should call Ulrich. The winery is pack property, and he should decide whether to call the chief. Meanwhile, Rain's right. Nobody touch anything."

THIRTY

Ulrich Burkhart arrived within minutes. To Rain's surprise, he didn't make a move to open the barrel. After a few questions regarding the discovery of the drum directed solely at Freddie, he called the chief and told her there was a mysterious bag in a chemical drum they suspected was a dead body, and then he called another person, saying only, "We have a situation in the fermenting room at Haven. Come now."

After the calls were made, Ulrich Burkhart didn't ask any more questions. He simply waited, like the rest of them, prowling the length of the room and running his hands through his gray hair. Fortunately, they didn't have to wait long. Charles Ericksen banged on the door, and Merrick let him in. At the same time, a huge, dark-haired man Rain had never seen before stormed in from the hallway door.

"What are you doing here, Klaus?" Charles Ericksen asked.

"I was notified that something was up."

"Ulrich and I have it under control."

"Sure you do." The man's fists clenched and unclenched at his sides. "Like always, you do."

Charles scanned the group. "Who else did you tell, Burkhart?"

"I only called you and the chief," Ulrich said.

"You should have called me, too. I'm pack security. My son sent me a text. It was the right thing to do. He's protecting the pack."

All eyes swung to Thomas. Rain looked from the man to his son. The family resemblance was obvious. From the look on Klaus's face as he glared at Ulrich, it was clear there was no love there.

The lock on the door made some clicking sounds as it was unlocked from the outside, then the door swung open with a *bang* and Chief Wanda Richter strolled in, eyes scanning the room, pausing on Rain for a moment, and ending on the blue plastic drum he was guarding.

"Who has touched the barrel?" the chief asked, putting her keys in her pocket.

"Only me," Rain said. "I was moving them to make room for the new ones. This one was obviously not empty, so I opened it."

"Tell us what's inside," Charles Ericksen said, wiping his glasses on a handkerchief.

"Something in garbage bags, sealed up with duct tape. The shape is human."

"We need to open it," Thomas's dad said.

"What if it's not one of us?" Freddie's voice was flat and harsh. "Then what? We cover up another murder? It will be a lot harder with an outsider than it was with my dad, don't you think?"

Gooseflesh rose on Rain's arms. She was testing the adults the same way he'd tested the kids. Hell, here she'd been warning him about playing it safe, and she brought on the nuclear option right out of the chute. He held his breath in the stunned silence that followed, watching their faces for reactions. Then, Thomas's dad shouted, "You stupid little girl!"

Merrick grabbed Freddie before she lunged.

"Watch your mouth, Klaus," Ulrich warned. "She's going to be your boss any day now."

"Over my dead body."

"Or my dad's!" Freddie shouted.

Rain's chest constricted at the sound of her voice. Anguish had a sound all its own. He'd heard it many times in his life. Sometimes from his own mouth. Freddie had hit her limit.

The four adults exchanged wary glances, but none even attempted to contradict the murder accusation.

"You're right about the ramifications if what's in the barrel is human, Friederike," Ulrich said. "If it's not one of our own, it could be complicated. That's why I texted Wanda: in case we need human protocol."

"Or the perfect cover-up." Freddie's face was red, and her entire body trembled.

"That's enough!" the chief said. Her voice was pleading as if she were warning Freddie off, rather than just shutting her up.

Charles snapped his fingers at Grant. "Get her under control. There's too much at stake."

The four adults exchanged dark looks that Rain couldn't interpret. Clearly, they didn't like one another, but they hated what Freddie was saying even more.

"Grant, take Freddie out for some fresh air," Charles Ericksen said.

"I'll go with her." Rain followed them toward the hallway door, not wanting her alone with a guy who could use his "power of influence" on her.

"No, you'll stay right here," Chief Richter ordered as the door to the hallway closed behind Grant and Freddie. "I want to talk to you first, since you found…" She gestured to the blue plastic drum with her head. "Whatever that is."

Rain shot a look around the room. There was a high

probability that one of these people was responsible for
Hans Burkhart's murder and wanted Freddie dead next.
Ulrich scowled and scrolled through something on his phone.
Thomas and his dad huddled, muttering under their breaths
in the far corner with Kurt. Merrick was leaning against one
of the stem-removing machines they'd shown Rain on Friday
night, and Charles Ericksen shifted his nervous gaze from the
barrel to the door where his son had taken Freddie.

"First, we'll take a look and find out what's in the con-
tainer," the chief said, pulling a pair of gloves out of her bag.
She pulled the second one on with a *snap*, then grabbed a
camera out of the same bag. "If you wouldn't mind, Klaus, I
need some photos."

Thomas's dad took the camera and shot a bunch of
photographs of the room, the blue plastic drum, and shots
down inside it at the contents, like he was used to this routine.
Since the chief, Ulrich, and Grant's mom were in the photos
with Freddie's dad's body, Klaus Weigl was likely the one who
photographed him strung up on the grapevines.

The chief approached the drum with a tool that looked
like a scalpel or art knife. Without prompting, Klaus continued
to shoot pictures as she reached down inside the barrel. Rain
stepped closer to get a better look as she sliced through the
plastic and duct tape. Like him, the others in the room moved
in closer.

She pulled the incision open a bit, revealing a partial
view of a human ear. "I need everyone to step back," she said.
"Except Aaron Ryland." She met his eyes, knife still in hand.
"I would like you to stay right where you are."

"Who is it?" Thomas asked.

"Mr. Ryland will tell you in a moment," she replied.
"Unless he'd like to tell us now."

What the hell? Rain's heart jackhammered against his ribs, and the room closed in on all sides.

"Do you know who this is?" Chief Richter asked.

He stared at the gap in the plastic. He could see only a part of an ear. No hair. Nothing. A sickening wave rolled through him, and he shook his head. *Not Ruby. Please, not Ruby.*

A lengthening of the opening revealed a whiskered jaw and then dirty, thinning hair.

Oh God. "Gerald," he said.

The chief straightened and put a plastic cap on the knife. "Yes. Gerald Loche. You knew him, didn't you, Aaron?"

"Only in passing."

"Well enough to know that he was selected for Friederike before you. Well enough for him to give you a confidential file from my office."

This was bad. She probably planned to frame him for this. No mention of the photographs, though, which he found interesting.

He took a deep breath, hoping he was wrong about being set up. He'd been wrong when the chief drove him down a deserted country road and he'd been certain he was going to die. Maybe she was like a cat that enjoyed playing with her catch for the sake of a thrill. He lifted his chin, determined not to let her intimidate him. "I knew him well enough to know he was a failed science experiment that posed no threat to me and wasn't suitable for Freddie."

The chief's eyebrow winged up in surprise.

Freddie and Grant entered the room from the hall door and froze.

"It's Gerald," Merrick announced to them.

Both of their faces registered surprise and then sorrow. Rain was a bit thrown off by Grant's obvious upset at Gerald's death. A quick scan of the room gave no clues as to people's honest reactions.

"Get the Sealer here, Charles," the chief ordered. "It's clear Gerald hasn't been dead more than a day, or he'd stink to high heaven, but we need a time and cause of death."

Grant's dad pulled out his phone and strode to the door.

Chief Richter circled behind Rain, but he refused to turn and watch her. "Where were you yesterday, Ryland?"

Freddie answered before he could respond. "He was home. I was with him. You know the effect of the wine on humans. It took him days to recover."

"That's true. He would have been hard-pressed to kill anyone when he probably felt like dying himself," Grant said as the chief circled back in front of Rain.

The chief gave Grant a quelling look, and he subserviently lowered his gaze.

"Besides," Freddie added, "he'd have to possess a key to this room to access the chemical drums. It's always locked up."

"Kurt was on watch duty yesterday, according to this list." Thomas's dad pointed to a sign-in sheet on the wall. "He signed in at noon yesterday and out at ten this morning." The man stalked to stand right in front of Kurt, who looked like he might piss his pants any second. "We all know you hated Gerald. Threatened to kill him multiple times. If you ask me, Wanda, I'd say you've got your killer right here. Motive, access, and too stupid to cover up after himself. I bet his fingerprints are all over that barrel."

Freddie rolled her eyes. "Of course they are. We're the ones who move the drums."

"What do you have to say for yourself?" Chief Richter asked.

"I…" He clamped his mouth shut.

Merrick stopped shuffling foot to foot. "I was here. I was the one on duty."

"Then why was Kurt signed in?" Klaus asked.

"Well…" He resumed the foot to foot weight shifting again, which always reminded Rain of Moth.

The big man's face went red. Like Thomas, he clearly had a temper. "Answer, you worthless little shit."

"That's enough," Ulrich said, moving closer to his sons. "You'll not treat my boys like this."

"You're nothing but an imposter," Klaus shot back. "A beta, just like your boys."

Merrick's voice was a tinge higher than usual, which Rain was certain wasn't the effect he was going for. "I took Kurt's shift for him, but nobody came in."

"Why did you take his shift?" the chief asked.

"That's not permitted," Klaus said. "You didn't clear it with me first. I'm head of pack security. Everything goes through me."

"You need to leave, Klaus," Wanda Richter said. "Now."

"Make me, Weaver."

A growl came from deep inside Ulrich's chest. Rain had never heard anything quite like it. Rumbly and primitive and deadly.

"Dad, no," Merrick said.

Freddie lowered into a half crouch, making a similar rumble. *Holy shit.* Surely they weren't going to go Moon Creature right now.

"If it weren't for the ward on this building that prevents shifting, you'd be in serious trouble right now," Ulrich said.

"Perfect!" Klaus said, turning on his heel and striding to the door. "Take up for the murdering children and fucking witches. When this pack implodes, it's on your head, Burkhart. You and your traitor brother and abomination of a niece."

Freddie snarled. Her eyes had taken on that odd glazed look Rain had seen in the cave at Enchanted Rock.

Klaus stopped at the door. "The wrong wolf ended up

dead in that barrel. Hopefully someone will get it right next time." He gestured to Thomas. "Let's go, son."

"No. He stays until I'm through questioning," the chief said.

"Suit yourself," Klaus said. "He has an ironclad alibi, though. He was with me. All weekend long. Loads of witnesses. Let me know if you need a list of names."

After he left, the air seemed lighter. Both Ulrich and Freddie straightened from their crouches, and their eyes cleared and focused.

Something crossed the chief's face when she turned back to Merrick. Something that looked like compassion, but that couldn't be right. Rain was pretty sure she didn't have a heart or feelings at all. "Why did you take your brother's shift?"

Merrick shot a look at Kurt, who nodded, encouraging his brother. "He wanted to go meet a livestock girl, so I agreed to swap shifts. He's taking mine tonight."

"Why didn't you just sign in yourself if you swapped a shift?"

His chin dipped, and he shook his head. "Mr. Weigl would have made our lives hell for at least a month if we changed his schedule."

Mr. Ericksen and Petra came into the room. Petra was dressed in a long, flowing black thing similar to the one she'd worn the last time Rain saw her. She looked tired, with black circles marring the eerie pale skin under her oversize eyes. She met his gaze briefly but gave no indication of recognition. She was keeping their friendship a secret.

"And nobody came in while you were here, Merrick?" the chief continued.

"No."

Petra looked inside the barrel. Her expression reflected only mild interest. No revulsion or surprise. Without putting on gloves, she reached into the barrel and appeared to tug the plastic. Rain couldn't see the body from where he was standing.

The chief continued her questions of Merrick. "You never left this room?"

He shrugged. "I had to go take a piss a couple of times."

"Strangulation with a wire of some kind," Petra said with a neutral tone, as if discussing the weather. She leaned back over the barrel and reached down to mess with the body. Rain was grateful he couldn't see exactly what she was doing.

"So someone could have gotten in here and killed Gerald."

"That's ridiculous," Ulrich said. "That means Gerald and the killer were here and did the whole thing in the time it took Merrick to go to the bathroom."

The chief arched an eyebrow at Freddie's uncle. "Or Merrick lured Gerald here and then killed him. If the livestock girl can't corroborate Kurt's story, I'm inclined to believe the boys worked together. It would take some strength to put the body in bags and in the drum."

Petra straightened and tilted her head, staring in at Gerald's body. "Based on swelling and rigor, he died sometime late last night. Someone put wolfsbane in the mouth to prevent post-mortem shifting. No other alteration or preparation, though. Can I leave now?"

"No," the chief, Ulrich, and Charles said at the same time.

Petra crossed her arms over her chest and stared straight ahead. "Today I weave the spell for Doctor Perkins. I need to go."

The chief nodded to Mr. Ericksen, who approached Petra. "Listen, Sealer. We need to know if you've seen anything."

"Ask Helga Goff. I'm inaccurate. And as your wife says, Mr. Ericksen, I only see conspiracies."

"Is there a conspiracy here?" Rain asked.

"Shut up," the chief ordered.

"Yes," Petra answered. "A large one, but I can't quite make it out, which probably means it's orchestrated by a Weaver. I'm blind to my own kind."

The chief looked down into the barrel, and her expression darkened. "Well, we know two things now: First, Gerald died from strangulation last night. Second, it had to be an inside job. Nobody else could have gotten in." She turned to Ulrich. "I'm sorry, but I'm going to have to take both of the boys into custody until this is sorted out. There's too big a flight risk to leave them on their own."

All color drained from Merrick's and Kurt's faces.

"Like hell you are," Ulrich growled.

"You can't legally do that without any evidence," Rain said.

The chief closed the gap between them until they were toe to toe. "Things don't work the way you're used to around here, Aaron Ryland. We have our own laws and punishments. They were the last ones with the barrels. The exterior doors are set to lock automatically. That's enough evidence for me."

"Look, just because they were here last doesn't mean they had anything to do with this," Rain said. "Anyone could have gotten in here." He pulled the lock tool from his pocket and strode to the door. Once out, he slammed it, then checked that it was locked and set to work. Within a few seconds, the tumblers clicked into place, and he opened the door. "Easy," he remarked.

"I guess that puts you back on the suspect list," the chief remarked. "Your alibi witness is not the most reliable in the world anyway." She shot Freddie a condescending look. "I'm taking these two and Aaron Ryland."

"Others can open the door," Petra said, barely loud enough to be heard.

"Who?" Charles asked.

She stared at the chief for a moment, then glanced at

Rain. "Mrs. Goff." She strode to the door, and her shoulders rose and fell with a breath. "And me." She placed her hand on the door handle, and it unlocked with a *pop*. "So holding Rain Ryland because he can pick the lock is a waste of time unless you plan to detain every resident of New Wurzburg who owns one of those tools, along with Mrs. Goff and me. Keeping the wolf boys because they were on watch is silly, too. Any pack member in the building could have done it, so you'll need to round up every Watcher." She put her hands on her hips. "I have a better idea. Leave everybody alone. I'll look for prints on the barrel and body and will get back to you with any evidence I find."

"Add this to her file, too," Ulrich said. "For when the tribunal has their hearing next year. Instead of my boys, you might want to look into this Weaver."

"Oh, stop it, Ulrich," the chief said, her voice softer. "In case you didn't notice, she just stood up for your boys. You're just looking for someone to blame for your brother's death."

"And you're just protecting your own kind."

"It seems to me, Watcher," Petra said, advancing on Ulrich, "you're blaming me for both of these deaths in order to deflect attention from yourself. Who has more motive to kill than you? You had access to both victims."

"That's enough," Charles Ericksen said. "Know your place."

"I know my place," she said. "And it's not burning on a stake, which is where Ulrich Burkhart would have me."

"Get her out, Grant," Charles Ericksen said.

Grant made a move toward her, and she held up both palms. "Touch me, and I'll knock you on your ass again, like I did in second grade. I'm happy to leave on my own, thank you."

Rain fought back a smile. *Go, Petra.*

She got to the door and stopped, her back to the room. "You never meet my eyes directly, Ulrich Burkhart. Why is that?" Her eyes flew wide in mock surprise. "Oh, wait. That's right. You don't want me to see your memories."

The slam of the door when she left ricocheted around the room, making Rain even tenser. Damn. Instead of all of this narrowing down the list of possible killers for both Gerald and Freddie's dad, it had been expanded. Ulrich, Klaus, and—as much as he hated to admit it—all three of Freddie's cousins, too. The whole pack or coven could be involved. Hell, even the chief could have done it.

Chief Richter straightened her spine. "One of you did this, and I won't tolerate it. I've put up with missing cats and dead deer and antelope, but this is too far. We don't need this kind of problem right now." She got in Merrick's face, not a surprise to Rain. Singling out the weakest is a common bully tactic. "Whoever did this will regret it. Mark my words."

God, Rain hated bullies. Rage swirled in his gut. "What about you, Chief?"

From the other side of the room, Freddie shook her head, but he was already in too deep.

"You hated Gerald. Treated him like a dog," he said.

She lifted her chin in what he assumed was an effort to look down her nose, but it didn't work, since he was a head taller. "And here, I thought you understood what was going on in New Wurzburg. Clearly I gave you too much credit. Gerald Loche *was* a dog. That's what Watchers are."

It took every ounce of self-control to not charge Chief Richter and punch her flat in her smug face. "Watchers are people, just like you. Perhaps you're the one who doesn't understand." He took a few steps toward her and gestured to the door. "You have a key. You used it to get in here when you arrived today." Her eyes widened, and a strong wave of satisfaction at her discomfort rolled through him like warm water. "You asked me where I was last night. You blamed my friends for murdering someone. Maybe we should be asking where *you* were last night."

Her eyes narrowed, and she stalked toward him, stopping only inches away. "Your loyalty to your *friends* is touching. Watch yourself, Aaron. The only reason you're still alive is because of me. If you weren't biologically suited for the Weavers' purpose, you'd have been killed at birth. You're useful to us, which is why I brought you to New Wurzburg."

"Ruby brought me here."

She made a *tsk*ing sound and shook her head in mock sympathy. "How do you think your aunt even found out about you? We wanted your father's DNA line. Natural-born Watcher candidates are hard to find. I always knew where you and your tramp of a mother were."

Merrick moved to his right side and Kurt to his left, like backup in a fight.

"Stay cool, man," Merrick whispered.

The chief eyed Rain and the boys, and she took a step back. "Be careful. All of you. Like Gerald, Aaron Ryland has no ties." Her face relaxed, and she gave Rain a sickening smile. "No one would even notice if you went missing."

"The judge in Houston who signed the court order that sent me here would."

She laughed. "The judge in Houston who sent you here is a Weaver. He sent you at my request."

Rain's whole body felt like the concrete under his feet had become soft, like sand, and he was sinking.

Chief Richter waved her hand dismissively. "The only person who would be a problem if you ended up like Gerald is your aunt Ruby. This whole thing could result in some unfortunate collateral damage if you continue to go too far. Keep that in mind, Aaron Ryland."

And at that moment, it dawned on Rain that his aunt

worked at the police station for a reason—not a reason that benefited her, though, but rather, the Weavers. If this whole thing had been planned since his birth, they'd probably arranged to keep her close as leverage. His stomach twisted as the chief strode toward the door.

She stopped as she passed Freddie. "Drop the foolishness about your father, Friederike. You can only make it worse."

Without looking back, Chief Richter yanked open the door. "Call the Reinhardts and have them pick up the barrel and take it to the funeral home, Ulrich. Charles, see that the case is documented properly, on the off chance someone comes looking for Gerald." She turned and met Rain's eyes directly. "Nobody go anywhere for the next few days. No spring break campouts at Enchanted Rock and absolutely no runabouts." Her gaze shifted to Freddie. "Is that clear?"

Freddie lifted her chin, not blinking. "A lot of things are clear now, Chief, and getting clearer every day."

"Careful," the woman warned.

"You be careful, too, Chief," Freddie said, arms crossed over her chest. "I may just be a dog to you, but I'm sure as hell not going to roll over on your command."

Wanda Richter's face flushed red. "I've found dogs are good at obeying lots of commands, little girl." Her smile was more of a grimace. For a moment, Rain thought she was going to just leave it at that, but right before the door closed, she stopped it with her hand. "My favorite command is play dead."

THIRTY-ONE

By the time Rain and Grant had dropped the truck off at Ericksen's and he'd clocked out and showered, it was way past dark.

"Why are you so hell-bent on seeing the old lady?" Freddie shouted over the wind and bike motor as they turned off the main highway.

"Petra said we should. Mrs. Goff has visions that could help solve your dad's murder."

She slid her hands higher and wrapped her arms around his ribs. "Mrs. Goff is a senile old witch. The only visions she has are hallucinations."

He pulled up in front of the house and killed the motor. "You're the one who said people only see what they expect. Perhaps she cultivated that negative image for a purpose—to throw someone off."

Freddie slid off the back of the bike. "She killed her own lover's revenant. She sealed his body in her barn. She's wacked. Anybody would be."

"She's also been systematically earning Ruby's trust and has been bringing her out here for years in order to get to me. I think there's more to this than a goofy old witch." He got off the bike and propped it on its kickstand.

The waning moon hung low in the sky, and all around

them, insects chirped in the long grass that hissed when ruffled by an occasional feeble puff of wind.

Rain wiped his clammy hands on his jeans. "Maybe we should've called ahead to let her know we were coming," he said, following Freddie up the old woman's porch.

"No need." Freddie's hand trembled as she rang the doorbell. "She knew we were dropping by long before we even knew."

He pulled her into his arms. "You okay?"

"No, I'm not. You see what I'm about now, right? You could be next." She blinked rapidly, then looked past him into the fields. "You could end up in a barrel like Gerald. You act like you're impervious to what's going on here, but you're not."

He loosened his grip on her. "And that's why we're here. She might have some answers."

She sniffed and rang the doorbell again.

Somewhere in the distance, an owl hooted. "Maybe she's not here," he said.

Freddie tilted her head back and sniffed. "She's here." She rang the bell a third time and knocked.

The fine hairs on Rain's neck and arms prickled as he scanned the surrounding fields. Something felt off—like the air was too heavy or something.

With a frustrated huff, Freddie cupped her hands to her temples and looked in through one of the panes of glass. "Dang. Doesn't she ever clean her freaking windows?" She wiped a section with the bottom of her shirt, then leaned down to peek through the cleared area. "She's in a rocking chair, but I can only see her from the back. It's too dark to make out much else." After banging on the glass with no response, she strode to the door and tried the handle, but it was locked. "That's weird. Nobody around here locks their doors."

Something was wrong. Really wrong. Rain's body dumped adrenaline like he was about to jump into a fight. He strode down the porch, hopped off the end, and hustled to the back of the house. There was no back door and only one window on this side, but it might give a better view of Mrs. Goff. Because the house was elevated on blocks, the window was up too high for him to see in.

"I'll lift you up," he told Freddie when she joined him under the window. "Take a look in."

"Lean down."

He did, and she climbed up on his shoulders.

"Oh yeah," she said, peering in. "I can see her now. Let me down."

"Is she okay?"

Freddie climbed off his shoulders and headed for the front of the house again. "Yeah, she's fine. She's weaving a spell over a bunch of spools of thread." Then she muttered something Rain didn't catch.

She slumped into a chair on the porch and gestured to the one next to her. "Might as well have a seat. It could take a while."

"Should we come back another time?"

"No. I have to stay here. She broke the rules by going into a trance without a Watcher present. Goofy old witch."

He paced the front of the porch. "You sure she's okay?"

Freddie's expression was completely relaxed in the blue light from her phone screen. "Yep. You're uneasy because of the discharge. The magic is thick this close to a new spell. I guess that's why she lives out here in the middle of nowhere; she can do whatever she wants. No discretion or caution necessary." She peeked behind her through the section she'd cleared in the dusty windowpane. "But you and I both know nobody and nothing is safe right now." She turned back around and moved some colored squares in the game on her phone. "At least she locked the door. That would slow the revenants down a little bit."

Rain scanned the terrain for walking dead things.

"They're drawn to magic. They seek out Weavers first, always, but go nuts if spells are being woven. I've only seen one once when I was a little girl. I'm told Europe has a much worse time with them. American covens have tighter sealing regulations and less free-roaming Watchers."

"What was it like, the revenant you saw as a little girl?"

"Like an animated corpse in a really bad low-budget movie. Nasty. And it stunk. Dad took care of it. No idea how it got by without being sealed. Must have been a rogue wolf wandering the woods alone when it died."

A mournful howl drifted from the distance.

"That's Merrick," she said. "He's looking for me."

Rain leaned back against the porch railing, facing her, and waited.

"What are you looking at?"

"I want to watch you answer him."

She laughed. "Oh, okay. You'll love this."

He wondered if she could make a wolf call in her human form or if he was finally going to get to see her transform fully.

With a sly smile, she stood, placed her phone on the chair behind her, and cleared her throat. Then, she stretched her arms over her head, twisting side to side, as if warming up for exercise.

His grip tightened on the railing as his heart kicked up in anticipation.

"You ready?" she asked.

"Yes."

Then she picked up her phone and typed something, her fingers flying over the screen. "Whoosh! Sent." With a smart-ass grin, she sat back down in her chair.

"You texted him."

"You didn't really think I was going to howl, did you?"

She shook her head and started back in with the game she'd been playing.

For a moment, he stood there, stunned, half amused and half disappointed.

She clicked off her phone and set it in her lap. "Listen to me, Rain Ryland. I'm grateful for your help finding my dad's killer, but you're never going to see me in wolf form. I like you way too much to see you stuffed in a barrel or zip-tied to vine wires. The chief already thinks you know too much to be set free, and Grant refuses to cancel your conversion, but I'm going to find a way to get you out of New Wurzburg unharmed."

"What if I want to stay?"

"You've seen what happened to Gerald. You saw what happened to my dad. There's nothing glamorous about this. We don't live longer. We don't have superpowers. We're bizarre abominations created to do one thing: what I'm doing right now—we protect Weavers from harm while they weave spells to perpetuate the sick cycle all over again. Magic to protect magic so they can make more magic."

"What do they do with it?"

"Lots of things. Make Watchers, for one. Compel people to do stuff they don't want to do." She shrugged. "Basically, they're assholes."

"There has to be more." He couldn't believe all this effort and power was used only for selfish reasons.

The front door opened with a harsh squeak. "There is, and she knows it."

Freddie turned in her chair to face Mrs. Goff and crossed her arms on her chest.

The old woman shook a finger at Freddie as she spoke. "If it weren't for Weavers, dark magic would break through to the human world, and that would be bad. Am I right, Friederike?"

"Yeah. There's that, too. Demons and all kinds of random

monsters they keep out."

"She's minimizing our role to lessen the appeal of our world to you," the woman pointed out. "But you're not buying it, are you, Aaron Ryland?"

"You were weaving a spell without protection from a Watcher," Freddie said before he could answer.

"No, I wasn't. You were here."

"Not until just a bit ago."

"I knew when you were going to arrive. I didn't enter a full trance until you were on the property."

Freddie waved a hand. "Whatever."

"Would you like to come in?" Mrs. Goff offered.

"Nope." Freddie rolled her eyes.

Rain took a step forward. "Yeah, we would. Thanks."

Freddie shot him a look that could kill as they stepped into Mrs. Goff's cramped living room.

"I made cookies. Want one?"

"Sure," Rain answered.

"No," Freddie said at the same time.

"I'll just go get them."

After Mrs. Goff was out of earshot, Freddie punched his arm. "Are you nuts? You think the wine was bad? These cookies are the worst."

"Are they part of the conversion process, too?"

"No. They can allow you to see her ridiculous visions. Personally, I think she only lets you see what she wants you to see, not the real vision. They're never relevant. You don't want to do it."

"What if it reveals something about your dad's death?"

"Why don't we just ask her instead?"

"Here we are," Mrs. Goff said in a singsong voice as she set a plate of burned cookies down on the coffee table. "Please help yourselves."

"Bad idea, Rain. Terrible," Freddie said as he reached for one.

"She fears what you'll see," Mrs. Goff said, pushing the plate toward him.

Shit, *he* feared what he'd see, too.

Freddie yanked the cookie out of his hand and pitched it on the plate. "Don't do it."

"You have a lot of rules," he said calmly, picking the cookie up again. "Lots of dos and don'ts. But one of these days, you'll figure out that I take all your warnings and rules into account, but inevitably, I do things my own way. Just like you, Freddie. It's how I've stayed alive this long and how I plan to keep staying alive."

"That cookie's gonna show you shit you shouldn't see."

"I'm sure you're right, but I'm going to eat it anyway."

"Huge mistake." Freddie sat back in her chair, crossed her arms over her chest, and pouted. If Rain weren't terrified she was right and that he was making a colossal mistake, he might've found it cute.

Mrs. Goff settled into her rocking chair and pulled some sewing onto her lap. It reminded him of the way Mrs. Ericksen had stitched the fabric inside the round frame at Aunt Ruby's book club meeting. The woman's fingers moved deftly, in and out of the fabric, while she watched him. Only she was sewing something that looked like a strap with leather backing rather than a pattern in a hoop.

"Go on," the woman urged. "The cookie only shows you what I've seen. It won't cause you physical harm like the wine they gave you did."

"Yeah. Won't cause physical harm but will screw you up mentally," Freddie grumbled.

He leaned close and took Freddie's hands in his. "Admit it," he whispered. "You like me."

"Too much," she whispered under her breath.

Leaning closer, he gave her a gentle kiss. "And I like you, too. But I have to do this."

Their eyes locked for a moment. She blinked rapidly, then looked away. "I'm not going to watch. I'll wait outside."

He understood why she had to leave, but he felt safer with her near. Despite his insistence on doing things his way, this was a world he hadn't grown up in like she had. But also, because it was so new to him, he didn't hold any prejudices or preconceptions about it, which as he examined the ugly, burned cookie, he knew was an advantage. The front door closed with a *bang*.

"Old problems, new eyes," he said to Mrs. Goff, who looked like nothing more than a harmless old woman hunkered over some kind of sewing nonsense.

He took a bite of the cookie, and an image flashed through his brain. It was from his perspective as he lay on his back, staring up at a cloudless night sky that seemed more blue than black, full of brilliant stars. The image terrified him for some reason, even though nothing in it seemed dangerous. As quickly as the vision came, it disappeared, leaving him confused and breathing hard.

He opened his eyes to find Mrs. Goff staring straight ahead as she sewed.

"What was that?" he asked.

"Can't rightly say," she answered, changing thread color. "That's the problem with having the sight; interpretation gets in the way. What do you think it was?"

"I think I was lying on my back outside somewhere, like in an open field."

She nodded. "Well, that probably means you'll be lying on your back outside somewhere." She tied off the thread and broke it with her teeth. "Here's the thing. It's what Petra calls a frizzy wig or a whizzy fig—something like that. It is what it is."

WYSIWYG... What you see is what you get. "So I'm for sure going to see that."

"Yep." She nodded to the cookie in his hand. "If you eat more, you'll see the complete vision."

"Do you know what it is?" *Or why it scared the shit out of me?*

She threaded her needle with red thread. "I do. I've had this vision for more than a decade now. Will be glad to have it gone. Once you eat the cookie, I'll no longer be burdened with it."

"What are you sewing?"

She grinned. "A magic spell. Stop stalling. Eat the cookie so I can get some sleep at night."

Something in him rebelled at witnessing a vision that kept someone from sleeping. "Whatever," he mumbled as he raised the cookie to his lips. With a deep breath, he popped the entire thing in his mouth at once and chewed the dry, bitter-tasting thing and gulped it down.

Immediately, he regretted not eating it in small chunks. Gripping the arms of the chair, he felt the world tilt, and he closed his eyes. He again found himself on the ground, staring at the night sky. He trembled and shouted for help; at least he thought he shouted. At the edges of his vision, leafy vines fluttered in the breeze. Grapevines. There was no sound whatsoever, like someone had hit the mute button on the TV. Then a huge black wolf's head filled his field of vision, blocking all view of the stars. Drool dripped in slow motion from the sides of its jowls as it narrowed its golden eyes on him.

In the vision, Rain shouted something, but there was no sound.

There was no pain in the vision, either, only his intense panic and a spray of blood. Crimson filled his eyes and coated the teeth of the black wolf as it raised its head and stared down at him with a hunk of flesh in its mouth.

His flesh. The wolf had ripped out his throat. He reached up to feel his neck, but the weight on his chest was too much and something had pinned his arms to his sides.

With one more attempt to get a full breath of air, he watched his view of the beast's bloody fangs dim at the edges and then fade to black. Rain knew without a doubt that he was dead, surrounded only by black, silent hollowness.

And then screaming. Lots of it. But it wasn't his. The screaming was Freddie's.

"Come out of it, Rain. Pull out." A harsh slap followed. "Snap out of it."

"He'll be fine," he heard Mrs. Goff say.

"I can't believe you let him do this!" Freddie shouted. "How could you give him that much at once?"

"He put the whole cookie in his mouth. I didn't force him."

"I'm okay," he said, still not willing to open his eyes until the weight lifted from his chest. "I'm good. Stop." He cracked open his eyes to find Freddie sitting on top of his chest on Mrs. Goff's floor, arm raised to slap him again.

"Oh, thank God," Freddie said, slumping down on top of him.

The residual panic dissipated, and his head cleared.

"What did you see?" Freddie's mouth was right at his ear.

"Nothing I can make sense of." Which was partially true. "I thought you didn't want to watch."

"I didn't. I only came in when you started screaming." She sat up, palms propped on his chest.

He attempted a smile. "I only heard *you* screaming."

"Because you stopped!" She flipped her hair behind her shoulder and out of his face. "God. You just lay there limp. I thought you were dead."

In the vision, he had been.

She got up, and his entire body felt cold where she'd been draped over him. He sat and shook his head to clear it. He didn't remember getting out of the chair. It was like the vision had taken over his body.

Freddie flopped back in the chair she'd been in earlier and gave the plate of cookies a burn-in-hell look, then shifted that same look to Mrs. Goff, who chuckled.

Earlier, he'd wanted Freddie to stay; now he wished she'd remained on the porch so that he could talk to Mrs. Goff in private. Until he found out exactly how accurate visions were, he didn't want to tell Freddie what he'd seen. She was already promising to find ways to get him out of New Wurzburg.

He stood, still a little dizzy, and then sat in his chair and watched Mrs. Goff plunge her needle in and out of the leather for a while.

"Most of the younger generation turn their backs on the old ways," she said, needle moving as if on its own. "A spell, cast and then sewn together, is far more powerful than non-woven magic." She tied a knot and cut the ends. "Gotta ground the magic in something tangible that touches the skin. That's what went wrong with Gerald. They changed him without a belt."

"What belt?" Rain asked.

"Oh, a wolf belt. A bite from a Watcher will turn the wearer. The bite has to be superficial, though, just enough to get saliva directly in the bloodstream. A fatal bite doesn't work because it's a long process and the candidate dies before the transformation takes effect."

"Why didn't they use a belt on Gerald?" he asked.

"They thought a spoken spell was enough, but it wasn't." Mrs. Goff shook her head and made some more stitches in the strap of leather.

"Well, good thing they're not going to change Rain, then,

isn't it?" Freddie said.

Mrs. Goff pushed the cookies toward her. "Would you like a cookie, dear?"

"Hell no. For all I know, you plant images you want to make happen."

Rain knew that wasn't right. That would mean the Weaver wanted him to die a horrible death, which made no sense. "How accurate are the visions?" he asked.

"Certain. What you see will happen exactly as you see it."

"So, nothing can change it?"

She continued her rhythmic in and out with the needle through the leather. "The future is not like a fortune that can be changed with one wave of a butterfly wing. It's a glimpse of what really will happen. No Ghost of Christmas Future's gonna show you things that won't happen if you take a different course."

Well, shit. That meant a wolf was going to rip out his throat. His hand instinctually crept to cover his neck.

"You okay?" Freddie asked.

"Yeah." But he wasn't. If this was 100 percent going to happen, he needed to find a way to make it work to Freddie's benefit.

"But," the old woman said with a smile, "like all things, what is witnessed is up for interpretation. Nobody sees the same event the same way."

Yeah, well, seeing a chunk of his trachea in that wolf's mouth wasn't up for interpretation.

"I told you not to eat that cookie," Freddie said.

"You certainly did." But Rain was grateful he had. On the streets, it seemed like he had nothing to live for. Now, for the first time in his life, he had something to die for.

THIRTY-TWO

"We have a visitor," Mrs. Goff said, setting her sewing on the table next to her rocking chair.

Freddie rose from her seat and peeked out the front window. "It's Petra." She shook her head. "Freak's driving a hearse. Figures."

Rain joined Freddie at the window.

"She comes here every Monday and Wednesday evening to continue her education as a Sealer," Mrs. Goff said with a smile. "She's not a fan of the newfangled spells. She's seen the failed results. Sealers use the most elemental magic, woven into the thread that seals the lips and binds the power." With effort, she pushed to her feet, and the rocking chair stayed in motion behind her for several seconds. "She's quite good for someone so young."

Freddie opened the door, and Petra swept in with a flurry of energy and flowing black material. "No fingerprints on Gerald's body," she said, slightly out of breath. "No evidence at all, other than the wolfsbane in his mouth, which was a rare European hybrid and not what we use around here. Lots of prints on the outside of the barrel, all from Haven workers. Nothing useful inside, either." She took several deep breaths. "His body was wrapped in common Glad fifty-five-gallon garbage bags that can be bought anywhere, and there was latex residue on the duct tape. The killer wore gloves."

"Hello, we're fine. Thanks for asking. How are you? Glad you dropped by for a friendly social call," Freddie said, closing the door.

"Oh, hey. Sorry. This is one of the only places my parents let me go alone, and I have to make it back by my normal time or they'll know something's up, so I just got right to it," Petra said. "I knew you'd both be here, so…"

"It's fine, sugar," Mrs. Goff said. "Did you begin Sealing the poor boy?"

Petra leaned against the closed door. "Yes. And I overheard Charles Ericksen talking to my mom. Turns out there was a retrieval order on Gerald. They planned to bring him in and euthanize him, so he'd have been on my table sooner or later anyway."

"Yeah, we were told to begin the search tonight if he hadn't shown back up," Freddie said.

"Who ordered that?" Rain asked.

"Uncle Ulrich." Freddie tied her hair in a knot on the back of her head.

Hot prickles burned across Rain's skin, and his fists balled. "Why would your uncle condone the murder of one of your own?"

"For the protection of everyone," she said. "Gerald was a huge risk, wandering around in his wolf skin all the time. If some pissed-off rancher or a hunter popped him, the news about what we are would get out. It's why we always have to hunt in packs. No Watcher bodies can be left behind to be found."

"They also have to be brought back and sealed," Petra added.

Mrs. Goff returned to her rocker and resumed sewing. Her pleasant expression was more appropriate for a conversation about the weather than the murder of a werewolf.

Petra smoothed the front of her skirt in jerky movements. She reminded Rain of a mouse—all action and twitch. But then, after watching her stand up for herself when Gerald's body had been found, he knew this little mouse had fangs. "When a Watcher is killed in wolf form, it reverts to its true human form when the heart stops beating. Gerald could have become a human homicide case with national attention if he'd been shot eating somebody's livestock. Our community can't bear that."

Rain shuddered at the image that brought up. A dead human slumped over a half-eaten animal carcass would certainly make the news.

"But you won't do something like that when you become a Watcher, Rain," Petra said with a smile. "You're too smart."

"You're right," Freddie said. "He's way too smart. Too smart to become a Watcher in the first place. It's not going to happen."

"Listen to me, Freddie," Rain started.

"No. You listen to *me*. Look what happened to Gerald. To my dad. No more murders." Her voice broke. "I can't take any more. As soon as I can get him to answer my calls and texts, I'm going to meet with Grant again. If they turn you into a Watcher, I'm stepping down. I'm not going to be Alpha."

Petra stood motionless, mouth gaping open. Mrs. Goff, pleasant look still on her face, continued to rock and sew.

Petra said, "If you do that, Friederike, you know you'll be kenneled for the rest of your life. Or killed."

Freddie flailed an arm in Rain's direction, her body out of control like her emotions.

"Better that than his being forced into the pack or being killed."

"Probably not," Petra said. "With Kurt at the head of the

pack, it will fall into chaos, and if he steps aside for Thomas, we're all screwed."

"What if I want to become part of the pack? What if I *choose* to do this?" Rain asked.

Freddie threw both arms up in the air. "You have no idea what you're choosing. There are no do-overs. You're in for life or you're dead. It's not like joining some club. It's a permanent choice, Rain."

Yeah, like joining a gang, which he'd avoided his entire life so far. The payoff had never been worth the danger until now. And after seeing the vision, he knew the danger was much greater than Freddie could imagine. But, even if the black wolf slaughtered him soon, it would have been worth it. To have had Freddie for real, if even for a few hours, was better than playing it safe. He'd do all of this again. For her. He took her face in his hands. "What if I choose you? No do-overs."

Her eyes grew huge. "Oh my God." She took a step back. "I should have left you alone. I should never have… You don't understand. No." She turned and left, closing the door behind her.

For what felt like forever, there was no sound but the pounding in Rain's ears and the squeaking boards under Mrs. Goff's rocking chair as she continued to sew.

"A little too much there, Romeo," Petra said.

Mrs. Goff folded her sewing project and placed it in a wicker basket next to her rocking chair. "She will never condone you becoming a Watcher. That doesn't mean she wouldn't accept it."

The image of the black wolf ran through his memory. It didn't really matter anyway. His time was limited. He needed to be sure he used it to convince Freddie to take her place as Alpha.

"Thanks for your help," he said, standing.

"Would you like some cookies for the road?" Mrs. Goff rose from her chair with a grunt.

"No, thanks." The last thing he wanted was to see that vision again.

"I'll just pack some up," she said as if she hadn't heard him, then headed to her kitchen with the plate of cookies and her sewing basket.

When he opened his mouth to object, Petra raised a hand to shut him up, and he slumped back down into his chair.

For a moment, they sat in silence while Mrs. Goff clanged and banged around in the kitchen.

"The thing you saw in my future memory," he whispered. "Was it my being killed by a black wolf?"

She didn't answer. She didn't have to. Her sudden interest in her lap was all the answer he needed.

"I'm not afraid of dying," Rain said. "I'm afraid of dying for nothing."

Looking up, Petra met his eyes directly, and it struck him again how large and nonhuman they looked. "You'll make a difference. It's not for nothing."

"How long do I have before the thing I saw in the vision happens?"

"Impossible to say. It's not obvious from what I saw. Could be tonight. Could be years from now. Who knows?"

"All righty, kiddo," Mrs. Goff said. "Care package for the road." She held out a brown lunch bag, but Rain couldn't bring himself to accept it. "Lemme help." She grabbed his backpack and unzipped it, shoving the paper bag in the main compartment. "Okay. Scoot on off. That girl on the porch is sick of waiting for you and so's her cousin."

Cousin? A wolf howl wailed from the highway as Rain stepped out on the porch and closed the door behind him. Freddie wiped her eyes with her sleeve and shoved her phone in her back pocket. "He doesn't have his phone with him, which means he's probably in his wolf form. He's looking for us."

"Merrick?"

"Yeah."

Another howl wavered over the fields between Mrs. Goff's house and the main highway.

"Look away," Freddie said.

"What?"

She put her hands on her hips. "Turn around and face the house."

He grinned. "You're gonna howl."

"Turn around."

"Come on. Let me watch."

"No way."

"You can't be for real. I've seen you completely naked. Multiple times, including in your bed and in that barn." He gestured to the old, dilapidated building behind Mrs. Goff's house. "Why are you shy in front of me now?"

"Our bodies are natural," she said, leaning against the porch post. "Sex is natural. Watchers are…" She stared out over the fields as Merrick howled again. "*Un*natural. Our wolf forms shouldn't exist."

He stepped closer. "But your wolf form does exist. I like you, Freddie. All of you. What I've seen and what I haven't."

"You're romanticizing a *monster.*"

"And you're vilifying it."

Chest heaving as she sucked in deep breaths, she studied him, and for a moment, he thought she would give in. He was wrong. "Please turn around. Merrick's freaking out."

And so was Rain. The entire Watcher/Weaver system was messed up. He turned away from her and faced the front door, placing his hands on the frame. "I won't watch."

Her answer to Merrick was eerie. It started low and increased in pitch and volume. It took all his willpower not to turn around and see if she answered in her human form or her wolf. Merrick answered her howl with a series of barks and yips.

"Okay. We're meeting him halfway to where this road meets the highway." She headed straight for the motorcycle. "Let's go."

When they reached Merrick, he was shuffling from foot to foot in human form, completely naked on the dirt road leading to Mrs. Goff's house. When he spoke, he gestured like crazy with his hands like Moth used to do. "After y'all left the winery with Gerald's body, Thomas and Kurt disappeared for an hour or so and didn't tell me where they'd been. They're up to something. I don't know what, but it's bad. They're upset but won't tell me what's bugging them." He shrugged. "I mean, they always include me in stuff, especially if they're going on runabouts. This is different. I'm really worried. Thought I should tell you, Freddie."

"Where are they now?"

"Back at Haven."

"Well, they know you're on a runabout. The whole pack heard you looking for me."

"Yeah. I told them I wanted to thank Rain, and I knew y'all were together." He met Rain's eyes. "It was pretty cool of you to stand up for us. I mean, after what we did to you, nobody expected it. Even Grant was going on about it." He ran his hands through his hair, his mannerisms still nervous, but he seemed oblivious that he was in the middle of nowhere stark naked. He didn't even have his weird necklace on. "And that Petra girl. Holy shit. How cool was that? She scared the pelt right off Uncle Ulrich."

"Yeah, the freak came through," Freddie said. "So, thanks

for letting us know about Thomas and Kurt. Keep us posted if anything else happens."

"Do you have my number, Merrick?" Rain asked.

He shook his head.

"I'll get your number from Freddie and text you my contact."

Still shuffling, he grinned. "Thanks. You're not so bad, Ryland. In fact, you're pretty damn cool."

"Okay. Next thing I know, you two will be making out," Freddie grumbled. "Go put some hair on, loser, and run home."

Merrick grinned and trotted away from them.

"And eat something. You're skinny!" she shouted as he waved over his shoulder.

With only the top of his head visible, Merrick crouched in the tall grass. Rain held his breath, wishing he could witness the change. Everything in him was fascinated… No, everything in him was *obsessed* with the process. It felt like when he was in middle school and all he wanted was to be in high school. Rain's instincts had always been excellent, and deep down, he knew this was right. He belonged with this pack for as long as he was alive, and he wanted to jump in with both feet and come out with four.

A brown wolf emerged from the grass and stared at them, tail wagging.

"Go home, fleabag," Freddie ordered.

Tongue lolling, he loped off down the road, then disappeared into another field.

"I thought Watchers could only change during The Five," Rain said.

"I said it was only free during The Five. Merrick lost some time doing that, but sometimes that's a price worth paying. He doesn't have a car, and traveling as a wolf is fast and effective."

"So when you change, you lose your clothes."

"We take them off first. It gets expensive replacing them when they're lost or destroyed."

He remembered the stark, haunted look on her face as she'd crouched behind the crate in the barn. "That's why you were naked when I found you in the barn and when you came to my window. You'd been in your wolf form."

She pulled a long piece of grass next to the road and twisted it around her finger. "You already knew that."

"Why?"

"Why, what?"

"Why were you hiding from your cousins those times? It was during The Five, so it wasn't a time-limit thing." He gestured to where her cousin had disappeared. "Nakedness isn't an issue for you guys, so why?"

She kicked a rock at her feet and dropped the grass. "Let's go. I've got work in the morning."

"I do, too, but this is a lot more important." He rested his hands on her shoulders. "*You're* important. I know it wasn't a game of hide-and-go-seek."

She sniffed and looked out over the road and field. The crickets and nighttime creatures had gone back to making a racket in the almost breezeless night. "I have a problem."

Rain remained very still, not wanting to interrupt or distract her.

"Since Dad died..." It was as if she couldn't look at him. Her smooth face glowed blue in the moonlight as her eyes remained on the field. "Since he died, I can't hold my wolf form."

"I saw you shift—"

"I can shift form fine. I just can't maintain it for long." She sighed. "I know it's because of what happened to Dad. The inability to shift form is often a side effect of depression or anxiety or fear. It's the ultimate weakness. If the pack found out… If *anyone*, including my cousins, found out, I'd be labeled weak and possibly destroyed."

Wordlessly, Rain pulled her into his arms. No wonder she had seemed terrified in that barn. One word from him, and her cousins would've heard from the field, and it would've been game over. He ran his hand up her spine and back down to her waist. She felt amazing in his arms. Strong and warm and soft in all the right places. "We'll find out who did this to your dad. We'll bring that person to justice." She nodded against his chest. "Promise me you won't carry through with the threat you made in Mrs. Goff's house about not stepping up to Alpha if I'm changed into a Watcher. Wait to make that decision until after we solve this murder."

"I don't want you to become one of us."

No problem there. He was probably going to die first. "I understand that. Let's just play it day to day and see how it goes, okay? First things first: Let's see what mess your cousins are into, then we'll figure out who killed your dad and Gerald."

He tied his backpack down to the rack on the back of the motorbike then got on, and Freddie slipped behind him. Nothing in the world felt better than when they were flying through the night, her legs on either side of him, her breasts pressed against his back, and her arms wrapped around his waist. Well, maybe there was a thing or two that felt better, but after seeing his future, he was determined to pay attention and revel in each moment. He grinned as her hands roved under his shirt and across his chest. This was a good moment.

You'll make a difference, Petra had said. *It's not for nothing.*

He was damn well going to make sure of that. For him, for Freddie, for Ruby…for his pack.

THIRTY-THREE

When Rain arrived at Ericksen Hardware and Feed the next morning, nobody was in the main part of the store. He was in a crap mood, so that was probably for the best.

He'd gotten home last night to find Ruby at the kitchen table waiting up for him. At first, he'd thought he was in trouble for getting in so late, but as usual, his aunt was chill. She simply asked him to keep tonight open because she wanted him to bring Freddie for dinner and then told him that she had an after-dinner surprise planned.

Surprises weren't his thing—especially when he thought about how intense it was going to be with Freddie there and his constant fear Aunt Ruby would pick up on something that would drag her into this Watcher/Weaver mess. Rain had accepted that his fate was sealed, but he was in control of his life until then. He didn't want his aunt's death to be his legacy.

He shook his head to clear the image of the wolf's face covered in his blood that had haunted him all night and transferred his backpack to his other shoulder. "Hello?" he called, wondering if Grant's weird little sister was lurking somewhere.

As he approached the counter, raised voices came from the office at the back. One voice he recognized as Grant's; the other was probably Grant's dad's. Occasionally, a woman would chime in, but he could only make out an occasional word.

He needed to hear this conversation. Nothing suspicious about taking a leak before work, right? He headed to the bathroom at the back, looking casual in case someone was lurking around. Once inside, he locked the door and leaned back against it.

The people on the other side of the wall were no longer yelling. Maybe the argument was over.

Something on the other side of the wall crashed, and a woman screamed.

Maybe not.

"Stop it, Dad!" That was clearly Grant's voice, and the woman who'd screamed was probably his mom.

"I'm tired of excuses. This male they brought in is as uncontrollable as the girl. Remove them both and go with Ulrich's oldest son."

"Go with Kurt? Are you crazy, Dad? He can't lead the pack."

Something else broke, and the woman shrieked, "Stop it, Charles. That was my mother's."

"Here's what you don't understand, son. We don't want one who can lead. We want one who can be led." Mr. Ericksen's voice shook like he was on the edge of losing his shit completely.

"By birth, Freddie's up next. She's my choice," Grant said.

"What you want doesn't matter. We can control Kurt easily," the man said. "And your…girl won't commit. The pack is in chaos. Wanda got wind of some kind of trouble brewing."

"What kind of trouble?" Grant asked.

"She heard talk of something called a 'blood-in' going on soon," the woman said.

Rain had heard that term often. Gangs initiated new

members in different ways. Most of the gangs he'd been in contact with "jumped in" new members by beating the shit out of them. To "blood-in" generally meant a prospective recruit had to kill or seriously injure a non–gang member to prove loyalty. God, he hoped that wasn't what Thomas and Kurt were up to.

"What does that mean?" Grant asked.

His father replied, "She doesn't know, but she thinks it's a hit of some kind. She has the thugs' phones bugged and will pass on information if more becomes available. Meanwhile, she's tracking all their microchips, your girl included. You know she was out at Helga Goff's place last night, right?"

"So?"

"So, she's snooping into things she needs to leave alone. Things that will get her killed, which might be a blessing in disguise, if you ask me."

There was a pause before Grant spoke again. "When we were at Haven after Gerald's body had been found, you didn't dispute Freddie's claim that her dad was murdered."

"You need to know what to leave alone, too, son."

"You know what, Dad? I think I should leave *you* alone. You might need to smash some more vases or something. Gotta go to work."

A door slammed, and Rain checked to be sure he'd locked the bathroom, then leaned his ear against the wall again.

"You can't treat your son like that," Mrs. Ericksen said. "He's a man now."

"He's still my apprentice. In the olden days, he would have been bound to—"

"Times have changed, Charles, whether we agree or not. Most of the younger generation relate more to Hans Burkhart's separatist ways than tradition."

"His plan would be the end of the coven and the pack,

too. I told Hans that and he wouldn't listen. Now look what happened."

"Maybe it's time for you to let Grant have more control, like you promised."

"Maybe it's time for you to quit nagging me, like *you* promised."

A twist of the knob, then a knock on the bathroom door nearly sent Rain launching out of his skin. "Just a second," he called.

After a minute or so in which he calmed his panicked heart, Rain flushed the toilet and then washed his hands to make the whole routine sound authentic. When he opened the door, Grant was leaning against the wall waiting. Rain stepped out and gestured to the open door. "All yours."

The only response was a lift of one blond eyebrow.

Busted.

"Brigitte said I'd find you here. Said you'd been in here a long time."

Brigitte must be the creepy sister's name. "Yeah, kinda queasy today."

From the skeptical look on Grant's face, Rain knew he wasn't buying it. No need to play games. Nothing to lose except time. Rain kept his voice low in case the creepy sister was nearby. "Microchips? Fucking microchips like they're dogs?"

"Let's load up," Grant said a bit too loud as he shoved him hard toward the back door they'd taken yesterday to reach the truck. "Don't ever eavesdrop on my family again," Grant warned as the door closed behind them. "If you want to know something, ask me."

Rain squinted in the bright sunshine. *Oh, sure. Just ask.* Like this guy would narc on his family. Mrs. Ericksen knew about Hans Burkhart's murder and was part of the cover-up, and the whole family was probably in on it, including this guy.

"And never, ever talk inside the store," Grant warned when they hit the parking lot. "My sister hears everything. And never say anything on your phone you don't want everyone to hear."

Yeah, because the chief has it bugged, no doubt. "Am I microchipped?" Rain searched his brain for when one could have been implanted. He'd blacked out several times after drinking the wine.

"Not yet," Grant answered. "But you will be. It's mandatory for Watchers. We need to locate bodies if something happens... for obvious reasons. Revenants are bad business."

"Sounds like the chips are useful for other things, like tracking people without their knowledge."

Grant stopped by an empty trailer parked diagonally through three spaces. "It's common knowledge. They all know." His voice was civil, but his body language was anything but— fists balled at his sides, lips turned down, brow furrowed. His tone was laced with threat as he enunciated his next words slowly and clearly. "Why was Freddie at Helga's place last night?"

"We had a hankering for some home-baked cookies."

Grant got right in Rain's face. No fear, only rage. "This is not a game, Ryland."

"No, it's not a game. So why don't you and your creepy-ass family stop playing with people's lives like this town's a chessboard and the people are pawns to move around and murder at will?"

Grant moved so fast, Rain didn't even see the punch coming. With a *crack*, Grant's fist met the side of his face, and familiar, searing pain bloomed all the way from his cheek to his jaw. The blow sent him reeling back a few steps, but he stayed upright.

"I don't want to fight you," Grant said.

Well, that made one of them. Rain charged and got in a solid punch to the gut that doubled the guy over. "Then you shouldn't have hit me."

Still bent over, he said, "You called my family murderers."

Because they probably were. They certainly covered up Freddie's dad's murder, which was the next best thing.

A door creaked, and Grant's dad stepped out on the landing behind the back door. "Everything okay out there?"

Grant straightened. "Yeah, we're just messing around. Practicing some wrestling moves from gym class. We're going to move the two-bys onto the flatbed now." His voice was surprisingly solid for a guy who'd just had his intestines rearranged.

"And the bags of concrete mix," his dad called.

"Those, too."

From his labored breathing, Rain cold tell Grant was still in pain from the punch, but from where his father stood, it probably wasn't evident.

His father nodded and went back inside the store.

Grant leaned over with a groan and put his hands on his knees. "I'm trying to save your life—both of your lives." He took several gulps of air and stood up straight again. "You and Freddie need to stop fighting the wrong people." His eyes flitted to the building where his dad was staring at them out the window closest to the door. "We've gotta get moving."

Usually, Rain felt better after a fight. Somehow, hitting Grant had made him feel worse. Maybe the wine Friday night had messed up his instincts, or maybe it was the guy's power of influence, but he felt like his anger was misplaced.

They walked through a gate in a chain-link fence surrounding the lumberyard. The tall fence with barbed wire on top was designed to keep thieves out of the yard, but it felt like a prison to Rain.

Grant rubbed his stomach with his palm as they walked. "When Gerald was found at Haven, the chief mentioned a file he'd passed you. Is that why you went to Helga? Why Freddie thinks her dad was murdered?"

Rain didn't answer.

"*Was* her dad murdered?"

It struck Rain that this was a genuine question, not a leading one. Maybe Grant really didn't know. After the conversation he'd overheard through the bathroom wall, it certainly seemed that way. Maybe Grant was on the outside just like Petra and Freddie. "Yes. Without a doubt."

"Damn." He ran his hands through his curly hair. "Poor Freddie. No wonder she's having trouble managing her wolf."

So much for nobody finding out. He wondered how Grant knew as he followed him to a pile of lumber up on a metal frame.

"Wait here," Grant said. "I'll get the flatbed." In a few minutes, a different truck than yesterday backed up to the rack of wood.

Without speaking, Grant pitched Rain a pair of work gloves and put on a pair himself. He picked up two of the long boards and slid them onto the flat metal surface of the truck bed. Then, he did the same with two more, then more.

Rain dropped his backpack on the pavement and fell into the same routine from the other side. "How many do we load?"

"All of them. Carter Ranch is building a new barn. They're sick of losing calves." He gave Rain a pointed stare. "The main load was delivered two weeks ago, but they came up a little short to finish."

He assumed the loss of livestock was due to the pack. He loaded another two boards. "You really didn't know about Freddie's dad?"

Grant didn't even slow his load of the lumber. "No. I had no idea."

"Petra thinks you framed her for it."

"How could I have framed her? I thought it was an accident until Freddie's announcement yesterday."

Rain threw two more boards on the stack. "Word is Petra thinks you hate her."

He shook his head. "Because she's paranoid."

"Maybe with good cause. There's some kind of tribunal convening next year to try her for his murder."

He stopped mid-lift. "Someone likes Petra for Hans Burkhart's murder?"

"Yes."

"No way." He added the boards to the stack. "She was in favor of his plan and, with the exception of her parents, she doesn't take orders from anybody. One of these days, she's going to realize she has a lot more power than her entire family combined, and she'll quit taking their shit."

Rain pulled two more boards off the rack. It didn't sound like Grant hated Petra at all. It sounded like he admired her. "Exactly what was Hans Burkhart's plan?" His boards hit the top of the stack on the truck with a crash.

Grant pulled off his gloves and shoved them in his waistband, then picked at something on his palm—probably a splinter. He clearly wasn't going to answer.

The hackles rose on Rain's neck. "You said that I should ask you, rather than try to find answers on my own, remember?"

Grant sucked on a place on his palm, probably to get the splinter out, then spat on the pavement. "Hans believed that the Weaver/Watcher system was out of date and needed a new direction. He wanted the pack to be self-sufficient and autonomous. He proposed that in exchange for the herbs in the wine and the necklaces that keep the wolf balanced inside them, the pack would protect the Weavers on the four high spell days and on request for additional spell weaving. No need for microchips and forced compliance. He wanted symbiosis between the Watchers and Weavers, not—"

"Slavery?"

He tugged his gloves back on. "It's not that bad."

"Not from where you're standing, anyway."

Grant grabbed two more boards from the rack. "Fair enough."

Rain wanted to trust the guy. He desperately needed an ally, and although his instincts said Grant was on the up and up, he remained on his guard. "So other than Petra, the Weavers were opposed?"

"Most." *Crash* went the lumber onto the stack.

"Who wasn't?"

"Petra, Brigitte, and I are the only younger Weavers in this region. Our numbers are carefully controlled."

So the Watchers weren't the only ones with a breeding program. "Who controls that?"

"It's complicated."

Rain waited, both of them adding boards to the piles.

"There's a finite pool of magic," Grant said. "When too many Weavers or Watchers are born, it strains the magic because there is less to go around. Our numbers are regulated to keep the magic constant."

"That makes sense." *Sort of.* He thought back on the question. Evidently, the younger Weavers had been on board with Hans's plan. "Why did the older Weavers oppose a trade-off with the Watchers?"

"It's all about the fear of change. It's hard to let go of the old ways and relinquish control. That's why this generation of Watchers is so important and a new male has to be created." Grant ran a strap through a cleat on the side of the flatbed and pitched the nylon strap over the top of the pile of lumber. Following that lead, Rain threaded it through the cleat on his side and snapped the buckle, then tightened the ratchet to secure the boards.

"So, what happened to Gerald? He seemed messed up," Rain said over the bed of the truck.

Grant shook his head, and an expression of genuine regret crossed his face. Maybe the guy wasn't a complete asshole after all. "In the old days, a senior coven member would weave the shifting spell into a wolf belt. The Watcher candidate would wear the belt either voluntarily or not—sometimes he was forced to wear it. If he was bitten by a wolf while the belt touched his skin, he would turn." Grant threaded another strap through the cleat closest to the cab of the truck and pitched the end over to Rain. "For the last few decades, an elder casts a spell, but it's not woven into material. The Weavers feel it's too risky to have a physical belt. It would be evidence against us if a human found it, and since the magic follows the item, not a person, it could get into the wrong hands. Too risky. After what happened to our ancestors in Bamberg and Wurzburg, Germany, four centuries ago, we're careful. Personally, I think doing it without the physical belt is a mistake. A spell that's cast and not woven is fragile. Seems to me, safeguards could be put in place to ensure the belt doesn't end up in the wrong hands."

"Do you do this a lot? Make new Watchers?" Rain threaded the tie-down strap though the cleat on his side of the truck.

"No. The only other one in my lifetime was Gerald Loche."

"Who turned him?"

Grant tugged off his gloves and pulled his car keys out of his pocket. "Wanda Richter cast the spell. It didn't work. His bones were too soft when he transformed, and his hair never came in right. She feels awful about the outcome."

Sure she did. Rain fought an eye roll as he picked up his backpack from the pavement. *Play dead*, he heard Chief Richter's voice say in his head as he got in the truck cab and shoved his gloves into the center section of his backpack.

THIRTY-FOUR

Bouncing over the dirt road to the Carter Ranch, Rain watched the sun rise to a spot in the windshield where it was too low to be blocked out by the visor. Grant had put on a pair of Ray-Ban Aviator sunglasses, and Rain held up his hand to block the rays. When he squinted, the place Grant had punched him throbbed. Hopefully the guy's gut hurt as bad.

"What did Helga Goff tell you?" Grant asked. "Did you eat a cookie?"

"She didn't say much. And yes."

He slowed the truck and looked over, his eyes invisible behind the dark lenses. "What did you see?"

None of your damn business. "It was jumbled. I saw a starry sky."

"That's weird."

He didn't know the half of it, and Rain had no intention of ever telling him. "Yeah. And the cookie tasted terrible on top of that."

Grant laughed. "Yeah, they suck."

"You've eaten one?"

"I have."

"What did you see?"

"You and Friederike…um…" He pulled back to the center of the dirt road and picked up speed. "You know."

Well, *that* was awkward. They rode in silence for a while, and Rain stared into the side-view mirror at the red dust from the road billowing in a cloud behind them.

"It was two years ago," Grant said. "I was beginning to think that for the first time ever, Helga's cookies were wrong and you weren't going to show up."

"They're always right, huh?"

He pushed his sunglasses up on his nose. "Yep. One hundred percent."

Well, that sucks.

They rode without speaking for a while longer until Grant broke the silence. "What did you really see?"

Rain hated this. Knowing how he would die added a whole new edge and intensity to things. Sort of like that timer shaped like a chicken on Ruby's counter—only he didn't know how many minutes were set on it. It could ding at any time. Minutes, days, weeks, years. He had no idea when he would see that wolf standing over him, so he had to plan for the worst. "I need a favor from you."

Grant pulled over to the side of the two-lane dirt road and put the truck in park. "Name it."

"I need you to promise me you won't kennel or kill Freddie."

"That's not solely my decision."

After hearing Grant's dad through the bathroom wall, Rain knew that was the truth. "Okay, then. Promise me you'll do everything in your power to keep her free and alive."

"You saw something when you ate Helga's cookie. What was it?"

"It doesn't matter."

Grant gripped the steering wheel so tightly, his knuckles paled. "It matters if you saw Freddie hurt. Please tell me you didn't see her hurt."

Whoa. The guy was intense. "I didn't."

A puff of air left Grant's lungs with a *whoosh*, and something clicked into place in the huge puzzle Rain was trying to solve.

Grant loosened his grip on the steering wheel. "I'll make a trade with you. My promise to keep her free and alive in exchange for information."

Well, Rain hadn't expected that. "What information?"

"My mom and dad said that Freddie's cousins are planning something. I need to know what's going on. Wanda called it a 'blood-in,' which she thinks is a hit of some kind. I can't keep Freddie safe from outside, but you can. I don't want her caught up in this."

The guy seemed genuine. Rain hoped to hell he was right about him because ordinarily, he'd have just blown the guy off. Again, the urgency of knowing he would die at any minute made him uneasy enough to throw away his usual caution. "Merrick told me that Kurt and Thomas were up to something but didn't know what. I'll look into it and let you know what I find out."

Grant put the truck in gear and pulled back to the center of the road. "Stay with Freddie twenty-four-seven until we know what's going down. Make sure you're seen together. Give her an airtight alibi in case those guys do something stupid. There are some folks who would love to see her out of the way."

"Like your dad." Rain knew that statement could cause Grant to punch him again, but he needed information fast, even if it meant getting some bruises. To his surprise, the guy simply answered.

"Yeah, my dad and every other Weaver over forty, as well as half the Watcher pack."

"Why?"

"Well, she's a girl for starters, which doesn't go over well with the older crowd. Add to that her temperament and her dad's agenda, and people oppose her for every reason imaginable, from bigotry to fear." The truck rattled and shook over the cattle guard at the Carter Ranch entrance. "But she's the best candidate for Alpha. She'll be fantastic if they'll just give her a chance. She's smart and powerful and born to lead." Even with those sunglasses covering a good part of his face, it was as if Grant glowed as he talked about Freddie.

Yep. The puzzle piece totally fit. "You're in love with her, aren't you?" Rain asked.

Grant's lips drew into a tight line, and he placed a hand over where Rain had punched him as they pulled into the parking area in front of a huge barn. "I always have been."

"Does she know?"

"No. She hates me, and I keep it that way." Grant snapped the gearshift to park. "It's best for everyone, especially me."

Rain swiveled in his seat to face him. "Why especially you?"

He didn't turn off the truck. "Relations between Watchers and Weavers are strictly forbidden. The ultimate taboo."

"I don't understand what the big deal is," Rain said, unfastening his seat belt. Petra had mentioned this, too. "Why can't Watchers and Weavers date?" Not that he wanted Grant to try. In fact, he'd do more than punch him in the gut if he so much as touched Freddie.

Grant shrugged. "Tradition."

"Or prejudice, maybe?"

He ran a hand through his hair. "Yeah. Maybe. Freddie's different, though. She has to be with a Watcher in order to pass the torch."

"Pass it on to kids, you mean?" Rain asked.

"Yeah. Mixed progeny are all non-magical. A Watcher

and a Weaver would have a human baby, which would be a nightmare for everyone involved, especially the child."

"So Freddie's kid will be the next Alpha."

"Alpha presumptive, like Freddie is now. Freddie could still be overturned before she turns eighteen. Being the Alpha is like being king, but it's not a concrete birthright. A vote of no confidence can cause an overturn in leadership if the challenger is successful."

God, this was a screwed-up system. "You lost me."

"Anyone who wants to contest Freddie's position as Alpha will join in a fight to the death for it. It's called a culling. The weak are culled from the pack. Anyone willing to challenge will either die or become Alpha."

Totally screwed-up system. "You think that'll happen?"

Grant took off his sunglasses and put them in a case under the visor. "I'm certain of it. And that's where you come in. You keep her safe until then, and during the fight and forever after that, you watch her back."

"What if she doesn't want me?" Not to mention forever would never happen based on the cookie.

"Like I said before: I ate Helga Goff's cookie…more than one, actually. Trust me—Freddie wants you."

Rain cringed at the thought Grant had seen a vision of him and Freddie together. What he saw wasn't proof, anyway. Freddie wanting him physically was not the same as wanting him forever. It didn't matter anyway. He'd be dead soon. He needed to keep her safe and be sure she was in power before that happened. He might be way wrong, but everything in him told him that this guy was legit and might be the only ticket for her safety once he was dead.

Grant killed the motor. "I'll go find the foreman so we know where to unload this stuff. Be right back."

Rain grabbed his backpack from the floorboard and pulled

his phone from the outer zipper pocket. Freddie had texted saying she'd be at Ruby's for dinner at seven. He grinned and unzipped the main compartment to pull out the work gloves Grant had given him. His fingers touched crinkly paper, and he remembered the cookies Goff had slipped him last night. Grant had said he'd eaten more than one of them. Maybe if he ate another, he'd see more of his future.

Grant was nowhere in sight, so he pulled out the bag and unrolled the top. When he reached in, his fingers touched leather, not cookies. He tipped the bag and looked inside. It was the sewing project Mrs. Goff had been working on. He pulled it out and examined the long leather strap, running a finger over the intricate needlework that was in tiny X patterns from one end to the other. There was no doubt in his mind what this was: It was the wolf belt Petra and Grant had mentioned. Looked like Mrs. Goff wanted him to transform old-school style.

All he needed now was a wolf bite. He smiled. He knew a wolf and knew she bit. His smile turned into a grin. Maybe this transformation business wouldn't be that bad after all.

He stuffed the wolf belt back in the brown paper bag in his backpack and zipped it up. Hopefully, tonight after dinner and Ruby's surprise, he and Freddie could explore that possibility firsthand.

THIRTY-FIVE

"Hey, will you bring me a dish towel from the clean laundry pile on the couch?" Ruby called from the kitchen when Rain arrived home.

"Sure." He pitched the bike keys next to Ruby's car keys and locked the door. It bothered him that she always left it unlocked. She put way too much faith in the safety of her small town. If she only knew how deadly it really was.

He scooped up a dish towel and strode into the kitchen to find her hefting a big pot onto the stove. "Need help?" he asked.

"No. Making pasta. I'm a terrible cook, but I can boil water." She smiled and took the towel. "Sometimes, anyway. One time, I forgot I had water on, and it boiled dry. Ruined the pan and the house stunk like burned Teflon for a week. Your dad thought it was hilarious." The stricken look that crossed her face was familiar to him now. It happened every time she mentioned his dad. Poor Ruby was dredging up pain every time she thought of him, and Rain ached right along with her.

With jerky movements, she turned her back to him and grabbed a package of spaghetti. With a harsh tug, she ripped the cellophane down the side instead of on one end, sending dried sticks of pasta skittering across the floor in all directions.

"Well, crap," she said. "So much for this fool pulling off

a foolproof dinner." Before he could react, she dropped to her hands and knees and began scooping up the pasta with shaking fingers.

"Hey," he said, joining her on the floor. "Aunt Ruby…"

"I can't believe I was so clumsy." She gave a hollow laugh. "Been like this my whole life."

"Ruby." He took her hands in his.

"Really, I don't know why it still bothers me when I drop stuff. I'll just clean this up while you go get ready for Freddie to arrive."

He spoke louder this time. "Ruby." He gave her hands a squeeze around her fists full of dried spaghetti. "I know."

She said nothing. Frozen, she raised her eyes to meet his.

"I know about my mom and Roger. I know he was your husband and that he cheated with her."

The pasta she clutched fell to the floor.

"I know you loved him and he hurt you. They both did. I know that seeing me, you see him and what he did to you, and that hurts."

Tears filling her eyes, she shook her head. "No, you're wrong."

"I read the letters. I know what happened."

"Not about that. You're right about his being my husband and my loving him—I did. I still do. And you're right about my sister…my sister doing what she did. But you're wrong about what I feel when I see you." She shifted her grip so that she held his hands instead. "You are the only good thing to come out of this. The only good thing in my adult life."

Oh shit, oh shit, oh shit, he chanted in his head, because although he was watching a tear zigzag its way down her cheek across the same constellation of freckles his mom had, all he saw was the black wolf with a hunk of his flesh in its bloody teeth.

"I love you, Aaron. You're the son I could have had…
would have had if things had been different."

For the first time since seeing the vision of his death, a
jolt of panic and remorse flared, causing his skin to prickle
and his heart to race. Moving here had given him purpose
and a reason to live, just in time to die.

Fate was a heartless bitch.

At almost any point in his life before coming here, his
response would have been, "Whatever," but somehow, that
was the last thing on the tip of his tongue.

He wiped her tear from her jaw with his thumb. "It's
gonna be okay, Aunt Ruby."

"Roger got into some kind of trouble. I don't know what
it was. One day he just up and quit his job at Ericksens."

"My dad worked for the Ericksens?"

"For his last two years of high school and his first year after
graduation, which is why his quitting was such a surprise. He
begged me to leave New Wurzburg with him. To move to a
new town and start a new life."

Are you going to run away now? Grant's little sister had
asked. *Cowardice is genetic.*

"I didn't think he was really serious. Besides, I couldn't
leave here. My folks…my sister…" Aunt Ruby stood and
dumped the spaghetti into the trash can. "That's when I was
offered a job at the police station. Chief Richter called me
out of the blue, asking if I'd like to leave my receptionist job
at the electric company and train to be a cop."

Out of the blue, my ass. They were looking for leverage to
keep him in town so they could change him into a Watcher.

She stooped and picked up more pieces of pasta. Rain
joined her cleanup efforts. Her hands trembled as she swept a
small pile together with her fingers. "Of course I was thrilled.
I mean, how often does a police chief recruit a total newbie

like me? And with him having no job, it was a godsend."

Rain concealed the anger rolling through him. What a young woman had perceived as a step up had actually been a setup.

"When I told Roger I was going to start working with Wanda Richter and train to be a cop, he lost it." Her brow furrowed. "I still can't make sense of it. The money was good. Twice what I made as a part-time receptionist."

Rain dumped his handfuls of pasta in the trash, resisting the urge to kick the bin across the room.

From the corner, she grabbed a broom and swept the last broken fragments into a pile. "When I refused to give up the police job, he moved out." She gave a rueful smile. "The next thing I knew, my sister was pregnant, and I found out third-hand. He didn't tell me, but he told the chief of all people. Why did he do that?"

To make himself less disposable and less desirable as new blood to mate with the pack. Rain knew she wasn't asking him the question. It was aimed at the universe, which he knew didn't give a shit. He leaned against the counter, heart aching for this woman who was the victim of a war she didn't know about. And now, to top that off, the same war was going to cost her another person she loved. The image of the black wolf's bloody face floated through his head, and he gripped the counter until his hands ached.

She dumped the dustpan full of pasta pieces into the trash can. "Roger left that same day. Ended up on a rig out in the Gulf of Mexico. I received word from the offshore drilling company that Roger had died of a heart attack the next month, which still strikes me as weird. He was young and healthy. He only had his mama growing up, and she died his senior year in high school, so they sent his body back here."

Roger fit the *disposable* profile perfectly. No doubt his

death had been arranged. Rain wanted to beat the shit out of some Weavers as he watched his aunt pull another package of pasta from the pantry.

"Reinhardt Funeral Home took care of everything for free, which was really nice of them."

Yeah, nice.

She tore the pasta open successfully this time. "For some reason, they brought his ashes here, to my parents' house, rather than to Roger's and my house. I should have told Lynn what had happened, but it all went down so fast, I was still processing it myself. She was living at home, and we weren't speaking, for obvious reasons. I always thought I'd find the right time to tell her he was dead. That was a huge mistake."

The spaghetti hit the pan of boiling water with a *hiss*.

"What happened when they brought the ashes?" Rain asked, slipping onto a stool at the island.

"Well, Lynn was two months pregnant with you. According to my mom, she snapped completely. Said she acted like she was running for her life from the moment she found out he was dead. She packed an overnight bag, withdrew all her money from her bank account, and caught the first bus out of town. She sent Mom a letter saying she had to keep you from 'them.' That she'd promised Roger she'd leave if anything happened to him."

Sonofabitch. His mom hadn't run away because she was a junkie. She became a junkie because she had been forced to run. Because she was terrified of monsters. How much had she known? he wondered. Of course she'd hated him. Everything wrong in her life was because of his existence. He was her rain cloud. Storming and killing her sunshine.

Ruby stirred the boiling pasta. "I had no idea where Lynn had gone. I didn't even know if she was alive or not. If you were alive." She tapped the water off the spoon on the side of the pan and set it on a plate. "I can't tell you how relieved I was when that judge wrote to me and told me you needed a place to live."

The judge in Houston who sent you here is a Weaver, Chief Richter had said.

Bile rose in Rain's throat. They were using Ruby like they'd used his mom. Like they'd used his dad. Like they were using *him*.

Things had to change. Freddie needed to step up as Alpha and follow her father's initiative, and he would make sure that happened, even if he died in the process.

The doorbell rang.

"That must be your girl," Ruby said, wiping her eyes.

Your girl. If only. Rain put his hands on his aunt's shoulders. "Sometimes people do things that seem totally random and hurtful when in fact, they're making calculated decisions to protect the people they love."

She stared at him, brow furrowed. Sadly, he'd never be able to explain it to her. His father had left to protect Ruby. Lynn had left to protect Rain.

The doorbell rang again, and he strode from the kitchen to let Freddie in.

Rain knew he wouldn't leave New Wurzburg to protect people he loved. He would stay here and die for them instead.

THIRTY-SIX

Dinner went down without any weirdness at all. Ruby and Freddie took to each other right away, laughing about stuff the townspeople had done over the years, like a guy who had greased his trash cans to keep out raccoons but ended up setting them on fire with sparklers one Fourth of July because the grease was flammable. Then there was a woman who never wore her glasses and thought it would be a good idea to bring the kitty living under her house inside during a storm. The kitty turned out to be a baby skunk. The woman always wore her glasses from that point forward.

As he watched the two of them laughing and talking, it struck him how much he'd missed out on in his life. How much he would miss in the future he'd never have. How much he wanted this. Normalcy. Belonging. Family.

His phone rang on the counter, and Grant's name popped onto the screen. He grabbed it and excused himself from the table.

"What's up?" he asked.

Through the doorway to the kitchen, Freddie's laughter mingled with Aunt Ruby's like music, drifting into the den.

"Well, turns out it was nothing to worry about. I dropped by Haven and talked to Merrick, who had grilled the boys until they told him what was going on," Grant said.

Rain let out a relieved breath. He had enough trouble without the boys kicking up more. A blood-in would have been terrible.

"Evidently, they were yanking his chain. It was a joke or something. Merrick said they told him the hit was ordered on a bug of some kind. They were going to prevent an infestation."

"Oh."

"Yeah. So, nothing to worry about. Looks like a practical joke among cousins."

"That's a relief. Thanks for letting me know."

"Still, stay close to Freddie until she steps up, okay?"

"Yeah." He planned to stick as close to Freddie as she would allow for as long as possible. It would be easier now that she and Ruby had met and got along so well. Maybe Ruby could be like the mom she'd never had. His heart constricted painfully in his chest. Like the mom *he'd* never had but had finally found too late.

When Rain got back to the kitchen, both women fell silent. "What?"

"Nothing," Freddie said with a smirk, looking him up and down.

Ruby snorted.

Rain looked down at himself to be sure he was zipped up and put together. "What?"

"Why don't you two go out on the porch while I finish up these dishes?" Ruby said. "The surprise doesn't arrive for a while yet, so you have time to kill."

Rain gritted his teeth. He really hated surprises.

The moon was visible over the trees, nowhere near full but big enough to cast moon shadows across the house. Freddie sat on the porch swing, and Rain joined her. "So what was so funny in the kitchen?"

She grinned. "We were just comparing notes."

"On…"

"Like father like son…" She winked and set the swing in motion. She patted the place beside her, and he joined her on the swing. For a while, they said nothing, listening to the squeak of the long porch-swing chains and the raspy song of the crickets in the fields behind the neighborhood.

"You gonna tell me what you saw in the vision at Mrs. Goff's that had you writhing on the floor screaming?" she asked, staring straight ahead.

"You gonna tell me why you left the room pissed off afterward?"

"I wasn't pissed." She continued to stare straight ahead.

He didn't respond other than to give the swing a push with his foot. He'd learned that Freddie needed to reveal things in her own time. Rushing her wouldn't help. That was true of most powerful people he'd met. And Freddie was powerful. He loved that about her. But he also knew she was a lot like him. She was struggling for words because under that tough exterior, she was tender inside and that was the part that was hardest to deal with.

She took a breath through her nose. "I was mad at myself." She shifted on the swing to face him. "I like you so much. That's the problem. If I'd followed the rules and stuck to my kind, none of this would have happened. You'd be safe in this house with your aunt, never knowing my kind even existed. Your life wouldn't be in danger."

The swing jerked to a stop when he planted his feet on the wooden porch. "Wrong, wrong, and wrong."

She turned her head away, mouth in a thin line.

Palms on either side of her face, he coaxed her to look at him. "This whole thing…my being here has been set up from before I was even born. The coven tried to convert my dad. He ran, so they killed him—at least I'm pretty sure they did.

For all I know, they killed my mom, too. When the time was right, they had a Weaver judge order me here."

Her eyes were wide with surprise and disbelief.

He stroked his thumb over the smooth skin of her lower lip. "They'd planned this all along, Freddie. Even if you'd followed the rules, this still would have happened. I would *not* be safe and ignorant in this house, like you said. I'd just be ignorant. Thank God you agreed to go out with me and accidentally shifted that night at Enchanted Rock, because if I were like Gerald and hadn't known anything before I drank that wine, I'd be in even more danger."

"Wow." Her expression changed several times as she processed. "I had no idea." Her eyes narrowed. "Those assholes!" She pushed to her feet. "How dare they? I'm gonna—"

He wrapped his hands around her waist and pulled her into his lap. "No. Don't." He held her close, burying his face in her hair. "Don't." Her body vibrated with anger and tension. "I'm grateful it happened."

She pulled back. "Are you nuts?"

"No. I'm not nuts. I'm…" As he looked at her beautiful face in the moonlight, a strange sense of calm flooded him. "I'm happy. For the first time in my life, I'm *happy*, Freddie. If the Weavers hadn't brought me here, I would never have met you, which—"

"Stop." She put her hand over his mouth. "I don't want you to become a Watcher."

"I do," he mumbled behind her palm.

"No, really. Listen." She dropped her hand from his mouth to his shoulder. "The night you drank the wine with the boys, Uncle Ulrich made me go to a hoity-toity dinner with leaders from packs in Russia and Germany, and I found out some stuff. In Europe, they've moved the age when an Alpha has to choose a mate from twenty-one to twenty-six. There's a movement to do that here, too—all initiated by men, of course, because there are hardly any female Alphas, and they want to screw around longer before settling down." She almost bounced with excitement. "See? It buys us time. You don't have to become one of us. I mean, the Weavers are down with you, clearly, which was one of my huge concerns. And if I don't have to pick a mate for eight more years, then…"

He put his finger to her lips. "Stop. I want to be a Watcher. I belong with this pack. I've never belonged anywhere before." She shook her head. "And I want to be with you," he continued.

"You can be with me anyway." She ran her hands over his temples and tightened her fingers in his hair. "Promise me you won't let them change you now."

He shook his head. "No deal." He had to change as soon as possible. He could defend Freddie better if her father's killer tried to hurt her. And deep down, he hoped converting would somehow help him with the black wolf. In fact, he'd hoped to get Freddie to bite him tonight to initiate the change.

She tightened her hold in his hair to the point it almost hurt. "I can't…" She turned her head to the side and took a deep breath as if gaining her composure. "I can't stand it if it fails and you end up a shift junkie like Gerald—or worse, you end up dead in a barrel. We still don't know who did that. Rain, you could die. Promise me."

It was clear she wasn't letting up until he promised her something. "I won't convert until it's absolutely necessary or you say it's okay. How's that?"

The kitchen window on the side of the house was slid open with a *thump*. "Ten minutes, kids!" Ruby called before the window banged shut.

After studying him for a few moments, Freddie released Rain's hair. "Fine. I'll take that as a promise."

Rain stretched his arm across the back of the swing,

wanting to change the topic before Freddie tried to override his bit about "absolutely necessary," because changing to a Watcher as soon as possible was "absolutely necessary." "What does Ruby have planned?"

"I don't know. She didn't tell me."

"I hate surprises."

"Really? I love them." A look crossed her face that made his heart kick up a beat. "I bet I can change your mind about surprises."

Before he could answer, she stood in front of him and then crawled up onto the bench swing, facing him with her knees on either side of him. He planted his feet to keep the swing steady. "You're going to knock us out of this thing," he said with a laugh.

"If I do this right, you won't care."

He stopped laughing when she leaned forward and kissed him. Just like every kiss he'd had with Freddie, it was hungry and set his entire body on fire. Feet braced on the wooden porch to hold the swing still, he gripped the back of the bench as their tongues twined and danced. On and on, the kiss went. She made a growl and sank her fingers in his hair.

God, he loved this. Freddie Burkhart got him going in ways he never knew he went. He would've given anything to wrap his arms around her and pull her against him, but he was afraid if he let go of the back of the swing, they'd tumble out, so he relaxed and decided to let her lead.

She's a born leader, Grant had said. *Ha.* The guy didn't even have a clue.

Spreading her knees wider, she lowered herself onto his thighs and pulled away from the kiss. Breathing hard, they stared at each other for a moment before she reached between them and unzipped his jeans. Parting the denim, she slipped her fingers through the opening in the front of his boxer briefs. When her cool fingertips met his heated flesh, he hissed in a breath through his teeth, fighting the urge to let go of the back of the swing.

"Surprise," she said, wrapping her fingers around him.

Oh shit. No way. She couldn't touch him like this here, on his aunt's porch. There were neighbors—not that he'd ever seen them out at night, but his aunt could come out at any second.

She kissed him again and began stroking him in a way that made him forget all about neighbors and aunts and anything but her.

"I like you, Rain," she said, running her lips down his neck. "Never liked anyone this much."

Unable to speak, he held his breath, amazed by her words and touch. She ran her free hand across his chest and down his abdomen, then froze.

Her body stiffened, and she pulled away. The swing almost tipped over backward as she scrambled off him like he was toxic.

"Wh-What?" he stammered, struggling to come back to earth and not lose balance.

"You're asking *me*?" She took a few more steps back and pointed at his waist with a trembling finger. "What the hell is that?"

For a moment, her words didn't register, then he realized she meant the wolf belt he'd put on after work. "Freddie, I—"

She threw her arms up. "No. Just shut up for a minute."

Anger and fear swirled in a sickening concoction in his gut as he pushed to his feet. The swing nailed him in the back of his knees a couple of times while he zipped his pants and waited for her to pull herself together.

"Where did you get it?" she asked finally.

He wanted to take her in his arms but was afraid to move

for fear she'd bolt. "Mrs. Goff."

"That witch! Is that why you wanted to go out there? So you could sneak this in on me?"

"No. She snuck it in on *me.*"

"Oh, sure she did. You went behind my back to become a Watcher even though I told you no." She paced to the end of the porch. "I trusted you. I wanted to be with you…like, long term. And now, you pull this shit."

"I'm not pulling any shit. And like I told you before, I take what you say to heart, but in the end, I make my own decisions. I'm not one of your cousins you can push around. Just like I can't push you around. I wouldn't even try. That's why you like me. Why we're good together. You need someone as strong as you are." He took several long strides toward her, but she stepped to the side. He'd worked hard for her trust and was desperate to keep it. "I didn't go behind your back. Mrs. Goff stuck it in my backpack. I found it in there today."

"So you decided to put it on. Just like that. Put on something that will ultimately kill you."

His heart skipped a beat. She wasn't mad; she was worried for him. Worried because she cared. "The belt isn't going to kill me. I'm hoping it'll save my life."

"Oh, so now you have the power of sight, too?"

"No. But Mrs. Goff does." He regretted saying it the minute it came out of his mouth.

Her arms dropped limply to her sides. "You saw something horrible after you ate that cookie, didn't you?"

"It's hard to interpret what I saw."

"And now you're going to lie, on top of everything else?"

The front door opened, followed by the squeak of the screen door. "Hey, you two. It's time." Ruby stepped onto the porch, drying her hands on a dish towel, studying them with a concerned expression. "Everything okay?"

"Everything's fine," Rain lied.

"Well, then. Let's go get your surprise." Her face lit up like one of the fireflies flickering in the yard. "You're going to love this." She pulled out her car keys. "We're going to pick up Jeremiah Brand at the bus stop for a three-day visit. I figure he can sleep on the couch." She studied his face expectantly, then her smile faded. "Your friend from Houston?"

Rain had never heard of Jeremiah Brand.

"You look confused. He said he was a friend of yours. That you guys were really tight and hung out all the time."

Rain shook his head. "I don't know anyone named Jeremiah."

"That's odd. He said he was with you on the night Lynn died."

It felt like the earth had opened and swallowed him whole. Pressure closed in on all sides as if he were far underwater. He grabbed his phone from his back pocket and shot off a text to Grant.

What kind of bug were the boys ordered to kill?

His answer came immediately: *A moth.*

THIRTY-SEVEN

"Listen, Aunt Ruby. My friend Moth… Um, Jeremiah is gonna be freaked out if he's picked up by a police cruiser. He's lived on the streets for a while."

Ruby's face flipped into that expression she wore when she was covering up how much his mom and dad had hurt her.

"I mean, I almost pissed myself when you came rolling up in a cruiser that first night." *Damn.* He was breaking her heart and he hated it, but he couldn't let her go to pick him up in case some magical Moon Creature shit went down.

Freddie must have picked up on how serious things were, because she pulled her keys out of her pocket and gave him a quick nod before putting her hand on Ruby's shoulder. "Why don't Rain and I go get him in my Explorer while you heat up that pie I saw in the fridge? We'll be back just in time for hot apple pie and ice cream. He can't freak out about a cop if she serves him hot pie, right?"

"I guess not," Aunt Ruby said with a shrug.

Rain could tell she was troubled from that crease between her eyes.

"Awesome," Freddie said. "And then you can finish that story about Mr. Parker's haunted chicken coop."

A smile broke through his aunt's frown, finally, and Rain headed for steps. "Thanks for the surprise, Aunt Ruby. Moth's a cool kid. You're going to like him. We'll be back soon."

Neither spoke as they ran down the walk to Freddie's car. Ruby watched from the porch as Freddie backed out of the driveway slowly, not punching the gas until she hit the end of the street. "So, it's the boys, right?"

"Yeah. They're going to hurt Moth."

She rounded the corner out of the neighborhood and took off down the freeway toward the gas station where Greyhound dropped off. "Why?"

"I was hoping you could tell me." Rain took his phone out of his pocket and put it in the glove box along with his wallet and motorcycle key. Last thing he needed in a fight was a lot of extra crap in his pockets to break the skin. "Chief Richter used the term 'blood-in.' That's a gang term used to describe an initiation into the group by hurting or killing an outsider to prove loyalty."

"Sonofabitch," she muttered, accelerating to well over ninety miles an hour.

"Is this something you guys do?"

"No. Not in the last hundred and fifty years." She passed a pickup truck and swerved back into her lane. "Up until the 1860s, in order to prove worthiness, when a male Watcher came of age, he had to demonstrate he was willing to take risks for the pack and his coven of Weavers by killing a human."

He could see the red and white sign of the Stripes gas station in the distance. "Do you think that's what's going on?"

"I have no clue what's going on." She shook her head, eyes never leaving the road. "Not with them, or Mrs. Goff, or you. Nothing makes sense anymore."

She slowed when they neared the station. A bus pulled out before they got to the driveway. Rain didn't see any sign of Moth or anyone else for that matter.

Freddie pulled into a parking space in front of the gas

station convenience store and killed the motor. Everything in Rain was on high alert, his skin prickling with gooseflesh. He put the window down, listening for the sounds of the nighttime creatures in the fields surrounding the place. It was silent. Dead silent, which wasn't right.

Freddie lowered her window, too, and put her finger to her lip to silence him, then pointed toward the dumpster past the far end of the building. Then, she swung her finger toward the field to the left. She tilted her head and held up two fingers. Her face pinched with concern and she added a third finger. With incredible speed and force, she shoved him down to where he couldn't be seen from outside the car. *Stay here*, she mouthed.

"Hello?" Moth's frightened voice called from the far end of the building near the dumpster. "Anybody here?"

Freddie clamped her hand over Rain's mouth before he could answer. "Stay here. If they see you, they'll kill him." She said it so quietly, he had to read her lips.

"Hey, Moth?" she called out, opening her door. "I'm a friend of Rain's. I'm here to take you to his house."

"Oh, thank God," he answered. "I thought I'd gotten off at the wrong stop."

Rain knew she'd told him to stay down, but he couldn't help peeking over the dash. Moth was striding toward Freddie, who was almost to the end of the building, with a huge grin on his face. Before he got within twenty feet of her, three sets of gold eyes appeared in the tall corn stalks in the far field. Freddie must have seen them, too, because she crouched as if ready to leap.

Moth spun to look behind him just as two brown wolves stepped out of the cover. His hands flapped at his sides as his eyes flew wide. "Oh shit."

Freddie stood straight, as if relieved by the sight of the

two wolves. "What the hell do you two think you're doing?" she asked.

One looked over its shoulder at the corn, then both moved between Freddie and Moth.

"Is that you in that corn, Merrick? I'm going to kick your ass if you're a part of this nonsense."

There was no reply or movement from the field. The bigger of the two wolves narrowed its eyes and growled. The thinner one next to it with the long legs looked back at the corn again.

"Both of you get back to Haven right now, or I'm going to make you suffer for the rest of your worthless lives for this stupid game."

A loud, deep snarl answered from the corn, and Freddie stiffened. She took a step back, and Rain knew right away, this wasn't a game.

"Who's there?" Freddie shouted.

Still crouching behind the dash so as not to be seen, he prepared to join in, muscles bunching, ready to go when needed.

Growls filled the air as both the wolves closed in on Moth.

"You so much as touch him, and you're both dead," she said.

Moth whimpered and flapped his hands frantically.

A vicious snarl came from the field, and the bigger of the two lunged, knocking Moth to the ground. The other wolf stood still, as if confused. Like a strobe light, his form wavered, and Rain was certain he saw Kurt, crouched on all fours, flickering back and forth to a wolf.

"Back off, Thomas." She shoved the wolf standing on Moth's chest, and he reacted quickly, lunging forward and biting her arm. She kneed him in the chest, but he didn't let go. With her free hand, she ripped the necklace out of her shirt and yanked it so hard the chain broke.

"Moth, run to the car," she shouted, then instantly fell to her knees, her back bowing. The transformation process was much faster than it had been in the cave at Enchanted Rock, probably because she wasn't fighting it this time.

Watching Freddie change was like a time-lapse film of horror makeup being applied. Her spine protruded and silver hair sprouted all over her body. Her pants fell away as her limbs thinned and shortened, but her shirt stayed around her ribs like an ill-fitting pet costume.

Rain found himself bouncing between horror and wonder, gripping the wolf belt around his waist as Freddie's ears migrated to the top of her head and peaked into triangles. As soon as her face elongated, she growled and sunk her fangs into Thomas's neck. He immediately released his bite with a yelp.

Moth, still on his back on the pavement, appeared too stunned to even flap his hands. While Freddie and Thomas fought, the other wolf, who'd flickered as Kurt earlier, stood over him, growling.

Freddie was holding her own with Thomas, but if Kurt lost his common sense and attacked Moth, he could kill the kid with one bite. Rain decided he'd had enough. It wasn't in his nature to stand by while people were in trouble. She'd told him to stay in the car, but that was before shit went down and before they knew there was someone else in the field making the calls. The wolf in the corn worried him far more than either of these two.

Rain checked under the front seats but found only some random clothes and shoes shoved underneath. Then he climbed over into the backseat, looking for a weapon of some kind. Nothing. The car was way too clean.

"Fuck!" He stretched over the backseat into the way back

of the vehicle. There had to at least be tools to change a spare stashed somewhere. He ripped up the carpet mat on one side. *Bingo.* He yanked the plastic storage sleeve off a tire jack and grabbed the metal handle. It wasn't as big as he'd like, but it could crack a wolf skull.

He opened the back door, planning to grab Moth and bring him back to the safety of the car, knocking the shit out of any wolf that got in his way. Surely Freddie would follow his lead and return to the car so they could get the hell out of there.

He transferred his makeshift metal club to his right hand, leaving the door open for an easy access for Moth.

Freddie and Thomas seemed evenly matched and not too serious about killing each other—mainly circling, nipping, and growling. Kurt in wolf form, no longer flickering between wolf and human, stood guard over a catatonic Moth.

Keeping his eye on Moth, Rain slunk around the door of the car. As he took his first step, his entire plan went straight to hell. He froze when a low, rumbling snarl came from only a few feet behind him.

As adrenaline coursed through every cell of his body, Rain tightened his grip on the tire-jack handle and turned, feet wide, ready to swing. For a moment, his body seemed to short-circuit as he met the eerie gold eyes of the black wolf from his vision.

Its lips drew back beyond its gums, revealing enormous teeth—teeth that Rain recognized. The growl turned into a snarl as it crouched lower to lunge.

Get your shit together, Rain coached himself silently. *You're gonna die lying on your back in a field full of grapevines, not here at a gas station.* He visualized his strike before he made it, but when he swung at the animal, instead of nailing it in the side of the head as planned, it reared up and took the hit in the ribs. The *thwack* of crunching ribs wasn't nearly as satisfying as it would have been to hear the dull crack of the black wolf's skull. Still, it would buy him time to get to Moth.

In a full sprint, clutching the tire-jack handle like a relay baton, he headed for Moth. Kurt, still in wolf form, went through the motions of defending his prey but backed off when Rain swung at him with the metal bar.

"Get up, Moth," he shouted as he grabbed his friend under the arm, trying to haul him to his feet. The kid was as floppy as a dead fish. When he made a scan of the parking lot, the black wolf was nowhere to be seen and the path to the Explorer was clear.

"Freddie, let's go!" He pitched the jack handle aside and grabbed Moth under both armpits, dragging him toward the car.

Thomas yelped as Freddie gave him a ferocious bite before she ran, still in wolf form, toward the car.

Rain shifted his hold on Moth when he got to the front of the car to make it easier to shove him in the open door when he reached it. Once around the door, he practically pitched Moth onto the backseat, only to realize his mistake too late.

The black wolf leaped over the seat from the far back where he'd been hiding and sank its teeth into Moth's neck just above the shoulder before Rain could intervene.

Reflexively, Rain punched the animal as hard as he could in the head, then the body. Over and over he slammed his fists into it, focusing on nailing the ribs he'd broken earlier, but it didn't let go of Moth, other than to adjust its bite to get an even better hold.

Freddie, in human form, wearing only a tattered shirt, flung open the back door on the other side of the car and climbed in. She grabbed the wolf's tail and yanked it, pulling the back half of its body from the cargo space in the back, fully into the backseat, then, using her leg for leverage, she tugged its tail out the door and slammed it shut. Once. Twice. Three times.

The wolf released its hold on Moth's neck and spun to face Freddie through the closed door, its blood gushing all over the leather seat, mixing with that pulsing from Moth's neck. She held up its amputated tail and flipped the bird.

Rain wanted the wolf dead but knew that wouldn't happen now. He just needed it out of the car and away from his friend. While Freddie taunted it from outside the car, he ran and grabbed the metal rod.

Before he made it back to the car, Moth screamed, and then the black wolf leaped from the car and bolted into the cornfield. Thomas and Kurt were nowhere in sight.

"Hurry, Rain," Freddie shouted. "Hurry or he's gonna die."

THIRTY-EIGHT

R ain's hand ached, but there was no way in hell he was
letting up pressure on Moth's wound. The kid had lost
consciousness before they'd even made it out of the Stripes
station parking lot. It seemed like they'd been on the highway
for hours, but Rain knew it had been less than ten minutes
from the time Freddie pulled on a pair of pants from her
floorboard to now. Were it not for the blood coating his hands
and Moth's T-shirt, it would look like his friend was sleeping.
"How far is the hospital?"

"Can't go to a hospital." Freddie turned on her blinker.
"He'll tell them he was attacked by wolves, or they'll figure
it out from the bite pattern. Wolves don't live in this region.
We can't risk that kind of exposure."

The entire backseat was slick with Moth's blood. "He's
bleeding out. We've gotta get him to a doctor."

"Petra will know what to do."

Hopefully they wouldn't need Reinhardt Funeral Home's
other services. Why the hell had Moth come to New Wurzburg
in the first place?

Freddie took a sharp turn, and Rain struggled to keep
pressure on the wound. The black wolf had given Moth a
parting bite on his side, too, but the wound on his neck was
much worse, though not as bad as the one Rain knew he'd

receive some time in the future.

Freddie pushed a button on her dash. "Call Grant," she said.

Moth moaned and turned his head. Blood oozed between Rain's fingers. "Stay with me, buddy. We're almost there," Rain whispered.

"Freddie?" Grant's voice said from her dash speakers.

"Yeah. Call Petra. We're bringing in an emergency. Meet us."

"Are you okay?"

"I'm fine. It's a human down. See you in five."

Rain knew now for sure that Grant was on the right side of this. His first question was to confirm Freddie was safe. He figured at least Grant, Merrick, and Petra had all stepped up to the plate and were allies. After tonight, he had no idea where Thomas and Kurt stood, other than at the top of his ass-kicking list.

"This is why I don't want you to be a Watcher. Nobody should be dragged into this," Freddie said through gritted teeth.

Rain remained silent, willing his friend to live.

As they pulled under the covered area at the back of the funeral home, Petra was pacing outside the loading door. Grant drove up right as they got out. In no time, Moth was transferred to a rolling gurney and wheeled into the same room where Petra had worked on Doctor Perkins. Rain kept his hand on Moth's neck.

"Put him here," Petra said, pulling on a pair of gloves from a rolling cart next to the stainless steel table where she'd sewn the doctor's lips shut. "Friederike, please go close both the doors in the hallway. I don't want to involve my family."

"I wonder why not," Grant said with a sneer.

She leveled her enormous eyes on him and sneered right

back. "For the same reason you won't involve yours."

Moth groaned, opened his eyes, and let out a sound like he was gargling with Scope. Blood trickled out the sides of his mouth and spurted between Rain's fingers from the wound. Grant paled and turned away.

"If you're going to vomit, do it in the basin on the far wall," Petra said as she put on safety goggles. "I need to keep a sterile field over here." She picked up a large square of gauze. "Please move your hand, Rain. I need to get a look at it."

When Rain lifted his palm, blood pulsed from the wound in time to Moth's frantic heartbeats. Petra wiped it and leaned close, then wiped it again. "Please reapply pressure for a moment, Rain, while I get the supplies I need. Friederike, thoroughly wash your hands and put on gloves. I'll need your help."

While Freddie scrubbed her hands, Rain pressed his palm over the worst part of the wound and held it there while Petra threaded a small, curved needle with a fine, dark thread. Nothing like the materials she'd used on Doctor Perkins.

"I don't stock anesthetics because corpses don't feel anything. Grant, could you please influence his thoughts to not feel pain?"

Grant took one of Moth's hands and held it between his palms, eyes closed. Immediately, the boy's strained features relaxed as he received the Weaver's magical novocaine.

"That's better," Petra said. "I need to sterilize it first. Freddie, please grab that tall bottle with the bent plastic straw on top and bring it here."

After the wound was washed and sterilized, Petra went to work. She repaired the damaged blood vessel first, then meticulously closed the wound in phases. When she was done, it didn't look anything like the gaping hole it had been. Then, she closed the couple of larger lacerations on his side left from the black wolf's parting shot. "I made a few incisions through the tooth punctures to disguise the bite pattern in case he dies and falls into the wrong hands."

"Dies?" Rain didn't even recognize his own frantic voice.

Petra dumped the surgical tools in a stainless steel pan and then pulled off her gloves. "Working on living things isn't my gig. He lost a lot of blood. Probably needs a transfusion."

"Can you do that?"

"Only if it's with embalming fluid." She winced at his scowl. "Sorry. Mortician humor isn't funny, is it?"

"No." He stared down at Moth's ashen face. He looked so young—like a little kid. "We can't let him die."

"I've done all I can do." She scooped up the blue towel on the tray and dumped the contents into the trash can. "I'm sorry."

Grant and Freddie were both silent.

"He *can't* die," Rain repeated. Still no reaction from any of the three, which made him want to punch a wall. "I'm taking him to the hospital where they can give him some blood."

"You can't," Grant said.

He held out his hand. "Give me your keys, Freddie."

She shook her head. "I'm sorry."

This couldn't be happening. Rain had never felt this helpless in his life. "You'll value your secrets over someone's life? He's gonna *die.*"

"We did our best," Petra said. "And he might live."

Grant's voice was level and calm—the exact opposite of Rain's. "It's not valuing our secrets over his life. It's valuing hundreds of lives over his. Maybe thousands, if it goes viral like it did during the witch trials in the 1600s. If you think people today won't pick up torches and pitchforks, you're wrong."

Rain refused to take no for an answer on this. "Give me your keys, Freddie."

She looked tormented—her brow furrowed and lips thin. "Even if you don't care about the Watchers and Weavers, please consider that you're choosing his life over mine. My life will end if he tells anyone he was attacked by wolves. If the humans don't kill every last one of us, my pack will execute me for not stopping you."

He closed his eyes and took a deep breath to keep from losing his shit completely. "You guys have infiltrated every single important job around here. Why isn't there a Watcher or Weaver doctor at the hospital?"

"There was. We buried Doctor Perkins yesterday," Petra said. "We're searching for a new doctor to put into place at our local hospital, but qualified Weavers with medical degrees willing to leave their home coven are hard to find."

He couldn't stand by and let his friend die. There had to be a way to fix this. He turned to Grant. "Can't you use your power to make him not remember what happened or something like that?"

"No. I only have the power of influence. I can influence people to feel or not feel something. I can't make them do stuff or forget events."

Rain wasn't sure about the forgetting part, but he certainly knew someone who could make people do stuff. It was risky, though. Really risky. "Chief Richter could do it."

"What? No! She might be in on the murders," Freddie said.

"It doesn't matter. If she is, she knew about this anyway. Hell, she might have even called in this hit." Rain's fingers ached from being balled up so tight.

Grant's eyes widened. "Yeah, and if she is in on it, she'll have to help us out to cover her tracks. Good thinking, Ryland. Can't do any harm. Might actually help us if she thinks we trust her."

Petra removed her safety goggles. "Who should call her?"

"The one with the most to lose," Freddie said.

Rain pulled his phone out of his pocket. "I only have the station number. I need her cell."

Ruby patted Rain's leg. "I'm sure Jeremiah will be okay. Good thing your friend Petra was there and able to stitch him up on the spot or he'd have died, according to the doctors."

Chief Richter was on the phone at the far end of the ER waiting area. Freddie and Grant had left ten minutes ago to pick up some burgers to bring back.

Aunt Ruby shifted in the uncomfortable plastic chair. "We closed down the junkyard and the dog-fighting ring behind the gas station months ago. Hard to believe we missed one of the dogs, and it was still lurking around. Poor kid. He's lucky to be alive."

"Yeah."

"And he's lucky you, Freddie, Grant, and Petra were there to greet him."

Yeah. Really lucky... Hey, Moth! Welcome to New Wurzburg. Home of your worst nightmares.

"The chief is trying to locate his parents. Evidently Brand isn't his real last name."

Imagine that. He wondered if Jeremiah was a fake name, too.

"Ms. Ryland?" a woman in a white coat said as she appeared through two wide, automatic doors.

"Yes." Ruby sprang to her feet. "This is my nephew, Aaron."

"Hi. I'm Doctor Lloyd. I'm the treating physician for Jeremiah Brand. The police chief told me you're his temporary guardian."

"Yes." Ruby twisted her fingers together in front of her.

"Well, I have good news. It looks like he's going to be okay. He's received some blood, and all his body functions are normal. He's still unconscious, which is probably a blessing. He's going to be in a world of hurt when he wakes up. Since the dog wasn't found, we started post-exposure rabies treatment. We're waiting on some more test results, and then we'll start another bag of blood if it's indicated. We'd like to keep him in ICU overnight and then move him to a room tomorrow."

Rain relaxed for the first time all night.

The doctor tucked the clipboard under her arm. "There's no need to hang out in this uncomfortable waiting room. I have your number and will call you if anything changes. You both look like you could use some sleep."

Sleep wasn't going to happen. Not for Rain. Not until he handled Thomas and Kurt and found out who that black wolf was.

"I'm going to wait here for Grant and Freddie," Rain said. "And my burger." He knew that last part would appeal to Aunt Ruby. She had a strong tendency to mother him. "I'll be home soon."

She smiled, and her face transformed into sunshine. He loved it when she smiled. He wished he could bask in her smile for years and years and give her some in return to make up for the last eighteen years of unhappiness. His chest ached as if someone had taken a crowbar to his rib cage and was splitting it open. He hated this ticking time bomb that loomed over him since he'd eaten Mrs. Goff's cookie.

He pulled her in for a hug. "Please know how grateful I am that I've gotten to know you."

She pulled back and didn't even try to hide her tears. "Freddie told me where your nickname came from, Aaron. I want you to remember something: The rain doesn't only bring gloom and destruction; it also brings life. Without rain, the world would be desolate—like me before you came here." Her voice broke on the last two words.

As he watched her practically run through the automatic doors at the patient drop-off, something in him crumbled. Just when life had meaning, it was going to be ripped right out from under him. He wanted to scream, *Fuck the universe!* but sat back down instead.

"She loves you very much."

He hadn't even noticed Wanda Richter sneaking up on him.

"It appears Friederike and Grant are enamored as well. You've even managed to infuse some life into poor little Petra."

He gave her his best whatever look and then leaned back in his chair and stared at the fish tank across the room.

"Maybe I underestimated you, Aaron Ryland."

He was counting on it.

"So, I'm going to tip you off to something that's about to happen."

That got his attention. He met her eyes and sat up.

"There have been several calls from the main office at Haven to a known rogue pack in Montana, and another in Germany. The lines are tapped, but the conversations are cryptic. All I know is whoever is in contact with these rogue Watchers is doing something this evening. He says the power will shift tonight. I'm assuming he means the power will shift from the Burkhart family. Freddie turns eighteen just after midnight, so she'll become Alpha if she's still alive at that time. I expect a culling has been called."

Holy shit. Freddie hadn't told him she turned eighteen tomorrow.

"Ah. You didn't know. I'd assumed as much. She's trying to shield you. She figures she'll have more power to protect you once she's Alpha and in control."

"What else did you hear?"

"Not much. One of them said, 'Kill all four.' Not certain who those four are. Of course, Freddie is one of them. Maybe the other three living Burkharts?"

Ulrich, Merrick, and Kurt.

She dropped her cell phone in her purse. "All are at Haven. In fact, every pack member is there, which would be expected the night before the transfer of power. Most of them are in the room where we found Gerald, which is where all pack meetings are held, since that room has been warded by the coven so that they can't shift and fight one another like the animals they are. Well, all of them are there except her cousins, who left that room and are in their cabin; Ulrich, who is oddly wandering the field where his brother died; and Friederike, who, when I last looked, was at McDonald's. I assume the pack is conducting a meeting about her stepping up to Alpha and deciding if there will be a culling."

"Why are you telling me this?"

"Because despite your opinion of me, I'm not your enemy. I'd like to know who the enemies are so that my coven isn't under constant threat of exposure and extermination." She leaned closer. "Because with the exception of one two-year-old child, my entire family line was burned at the stake in Wurzburg, Germany, and I intend to never let that happen again at any cost."

Even though she'd used some hocus pocus to rearrange Moth's memory to remember an attack by a junkyard dog, there was no way he could trust this woman. "You say you aren't my enemy, but you threatened Aunt Ruby's life."

"Like I said, I will protect my coven at *any* cost. Do you know why they call it Haven Winery? Because like us, the Watchers came here seeking a safe haven. We've found it, if someone from inside doesn't screw it all up."

Freddie and Grant entered through the sliding doors carrying bags of fast food.

Chief Richter tapped him in the chest to get his attention. "That girl must become Alpha. She must go face down the opposition tonight and win the culling if one occurs. She's allowed to name a second to fight with her if her opponent does so. It's why I brought you here. It's why I lied for you to this hospital and compelled your friend to remember a dog attack, rather than a wolf attack. It's why your aunt is alive and your father is not. This girl becoming Alpha is why you were born in the first place."

"So, it's all been a big game of manipulation to you. My life means nothing."

"Aaron Ryland, right now, your life means everything. Make it count." And without even acknowledging Freddie and Grant, she stalked out the doors of the ER.

"Oooh. What's got her panties in a bunch?" Freddie asked.

Rain held his breath until the doors closed behind the chief with a *whoosh*. "Your birthday party."

THIRTY-NINE

"Look, Rain, I was going to tell you about my birthday," Freddie said as she pulled out of the hospital parking lot. Grant was in the backseat, which had been wiped clean of the blood from earlier with some solvent that Petra had at the funeral home.

Rain was so furious he had to cross his arms in order to not shake. "And the culling?"

"Yeah."

"No, you weren't."

She rolled her eyes. "I sure was. Just like you were going to tell me about the wolf belt."

Grant leaned forward. "Wait! He has a wolf belt?"

"Yes." Freddie turned onto the main road that ran through town. "Goff slipped him one."

"Well, pull over and bite him right now, Freds."

"What?" Her eyes narrowed as she stared at his reflection in the rearview mirror. "No, Grant. He's *not* going to become one of us."

"We need him. You need him tonight."

She shook her head. "I highly doubt there'll be a culling. Kurt is next in line after me, and nobody in their right mind would want that." She slapped her hand on the steering wheel. "And even if they're dumb enough to try to overthrow me,

Rain would be so new to his skin he wouldn't have a clue how to use it."

"I can help in my human skin," Rain said. "If there's a culling tonight, I'm going."

She made an exasperated growl. "No, I'm dropping you off at Ruby's house. You're going to have a piece of pie and a good night's sleep, and I'll see you tomorrow."

Prickles crawled up his scalp. "Don't treat me like livestock. Chief Richter said you could have a second stand with you."

"Oh, now you're chummy with Wanda freaking Richter. You're just full of surprises tonight, aren't you?" She turned off into Rain's neighborhood and pulled over to the side of the road with a screech of tires.

"You need me for backup," Rain said.

"That's what Thomas, Kurt, and Merrick are for."

"Oh, the same Thomas and Kurt who were at that gas station tonight? And Merrick, who's afraid of all three of you? Perfect. I suppose if things get really wild and crazy, Grant's little sister could jump in and protect you by reading out of her fucking book until the opposition dies of boredom."

"I might do that myself right now," she said, faking a yawn.

Rain pulled her hand away from her mouth. "Who's the black wolf?"

She shook her head. "I don't know. Only those over eighteen are allowed to guard the Weavers on the high magic days. The only older wolf I've seen in his skin is Uncle Ulrich, and he's almost silver. It could be anyone."

"Whoever it is has an agenda," Rain said.

Grant leaned forward from the backseat. "What agenda would be forwarded by killing your friend?"

"Maybe it's a distraction to shake me up and take me out of play for the culling tonight," Rain said.

Grant leaned back and crossed his arms over his chest.

"It would also send a clear message to the Weavers that the pack is out of control."

Freddie gave Grant a glare. "It's not."

"Your cousins are. And every Weaver in the coven is going to demand they be euthanized after what happened tonight," Grant said.

"No," Rain said, slamming a fist on the dash. "It's not their fault."

Grant's voice remained level, but his body tensed. "Why do you even give a shit?"

"Because it's my pack, too."

Freddie growled.

Rain twisted in his seat to face Grant more fully. "I know the black wolf made them do it. People do things they'd never do when they're backed into a corner. I got Moth out of a gang that had him knocking down old ladies in grocery store parking lots and stealing their purses. He would never in a million years do that on his own." When Grant's only response was a lift of a blond eyebrow, his fingers curled into fists.

"It's not your pack. You're not a part of this," Freddie said.

"Really? I'm not a part of it? Besides the fact that there have been two murders, my aunt has been threatened repeatedly, and someone just tried to kill my friend, I'm supposed to walk away? Would you do that, Freddie—just walk away?"

She let out a long breath before replying. "No."

"But *I'm* supposed to." Rain knew he'd scored a point when Grant and Freddie winced. "I wanna know how the black wolf and the boys knew Moth was coming to town."

"I've been wondering that myself," Freddie said. "Maybe you should ask your friend the chief. She would have known because she has Ruby's phone tapped."

A minivan turned into the neighborhood and pulled into

a driveway halfway up the block.

"I knew your friend was coming." Grant cleared his throat and shifted position in the backseat. "Aunt Wanda was at our house last week when Moth called Ruby. She had the call on speaker on her phone. He got her number from the judge who sent you here."

Rain couldn't believe these people. "Who all heard that call?"

He shrugged and ran a hand through his curly hair. "My whole family. Mom, Dad, Brigitte. But, look. No one would have told a Watcher. Chief Richter and my parents are elders in the coven. All information is shared among us. It's not shared with Watchers." When Rain's eyes narrowed, Grant continued. "But clearly this was."

"Weavers consider us a lesser species," Freddie said, not even bothering to hide her hostility toward Grant. "We don't socialize with them, but we're forced to deal with Wanda Richter. It had to be her. I bet she's behind this whole mess. She certainly knew my dad's death was murder, and she covered it up."

"Grant socializes with the pack," Rain said. "He talks to your cousins all the time. Even teams up with them to drug people."

Grant's fists balled in his lap. "Look, Ryland, if you're accusing me of having your friend jumped, you're way off. I'm one of the good guys."

"Funny, Chief Richter said the exact same thing less than an hour ago."

For a long time, they glared at each other. Rain was pretty sure Grant wasn't involved in Moth's attack, but he probably had a good idea who was behind it. Muscles bunching, readying for an attack, Rain almost hoped Grant would make a move and lunge at him from the backseat. A fight would feel good right now.

"Put the testosterone away, asshats," Freddie said, turning the key. The Explorer hummed to life. "If you beat each other up now, you'll be worn out if there's a culling, Sprinkles. And I might need you."

Rain and Grant exchanged surprised looks.

She sighed and put the car in gear. Without another word, she U-turned, just like she had in her decision to include Rain, and headed out of Ruby's subdivision, turning on the highway in the direction of Haven Winery.

After a few minutes, Rain broke the silence. "What happens at a culling?"

"A weak Alpha is removed from leadership if the opposition is successful," Freddie said.

"But it might not happen. We haven't had one in three turnovers. It's been peaceful for well over a century," Grant added. "Though, in Freddie's case, there's been a lot of voiced opposition. Not from the coven but from her pack."

"Only because Thomas's dad, Klaus, is a bigoted asshole who thinks girls shouldn't be in power. He'll get over it."

"It's not just that," Grant said. "Klaus fought with your dad all the time about the direction of the pack."

"So did my uncle. So did lots of people, including the chief and your parents," she said. "Your parents hate me."

"My parents don't know you." Grant turned his attention to Rain. "Klaus Weigl didn't agree with Hans Burkhart on anything."

"Only because his family was overthrown at the last culling in 1916," Freddie snapped.

"No. Because he fundamentally disagreed with the direction of the pack."

"My dad was a visionary. Klaus is a hateful bigot. And he's trying to poison his son to be the same way. Your dad's just like him. Have you been poisoned, too, Grant?"

"No."

Knowing how Grant felt about Freddie, Rain almost felt sorry for the guy.

Freddie huffed and sped up. Outside the window, fields whizzed by in a blur as Rain's thoughts did the same. He knew all major disputes resulted from a desire for more power. Money was power. Sex was power. Hans Burkhart and Gerald Loche were both dead as a result of someone's quest for power. Who in the pack or coven would kill for money or sex? Thomas came to mind immediately. He wanted Freddie. Whoever had Freddie had power if she became Alpha. But then, there was this culling bullshit. Whoever displaced her from becoming Alpha had power. Probably not sexually motivated, which left money as the motive.

Rain shifted to face Freddie more. "Tell me about your dad's plans for the pack that pissed people off." He'd heard of Hans's approach from Petra and Grant but wanted Freddie's take on it.

"My dad wanted us to modernize. He proposed a new structure. Watchers would protect Weavers voluntarily in exchange for herbs and the charms used to control our inner wolves. We'd be liberated from coven control and breeding programs but would consult and pay the Weavers for services regarding breeding and power stabilization. We'd work together equally." She shot a look over her shoulder at Grant then back at the road. "No more threats of kenneling and euthanasia. No more forced pairings or trading with other packs. No more phone taps or microchips. We'd handle it ourselves."

"That sounds like something everyone in the pack would approve. Why was there opposition?"

"Because some people are closed-minded assholes."

"It's more complicated than that," Grant said. "Hans Burkhart's plan, according to the elders on both sides, wasn't in the best interest of the region. He wanted to close in and isolate the pack from the global community and make it self-sufficient, only producing what it needed to survive and stay just large enough to protect the local coven. Many elders disagreed and wanted economic growth."

There it was. Less money meant less power. Somebody didn't like that. The question was, who?

The lights at Haven were on when Freddie pulled into the gravel parking lot. Rain unclipped his seat belt. "So, who killed Hans, Gerald, and tried to kill Moth?"

Freddie turned off the engine as a group of people poured from the building holding flaming torches. "Probably the same person who's about to try to kill me."

Rain studied her face, flickering gold in the torchlight through the windshield, and knew two things for certain. He'd never felt this strongly for any person in his life and he'd do whatever it took to protect her. Someone wanted her dead, and they were about to find out it wasn't going to be that easy.

Over my dead body, he vowed.

FORTY

"I can't believe you're actually going to do this," Freddie
shouted at her pack through the open window before
she even got out of the car.

There were some muted, surprised remarks from the three
dozen or so people who had gathered around the Explorer at
this point. Somehow, Rain thought the pack would be larger.
That explained the need for new blood. Kurt and Thomas
stood apart from the others and didn't have torches. Rain
didn't see Merrick anywhere.

Freddie slammed the door of her car. "Who's the
challenger? Whose throat am I going to rip out?"

A shudder ran through Rain as glimpses of the black wolf
flashed in his brain.

More people joined the group, which had grown to about
fifty now, while yet more lit torches at a fire pit near the
pavilion where humans had danced and drunk wine during
business hours only short while ago, completely unaware that
their hosts were not like them. Not at all.

"My son, Thomas, challenges Friederike Burkhart for the
position of Alpha," Klaus Weigl shouted from the far side of
the circle.

"Thomas? Are you kidding me?" Freddie yelled back.

"So be it!" called someone.

"So be it," replied the rest.

The crowd struck out toward the vineyard where Hans Burkhart had been murdered. Fire contorted in a macabre dance on the ends of the torches, flickering in time to their strides. Nobody else would have noticed it, probably, but Freddie's fingers trembled as she rested her hand on the hood of her Explorer. "I can't believe this is happening."

Thomas and Kurt, chins down, were the last to join the others. If they'd been in their wolf forms, their tails would have been tucked between their legs.

"That's it? They can just spring this shit on you. No heads up or anything?" Rain joined her at the driver's side of the car.

"Yep. That's it," Freddie said.

"Well, at least it won't last long." Grant slammed his door. "Thomas is no match for you."

Rain looked up at the brilliant stars that sparkled like pinholes in an indigo piece of paper. A breeze rolled across the grapevines, rattling through the leaves—sounding like a snake ready to strike. Rain took a deep breath and shuddered again.

"You okay, Ryland?" Grant asked. "You look like someone just stepped on your grave."

What the hell was he talking about?

Grant shrugged. "We say that when somebody shivers for no reason."

Except he had a reason. This was the sky in his vision. Crisp. Distinctive. The person metaphorically stepping on his grave was himself.

Freddie struck out in the direction of the others. "If y'all are done with the chitchat, I've gotta go rip out my cousin's throat now."

"You wouldn't do that, would you?" Grant asked.

She turned to face them. "I hope not, but it's what he'll

have to do to me to get me to back down. He's too hotheaded to be Alpha and is too deep into his dad's ideology. I can't let Klaus Weigl call the shots like this." Her lips drew to a thin line, and she blinked rapidly. "I owe it to my dad to fight. To do whatever it takes to keep his dreams alive. Even if it means killing one of my best friends." A tear breached her lid before she spun around and stomped through the gate to the vineyard.

For a moment, Rain found it hard to breathe. Freddie was in a horrible position with no way of winning, no matter the outcome. She either killed Thomas or died. As she moved in large strides through the row of vines, she looked confident, but he knew she was collapsing inside.

"I'm not allowed to witness this," Grant said as she disappeared into the vineyard. "They'll let you in because you've passed the first test. You're not really human or Watcher."

Rain could tell the guy was worried; he'd never seen him fidget before. As if Grant realized he was drumming his fingers on his leg, he shoved his hands in his pockets. "Keep her safe. I don't trust any of this. Thomas would never challenge Freddie. He loves her. Damn, I hope she doesn't have to kill him." Then, he shook his head and wandered back to Freddie's car and got in the driver's seat. She must've left the keys, because he drove off in a cloud of dust from the gravel parking lot. Rain watched the cloud settle, realizing nothing else would be settled until Freddie was safe.

It must've been hard for Grant to leave like that. No way in hell could Rain have driven away with Freddie in danger. For the first time, he wasn't pissed about being tricked into drinking the poisoned wine.

The torches had been speared into the ground in a lopsided circle about fifty feet across in the vineyard. They filled the air with the acrid smell of cinders and cast a wavering amber light on all the Watchers circling the space. The entire scene was like something out of a monster movie. Only it wasn't a movie. These monsters were *real*…and they wanted to hurt someone he cared about. Rain wondered how many of them really supported this culling. Again, he stared at the brilliant stars overhead, knowing his time was running out.

"The rules of our forefathers are absolute," an older guy with a beard bellowed from the north side of the circle of torches. "Once a challenge is made, it cannot be retracted."

Thomas shifted his weight from foot to foot, avoiding Freddie's stony glare as she stood stock-still on Rain's left.

"The only way to end the match is surrender or death."

"As if," Freddie muttered under her breath. It was a good bluff, but Rain knew she was worried. Not about if she could beat her cousin but about the fallout after she did.

The man stroked his beard as if remembering his lines. "The challenge must commence and remain within the circle of fire."

Which basically meant they were confined to the narrow rows between grapevines. The only way from one row to the next within the circle was under the wires holding the vines or over them.

"The challenge must be conducted without the weapons of man but is not limited to the wolf form. Are the combatants ready?"

"The challenger and defender are allowed seconds," Thomas's dad bellowed.

"We don't need seconds," Freddie said.

"Thomas calls Klaus Weigl," Klaus shouted.

Oh shit. That put a new spin on things. Rain gritted his teeth as Thomas took a step back, shaking his head. Clearly, he hadn't known about this. He probably had planned to throw the fight away and just get on with things. As Klaus balled his fists and grinned, it was obvious he had no intention of throwing anything away, except maybe his son.

"The boy is supposed to name his own second!" someone shouted.

The guy with the beard cleared his throat and rubbed his chin. "Um, that has been tradition, but it's not written in the rules."

Whispers hissed through the gathered Watchers as Freddie searched the circle. "Where's Merrick?" she asked.

Merrick would be a terrible choice. He was scared of his own shadow. Rain was relieved he wasn't there.

"Must be changing his pants," Klaus said. "Probably soiled himself when the culling was called. He was highly opposed. I can't imagine why…"

Freddie gave Kurt a pleading look. He wouldn't even meet her eyes. He wouldn't fight for her. She had to be stopped before she named Kurt to back her up.

"Friederike Burkhart calls Rain Ryland as her second," Rain said in a voice that, to his relief, came out strong and loud.

"Not a chance," she hissed.

The grin on Klaus Weigl's face stood all of the hairs on Rain's neck at attention. This was exactly what Klaus had wanted. And he'd walked right into it.

"It has been called," said the guy with the beard.

"He's not a Watcher." Freddie wasn't even trying to hide her panic. "Humans are untouchable. He can't participate. You can't hurt him."

"He's in between," Kurt said, still not looking in Freddie's direction. "I was there when the wine was administered."

"You asshole!" Freddie shouted. "I'm going to skin you for this."

The hurt on Kurt's face was clear. "H-He passed the test."

"He's trying to help you," Rain whispered in her ear. "You don't stand a chance against both of them. I'm your only hope."

"You're going to die," she said.

"Not if I can help it."

It seemed like an eternity, waiting for her answer. All around them, torches crackled and the wind hissed through the grapevine leaves. Above, the stars beckoned him to look up and remember the vision. To follow his instinct to protect himself and survive. But he didn't. He studied Freddie's beautiful face instead and knew that even if the black wolf appeared and he died tonight, it would have been worth it. He would do it all again, just to be with her the short time they'd had together.

She turned away from the circle and moved to the bare spot where the vines hadn't grown back after her dad's murder. She skimmed her fingers over the naked wire, then wrapped them around it, as if it were some kind of anchor. "Everything I've done has been to protect you." She blinked several times and notched up her chin. "It was a mistake, but I wanted you and was selfish. I've never felt…" Her voice trailed off and she took a deep breath. "I wanted you. I didn't want *this*."

He placed a hand over hers, and her grip on the wire loosened. "It wasn't a mistake." His emotions bubbled up, but he kept his cool. She needed him level. "It wasn't a mistake, Freddie. I want to do this. I have no doubts about this. About you. Let me do this."

"I can't." She didn't meet his eyes. "I like you too much. Way too much."

"Not too much. Never enough. I'll never get enough of you, no matter how long I live." As he stared at her face, for the first time since the vision, he was truly scared. Terrified. Not of death. Not of pain. But of losing her. "Let me be your second."

She took a deep breath. "I didn't want you involved. I don't want this."

He tightened his grip on her hand. "I do. It was my choice."

"You really suck at making choices, Sprinkles."

"You really suck at accepting help, Burkhart." He slipped his arm around her waist. "You told me you felt alone after your dad died. You're not alone anymore. Neither am I. For the first time in my life, I have something worth fighting for. Worth living for." *Worth dying for.*

He stepped back, holding his breath, praying she wouldn't insist on doing this alone, and headed to join the circle. *Sprinkles.* She'd called him that the first day they met. It seemed so long ago. She'd fascinated him immediately. She still did. She always would—until his very last breath.

After several moments, she joined him in the circle but said nothing. The tension was as thick as the smoke from the torches encircling them. Rain found it hard to get a full breath. Then, she laced her fingers through his and gave a squeeze.

"So be it," she said.

"So be it!" the Watchers chanted.

"Begin!" the man with the beard shouted.

With a sharp tug, Freddie ripped off her shirt, striding to the center, and the circle widened, the Watchers moving back behind the torches. In the firelight, she looked golden and alive...and powerful. An invisible band tightened around Rain's chest.

Thomas tugged off his shirt and shuffled forward several steps. Rain had seen guys fight against their will, and he had no doubt that's what was happening here. Slumped shoulders, glazed expression, even his arms hung limply by his sides; Thomas wanted nothing to do with this. His father was a whole other story. Studying Rain as if summing up his weaknesses, Klaus didn't move a muscle as Freddie and Thomas stripped out of the rest of their clothes.

"Let's go, Tommy," she said, ripping off her necklace and tossing it toward the spot where her father's body had hung.

"Where's Ulrich?" a woman shouted. "The acting Alpha has to serve as judge."

"He's not here," Klaus said. "Pity. I'm second in command. I'll judge."

"You can't be a judge *and* a participant," Freddie said.

With a smirk, Klaus turned his attention to the man who had called out the rules. "Is that correct?"

The guy shrugged. "There is nothing in the rules prohibiting it."

He waved his hand in a smart-ass twirling gesture. "Carry on, children."

Rain had no clue what to do as Freddie dropped to a crouch and Thomas did the same. All he knew was he didn't trust Klaus at all, but the man did nothing but stand there grinning as Freddie and Thomas shifted fully to their wolf forms, surrounded by a pack of shifters that looked like they were ready to lose control at any second.

A quick scan of the circle revealed that Kurt had slipped away. The chickenshit probably couldn't bear to watch. If Rain lived through this, he planned to kick all her cousins' asses.

As they circled, Freddie was the first to lunge, getting a good bite on Thomas's shoulder. Her gray and white fur rippled over flexing muscles. He yelped, and his form flickered back and forth between wolf and human. The crowd remained silent, as if in a church service or something, which made things even eerier. In gang fights, the combatants were cheered on. This was weird—well, that went without saying, but weirder than anticipated.

Again, Thomas flickered between forms, and Freddie bit down harder. Still, Klaus remained motionless, watching Rain.

Did the seconds only step in if their partners asked them to? Maybe he was supposed to intervene if she appeared to be losing. Rain felt way out of his depth as Klaus studied him without any apparent interest in what was happening in the center of the ring. He wished he knew the fucking rules.

Thomas flickered and this time stuck in his human form. Freddie didn't let go. He glanced at his father, fear clear on his face, but the man didn't even look his way. Then Thomas stared at Rain, whose breath caught. The poor guy was terrified. He looked like Moth had when the black wolf had stepped from the corn. Eyes wide and mouth drawn tight, he dropped to his knees. He was going to give up without even trying to fight back. Without delivering one bite.

"He can't shift," someone shouted.

"Worthless!" someone else yelled.

Freddie flickered, too, but only briefly, never fully leaving her wolf form. She'd said the inability to hold a shift was seen as weakness. She couldn't appear weak in front of her pack. Rain held his breath, willing her to fight and stay in her wolf skin.

With a growl, she turned loose of Thomas, then focused her gaze on Klaus Weigl, growling a challenge deep in her chest.

"No, Freddie," Thomas shouted. "This is what he wants. Kill me and end it. You'll be Alpha."

She swiveled her head from Klaus to Thomas and back again, tail rigid behind her, paws planted firmly apart. The only thing familiar were her icy-blue eyes, which narrowed on Klaus.

"You're not willing to die for her, Thomas. You've never been that strong. Forfeit and call me in, son," Klaus ordered.

"Kill me, Freds. Please. End it."

"Forfeit, you little piece of shit," his father shouted, "or

I'll make you *wish* she'd killed you."

Well, that answered that. The second stepped in if the primary couldn't continue but was still alive and called him in. *Shit.*

Saliva and blood dripped from Freddie's jaws as she drew her lips back in a snarl. She was terrifying and magnificent, and Rain knew then and there that without a weapon, he didn't stand a chance against a wolf.

"Thomas Weigl forfeits and calls his second," Klaus announced.

"You may not do that," the guy with the beard said. "Only the combatant can call you in."

Klaus sneered. "Only the combatant can name a second, and you didn't enforce that."

"Because last night, you said—"

"I said a lot of things last night. So did you. Would you like to revisit everything you said last night about how to incapacitate Ulrich and Merrick? Let everyone know what you did and where they are?"

Oh shit. They'd hurt Freddie's uncle and Merrick.

The man's mouth opened and closed a couple of times, his beard quivering with the movement. He looked like one of those puppets on strings Rain had seen when a theater company had visited the homeless shelter. In fact, the guy probably *was* a puppet who'd gotten in too deep with Klaus's twisted plan.

The pack had grown agitated. Four dozen or so freaked-out werewolves couldn't be a good thing. Rain fought the urge to take a step back.

"Where is Ulrich?" a woman shouted.

"The culling is invalid," yelled a man near Rain.

Klaus squared his shoulders. "The only thing invalid is the Burkhart family's leadership. Everyone in that room tonight agreed it was time for a change. *I am that change.*"

Freddie shifted back into her human form, standing naked in the middle of the circle. No one seemed to even notice she was there, except Rain. All the rest were focused on Klaus Weigl.

"No!" someone shouted. "Your son was going to fight her, prove himself, and step up as her mate. You were going to run off the human. Where is Ulrich?"

Klaus's voice was level and calm. "Perhaps you should ask our esteemed rule keeper."

All eyes turned to the man with the beard.

"You guys all were in on this?" Freddie said. "The entire pack? Are you shitting me? This whole thing was a setup? To what, get rid of Rain Ryland? This is so fucked up."

As Rain looked around at all the angry faces and the naked girl in the middle of a circle of torches, he couldn't agree more.

And then, *fucked up* took on a whole new meaning.

Klaus Weigl, without removing any clothes, crouched, and in a span of less than a breath, morphed into the black wolf.

FORTY-ONE

"Run, Rain!" Freddie screamed, crouching to shift forms. Like hell, he'd run. He had never run from a fight in his life. He lifted his fists and spun to face the black wolf stalking his way, fangs bared. Half of the animal's tail was missing, but the wound appeared fully healed. As Rain readied for the wolf's lunge, a blur of white and gray fur sailed through the air, knocking the larger animal to the ground. The black wolf wasn't down long, though, and immediately spun to bite Freddie in the side of her face and drag her to the edge of the circle. The Watchers parted.

"You must stay within the circle," the man with the beard shouted, and the guy next to him punched him in the mouth. All the Watchers seemed on the edge of frenzy. Rain understood this, the pack mentality—it was the same with the gangs he'd encountered. One trigger and they would all be out for blood. Hopefully not his.

"You tricked us," the man shouted at the bearded guy. "Where's Ulrich?"

Two men morphed into wolves and stalked closer to the guy with the beard. Rain didn't wait for the man's answer. He darted away from the circle and ran down the row of vines, searching for Freddie and Klaus. When he looked back, the circle had closed in on itself and the man who, no doubt, would pay for betraying his pack.

He sprinted faster between the rows of vines but saw no sign of Freddie or the black wolf. A man's cry of pain came from somewhere behind, followed by a chorus of howls.

After some distance, he paused to listen, stretching the cramp in his side and gulping air. The wolves were much better equipped for this sort of thing. The pack had moved to the far end of the vineyard, still snarling and howling, but he couldn't detect any sign of Freddie or the black wolf.

And then he heard it. He couldn't make out any words, but it was Freddie's voice. If he were a wolf, he'd be able to hear what she was saying and locate her. He turned toward the northwest corner with dread. Klaus had taken her to the spot where her father had died.

He ducked down and slipped through the vines and, once he was two rows over, sprinted back toward the dead spot. Freddie's voice sounded as outraged as it did pained. And human.

"You killed my father, didn't you?"

Rain crept on all fours to not be seen over the vines, stopping when he was even with them. At the far end of the vineyard, the pack of Watchers had gone feral, snarling and snapping and yelping, Freddie and Klaus forgotten in their blood frenzy.

"Someone had to stop him." Klaus's voice sounded choked, like he was about to lose control. "He wanted us to continue serving Weavers. The Weavers should serve *us*. We are the real power. But I didn't kill him. I didn't need to."

Rain carefully pushed aside some leaves to peek through. Everything in him wanted to rush in with his fists flying, but he knew he was at a huge disadvantage against a wolf if the guy shifted. His objective was to keep Freddie safe, and that meant waiting until he could for sure gain the upper hand.

Klaus held Freddie by the hair, bending her almost backward over the wire where her father's body had been found. Blood oozed from the bite mark on the side of her face.

"But I'm going to kill *you.*" Klaus wound her hair around the top wire and tied it off in a knot, binding her to the wire as she thrashed and clawed at his face. He grabbed her wrists and held them to her sides. "Look at you," he taunted. "You can't even maintain your wolf." She kicked and twisted to free herself. "And the beautiful thing about my whole plan is, your precious Rain Ryland will take the blame. Human bites are very distinctive. I will have witnessed the murder with my very own eyes. He bit your neck. Ripped out your throat—like an *animal.* And the Weavers will believe me. What self-respecting Watcher would kill in his inferior human form?"

"And the bite mark on my face?" she said, eyes narrowed.

"A scavenger. In fact, your insides will no doubt be devoured by some wild animal." Howls sounded from behind. "A whole pack of them, perhaps. The chief will have her hands full hiding this one from the human press. Maybe she shouldn't. Maybe I'll call the local news station. The humans should know what's coming their way when we're finally liberated."

Before Rain could react, Klaus bit her neck, and she screamed. By the time Rain crashed through the vines, she had shifted and twisted out of the man's grip, leaving him with a mouthful of fur. Klaus snarled as he shifted, then lunged, catching her back leg and chomping down. The crunch of bone was unmistakable, and she collapsed into a writhing ball, whimpering, tail tucked. He must have smelled or heard Rain over the commotion, because he released her and spun, hackles raised, teeth bared, then he stretched and twisted into his human shape.

"Rain! No!" Freddie screamed, having shifted back to her human form. She tried to stand but fell back to the ground with a shudder. No doubt her leg was broken in multiple places.

"Oh, but he can't help himself. He has to fulfill his destiny. Don't you, Aaron?"

He stood his ground, watching the man for clues as to his next move. If he could catch him before he shifted back to a wolf, Rain had no doubt he could take him. The wolves behind him launched into a chorus of howls.

"They're still hungry," Klaus said with a sickening smile. "Didn't you eat one of Helga Goff's cookies, Friederike?"

She didn't answer. She simply rocked, clutching her leg, with a look that could kill.

"I did," he said. "Aaron cast it off during his first trip out there. Thomas brought it to me after he found it while looking for you. You had disappeared. You do that a lot, I'm told. Maybe you were having trouble keeping your form…"

She growled.

"See, I'm doing the pack a favor. You're not fit to lead."

Rain hated guys like this. Guys who had to talk shit all the time. Usually it was nothing but a bluff. With this guy, though, he was certain it was the real deal. He genuinely enjoyed torturing them.

"Tell her what your destiny is, Aaron Ryland. Tell her what you saw when you ate one of Mrs. Goff's cookies. I saw the same vision. Just from a different viewpoint."

Rain stood very still so as not to provoke him. Freddie struggled to get to her feet again but fell back with a grunt. Klaus didn't even turn to look at her.

"Grant told his sister you'd eaten one. She told her mom, who told her dad, who told me, of course. Charles Ericksen and I have an understanding…sort of. I understand him, and he thinks he understands me." He arched a black eyebrow. "He didn't see this coming, though. None of them did. Surprise!"

This was off. The guy was way too relaxed and chatty. Maybe Rain could lunge and take him by surprise. He'd need to break something quickly so that he couldn't fight well in wolf form.

"So, are you going to tell her what happens next?"

I'm going to kick you in the gut, then dislocate or break both shoulders and hopefully some ribs in the process.

"Because I plan to kill her first, and I'm sure she'd like to know what will become of you."

Behind Klaus, Freddie got to her knees and bowed her back. She changed into a wolf almost instantly and leaped, three-legged, at his back just as Rain lunged for Klaus and kicked as hard as he could, waist-high.

In horror, he watched as his boot made contact, not with a man's gut but with Freddie's face as Klaus dropped in wolf form to all fours between them.

Freddie was catapulted backward by the blow that was strong enough to shatter bones.

"My God!" Rain shouted, lunging to her and falling to his hands and knees over her body, insides twisting as if he were the one who had received the blow. He buried his face in her soft gray and white fur. "Freddie, no. No!"

She curled up and whimpered. Her eyes opened, and she took a deep breath. And then she licked his face and closed her eyes. For a moment, he thought she was dead, then he remembered what Petra had said about returning to human form when they died. Freddie remained a wolf. Beautiful, powerful.

Behind him, a low rumble began and then got louder.

A puff of wind rustled the leaves of the vines around him, and he sat back on his heels and stared up at the stars for a moment, his chest too tight to expand for a breath. *He has to fulfill his destiny*, Klaus had said. Yeah. Maybe so. But he sure as shit wasn't going to do it without a fight. He was going to inflict as much damage as possible before that vision played out.

The rumble behind him got closer, and the hairs on the back of his neck prickled.

The chief's voice rang in his head. *Aaron Ryland, right now, your life means everything. Make it count.* The constriction of his chest loosened and was replaced by hot fury.

He got on all fours again, hovering over Freddie's unconscious wolf form, pretending to grieve. He had to keep her safe. Get the wolf away from her and inflict as much damage as possible and buy her time to heal or get to safety. The black wolf behind him was so close, he could feel its breath through his T-shirt.

"I'm so sorry, Freddie," he said, hoping the wolf thought he was drawing up his knee to his chest from pain. *Make it count*, the chief's voice echoed in his brain again. Damn right he would. After a slow, deep inhale, he kicked back with all his might, making solid contact with the wolf's chest in a loud *thunk*, followed by a yelp.

He leaped to his feet and spun, chasing the black wolf down the row of vines, then tackling him. Once the wolf was off balance, Rain delivered another solid kick to the beast's abdomen. Then another and another. When he kicked out a fourth time, the wolf caught his calf in its jaws, biting down, sending pain like boiling water shooting up his leg to his thigh. The animal yanked hard and pulled Rain off balance. The wind was knocked from his body as he hit the dirt, and his skull hit something with a loud crack and he found himself unable to move. He could only stare at the star-filled sky above him. Nothing like the skies back home in the big city. No. The city wasn't home. *This* was his home. *Freddie* was his home, and from the corner of his eye, he saw she was no longer lying at the end of the row of vines. He'd done it. She'd escaped.

He grunted as a weight pushed in the center of his stomach when the black wolf crawled up his body snarling and wheezing. Good. He'd hurt it. He wanted to kill it, but he couldn't make his body move. He'd hit the ground too hard. Maybe he'd hurt Klaus Weigl enough to keep him from defending himself against the pack, and all of this wouldn't be for nothing.

The stars twinkled like the Christmas lights on the huge tree they used to put up in the church near his shelter. He and Moth used to sneak in at the end of services to get a look at it. *Moth.* At least his friend had lived.

Fire shot through his leg from the bite, as if he'd been branded or something.

The wolf's black head now blocked his view of the stars. He could lift his arms, but the rock to his skull had done something to him, and he couldn't make a fist. This was it.

You'll make a difference. It's not for nothing, Petra had said. He hoped that was right.

The animal snarled and drew its lips from its teeth, and his thoughts went to Aunt Ruby. The wolf went blurry for a moment, and a hot tear slid down his temple. All his life he'd brought nothing but unhappiness until he came to New Wurzburg. *Without rain, the world would be desolate—like me before you came here*, Ruby had said.

Maybe the chief was wrong, and he wasn't totally disposable. Even if he disappeared without a trace tonight, Ruby would feel it. Freddie would, too. And Petra and Moth. So would Grant and Merrick and Kurt and maybe even Thomas. A disposable had no loved ones. He did. Petra was right. It hadn't been for nothing.

A fierce growl came from the black wolf, and a drip of

hot drool and blood hit Rain's cheek. Another attempt to make a fist failed.

In the silent vision at Mrs. Goff's house, he thought he had yelled for help, but that wasn't it at all.

"Do it!" His voice came out as a bare whisper. "Just fucking do it."

And the black wolf did. The pain was so overwhelming it was almost like it was happening to someone else, which didn't really make sense, but then, maybe the thoughts of a dying person never made sense. His breath choked off with a gurgle, and the wolf pulled back with blood and tissue in its teeth, then bit again, tugging so hard Rain's head fell back. He raised his hands to his throat, mouth opening and closing silently as the wolf seemed to grin around what Rain knew to be a chunk of his own flesh.

Like a band of fire, pain encircled his body, overshadowing the searing in his neck. And mercifully, the pain receded. So did the stars as his field of vision faded to black from the outside. *Home*, he mouthed. As his head lolled to the side, the last thing he saw in a shrinking ring of vision was the moon, beautiful and clear blue, like Freddie's eyes.

FORTY-TWO

The ceiling of the tank room at Haven Winery wasn't something Rain had ever expected to see again. Even if he was fool enough to think the white ceiling was heaven, the pain in his body let him know it was closer to hell. Flames of pain scorched his body from the inside out.

Definitely hell.

His groan sounded distant, like it was coming from somewhere else.

And then it all came back. The torches, the fight, the black wolf, *Freddie.*

He tried to sit up, but something pinned him down, and the pain flared.

"Easy, dude. Relax." He recognized the voice as Merrick's "We thought you were a goner."

"How long does it take?" That one sounded like Kurt.

An adult male voice answered. "I've never witnessed it before."

"It shouldn't be happening here," Merrick added. "It shouldn't be possible."

Gotta get to Freddie. Rain cracked his eyes to find Kurt, Merrick, and Ulrich Burkhart huddled over him.

Ignoring the searing deep inside his bones, he tried to sit up again but hardly budged. "Freddie!" His voice came out in an indistinguishable growl.

"Easy," Ulrich said. "You lost a lot of blood. It's going to take you a while to heal."

"We should bring him outside," Merrick said.

"No, he's safer in here. The pack will tear him apart." Ulrich's voice was calm.

"But he'll—"

"I said no! He's doing fine inside. He's clearly not like us." A heavy hand patted his shoulder, and pain raged through his body from the touch. "Relax and let the beast take over. Here, drink some more of this."

Rain swallowed, and a familiar bitter taste made his stomach roll. He tried to sit up. *What the hell?* The guy was holding him down. They all were. He struck out and froze mid-punch when he got a glimpse of his forearm. A sickening churn joined the unchecked fire under his skin as he stared at his elongated bones and thick hair covering his limb. He uncurled his fingers tipped in razor-sharp black claws.

The belt. It had worked even though he'd been fatally bitten. Mrs. Goff had said the bite had to be superficial. The black wolf had bitten Rain's leg before he'd ripped out his throat. Maybe that was the reason. Eyes closed, he grasped his throat, running his unnaturally rough fingertips over the fur and sticky skin. It should have been gaping open, with chunks of his esophagus and trachea missing. He'd seen them in the black wolf's mouth. Instead, it was rough and wet but closed.

He should be dead. A whimper... *His* whimper.

Holy shit. He was a werewolf.

He called out for Freddie, but it came out as an eerie howl.

Sonofabitch. She was out there in the vineyard bleeding with broken bones and he had no way to talk. She might even be *dead*. A flash of scorching pain raged, moving from his bones to his heart, and he held his breath to keep from crying out.

He had to do something. With a gulp of air, he rolled over, snarling when Ulrich attempted to restrain him.

"Don't try to regain your human skin yet, Rain." Merrick had sprung to his feet, eyes wide and frightened. Clearly Rain was only partially shifted and must look like something out of a nightmare. No. This *was* a nightmare. "You heal thousands of times faster in Watcher form," he added, shuffling foot to foot.

No problem there. He had no clue how to regain his mind, much less his human form. When he looked down, his fingers had shortened and his hands were almost paws. His skin showed through the hair, but it was thicker on his arm than it had been moments ago. And everything hurt. Freddie had said it felt good to shift. Way wrong, there.

He twisted his head and took in the horrifying, raised knobs he'd seen on Freddie's spine when she transformed. And a tail with black fur tipped in the color of ashes.

This was what he'd wanted. To be a part of them. To be with Freddie. To belong.

Too late.

The main door slammed open, and Grant and Petra burst in. Grant wielded a baseball bat and Petra had a giant blade that looked like a curved garden tool—or that thing Death carried in the movies, which suited her. She raised it in front of her with two hands, eyes narrowed on him.

"It's Rain," Kurt said. "Back off, Xena: Warrior Princess."

Her eyes widened, and she lowered the blade.

"Wolf belt," Ulrich supplied, still holding the bottle of Full Moon wine they'd been pouring down his throat. "He's only a quarter of an hour into the transformation. We'll have to chain him up soon."

Like hell, they would. He had to get to Freddie.

"Wait a minute," Grant said. "This room is completely warded. It's the pack safe room. It's impossible for a Watcher to shift in here."

"Well, behold your handiwork, Weaver," Ulrich said. "Clearly something went terribly wrong."

"Or terribly *right*," Petra said.

Nothing would be right until he found Freddie. What he'd intended to be a surprise sprint to the door turned into a face-plant when his partially formed paws and legs didn't work as intended. With a groan, he rolled to his side and gnashed his…fangs?

"Where is Friederike?" Petra asked. "And Thomas."

At least someone in the place had her wits about her.

"We don't know where Freddie is. Thomas is out looking for her now."

"How can you not know where the Alpha presumptive is?" Grant's voice was harsh. "You should be witnessing the culling. Her family should be present."

Merrick shuffled his feet. "Yeah, well, the pack met and decided she wasn't strong enough to step up. Then, Klaus Weigl locked Uncle Ulrich and me in the cellar. Kurt pretended to be down with his plan, so he wasn't locked in with us. He doubled back and let us out."

"He was going to kill me anyway," Kurt said. "Thomas heard him on the phone with someone. He plans to kill all of the Burkhart family. Tommy and I came up with a better plan. He'd pretend to fight Freddie while I freed Merrick and Dad."

"I'm proud of you boys," Ulrich said, squeezing his son's shoulder.

Enough self-congratulatory bullshit. The plan had only partially worked. Freddie was out there somewhere, in pain or dead. "Find Freddie!" Rain shouted. It came out as random garbled snarls.

Thomas ran in from the door at the back that opened from the hallway lined with offices, sucking air in wheezing gasps. "Can't find her. Or my dad."

"Maybe you didn't really *want* to find her." Grant, bat in hand, advanced on Thomas. "Maybe you're working with your dad so you can be Alpha."

"Maybe you're gonna kill me so *your* dad's agenda is possible," Thomas shot back.

"What agenda?"

"He wants Kurt to be Alpha."

While the two circled each other, Rain struggled toward the back door on four wobbly legs. He had an agenda, too: rescue Freddie.

"We're going to play it safe here," Ulrich said, banding his arms around Thomas's arms and ribs and lifting him from the ground.

Thomas struggled against the much larger man, legs kicking out and head thrashing from side to side, but he was still too winded to break away. "No. I'm not with him. I would never hurt Freddie. I tried to stop h—"

His last word was cut off when Ulrich shoved him in the cellar and slammed the door.

Glances were exchanged as the three Watchers and two Weavers sized one another up. The huge room seemed to swallow sound, like being underwater. Rain took another couple of steps toward the door, feeling a little more stable on his feet...paws.

"What do we do now?" Petra asked.

"We round up the pack and someone goes to get Wanda Richter," Ulrich said.

"No!" Grant, Petra, Kurt, and Merrick answered in unison.

Another five or six steps closer to the back door—and Freddie—went unnoticed by the others.

"The chief needs to be notified," Ulrich said. "And all phone calls are monitored. We don't know the extent of what's going on here, so we can't phone her. Do the right thing, Grant, and go get your aunt. You know I'm right. She's head of the coven."

"What if she's allied with Klaus?" Kurt said. "What if Freddie's dead?" His voice broke on the last word.

Two more steps. Almost there.

"Then we'll take appropriate action."

They should take appropriate action right now to find Freddie, not stand around talking.

When Grant pulled his car keys out of his pocket, Rain took the opportunity to dash the short distance to the door. Pain still turning his insides to cinders, he headed down the paneled hallway lined with offices, straight through the back door of the building that led to the pavilion.

Once outside, his senses were assaulted. Too much sound — leaves rustling, wind whistling as it hit the wires holding up the vines in the vineyard beyond the pavilion, bugs and who knew what else crawling around in the soil. Intense smells that churned his gut more — decaying vegetation, smoke from the torches out in the vineyard, and the copper tang of blood. He sniffed the air but got no sense of Freddie. He reeled momentarily at the overload, shaking his head to clear it.

"It takes getting used to."

Rain's hackles prickled all the way down his spine as he wheeled to find Klaus Weigl leaning against a tree in human form, completely at ease, as if he were observing a game of checkers, not standing half naked with bruises and blood covering the front of his body. His black pants were torn in several places. The skin of his shoulders almost glowed in the speckles of moonlight filtering through the tree.

"Too bad you won't be around to get used to it." Still,

Klaus didn't move. "She thinks you're dead, you know."

Thinks, not *thought*, which meant she might still be alive. On its own, a deep, feral growl rumbled through Rain, his body running on adrenaline and instinct rather than choice.

"We are going to make a deal, Friederike and I."

Rain's mouth filled with saliva, as if prepping to bite.

"In exchange for my letting her family live, she will waive her right to become Alpha, abdicating to my son, Thomas, who, being newly of age, is next in line. No one in the pack took her seriously anyway."

Still, his chest rumbled, and he clamped his jaws shut to keep from snapping them together. A glance down confirmed he had turned full wolf.

"Once her family is out of the way"—he extended the last word menacingly—"safely in another pack, of course…" He cleared his throat. "She'll become Thomas's mate." He stretched out the last word, ending it with a *T* like a finger snap. "That will placate the few pack members who believe she should step up. We have a problem now, though, because she'll never make this bargain if she thinks she can still have you. Good thing that's easy to take care of." The asshole was clearly enjoying himself. So much, in fact, he didn't notice the gray and white wolf limping silently among the moon shadows under the grove of oak trees behind him. Freddie paused momentarily, staring at them, then slipped behind the far side of the building.

If she recognized Rain in his wolf form, she'd know he wasn't dead. She wouldn't agree to step aside for Thomas. She'd fight, just like Rain planned to fight.

From the other side of the building, gravel crunched. In human form, Klaus couldn't possibly have heard it. A car door opened, and Grant's and Petra's muffled voices were cut off by the door closing. Good, they were leaving before anything else went down.

"Thomas and I will go warn the pack," Ulrich said from somewhere inside. "You stay here with Freddie until we get back."

Rain's chest tightened. She'd made it inside safely.

"What about Rain?" Merrick asked.

The metallic groan of a door hinge cut off the first part of Ulrich's response that ended with, "...can't get far partially shifted."

For once, Klaus was quiet, which was a lot more disturbing than when he shot off his mouth. His eyes narrowed on Rain. "You heard something inside the building, didn't you?"

Shit. Shit, shit, shit.

"The head tilt gave you away. She's in there, isn't she?"

Rain didn't know if his wolf face showed expressions, but he focused on not reacting from head to tail, just in case.

Somewhere in the vineyard, a chorus of howls erupted. From closer, a larger group of wolves answered back.

Klaus stiffened, then reached behind him and pulled a gun out of his waistband. It was small and dark, glinting almost blue in the moonlight. "Get inside." He opened the door and gestured for Rain to enter.

Somehow, he had to let Freddie know Klaus was coming and give her time to get away. Pulling his lips back from his teeth, he growled, relieved it came out exactly as planned— and loud. Surely Freddie had heard him through the open door.

Klaus gave an exasperated growl of his own. "I don't have time for this. It would be so much easier to shove you in a barrel like that other mongrel, but I can't kill you right now or she won't cooperate."

The wolves howled again, closer still.

Holy shit. This guy had killed Gerald. Rain's stomach

churned. And despite the fact he'd told Freddie otherwise in the vineyard, he'd probably killed Hans Burkhart, too.

"Move it, Ryland." Klaus had totally lost that casual demeanor, and the gun tip vibrated slightly. Whatever he made of the wolf howls had shaken him. He probably wanted to get inside where the pack couldn't keep wolf forms, and he'd stand a better chance if they turned on him.

Rain slunk toward the door and stopped short. *Freddie.* Her smell was everywhere. He'd never been close to her in his wolf form, and it took everything in him to not lower his nose to the ground and track her.

An odd tugging sensation shuddered through him the moment he set foot over the threshold. The wards on the place were trying to force him into his human skin, but for some reason it didn't work on him, which Klaus didn't know. Rain planned to keep it that way. He needed every advantage. How the hell was he supposed to force a shift back to his human shape, though? Glancing down at his fully formed paws, he silently bid himself to change form. No luck.

When Klaus locked the door behind them, Rain could actually hear the tumblers rolling over inside the doorknob.

Shift, Rain ordered his body. Still nothing. He sat and closed his eyes, imagining himself in human form, but didn't feel any different. He had to hide his secret from this asshole. He *had* to shift. Had to do it for Freddie. This time, he pictured her instead. Long, wild hair. Unearthly pale eyes. Strong, sexy body… Strange aches crept through his limbs. Freddie's mouth… More pain in his limbs. Her mouth on his skin. Yep. It was working. In amazement, he watched his fingers elongate and the black claws recede.

Then, the raging pain from before seared him from deep inside, bones shifting and contracting. *It's like crack*, Gerald had said. No. It was like torture. Bowing his head to bear the pain, he thought of the guy. *Disposable.* Gerald wouldn't even have a funeral. Bones crunched in Rain's nose as it shortened. And this man, Klaus, had killed the poor guy. Whatever it took, he was determined to not end up like that: in a barrel to be disposed of without a trace.

"I don't have time for this," Klaus growled.

Neither did Rain. With a final shout of pain, he pushed to his feet—his two human feet—and staggered several steps.

Klaus flipped the switch, and Rain blinked as the fluorescent light vibrated and bounced off the dark paneling in the hallway. "Friederike!" he shouted, gun pointed at Rain. "I know you're here. I have something that belongs to you." From a hook on the wall, he grabbed what looked like doctor's scrubs and tossed them to Rain. "Put those on. Nothing more humiliating than dying naked."

Good thing Klaus had on pants, then, because Rain fully intended to turn this thing around.

FORTY-THREE

With a growl, Rain pulled on the scratchy garment and tied the waist with clumsy, aching, newly formed fingers.

Klaus gestured to a support beam running from the concrete floor to the apex of the ceiling with the gun while he grabbed a roll of rope off a hook. "Stay calm and I won't kill you."

Scanning the room, Rain moved to the beam. He'd lost his keen wolf senses when he morphed into a human again, and he couldn't see anyone else in the room. Maybe they'd left or were hiding behind the gigantic stainless tanks. Either way, it was best to go along with the guy to buy them more time. Klaus was clearly on the edge of losing his shit completely, and compliance seemed the best tactic.

With a shove to Rain's bare chest, Klaus slammed him against the beam and lashed his arms together behind him with the rope so tight it made his eyes water. "My best bet is to turn you over for the Weavers to euthanize." He pointed the gun at Rain's gut. "Move or kick, and I'll kill you." He then wrapped the rope around Rain's ankles, tying it off impossibly tight as well. "Charles signed your kill order yesterday, but I told him he wouldn't need it. You were supposed to die out in the vineyard." He gave a dramatic sigh and stood so that they were eye to eye. "I hate being wrong."

"You're going to hate being dead worse."

Klaus leaned back against a fermenting tank, gun still trained on Rain. "If you had stayed out of it when Gerald's body was found, none of this would have happened. Kurt and Merrick would have already been in custody. Instead, I killed that failed experiment for nothing."

Rain's gut churned. How could anyone be so heartless? Again, he pushed back an animal rage he wasn't used to and focused instead on figuring out a way to get out of this mess. He tested the rope on his wrists, but it was so tight his fingers were doing that pins-and-needles thing that happened when he slept funny.

Klaus, obviously feeling safe now that Rain was tied up, lowered his gun. "Then, when that fell through, I had a plan B, which was no easy feat. I had to threaten to kill my own son if he couldn't convince Kurt to go with him to the gas station. They both thought they were simply going to scare the boy." He began to speak faster, his words flowing like an ordinary conversation. "This whole culling could have been avoided if you hadn't interfered. I would have killed the boy and Thomas would have implicated Kurt and Merrick, who would have been kenneled for the boy's murder. Ulrich would have been wrecked, which would have affected Friederike, and she would have had even more trouble shifting. Voilà. Instant discredit in the eyes of the pack. Brilliant, yes?"

Brilliantly evil. This asshole was going down.

"It was a fantastic plan, right, Friederike?" Klaus shouted.

From the corner of his eye, Rain caught a flash of blue reflected in the tank on the back wall. He kept his gaze straight forward so Klaus wouldn't notice. The bottom fell out of Rain's stomach when Klaus raised the gun and pointed it at Rain's head and shouted. "I saw you. Come out or he's dead."

"Don't do it!" Rain called. "He's bluffing." Before he'd even finished the last word, a deafening bang and searing pain ripped through his thigh. *Sonofabitch*. Klaus had shot him. The pain was so intense, he had to close his eyes and grit his teeth through the waves radiating from the outside of his leg. At least it was only a flesh wound and hadn't shattered a bone or hit a major artery.

"That was just a warning. Come out or I'll get serious." He raised the gun to Rain's crotch.

Game over on this one. Rain took a deep breath and readied himself, praying Freddie had made it out safely.

"Stop. I'm coming out."

His frustrated groan turned into an inward sigh of relief when Rain realized the flash he'd seen was Merrick. Hopefully Freddie was long gone, because this kid wouldn't hold out under pressure.

He emerged from behind a tank with his arms up, visibly trembling.

"Where's Friederike?" Klaus swung the gun to point at Merrick, who was now in the center of the room.

"Dunno." Even his voice shivered.

"How did you get out of the cellar?" Klaus was shaking, too, but not from fear.

Merrick cringed. "Kurt let me out." When Klaus's eyes narrowed, the boy continued. "I was kind of freaking out."

"Imagine that. Ulrich is still inside?"

"Yeah. Kurt only let me out," he lied.

"Where is Kurt now?" The gun was pointed right at Merrick's face.

"O-Out rounding up the others. He…" Rain could tell the kid wasn't used to covering or lying. "He told me to wait here…alone."

Rain almost rolled his eyes at the awful tells from the boy, complete with the inability to meet the man's gaze directly.

"You're alone except for Friederike."

Merrick's eyes widened, totally giving him away. Rain scanned the room for Freddie, cursing his weak human senses. Her scent had hit him like a head-on collision when he'd entered the room in his wolf skin. Now he was clueless as to whether she was nearby or not.

"Come out, Friederike! I saw you sneak around the back of the building. Naturally, you were ordered to stay with your weakling cousin in the only room safe from the pack." In a lightning-fast move, he grabbed Merrick by the back of the neck and threw him facedown on the concrete floor, then ground his heel into the boy's thin spine. "But it didn't protect you from *me*, did it, Friederike?" He twisted his bare heel, and Merrick groaned in pain. "Come out or I'll break your precious little cousin. Show yourself and we can cut a deal."

"Don't do it, Freddie," Merrick choked out.

Rain had never felt this helpless. Twisting his wrists in his bonds, he glanced down at his leg. Blood was seeping out, and it hurt like hell, but the wound wasn't life-threatening—at least not immediately. If only he could get the bonds loose… or shift. He could wiggle loose if he had long, slender wolf legs again. He focused on his mind's image of Freddie, willing his body to change shape, but nothing happened.

Klaus yanked Merrick to his feet and pointed the gun at his head while forcing him toward one of the waist-high stainless machines Rain had been told were stem removers the night he'd drunk the wine. "I'll hurt him if you don't come out." With his much larger body, Klaus trapped Merrick against the machine and flipped on the switch. The workings whirred to life with a rhythmic hum.

Rain closed his eyes and played the same thoughts of

Freddie that had worked before to help him shift, but the struggle next to him made it impossible to focus.

"Ah, God. No!" Merrick rasped as Klaus, gun arm wrapped around his chest, grabbed the squirming boy's arm with his free hand and held it over a spinning thing that looked like a corkscrew on its side that fed into another chamber.

Change, change, change, Rain willed his body.

"Come out, Friederike!" Klaus shouted, lowering Merrick's hand close enough to the spinning blade he could have touched it if his fingers weren't balled into a fist.

Holy shit. The bastard was going to grind the kid's hand off.

"As you know, the purpose of this machine is to separate the grapes from the stems. I wonder if it will separate flesh from bone… If you come out, Friederike, we'll never know."

"No, Freddie. Don't," Merrick squeaked. Rain was amazed he was still hanging tough. He had a lot more strength and loyalty than he let on. Fighting against the ropes, Rain gritted his teeth, willing his body to shift to wolf form and praying Klaus didn't go through with it.

"Last chance!" Klaus called to the huge room. There was no answer over the hum of the machine and Merrick's wheezing breaths.

"Hey, asshole!" Rain growled, trying to incite him to let the boy go or distract him enough for Merrick to twist out of his grip. "Come untie me and let's see who ends up as hamburger."

Klaus's only answer was a lift of one dark eyebrow before he shoved the boy's hand into the de-stemmer. The calm whir of the machine motor choked and was replace by a wet, grinding sound, barely audible over Merrick's agonized screams.

Rain fought his bindings as the machine struggled to chew Merrick's bones, which were much stouter than grape stems.

Rain prayed the machine would jam. From the far end of the long metal device, blood dripped in a slow, steady stream to the floor, and Rain fought the urge to scream himself.

"Stop!" Freddie was louder than Merrick at this point because the poor guy had gone limp and was most likely in shock. Rain's entire body went numb with dread.

Immediately, Klaus turned off the machine and stepped away from Merrick, who collapsed in a ball on the floor, wrapped around his injured arm.

"He needs help," Freddie said, stepping out from behind one of the tanks.

A puddle of blood oozed from under the curled-up boy, and Rain shuddered.

Freddie limped closer, wearing the same kind of scrub pants Klaus had thrown Rain. Obviously, her broken bones from the vineyard weren't fully healed. Her long, tangled hair covered her top half, and Rain's throat tightened at the sight of her troubled face as she watched her cousin writhe in pain. If only he'd been stronger or had shifted, he could have prevented this. If only...

"Get him help and I'll do whatever you ask," she said.

Klaus remained perfectly still.

"At least let me take him outside so he can shift to heal. He's going to die."

"Yes, he is. And so are you once Charles Ericksen gets here to execute the kill order on your entire family—unless you do as I say."

Her eyes widened for only a moment, then flitted back to her cousin as the pool of blood on the floor continued to spread. "Let me get him outside."

"In time," Klaus said.

"He doesn't have time," Rain said. Freddie met his gaze and shook her head. Like hell he was going to stay out of it. "He's bleeding out. She said she'd do what you say. What more do you want?"

"You dead." Klaus leveled the gun at Rain's head, and he gritted his teeth in preparation for the pain, but none happened. Instead, Klaus grabbed Freddie by the hair and placed the gun to her temple and pulled her toward the cellar. "You can wait with your uncle for the coven leaders to arrive while your boyfriend and I have a chat."

Freddie put up no resistance, perhaps because she was unnerved by the gun, or most likely because she knew her uncle was not in the cellar.

"What? No plea for your boyfriend?" the man taunted.

She glanced at Rain over her shoulder with an unreadable expression, then sneered at Klaus. "Not my boyfriend, asshole. Not even close. Do whatever you want to him."

For a brief moment, Rain's heart stopped dead in his chest. Then, he realized she was playing Klaus—diminishing Rain's value so the guy wouldn't kill him, right? Because if she didn't want him, he wasn't a threat. His heart stuttered, then kicked back up as his vision blurred a bit. Surely that's what was going on.

"Okay, I'll play along." Klaus shoved Freddie away but kept the gun aimed at her. "Untie him and do as I say, and I'll let you take Merrick outside to heal." His gun was steady as he scanned the room, as if looking for something. Then, a horrible grin stretched his lips. "Hurry up."

Freddie's breath fanned across the back of Rain's neck as she struggled with the knots in the rope. "They're too tight."

"That's a shame," Klaus called from the other side of the room. "Merrick isn't looking so good."

Freddie tugged the ropes at his wrists, leaning down behind his back so that Klaus couldn't see her. "Shift. Ulrich said the wards don't work on you," she whispered almost inaudibly.

"Can't."

"Shit."

No kidding. Again, Rain closed his eyes and focused on her sounds as she struggled with the impossibly tight knots.

"I need a knife," she said.

"Too bad," Klaus replied, leaning against the cellar door. "Better hurry if you're going to save your cousin."

Then she crouched and pulled on the rope with her teeth. Her breath puffed hot on his wrists and he felt a faint shudder in his bones, like his wolf was waking a little bit. The rope loosened, and his fingers throbbed, then stung, as blood began to circulate through them.

"When you have him untied, I want both of you to climb the steps to the landing of the first fermenting tank," Klaus said, still smirking at whatever plan he'd concocted in his screwed-up brain.

The rope on Rain's wrists finally fell away, and it was all he could do to not reach around and pull Freddie to him. The sound of her bones breaking in the vineyard had played through his mind a million times, and what he wanted more than anything right now was affirmation she was whole and alive. That *he* was truly alive. When his throat had been ripped out, he thought he'd never see her again. But here she was, close but untouchable—like the life he'd dared to dream of only days ago.

Untying the bond on his ankles took less time, and soon Rain found himself stepping out of a nest of coiled rope.

With his first step, the pain in his wounded leg almost sent him to the ground. If he hadn't caught a bullet, he might try to find a way to maneuver closer to Klaus and then lunge. As he took another step, it was clear that walking was almost impossible and lunging was totally out of the question. Better to just go along with the asshole's orders and see if he could figure a way out.

Leading each step with his good leg, he'd climbed only three steps up by the time Freddie had made the landing way above his head at the top of the gigantic stainless steel tank.

"Move it, Ryland. The boy's life is leaking out while you dillydally."

Dillydally. When he got his hands on Klaus Weigl, he'd make sure his life didn't leak out. It would gush like Niagara Falls.

Rain gritted his teeth and struggled up to the landing, not able to bring himself to look down at Merrick. No matter how much his leg hurt, he was sure it couldn't hold a candle to what having a hand ground off felt like.

"Now what?" Freddie shouted, helping Rain to the rail on the landing.

"Now he goes in the tank, of course," Klaus answered.

Of course.

Freddie tensed, but before she could say anything, Rain whispered, "Go with it."

"Take as long as you like for your sorrowful good-byes," Klaus called before giving a pointed look in Merrick's direction.

Rain made the mistake of looking straight down. The landing surface was made of a ridged, open metal grid, and the sight of Merrick's blood on the concrete below made him light-headed.

"You'll die in there," she whispered.

He gestured to Merrick with his chin and whispered into her hair. "He'll die down there, and so will you if we don't go along with this. I have a plan."

"What kind of plan could you possibly have that—"

"Hurry up!" Klaus shouted.

"Go get Merrick outside," Rain whispered.

"You're gonna die." Her voice broke. "You're gonna die for…" She blinked a couple of times. "You're stupid, you know that?"

"I've been told that on more than one occasion."

"Are you done yet?" Klaus called.

"I'm going in this tank, but you're going to let Freddie get Merrick outside first."

"You don't trust I'll keep my end of the bargain, Ryland?"

"Not a chance," Rain answered.

"You're right." And faster than Rain could process what was happening, Klaus aimed and fired, knocking him off balance into the guard rail and sending a trail of searing heat through his right shoulder that nearly drove him to his knees.

Freddie's scream ricocheted through Rain's skull, and he grabbed her shoulders, scanning her to be sure she hadn't been hit, too, then he pulled her against him, reveling in her smell and the feel of her hard muscles as she clung to him. *This.* This was what he'd lived for. What he'd willingly die for… Unless his plan worked, and the tank held the Full Moon wine that would help him transform into his wolf so that he could heal.

"Believe in me," he whispered in her ear. "Like I believe in you. Don't give in. Lead."

"Lead?" she choked out. "I won't even live through this."

"Fight to live. Like I'm doing." Struggling to breathe through the pain, he tugged the handle on a door that looked like a submarine hatch but couldn't manage to open it. He knew if he looked down, he'd see his own blood splattering the floor below as it ran through the grated surface of the landing. "Help me."

"Help you die? No."

"I'm going to die anyway." He gestured to the gaping wound under his clavicle, just inside his armpit. No doubt this injury would kill him if he didn't do something quick. "Open the hatch, Freddie. I have a plan."

"Your plans suck, Sprinkles," she said as she twisted the latch and popped open the door.

"You've said that before." Leaning over, he cleared his head, balancing his hands on either side of the wide opening at the top of the tank. "And I plan to make you take it back when this is over." He knew that he might not get that chance if the wine didn't work. If it was the Hair of the Dog wine, he wasn't coming out of that tank on his own feet...or paws. "You need to go save Merrick. There's nothing you can do for me here, except know one thing." Looking through the grates, he could see Merrick's chest rise and fall with life. "Know that you matter. That you mattered to your dad. You matter to your cousins and your pack."

Tears rolled unchecked down her cheeks, and his heart pinched. Her lips moved, but no sound came out as she touched his face.

"And know this, Freddie. You matter to me. More than anything in the world. I..." He had always sworn, even before he'd ever heard of New Wurzburg or Ruby Ryland, or Freddie Burkhart, that he'd die without a single misgiving. *No regrets*. He swung his legs into the round opening, balancing on the edge. "Even if this doesn't work, know that you've made my life better than I'd ever expected. More than I've wished for. I love you, Friederike Burkhart."

Before she could respond and without looking back, he drew a final breath and pushed off the edge into the tank, falling a short distance, then sinking below the surface into total blackness.

FORTY-FOUR

It struck Rain that life had never been as precious as it was when he was dying. And death was certain if he didn't get his shit together and luck didn't cooperate. Eyes squeezed shut against the harsh wine, he concentrated on the direction his body was floating to determine which way was up, then with a kick, he broke the surface of the muck in the tank, spitting out debris and liquid. After several harsh coughs, he fought for focus in the absolute darkness, concentrating on the sharp pain slicing through his leg and upper body to ground him in reality—and at that moment, reality sucked.

Every time he moved his arms or kicked to keep his head above the surface, Rain thought he might pass out from the pain, which wouldn't have mattered a month ago. A month ago, he didn't have Ruby, or the boys, or Freddie. Hell, he didn't even have a life. But now he did, and he'd be damned if he'd drown in a slog of nasty-tasting almost-wine and grape rinds.

He took a small gulp of the brew, hoping it was fermented enough or whatever it took in order to help him shift into his wolf form, which was the only way he'd make it through this alive. He shuddered as the bitter swallow of the wine went down and groaned at the pain in his shoulder from the movement.

The blackness in the tank was overwhelming. When he

looked up, he couldn't even see where the hatch was. Klaus must have forced Freddie to close it. *Shit*. He hadn't counted on that. He tamped down the terror rising in his gut but couldn't slow his frantic fears. What if the wine didn't work? What if the hatch was locked and he couldn't get out? What if Freddie was dead?

"Oh, hell no," he growled, wincing as he reached out to locate the wall. The wine level was about five feet from the top of the tank, Hopefully, he'd find something to climb to get to the top. He regretted not paying attention when he slid in.

Kicking with his non-injured leg, he made his way along the wall of the tank, feeling for anything to hold on to. The problem was, he'd been distracted when he slid down into the tank. He'd just told Freddie he loved her, and instead of looking for a way out of this damned metal tomb, he'd focused on her instead.

Stupid.

No, not stupid. She was the least stupid thing in his life, and he planned to keep her in his life—which meant he had to fight to survive.

His hand hit a rail, and then another. Yes! A ladder. Gasping for breath, hoping his dizziness was from the wine and not blood loss, he hung on and imagined Freddie like he had before, willing his body to change. He didn't feel anything, but if it worked and he could shift, he'd need to get to the top of the ladder before he changed fully and couldn't climb. There was a lot to be said for human hands—especially Freddie's hands. He relaxed against the ladder, letting his body float in the cool muck, imagining the things she could do with those hands, and his heart rate slowed, along with his breathing, in a moment of blissful calm.

There was no sound in the tank except a soft hum and the liquid lapping the edges because of his earlier struggle.

In the pitch-black, he took a deep breath and buzzed with an odd numbness, letting his body submerge up to his chin, wanting nothing more than to rest…to sleep.

With a splash, he kicked upright, pain searing his leg and shoulder. "No!" His voice bounced off the metal walls like thunder. He shouldn't be calm. *Couldn't* be calm. "It's not blood loss," he told the blackness. He shook his head to clear it. "Focus, Ryland."

He couldn't die. Not now. Not after finding home…finding *her.*

After another gulp of the nasty mush, he grabbed a rung of the ladder well above the liquid line, then felt around with his bare feet to find a rung. He ran a hand over his face—his still regrettably human face—to clear away the pieces of grape pulp. Maybe it just took time for the wine to work.

Or maybe it was the wrong wine, and he was truly and totally screwed.

Muscles straining, he attempted to pull his chest above the pulp line but was too weak to grab the next rung up. With a groan, he sagged back down where it was easier to hang on.

He'd imagined his death frequently while living on the streets, but never, ever had he imagined drowning in a vat of wine. But then, he hadn't imagined people who morphed into Moon Creatures, either—powerful, primal things. A vision of Freddie in her wolf skin flickered in his brain. Silver and white with pale-blue eyes. Then he thought of the sight of his own paws and tail with dark fur and ashen tips. He imagined running in the moonlight next to her.

It started as a tingle. Like a toothache before it got bad, only it was deep in his bones, stretching to be freed. Heat pulsed in the wounds in his leg and shoulder as the wolf swelled closer to the surface, growling with rage. Growling for its mate.

Wearing what was certainly a goofy grin, Rain wrapped his shortening fingers around a ladder wrung and pulled up, lifting himself several rungs, one after another. And while the pain was still unbearable, the weakness started to subside.

Please let it be open. He reached the top and pushed open the hatch right as a gunshot sounded, reverberations rocketing around the tank along with his terror. Rain pulled himself up enough to look out the top.

He couldn't see anything close to the tank from this vantage point, but on the far side of the room, Klaus and Thomas were squared off, both breathing heavily. Klaus had the gun pointed at his son, whose body language screamed defeat—shoulders slouched and arms limp at his sides. For a moment, pity flared, trickling like ice water in Rain's chest. Maybe not ever knowing your father was better than knowing he was an evil prick.

As silently as possible, Rain climbed out of the circular hatch. Other than some extra hair on his arms and a darkening of his fingernails, he was still completely human. The wine hadn't worked, but at least he wasn't dead. And the partial shift he'd experienced seemed to have helped with his strength and wounds. If only his wolf had fully emerged…

Once on the landing, he crouched and peered through the metal grating. There was no sign of Freddie, but a wide crimson trail led from the pool of blood under the landing to the front door. She'd gotten Merrick out where he could heal—hopefully far, far away from Haven, where she was safe, too.

Klaus's voice was a growl. "How did Ulrich and Merrick get out of the cellar?"

Thomas shook his head and took a step back. "I dunno. I was in the vineyard looking for you and when I came back, he was out, and he locked me in there."

"You attacked me." Still advancing on his son, Klaus lowered the gun.

"When you opened the door, I-I thought you were one of them."

In a flash, Klaus backhanded his son with the gun handle, sending him to the floor. "And now I've lost the girl, too. I'd intended to put her in the cellar with her family, but she bolted when you lunged at me."

Thomas stayed down, which was probably a move he'd used with his dad before. For a brief moment, Rain felt sorry for him—until he realized he might have known about his father's plan all along.

Klaus leveled a hard kick at his son's side, sending him into a ball facing the stairs to the tank. "Charles Ericksen issued a kill order on all of them before the culling. He's coming to collect them any minute and they're gone!" Another kick landed in the middle of his back, but Thomas didn't make a sound, he just rolled tighter. "I did this for you."

"No, you didn't." Thomas groaned. He opened his eyes, and they widened as he stared at the puddle of blood where Merrick had been, then he looked up—directly at Rain, drawing Klaus's attention as well.

Shit! He was dripping through the grating. Wine and blood steadily dropped from where Rain crouched on the landing. How could he have been so stupid? As Klaus raised the gun, Rain made a lunge for the tank opening but never made it. This one wasn't a flesh wound. This time, Klaus hit his mark. A shot to the gut took Rain out of play like flipping off a light switch.

"Rain!" Freddie's voice cut through the haze in Rain's brain. "Oh God. No."

Curled on his side on the grate above her, arms across his middle where he'd been shot, he could only watch as she sprinted across the room from the front door toward the stairs. He couldn't even warn her when Klaus turned and started to level the gun at her.

And then, everything transitioned from hazy to slow motion—like an underwater scene with smooth movements as his brain and body began shutting down. Rain wondered if there was really a heaven. It couldn't possibly be better than the time he'd spent with Freddie. And as Klaus leveled the gun at her chest, he wondered if they'd find out about heaven together.

From his ball on the floor, Thomas kicked out in a circle, catching his dad's ankle, sending him down right as the gun went off, the bullet lodging somewhere in the front wall. Freddie lunged, plowing into Klaus before he even hit the ground, and the gun flew from his hand, crashing across the concrete and sliding under the de-stemmer. Freddie wrapped her body around Klaus's legs and kept him from reaching the gun while Thomas, no doubt with broken ribs and internal injuries, crawled across the floor and snatched it.

"Go take Rain outside, Freds," Thomas said, voice raspy. "I've got this." It was as if his voice were from far away and in a sound mixer of some kind. Almost liquid.

After looking from Thomas, who had the gun pointed at his father, to Rain, then back again, Freddie bolted up the stairs, taking them two at a time. Rain wanted to tell her not to worry, not to cry, but all he could do was stare at her beautiful face and blink back his own tears.

Worth it, he mouthed. And it was. She was safe, and it had been worth every bullet and bite.

"You've gotta shift," she said, moving his hand to look at the new wound. "Oh shit. You've gotta shift *now*, Rain."

He couldn't answer. Could only stare.

"You're too much of a coward to use that gun, Thomas,"

Klaus taunted. "You're such a coward, you wouldn't even fight a girl."

"She's not a… Well, she *is* a girl… She's the Alpha *and* a girl."

"Pathetic little wimp. Give me the gun. Now!"

"Shift, Rain. Do it for me," Freddie urged, scraping her nails across his scalp like he loved. "I can't carry you down to get you outside. You've gotta do it here."

"I'm not a wimp or a coward," Thomas said, voice trembling like the tip of the gun. "I won't let you hurt anyone else. I stand behind my Alpha."

Klaus barked a laugh. "She'll never be Alpha. There's a kill order on her, you idiot. I tried to give Alpha to you and was even willing to save her by making a plea to Charles to make her your mate, but you're throwing everything away. You'll be kenneled and euthanized like the rest of them."

Freddie's hair brushed across Rain's face, and he smiled at the memories of when it had done that before. "Rain. Are you listening? Shift, dammit. You're gonna die."

Whatever, his mind whispered like it always did when he was frightened, only the fear was tempered with a bizarre calm, probably from the lack of blood to his brain from taking three bullets. How many fucking bullets did Klaus have in that gun, anyway? His mind wandered to Ruby, and he wished he'd told her he loved her like he had Freddie. *No regrets.* She knew how he felt.

Freddie huffed. "Well, screw you, then. I don't have time to wait around for Klaus to get the gun."

Rain's Zen-like calm shattered when Freddie reached under him and then shoved him off the side of the landing, sending him plummeting to the concrete below. And this time, things didn't move in slow motion.

FORTY-FIVE

E verything in his body was broken. No doubt about it. Three bullets and pulp for bones—this was far more in keeping with how Rain had imagined his death during his years on the streets.

Freddie had shoved him off the landing. Maybe she considered it a mercy killing. Maybe it was because he was too weak to shift and therefore useless, or maybe she didn't want him or... *No.* He wouldn't go there. He'd keep his mind positive. His last thoughts would be positive.

"What did you do that for, Freddie?" Thomas practically shrieked. "You killed him."

"He killed himself," she said, coming down the stairs. "I'm trying to save him."

"Give me the gun right now, Thomas, or I'll end you myself, rather than let Charles do it," Klaus ordered.

"Shut up, Dad," Thomas shouted. "Shut up or I'll shut you up."

Freddie's face wavered as she leaned over him. "Stay with me, Rain." She gently kissed his lips, and things came back into focus slightly. "I'm going to drag you outside where you can shift. I'm...I'm so sorry. Rolling you off the landing was my only choice; you're too big to carry."

His smart, brave Freddie. No way in hell would he have

had the balls to throw her to her death like that. And it didn't matter whether she got him outside or not; he was done. He groaned as she lifted his arms to drag him out like she'd done Merrick. The pain that shot through his body like lightning with each of her steps revived him a bit.

After being lugged a few excruciating feet, several things happened at once: The front door slammed open and people poured in. While Thomas was distracted, Klaus tackled him to the ground. There was a lot of shouting and movement in the crowd that muddled Rain's brain as father and son wrestled in the middle of the floor. Then, the gun went off and everyone froze.

Silence. Silence so loud it hurt—or maybe it was just that everything already hurt. The only thing that grounded Rain was Freddie's tight grip on his wrists.

"Dad." Thomas's voice came out in a wheeze as he pushed his dad off him and backed up several steps, where Ulrich Burkhart caught him.

"Self-defense, son," Ulrich said, holding Thomas steady. "Grant, where's the chief? You were supposed to bring her."

"We did. She took off toward the vineyard."

"He murdered Klaus," someone shouted.

"I've gotta get you outside," Freddie said, setting back into motion and dragged him past Klaus's body lying facedown on the concrete.

"I'll take it from here," a voice behind Freddie said.

She came to a halt but didn't loosen her grip on Rain's wrists. "I'm taking him outside to shift so he can heal."

"No need. You'll be healing him for nothing. He's slated for euthanasia. It didn't work out. He's defective."

"Defective my ass," Freddie growled, resuming the excruciating pull toward the door. "The only things defective about him are the bullets Klaus put into him."

Charles Ericksen leaned in so that he was in Rain's range of sight. So close to Freddie that only she could hear—and Rain, of course, but the guy had clearly written him off as dead. "Listen to me, Friederike. It's over. I'll allow Kurt to live and become Alpha if you go along quietly. Otherwise, he will be put down with you and the rest of your family."

"Try it," she said, loud enough for everyone in the room to hear. "My pack won't allow it."

"You don't have a pack. Nobody would follow a Watcher who can't even hold her shift," he answered with equal volume.

The people in the room reacted in a burst of noise. It sounded like a beehive in Rain's fuzzy brain.

"It's true," Charles announced. "She hasn't been able to hold her wolf form since her father's tragic accident."

More angry, fuzzy bee noises and several calls for another culling. With that much noise, the entire pack must have been in the room.

Freddie released Rain's wrists and got on all fours next to him. "I'm not going to be able to get past them. I'm so sorry. I tried. I…" She leaned closer to where her lips were against his ear. "I love you, too, Rain Ryland."

His heart squeezed painfully, surpassing his other injuries.

"Hans Burkhart's death was not an accident," Petra's voice rang over the buzzing. "He was murdered."

"You would know, because you did it, witch," someone else called.

"That was a rumor started by the coven." That voice belonged to Grant. "By my dad."

Everything in Rain wanted to simply let go, to sleep, but he couldn't—not with Freddie in danger.

"Unfit to lead, just like Klaus said," another person shouted.

"She can't maintain her wolf," Charles repeated. "The rules

are clear." He was still near enough to hear papers rustle as he pulled them out of his pocket. "I hold in my hand kill orders for the entire Burkhart family. They are a detriment to the pack. And with the murder of his father, Thomas Weigl will be added to the list."

"This whole thing is a setup," Freddie shouted. "Nothing but manipulation to take the power my dad fought so hard for away from the pack. Away from *all of us.*"

The buzzing of voices got louder as the pack's control teetered on the edge, reminding Rain of a street gang. Growing up, he'd seen the destruction caused by group frenzy. If someone didn't do something soon, Charles's kill orders wouldn't be necessary; Freddie's own pack mates would take care of it, just like they had with the guy with the beard in the vineyard.

"She can't lead!" Someone shouted.

"Get her outside and we'll handle it the old way," someone else said. "We don't need Weavers to take care of this."

Cheers erupted.

Oh, shit. They were going to hurt her.

Freddie screamed in rage. "Get your hands off me!"

There was a scuffling of shoes and grunting along with the unmistakable sound of fists hitting flesh. They *were* hurting her.

Rain rolled to his side. He was broken—more than broken, he was smashed to pieces—but he'd be damned if he'd let this happen. Something in him—something primal and powerful—willed him to fight. That beast inside wasn't going down with a whimper. Not when someone he loved was in danger. *The inability to shift form is often a side effect of depression or anxiety or fear. It's the ultimate weakness,* Freddie had said that night she'd snuck in through his bedroom window. Nobody would ever accuse him of being weak, but he was afraid, no doubt about it. More than anything, though, he was mad. So mad, his insides felt like they were boiling.

His heart pounded so painfully, it felt as though every beat would be its last. He squeezed his eyes shut, but this time, he didn't imagine Freddie in her human form. He saw her in her wolf skin, and she needed him. Needed his wolf. And as he howled in pain and anger, he realized that the beast inside him needed her, too, and the only thing in its way was *him*. It was time for his fear and weak, broken human body to get the hell out of the way.

FORTY-SIX

The shift happened quickly and was evidently spectacular because the room fell completely silent as Rain pushed to his feet—his *four* feet. He could actually feel his flesh stitching back together as his body healed itself. Teeth bared, he growled, scanning the room for the people hurting Freddie.

Twenty or so feet away, the three men and a woman dragging her toward the door stopped in their tracks and released her in stunned disbelief. Freddie spun to face him. Her expression of desolation changed to one of absolute joy, which made his body buzz with power.

"He's impervious to the wards," someone said.

"He's an abomination!" Charles shouted. "Dangerous to the pack."

The several dozen shifters in human form were clearly confused, gazes darting around the room for an answer or direction. Like a gang, they were seeking instruction from a leader. Freddie ran to Rain right as the door where they'd been dragging her slammed open.

"Dangerous to you, maybe, Mr. Ericksen," Merrick said, striding in the room. "But not to the pack." His right hand and arm were missing halfway to the elbow, but he wasn't bleeding anymore.

Freddie's fingers tightened in Rain's fur, and his body

buzzed with power, like she was supercharging him with her touch. "You did it," she said, crouching to put herself at eyelevel. "I knew you were strong enough." She clutched a handful of his ruff, as if seeking strength of her own. "And so am I. You were right. It's time for me to step up," she whispered in his ear before standing and holding up a hand to silence the room.

"It's time for the pack to stand on its own," Freddie said, voice strong. "To follow the path my father forged and died for."

"Enough," Charles said. "We'll hear no more."

"*I* want to hear more."

Rain swiveled toward the voice and found Chief Richter in the back entrance to the building and wondered how long she'd been there. How much she'd heard.

"I also want to know who cosigned the kill orders on the Burkhart family," she said.

With his wolf ears, Rain could hear Charles's heartbeat speed up. The whole room was awash with sound and sweat and fear.

Klaus's body lay facedown in the middle between Freddie and her pack mates like a bloody line in the sand. Freddie's fingers gripped Rain's shoulder as she addressed the pack. "Klaus convinced you that I wasn't fit to lead. For years, he spread rumors that I was unpredictable and weak and what a loser I'd be as Alpha." Her fingers tightened in his hair. "And you believed him—a guy who admitted to killing Gerald and tried to start an uprising by ordering the attack of a human. A man who was going to kill his own son and all his cousins."

She pointed at his body. "You'd believe and follow him, forsaking all my dad did for you, and now, you're taking orders from a Weaver who says this wolf"—she gestured to Rain—"is defective. Why? Because he's powerful enough to shift in this room? Because he doesn't succumb to the coven's wards? Maybe none of us should. Maybe it's time for the subordination and brainwashing to stop." She narrowed her eyes. "If you'd follow them like mindless sheep, rather than listen to your inner beasts, then I'm not sure you're worth leading anyway."

And with that, she strode toward the back door and Chief Richter.

"Stop," Charles ordered. "As leader of the Weaver family in charge of lupine primogeniture, I cannot let you leave."

Freddie spun so quickly, even the chief's eyes widened in surprise. "As Alpha of this pack, I cannot allow you to stay."

Charles's pale face flushed red all the way up to his hairline. "You dare tell me what to do, you pathetic little dog? You're just like your father. He spouted this independence and liberation crap, too. Even with no tongue, he wouldn't stay quiet."

A hush came over the pack, and all color drained out of Charles's face as he realized his blunder. "I acted in the best interest of the pack," he said, scanning the room. "Those of you loyal to Klaus understand."

Merrick crossed the room, stepping over Klaus's body to stand with Freddie. Then Kurt, Ulrich, Thomas, Grant, and Petra followed, flanking her on either side. Rain's heart soared as one by one, the pack moved to stand with Freddie, who remained stock-still, hands balled into fists at her sides, until none remained, leaving Charles Ericksen and his old-school philosophy totally alone on the other side.

"You killed my dad," Freddie growled under her breath.

"The rules on this are crystal clear, Charles," Chief Richter said from behind them. "A Weaver or Watcher may not take another life without authorization, under the penalty of death, unless in self-defense or in defense of the magic."

"You've always been a staunch supporter of keeping the

Watchers in their place, Wanda. You've been very vocal since Hans's death."

"I was waiting for you to misstep," she said calmly. "To give me the evidence I needed to solve the murder. I knew you did it. I just couldn't prove it."

He shook his head. "I was defending the magic from being destroyed. From being taken from us. Liberating the Watchers would be disastrous. They cannot manage power of any kind. Especially her." He pointed at Freddie.

With his wolf ears, Rain could hear Freddie's rapid heartbeats and quick breaths.

She took several steps forward, stopping just short of Klaus's body. Behind him, he smelled the aggression of the pack as they readied to defend her. "I don't need to manage power, I *am* power. I'm the Alpha, asshole, and I'm your worst nightmare."

Crouching to place her fingertips on the ground, she closed her eyes, and with his acute hearing, Rain made out the crackling of her bones stretching and contracting, right before she launched over Klaus's body, turning full wolf by the time she reached Charles Ericksen.

For a moment, Rain was too stunned to move. She'd shifted despite the wards. She was also tearing into Charles's face and would kill him if not stopped. He leaped, hitting her full body, knocking her off the screaming man. Once they were clear, he shifted to his human skin so he could reason with her.

Knowing she might be frenzied enough to attack him, Rain wrapped his arms and legs around the silver and white wolf, praying she'd listen. "Don't do it," he said in her ear. "You'll get the death penalty for killing him."

She growled and fought but didn't bite him, which he found encouraging. Charles screamed in the background as Rain spoke in her ear. "Let the coven handle him. Your dad would want you to carry on his legacy. Your pack needs you." He tightened his fingers in her hair. "*I* need you." She relaxed in his grip, and he placed his mouth close to her ear. "Let's make this a beginning, not an ending."

Her form changed beneath his body, going from wolf to familiar hard muscles and curves, and it was clear that Rain's wolf had worked miracles on his injuries because he felt no pain at all except an acute ache in the middle of his chest and an overpowering need to kiss her.

They were alive. The pack was safe.

"This isn't over," Charles slurred as Wanda Richter and Ulrich Burkhart pulled him to his feet. He looked like something out of a monster movie. Freddie had done a real number on his face—or what was left of it. "I'm only the tip of the iceberg. The revolution goes deep."

Freddie rose to her feet. "Yeah, well, so does pack loyalty. And so does our commitment to protect and defend not only the Weavers in our community but our loved ones." She slid her hand in Rain's. "So bring that shit." She made her way through her pack to the back door. They lowered their eyes in submission and offered promises of loyalty as she passed.

The moonlight on Freddie's skin had an almost magical effect, causing Rain's entire body to buzz. They were safe and alive. So were Freddie's family and Ruby and Moth. His heart expanded to the point he thought it would bust out of his rib cage—with relief, with love, with pride. "You shifted in the warded room."

Her grin was beautiful.

He grinned back. "You must have one kickass beast inside."

"The Watchers have come to rely too much on the magic when sometimes it's really mind over matter. You taught me that." Freddie stopped outside her cabin door and picked a grape husk out of his hair, then ran her hand over his cheek. "You didn't know the rules the first time you shifted. You hadn't been frightened or brainwashed into believing you were limited, so you didn't let it hold you back. Once you knew about the wards, you let it get to you."

"But I also knew about the wine, and it didn't work."

"Because that was a Merlot we make for humans. Nothing magical about it, Sprinkles, except the shade of pink it stained your skin." She laughed. "Uncle Ulrich is gonna be so pissed the batch is contaminated and will have to be trashed."

He must have looked horrifying, covered in blood and wine and grape pulp, but she didn't seem to mind as she pulled him in for a kiss that made him growl deep in his chest. She growled right back, and for the first time in his life, Rain felt complete. Nothing was missing. No regrets. Without his painful, lonely past, he wouldn't have gotten to this point, held in the arms of someone who saw him for exactly who and what he was, and loved him anyway. With Freddie, anything was possible, he realized as he pulled her even closer, wishing he could somehow find the right words to tell her what she meant to him.

"You're…" She ran her hands over his shoulders, clearly searching for words. "I…" Taking several deep breaths, she studied his face as if memorizing it, and his chest ratcheted tight around his heart. And then, as if she'd read his thoughts through his face somehow, she grinned and pulled him back for another kiss and he lost himself in her touch. Words weren't necessary. She knew.

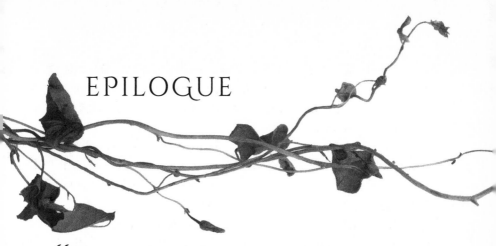

EPILOGUE

"So, how was school today?" Aunt Ruby asked, passing the plate of cookies to Rain and Freddie on the porch swing before settling back into her rocker.

"Great," Freddie answered, grabbing a cookie.

Rain nudged Freddie's thigh with his, recalling the hot moments in the janitor closet that got both of them a detention for being late to calculus...again. "Same as usual."

Ruby took a bite of her cookie. "I got a text from Jeremiah's...I mean Moth's mom. He's settling into school nicely, and she says he loves having his own room."

He could still see the fear turn to joy on Moth's face when his parents drove up to take him home. It had evidently been a while since they'd seen him, because his mom had remarked on how tall he was a billion times.

The swing creaked on its chains as it swayed, and Rain put his arm behind Freddie, wrapping her hair around his fingers. "Work at the station going okay?"

Ruby's sunshine smile made him feel warmer. "Yes. Thomas Weigl is fantastic with car motors, and he fixed the door and replaced the burned-out lights. The chief says he'll make a great cop after he graduates at the end of the month. Merrick is a master at filing. He does better one-handed than I do with two. Poor kid. I'm glad he's not working dangerous machines at the winery anymore." She leaned closer conspiratorially. "He's been spending a lot of time after work at the library with your friend Petra." She winked. "Might be something there."

Merrick had been acting unusually goofy the last couple of weeks. Kurt had noticed it, too. Maybe Ruby was right. Watchers and Weavers mixing it up was a huge taboo, so this should be interesting.

Kurt was learning the financial aspect of Haven Winery from Ulrich while his brother and cousin were at the police station. Rain leaned back and stretched, causing the swing to wobble. There hadn't been a missing cow or chicken or cat since the boys had been put to work. Wanda Richter was one smart witch.

"Are you two going to stay for book club tonight? Grant and his mother will be here. He's been such a help to her since his father was called away on business." Aunt Ruby's brow furrowed. "So odd, if you ask me."

Grant had also been working hard with Freddie and Rain to iron things out between the Weavers and the Watchers. They liked Rain's "outsider" viewpoint in the mix. The pack had rallied behind the collaboration so far. Freddie was an amazing leader. Alpha with a capital *A*, and Rain loved it.

He closed his eyes and listened to the crickets cranking up in the fields surrounding the neighborhood. "We're going to skip book club tonight, if that's okay. We'd like to go hang out at Enchanted Rock."

"Good night for a hike," she said, picking up the cookie plate to take it inside. "Gonna be a full moon, you know."

I sure do. The screen door closed, and he stared up at the moon and his wolf stirred. "So, did you eat Mrs. Goff's cookie?" he whispered in Freddie's ear, intentionally brushing her with his lips, which caused her to shiver.

She placed her sneakers flat on the porch and stopped the swing. "You bet I did." The look she gave heated him all the way through.

He pulled her to her feet, and she leaned into him in that way he loved. The way that made him feel whole and solid and complete.

"I'll be back late, Aunt Ruby," he called through the screen door. "Don't wait up. See you in the morning. Love you."

"Love you, too, Aaron. Y'all have fun."

If Goff's cookie was correct, she could count on it. "Wanna take the bike?" he asked.

Freddie tipped her face to the moon. "Nah. I need to run."

The moonlight danced across her skin, making his breath catch and his chest ache. "I need more than that."

"Down, boy." Laughing, Freddie jumped off the porch and sprinted toward the garage. He followed, catching up with her before she made it to the back fence where they left their clothes piled under a bush. This time the shift didn't hurt, not even a little bit, and as they ran through the night toward Enchanted Rock, one word tumbled over and over in Rain's head: *home.*

ACKNOWLEDGMENTS

First and foremost, thank you to Liz Pelletier, who convinced me to write a story about teen shifters in the Texas Hill Country and made the process a blast.

Love and thanks to my agent, Kevan Lyon, and to Stacy Abrams, Melanie Smith, and the entire team at Entangled.

Leah Clifford, your input on those first fragile pages made them fierce. Thank you.

Chris Smith you're always a rock when I need one—which is more often than I like to admit.

To my amazing family, Laine, Hannah, Emily, and Robert: you are champs. Not a day goes by that I'm not humbled and overwhelmed by your love.

And to my readers, from those new to me to those who have been with me since my first book, thank you.

GRAB THE ENTANGLED TEEN RELEASES READERS ARE TALKING ABOUT!

BLACK BIRD OF THE GALLOWS
BY MEG KASSEL

A simple but forgotten truth: Where harbingers of death appear, the morgues will soon be full.

Angie Dovage can tell there's more to Reece Fernandez than just the tall, brooding athlete who has her classmates swooning, but she can't imagine his presence signals a tragedy that will devastate her small town. When something supernatural tries to attack her, Angie is thrown into a battle between good and evil she never saw coming. Right in the center of it is Reece — and he's not human.

What's more, she knows something most don't. That the secrets her town holds could kill them all. But that's only half as dangerous as falling in love with a harbinger of death.

THE NOVEMBER GIRL
BY LYDIA KANG

I'm Anda, and the lake is my mother. I am the November storms that terrify sailors, and with their deaths, I keep the island alive. Hector has come to Isle Royale to hide. My little island on Lake Superior is shut down for the winter, and there's no one here but me. And now him.

Hector is running from the violence in his life, but violence runs through my veins. I should send him away. But I'm half-human, too, and Hector makes me want to listen to my foolish, half-human heart. And if do, I can't protect him from the storms coming for us.

27 Hours
by Tristina Wright

Rumor Mora fears two things: hellhounds too strong for him to kill, and failure. Jude Welton has two dreams: for humans to stop killing monsters, and for his strange abilities to vanish.

But in no reality should a boy raised to love monsters fall for a boy raised to kill them.

During one twenty-seven-hour night, if they can't stop the war between the colonies and the monsters from becoming a war of extinction, the things they wish for will never come true, and the things they fear will be all that's left.

Never Apart
By Romily Bernard

What if you had to relive the same five days over and over?
And what if at the end of it, your boyfriend is killed…
And you have to watch. Every time.
You don't know why you're stuck in this nightmare.
But you do know that these are the rules you now live by:
Wake Up.
Run.
Die.
Repeat.

Now, the only way to escape this loop is to attempt something crazy. Something dangerous. Something completely unexpected. This time…you're not going to run.

Combining heart-pounding romance and a thrilling mystery Never Apart is a stunning story you won't soon forget.

entangled teen

an imprint of Entangled Publishing LLC